Praise for Tamera Alexander

In These Hills is a powerful, deeply satisfying novel of courage, forgiveness, and grace that reminds us that passion must be tempered by wisdom—and that true wisdom is forged through life, faith, and God's gentle leading. From the harrowing opening to a richly rewarding epilogue, the story brims with unforgettable characters, beautifully rendered dialect, compelling chemistry between the hero and heroine, and memorable themes that resonate deeply.

FRANCINE RIVERS, *New York Times* bestselling author

As soon as I started reading *In These Hills* I couldn't stop. Tamera Alexander has created a riveting tale, beautifully told, that shines light on the sacrifices women made for the right to vote. The story is excellently researched and peopled with endearing characters, including a fun peek into the life of Jack Daniel of whiskey fame. This is a tender romance with rich, spiritual depth. A must-read.

LYNN AUSTIN, award-winning author of *The Lumber Baron's Wife*

In These Hills is a beautiful tale of struggle and redemption, fear and faith, love and forgiveness. Real history is woven throughout, and a reader can't help but feel the love of the writer for the places as well as the characters (whether real or imagined) that people this story. . . . An absolutely wonderful novel that should not be missed!

ROBIN LEE HATCHER, Christy Award–winning author of *To Find Where She Belongs*

[*In These Hills* is] such a unique combination of history, humor, and hope! Never predictable, the tale offered numerous surprises along the way and compelled me to keep turning pages—yet feel bereft when I reached the last one. Highly recommended.

DEBORAH RANEY, author of *Playing for Keeps* and The God Who series

[*In These Hills*] captivated me. I've studied the history of this area and the distillery . . . and Tamera has brought Jack Daniel and Miss Mary Bobo to life in a way that feels true and genuine. . . . She's worked hard to get it right.

MIKE NORTHCUTT, historian and president of the Moore County Tennessee Historical and Genealogical Society

A propulsive tale of marital infidelity and a historical Southern home overrun with secrets. . . . A heartfelt commentary on faith and the redemptive power of forgiveness.

PUBLISHERS WEEKLY on *A Million Little Choices*

In *A Million Little Choices*, Alexander skillfully weaves the past with the present, bringing out long-buried secrets that captivated me and had me turning pages well past my bedtime. This hope-filled story will undoubtedly serve as a beacon of light for each and every reader.

MICHELLE SHOCKLEE, Christy Award–winning author of *The Women of Oak Ridge*

A vivid portrait of Southern life near the end of the Civil War. . . . Alexander has created an exceptional tale of faith, hope, and love based on a real-life romance.

PUBLISHERS WEEKLY starred review of *With this Pledge*

To Wager Her Heart is a poignant glimpse into our country's history and conflict after the Civil War. . . . Tamera Alexander invites readers on a remarkable journey, traveling alongside resilient characters determined to do what's right even when family and peers choose prejudice and contempt.

MELANIE DOBSON, award-winning author of *The Lost Story of Via Belle*

Strong characters, a sense of the times, and the themes of love, friendship, and the importance of loyalty and determination make this triumph.

LIBRARY JOURNAL starred review of *To Win Her Favor*

IN THESE HILLS

Tamera Alexander

In These Hills

Tyndale House Publishers
Carol Stream, Illinois

Visit Tyndale online at tyndale.com.

Visit Tamera Alexander's website at tameraalexander.com.

In These Hills

Cover design by Sarah Susan Richardson

Interior design by Laura Cruise

Edited by Kathryn S. Olson

Published in association with the literary agency of Natasha Kern Literary Agency, Inc., P.O. Box 1069, White Salmon, WA 98672.

Library of Congress Cataloging-in-Publication Data

A catalog record for this book is available from the Library of Congress.

ISBN 978-1-4964-7562-6 (HC)
ISBN 978-1-4964-7563-3 (SC)

Printed in the United States of America

32 31 30 29 28 27 26
7 6 5 4 3 2 1

For Rabbi Jesus
who never changes,
yet who changes everything.
And for Leo and Ari,
my utmost prayer for you both,
always and forever,
is him.

But even after all he did, you refused to trust the LORD your God, who goes before you looking for the best places to camp, guiding you with a pillar of fire by night and a pillar of cloud by day.

DEUTERONOMY 1:32-33 (NLT)

You are always one decision away from a completely different life.

BANKSY

1

MARCH 1905

ATLANTA, GEORGIA

"Remember, Miss Dunham, you're an intelligent, independent young woman. Don't let them intimidate you!"

"No, of course not." Josephine followed the head of the local American Woman Suffrage Association to the foot of the makeshift outdoor stage, her insides thrumming with anticipation—and panic. Crowds filled the street, women *and* men alike. Far more than expected for so early in the morning and—judging by the hecklers—not all of them supportive of the cause.

She still couldn't believe they'd invited her to speak, and on the heels of Miss Susan B. Anthony herself. Even now, the venerated Miss Anthony, eighty-five years old, wearing her customary round-rimmed glasses and hair pulled back in a no-nonsense style, commanded the podium as she delivered her closing remarks.

"I wish I could live another century and see the fruition of all the work for women, including that of this next generation who joins the revolution with such unwavering enthusiasm and commitment. Like their foremothers, they have vowed to carry forth the fight for temperance, for voting rights for women, for equal pay for equal work . . ."

As Miss Anthony's voice rose, so did the jeers.

A biting wind whistled through the alleyways between downtown brick buildings, sharpening the unseasonably cold spring air. Josephine turned up her coat collar and adjusted the *Votes for Women* sash she and her fellow suffragists wore to such gatherings.

The past week of canvasing Atlanta's familiar streets and neighborhoods publicizing this event had made a real difference. Josephine took a deep breath. Now if only *she* could.

"Next we shall hear from Miss Josephine Dunham"—Miss Anthony motioned for Josephine to join her—"one of our young revolutionaries herself. So in conclusion, may I remind us all . . . There will *never* be complete equality until women themselves help make laws and elect lawmakers. Justice is better than chivalry—if we cannot have both!"

Triumphant cheers rose amid a wave of boos and hisses from men, and even some women, scattered throughout. "Go back home where you belong, you ol' cow!" one man yelled. "Leave decision makin' to men," added another. "Y'all ain't got the brains for it."

Miss Anthony grasped Josephine's hand, her gaze clear-eyed and determined. "Miss Dunham, their ignorance and chauvinism is no match for what we know to be true. God created *all* men and women to be equal. It is up to us to illuminate their minds, however narrow and dark they may be. Yes?"

"Yes," Josephine whispered and stepped resolutely to the podium. The number of eyes staring back at her seemed to double. "Friends and fellow compatriots, I should feel exceedingly diffident to stand before you today as I am wholly unaccustomed to public speaking, but—"

"Then best learn your place and get back in the kitchen!" a young man close to the front called out. The men around him snickered, and a satisfied grin split his face.

"But," Josephine continued, "I am driven by a moral sense of right and duty to speak to you today. To *all* of you, regardless of lack of decency—or intellect." She drove a brief but well-aimed look at the young man whose grin swiftly faded. "The time is long past for the question of woman's wrongs to be laid before the public, and women alone can understand the length and breadth of that degradation. We *must* speak for ourselves. We cannot depend on men to take up our cause. Because they have been educated to believe themselves far superior. No, we—"

"That's because we *are* superior, you dim-witted . . ."

The derogatory name he used drew gasps, but his brazenness only emboldened her, especially as she looked into the faces of women who had become the sisters she'd never had. Sarah, especially, who stood near the front, her confident nod fueling Josephine's determination.

"In this gathering today are women who have endured beatings by drunken fathers and husbands. Women abused by men given to heavy drink. Property rightfully theirs by God's moral law has been stolen and squandered, while others have been left to starve, along with their children, as wages meant for sustenance are frittered away on alcohol. Some women in our midst have been burned in effigy for daring to state that a woman is equal to a man, and that she should be treated as such in the eyes of the law." She looked at Miss Anthony, thinking of all she and her compatriot, the late Elizabeth Cady Stanton, had endured. "Our motto has been and always will be: 'Men their rights and nothing more; women their rights and nothing *less*.' So together with you, we, as the next generation, firmly take hold of the baton passed to us and vow to—"

Something struck her in the chest. And splattered.

The rank odor registered first, then the rancid taste in her mouth. Wiping her lips, she looked down to see the broken eggshell. The cocky smirk of the younger man who'd earlier yelled the obscenity identified him as the instigator. But it was the little girl a few feet in front of him, no more than seven or eight years old, who drew Josephine's full attention.

The child clutched a young woman's hand and stared wide-eyed at Josephine. In a blink, the tug of childhood wounds and years spent attempting to be *enough* threatened to undermine Josephine's confidence. But she refused to give in—to such a man, and to the cruel patriarchy he represented in the majority of men she'd known.

While she'd never endured a physical beating from her father or any other man, she understood paternal authority only too well. And she still struggled to understand why some women, especially mothers with children, who suffered continual abuse from such men, didn't seek to leave at all costs. Some did and paid dearly—but in the end, they were free. Others seemed paralyzed, unable to take that next step. Why, she would never know.

Of all the men in her life, only one had truly acknowledged her worth—her equality . . . Todd.

Her brother had been her dearest friend and closest confidant. While she'd realized early on that having a twin brother was special, she hadn't known how lonely the world would be without him. Until a handful of months later when the world had shown her what lonely really was.

"As is so evident today," she continued, drawing courage from Todd's memory, "we cannot and must not depend upon the protection of man. Yes, some men have chosen to support our cause and for that we are most grateful. But they are few and greatly outnumbered. Instead, woman *must* be taught to protect herself. And the best way to protect women and children is not by trying to change men, but by giving women the right to participate in making the laws. And by granting them the right to *vote*!"

"Here, here!" women yelled, waving their placards high and chanting, "Votes for women! Votes for women! Votes for women!"

Resolution coursed through her. "Here we take our stand!" she shouted over the hubbub. "And here we shall remain unmoved until the time women are granted *every* right that men have so generously granted to themselves since the beginning of—"

The object registered in her peripheral vision, but she couldn't react quickly enough. The rock struck her in the right temple, and she staggered back, dazed. Miss Anthony rushed to her side, followed by another fellow member.

"Miss Dunham, are you all right?" Miss Anthony's arm came around her shoulder.

"I-I think so." Josephine touched her temple and her fingers came away bloody—just as a group of men unleashed a volley of empty whiskey bottles and rotten eggs onto the stage.

Unsteady on her feet, Josephine attempted to shield Miss Anthony as they hurried from the platform. People ran screaming as glass shattered and rocks thudded against the heavy canvas backdrop. The putrid smell of rancid eggs hung in the air. Something hit Josephine in the back just as they reached the street, but her woolen coat helped soften the blow.

Her temple pounding, she ushered Miss Anthony around the corner of a building to protect her when she noticed a small cut on the woman's jawline. "Oh, Miss Anthony, you're hurt!"

"I've suffered far worse, Miss Dunham." The older woman made a dismissive gesture. "You're the one with the bloody temple. You, my dear, struck a nerve up there today. Well done. But you've never before spoken publicly?"

Josephine shook her head.

"You speak with such determination and confidence. Where did you acquire such skill?"

It was Josephine's turn to smile. "My brother and I used to debate on all sorts of issues. Our parents actually encouraged it. My father was an attorney, and Todd and I would hold court and present different sides of an argument, whether we personally agreed with it or not. My parents were considerably older when my brother and I were born. They both lived through the Civil War—or the *Rebellion*, as they often referred to it. They were abolitionists. They strongly believed that those exchanges would teach us perspective, and respect, and open-mindedness."

"Indeed." Wonder swept the woman's features. "My father, as you may know, believed women deserving of the same education as men and took my schooling upon himself. Thus the ideal was planted early. Even so, I learned much by eavesdropping on his conversations with clients and colleagues. Such opportunities for a girl to develop leadership of thought are rare."

"Well, in all candor, my parents' intent was for my brother to be the primary beneficiary of those exercises. But with us being the same age and the only two children, I was permitted to . . . eat the scraps that fell from the table, as it were."

Josephine had attempted a more nonchalant tone, but Miss Anthony's thoughtful nod encouraged her to continue.

"My father, though kind and generous in many ways—" Josephine paused, hearing another wave of angry voices and shattering of glass behind her. She felt pulled to rejoin her fellow suffragists, but this was Susan B. Anthony, the woman who had inspired them all. The opportunity to speak with her would likely not come again. "He was a very religious man and held steadfast to patriarchy. And my mother, she never once sought to challenge him. Not in word, or in deed. At least not in front of my brother or me. She taught me it was a wife's duty to love, honor, and *obey*."

Even now, the word rankled, and the shadow chasing across Miss Anthony's countenance seemed to convey agreement. Either that or concern, Josephine couldn't be sure. She so wished her mother had enjoyed greater liberty, both within her marriage and in her world. One thing Josephine knew for certain . . . She would never place herself in that kind of subservient role to a man. She wouldn't marry until she could find a man who esteemed a woman as his equal in every way. Which meant she would never marry. And she'd accepted that.

"But . . ." Josephine continued, feeling Miss Anthony's patient attention. "Somewhere along the way—"

"The brilliant, hungry mind of a young girl," Miss Anthony interjected, "didn't let stilted patriarchy or blind tradition stop her. She feasted upon the knowledge along with her brother, who, I sincerely hope, encouraged her to learn just as he himself was encouraged."

"Oh, he did." Josephine's eyes watered. "Todd was my twin brother, and my champion in every way."

"Was?" Miss Anthony questioned softly.

Josephine hesitated. "He was killed . . . two years ago. He'd been working on behalf of freedmen to uncover corruption in the Georgia prison system. Freedmen were being jailed on minor or trumped-up charges, then indentured to companies under brutal conditions. One night, following a meeting at the jail, Todd didn't come home . . . They found his body the next morning behind a warehouse, only a few blocks from here. The officers said it was due to an attempted mugging, but . . ." Her gaze trailed toward that part of the city as memories of how he'd died—had been murdered—still haunted her. All the unanswered questions. "A handful of months later, my parents also died. As I shared, they were considerably older when Todd and I were born, and . . . I think Todd's death just—" Her voice broke and she shrugged, letting the silence finish for her.

With a frail hand beneath Josephine's chin, Miss Anthony urged her gaze back. "I am certain your brother *and* your parents—viewing this world from their current vantage point—are very, very proud of you."

Josephine's throat knotted.

"The older I get . . ." Miss Anthony searched her expression. "The greater power I seem to have to help the world. I am like a snowball . . ." She smiled. "The further I am rolled the more I gain. And I believe with all my heart that I am looking into eyes remarkably similar to those of my younger self."

Josephine blinked and a tear escaped. "Thank you, Miss Anthony. I do want to help change things, but sometimes I don't know how to do that. Or if what I'm doing is making any difference. There's so much opposition."

"Stay the course, my dear young woman. Cautious, careful people, always casting about to preserve their reputation and social standing, never can bring about a reform. So forget conventionalisms, forget what the world thinks of your stepping out of your place. Think your best thoughts, speak your best words, work your best works, looking to your own conscience for approval. Trusting, of course, that your conscience is guided by God."

"Miss Anthony!" a man called out, and they both turned.

One of the handful of men Josephine recognized as attending in support of suffrage raced toward them. "Make haste, ma'am. It's not safe. The violence is escalating. We have your carriage waiting."

"Yes, yes." Miss Anthony's steady voice belied the chaos. "Miss Dunham, you are most welcome to accompany us. In fact, I would encourage it."

"Thank you, ma'am, but I want to find my friends. Make sure they're all right."

"Very well. But promise me, no matter what comes, you'll remember"—Miss Anthony gently grasped her shoulder—"we must prevail in this. Failure is impossible."

Josephine nodded. "I'll remember."

As the two hurried away, she caught the boisterous laughter of men and walked back to the corner to see a group of them pelting suffragists with rotten eggs. The seasoned cluster of women stood shoulder to shoulder, placards held high, vigorously chanting the mantra, "Votes for women! Votes for women! Votes for women!"

Josephine's resolve hardened even as her heart ached. This was not the change she'd hoped to inspire. Her parents, God rest them, had taken her and Todd to abolitionist rallies after coming of age, so she knew this kind of ignorant hostility. They'd taught her that words carried the power to change hearts, and that God Almighty could be trusted to work in his often-mysterious ways.

She still wanted to believe that, and she still knew the Scriptures instilled in her from childhood. But mysterious was one thing—seeing no sign of his hand at all was another. Had he simply turned away from her? Was he weary of her repeated disappointments, as her earthly father had once been? If so, the feeling was mutual.

Across the street, younger compatriots huddled en masse as a half dozen men poked and prodded them with sticks as though they were cattle, laughing and making fun. A few tore off the women's sashes, the ribbons snagging their upswept hair and drawing even louder jeers.

Fuming, Josephine started toward them just as pea whistles shrilled. A horse-drawn police wagon rounded the corner. Finally. It was about time. The authorities would disperse the crowd and protect the—

"No!" she screamed as officers seized the young women instead, shoving them toward the patrol wagon. When the suffragists resisted, the policemen raised their clubs.

2

"Officers, please!" Josephine called, approaching the man who appeared to be in charge. "These women have done nothing wrong. Our organization obtained the necessary permit with the city to hold a public—"

"That permit was for a *peaceable* gathering. You call this peaceable?" He glanced down at her sash. "You women are inciting a riot."

"Inciting a *riot*? It's the *men* who resorted to violence!"

"You best get in the back of the wagon, ma'am." His jaw firmed. "Or I will forcibly install you there."

Josephine's chin lifted of its own accord. "You will no more place me in the back of that vehicle than—"

He grabbed her by the arm and shoved her forward. She'd counted the cost when joining the suffragist movement two years ago, inspired to fight for women as Todd had fought for freedmen. "Great change requires great sacrifice, Jo," he'd always said. His passion for justice had inspired her—and had cost him his life.

She thought of the women still in jail. Three weeks earlier, eight suffragists—mothers all—had been arrested while picketing outside the courthouse. The women had agreed beforehand that, if taken into custody, they would, in solidarity, refuse food. But the mayor, a fierce opponent of suffrage, ordered them force-fed. Three nearly died from liquid being pumped into their lungs instead of their stomachs. The others suffered cuts to their mouths and throats resulting in sickness and fever. So while Josephine was willing to suffer for the cause, she had no intention of going to prison under Mayor Darden's rule without a fight.

Seething, she resisted as the others did and took a hard blow across her backside. When the officer raised his club again, she lifted her hands in surrender. His grip tightened on her arm as she fell into step beside him, glancing back and hoping the others would follow her lead.

Todd—older by only seven minutes but a true big brother—had taught her much about the differences between men and women: how men often underestimated women, and how women mistakenly assumed men reasoned as they did. Those lessons, sometimes humorous and sometimes maddening, had proven useful. Especially now.

She reached for the back of the patrol wagon as if to climb in. The officer loosened his grip—and she tore free. He lunged for her, but she ducked, twisted away, and bolted into the crowd with the other suffragists. Not looking back, she cleared the electric streetcar rails and kept running.

At the corner she finally glanced back. No sign of the officer. But she did see Sarah. A man had her friend by the coat collar, shouting in her face. Sarah, well acquainted with cruelty, fired back something Josephine couldn't hear, but the smirk said enough. The man drew back to strike her, and Josephine rushed at him from the side, trying to get there in time—but couldn't. Sarah's head whipped hard to the right as Josephine, shoulder down, sent the man sprawling.

She grabbed Sarah by the hand and helped her up. "Are you all right?"

Sarah nodded, her cheek bearing a handprint that all but matched the fiery red of her hair. "Thanks, Finny girl." Sarah turned and kicked the man in the abdomen. "That's what I'm thinkin' of your opinions on me friend's speech today—and of your *asinine* views on givin' women the vote."

Hand in hand, they set off through the crowd, Josephine unable to quell a smile. Sarah's language, matching her Irish temper, could be quite colorful, so Josephine had taken to suggesting more acceptable vocabulary. *Asinine* was one of Sarah's recent favorites. Never mind that she emphasized the first syllable far more than needed.

They reached the corner and broke into a run, but Sarah tripped and went down hard. Josephine bent to help her when someone grabbed her hair from behind, snapping her head back. White-hot pain radiated across her scalp.

"I'll show you lack of decency and intellect." The young man from earlier grabbed Josephine around the waist.

Sarah helped her fight him off until another man yanked Sarah away and hurled her to the street. The last Josephine saw, Sarah lay motionless on the roadway.

It took Josephine a moment to respond, the depth of deception within the local authorities—and the evil behind Todd's death—hitting her full force again. "No, but—"

"Here." Sarah dug into her skirt pocket. "I got me week's wages from the mill this mornin'. It's not much but it's yours."

"Sarah, I'm not taking your money, and I have no intention of—"

"You just killed the mayor's son, Finny! In self-defense, I know, I was here. I seen it. But a woman's testimony counts for nothin', do you hear me? *Nothin'*. So if you want to live, you will run!" She shoved the money into Josephine's hand. "Now come on."

Josephine struggled to think clearly. As much as she wanted to argue, she couldn't. Sarah was right. Todd had been, too.

They stuck to the alleyways Sarah knew well and were halfway across town to Union Station when police whistles sounded again, distant this time, followed by the clanging of a bell—the alarm on one of the patrol wagons.

They both paused, breathless.

Sarah glanced back. "They must have found his body. Come on! We have to hurry."

Numb, still trying to make sense of it all, Josephine raced to catch up. Sarah, twenty-three and younger by only a year, was the kindred sister she'd never had. They'd shared a room at Mrs. Lowery's Boarding House for Women for months now, and Sarah was forever thanking her for allowing her to move in. But Josephine knew the real truth. It was Sarah who had rescued her following a time of such loneliness and grief there had been moments when Josephine hadn't been sure she would live through it. Or even wanted to.

Minutes later, Atlanta's Union Station came into view, and Sarah stopped abruptly. Josephine followed suit, her gaze trailing Sarah's past the barrage of freight wagons and horses and buggies to the two police officers standing guard at the entrance of the terminal.

"Surely they don't know yet," Josephine said.

"Nay, but they'll be knowin' it soon enough." Sarah turned to her. "Buy a ticket for whatever train is leavin' next. No matter where it's goin'. What matters is—Finny, are you listenin'?"

Josephine nodded, feeling as if she were in a fog.

"What matters is you gettin' out of the city as soon as you can. Now take off your sash." Sarah gestured, then did likewise, stuffing hers into the pocket of her coat. "Oh Finny . . ."

Josephine looked down to see blood smearing the front and right sleeve of her already-soiled woolen coat, the remnants of rotten egg dried and crusted.

"Here." Sarah shrugged out of her coat. "Mine's not near as fine, but you can't be travelin' in that. You'll set tongues to waggin', mark my words."

Josephine put on Sarah's coat, the garment thin compared to her own and snug about the shoulders. Sarah being a few inches shorter and more slender, her coat barely fell past Josephine's knees. Whereas Josephine's all but swallowed her friend's lithe frame.

Sarah gently touched her cheek. "He got you good, didn't he?"

"It's that bad?"

Sarah shook her head. "Get somethin' cold on it soon as you can. That'll help with the swellin'."

The blast of a train whistle sounded and smoke plumed into the cloudless afternoon sky.

"You best go." Sarah pointed, her voice tight. "I'll tell the schoolmaster you've taken an unexpected trip and didn't have a notion as to when you'd be returnin'. Write me soon as you can, lettin' me know where you are. And that you're safe."

"I will."

"And remember what address we're to be usin' in situations like this. Don't dare send it to ol' Miss Lowery's or to one of the group. The authorities will for sure be—"

"I know. I'll remember." Josephine hugged her tight. "What will I do without you?"

"Well, you'll have to be learnin' how to cook, for one thing," she whispered with a strained laugh. "You can't go back to eatin' flapjacks that taste like sawdust and drinkin' that brew you try to pass off for coffee."

Josephine tried to smile, and found Sarah struggling to do the same.

"Watch out for yourself, Finny girl. And don't trust *anyone*. That's one of your most noble faults. You think all people have good in them, but they don't. Some are dark through and through. So when someone like that shows you who they really are, believe them the first time, all right?"

"I will." Josephine started toward the street when fear rushed to meet her, overpowering and foreboding. She couldn't move.

"You'll find your way, love," Sarah said softly, coming alongside. "You're smart as they come and know more about the world than anyone I've ever met."

"All I know of the world is what I've read in books, Sarah. I've never even been outside of Atlanta. We were going to travel to so many places together. See the world. Paris, Italy, Spain, Switzerland. All of Europe."

"And we still will. Someday we'll go to all of them places and more. But for now . . ." Sarah leaned closer. "Remember what me mam said to me, 'fore she took her last breath?"

Josephine nodded. *"This isn't forever—"*

"It's just for now," they finished together.

"We'll be together again soon, Finny Dunham. And I don't mean in the hereafter." A smile softened her voice. "I'm meanin' this side of the great beyond."

"Not if it means putting you in danger. I would never—"

"I know you wouldn't. Now go. And look for a small town. Somethin' off a rugged road. Used to be, a person could hide in big cities. Not anymore. Not with newspapers and police—and mayors who hate suffragists. When faced with a choice, Finny, trust your instincts. And trust God. He'll guide you. After all, he led us to each other after an awful time for us both, now didn't he?"

Understanding that Sarah knew every corner of her heart, Josephine gave her friend a last, tight hug. "I love you, Sarah McFee," she whispered, then hurried across the street toward the entrance to Union Station.

Josephine smoothed a hand over her hair, disheveled strands now loose from their pins, and did her best to look as though she belonged. But when one of the police officers out front caught her eye and frowned, his gaze narrowing, her heart all but stopped.

3

Fighting the instinct to run, Josephine schooled her features and walked past the officers. She forced herself to match the pace of other travelers, fearing at any moment she'd feel a hand on her shoulder or a firm grip on her upper arm.

Uncomfortably aware that everyone around her had either a satchel or trunk, she joined the queue at the ticket office and discreetly counted the money Sarah had given her. Four dollars and thirty-five cents. Sarah's unflinching generosity encouraged tears again. How would her friend get by? Then again, how would *she*? They both basically lived week to week. At least they'd already paid Mrs. Lowery room and board this month, so Sarah wouldn't have that to worry about.

Josephine checked the clock on the wall—10:20—then the departure board beneath, feeling a *tick tick tick* inside her. A train bound for Charleston left in thirty minutes. Richmond, Virginia in an hour and a half. New York City in two hours. She didn't have that long to wait. And all those places were so far away.

"Next!" the ticket clerk said, only then looking up. A shadow flitted across his face as Josephine stepped forward.

"Yes, sir, thank you. What is your next departure?"

"That'd be Charleston, ma'am. Standard fare of fourteen dollars."

"Fourteen?" Josephine searched the board again as though something might have changed.

"All aboard!" a man called from behind her.

She looked back. "Where is that train going?"

"That's the Chattanooga-Tullahoma line, continuing to Nashville. It's a Limited, only two stops. But it's already boarded and ready to—"

"Please," she whispered. "I need to be on that train. How much is the fare?"

The train gave two sharp whistle blasts.

"That train is full, ma'am. All except for the colored car, so you'll need to wait and—"

"That's fine with me. What's the fare?"

His brow furrowed and his gaze moved pointedly to the left side of her face. Josephine clearly read his assumptions, along with pity. Which told her the injuries were likely worse than Sarah had let on.

"Miss, it's clear you're going through a very difficult time, but as it states right there—" He pointed to a printed sign. "It's against the law for a white person to travel in a car designated for—"

"I am well familiar with the ruling in Plessy v. Ferguson, sir. But tell me, what ruling gives a man the right to beat a woman?" Her voice tightened. "I *must* get on that train."

He hesitated, his mouth forming a thin line. "Fare to Chattanooga is four dollars even. Tullahoma, four dollars and twenty cents."

Chattanooga, a growing city, she knew, but . . . "What kind of place is Tullahoma?"

"Mid-point stop between Chattanooga and Nashville. Tiny speck of a town. Not much to it compared to Atlanta."

"Tullahoma, please."

He took her money and pushed a ticket toward her. "Last passenger car." He gestured, lowering his voice. "There's a brief stop in Chattanooga but no changing trains. Don't let a porter see you getting on or off. If you do, you're on your own."

Josephine walked briskly down the terminal, past porters closing doors, until she was nearly to the end. Somewhere behind her, a train whistle bellowed a long, echoing blast and the Chattanooga-bound train lurched forward. She started toward the car when a porter exited the rear door, torn ticket stubs in hand.

She immediately feigned searching for someone, peering down the long terminal, certain she was fooling no one. The man walked past her as the train chugged forward.

Glancing around one last time, hoping no one would see her, she spotted a woman watching her from inside the car. Curiosity and mild disbelief registered in the woman's expression and, for an instant, Josephine wondered if the woman might alert someone in authority. But having no choice or time to waste, Josephine raced for the rear stair step, grabbed hold of the railing and pulled herself up, then climbed to the open platform as the train picked up speed.

Breath coming hard, her palm raw and aching, she opened the door to the car and stepped inside, and quickly realized it wasn't only the one woman who had been watching her.

All eyes in the passenger car were fixed on her, and Josephine, a teacher for close to half her life, could think of nothing to say that her actions hadn't already announced. They looked at her and knew her story. Or *thought* they did.

She moved to claim an empty space on one of the cushioned bench seats but the older woman occupying it scooted to the middle, preventing it. Eyes lowered, Josephine looked to the right and although the elderly man seated there didn't move an inch, his demeanor exuded unwelcome. Same as every other person she passed as she walked toward the back of the car.

She reached the last row and glanced outside to see a porter looking in that direction. Instinctively, she ducked, fear outweighing shame even as the back of her neck heated. Once the passenger car was clear of the terminal, she raised her head.

"I hope you done give him hell right back," a woman said, her voice barely audible.

Josephine peered up to see the woman she'd exchanged glances with before she boarded.

Similar in age, judging by her appearance, the young woman stared unblinking, challenge in her eyes. "Did you? Give him hell back?"

The image of Clay Darden's lifeless body returned with painful clarity. "Yes," Josephine whispered. "I . . . think I did."

"Good for you then," she said beneath her breath and indicated with the slightest nod that Josephine could share her bench. Yet no sooner did Josephine sit than the woman abruptly stood and moved a few rows up. Josephine stared after her. Had she mistaken the woman's kindness? Or perhaps that kindness, if made known, would come at too great a personal cost.

Grateful no matter the woman's reasons, Josephine rested her head on the window, the glass cool against her forehead. Recalling what Sarah had said, she lightly pressed her cheek to the chilled pane and winced at the sting, but forced herself to repeat the act several times.

As the train sped north, eating up miles of countryside and leaving behind everything and everyone she knew, the air inside the compartment grew colder. Which came as no surprise, because this particular car lacked the customary amenities such as cast-iron wood stoves, overhead luggage compartments, and even a water station. A few of the many injustices her father and the firm he worked for had addressed repeatedly with the railroad commission, including the harsh working conditions of the nearly twenty thousand black men who served as porters on the railroad.

Justice will not be served until those who are unaffected are as outraged as those who are. How often her father had quoted that. Yet when it came to fighting for women's rights, he had explained that the wheels of justice ground exceedingly slowly, and that just as in a great war, battles had to be fought strategically. Yet the battle for women's rights was one he had never seemed eager to fight. Only later had she begun to understand why.

He'd long attempted to dissuade her from joining the suffrage movement, stating his and her mother's concern for her safety. Those attempts had only intensified following Todd's death. Yet as she'd learned more about the movement and witnessed repeated efforts by local authorities to stamp it out, Todd's mantra had become like a steady drumbeat deep inside her.

One specific exchange with her father returned with striking clarity. Even now, she felt the heat of her anger from that day, and the deep disappointment she'd felt in him, both emotions exacerbated by Todd's death just weeks before. "But Father, it's impossible to struggle for civil rights, or even equal rights for black men, without including *all* men. And all *women.* Every tribe, nation, tongue, and people. Isn't that what you always say? Because equal rights, fair pay, justice, all of it . . . It's like the air we breathe. Either we all have it or none of us do. That is why women *must* be granted the right to vote, same as men. You of all people must understand that and take up the cause of suffrage now . . . as I am doing. And should have done a long time ago."

Steeled determination had slipped into her father's eyes. "Daughter, you well know that I forbid you from joining that organization. The women involved are not of sound mind or judgment, so again, I must—"

"Todd died fighting for justice, Papa. For a cause he believed in. He was doing something lasting with his life. I want to do that, too."

"You *are* doing something lasting with your life. Teaching children is helping to prepare you for marriage, Josephine. To be a wife and a mother. For raising children of your own and organizing a household. That is what is most important for you." His placating smile seemed intent on shutting down argument. "Your mother and I knew you'd be a wonderful teacher. That's why we encouraged you to sit for your advanced certificate when you were yet so young. *The youngest but most mature candidate they'd ever considered.* And now look at you. Already instructing upper grades for years now."

"Redirecting the conversation no longer works, Papa. I'm not seven years old anymore. I'm a twenty-three-year-old woman with a mind of her own that *you* helped shape and mold, inadvertently as those efforts might have been . . . now that I look back."

He rose from his desk chair, his movements slow and deliberate, more frail now than fierce, as though he'd aged decades in the weeks since Todd's death. "Politics is dirty, ruthless, and unfeminine, Josephine. Women are emotional creatures by nature, guided by sentiment, and are not equipped for political decisions."

"But that's simply not—"

"Allowing you to participate in such an organization," he continued with force, "would expose you to ridicule and hostility. And I will *not* have you, or this family, thus humiliated."

How small he'd looked in her eyes then, regardless of how still beloved as her father. "I attended my first meeting some weeks back, and will march in an upcoming rally. We must fight for change or change will never happen."

The gaze he turned on her felt almost foreign. "As your father and spiritual head, I will not allow you to throw away your education *or* to tarnish this family's reputation by associating with that group of women. And that is my final word."

"I know what you believe, Father. But I simply do not hold the same—"

The slam of his fist on the edge of his desk all but choked the words in her throat. "*I will not abide this, Josephine!* I did not raise my own daughter to disrespect me. To cast aside good reason for this foolish notion of equality with men. Men and women were made for very different purposes. The Scriptures clearly establish this. Women are to submit to men. It's God's divine order, and seeking the vote violates that sacred structure. If women get the vote, what next? Women running businesses? Women demanding to have a say in legal matters? Running for public office?"

"I would say yes to all of those things, Papa. Women are equally as intelligent as men and have every right to choose the course of their lives. How many times in our studies were my marks equal to, or oftentimes higher, than Todd's?"

"You *dare* compare yourself to your brother? To try to establish equal footing with him? As if you could ever take his place?"

The words sliced deeper than she would have imagined, even having long suspected them to be true. But to hear them stated aloud and without the least trace of regret . . .

"You always were far too curious," he continued, eyes narrowing. "I was wrong to have indulged you as I did. But try as you might, one cannot change the natural order of things. The change you desire must be tempered with the immutable truth of a woman's God-given duty toward hearth and home, and for childbearing. So with my opinion on the subject firmly established . . ." He eased back into his chair, his mouth a firm line. "You will align your actions accordingly, daughter. And you will govern yourself by what you have been taught to be good, and right, and true."

How often that conversation replayed in her mind, awaiting a resolution that, with her father's passing weeks later, had never come. Her mother followed him in death soon after. The doctor said they both succumbed to pneumonia, but she wondered if grief had not been the real killer. And if she'd been partly to blame.

Yet, she could never have imagined this sudden turn in her life.

Regret and doubt crowding close, she shivered as hunger pangs reminded her she'd foregone breakfast that morning due to nerves over speaking publicly. The rally had started less than three hours ago, yet how distant that gathering seemed now.

What had her students thought when she hadn't relieved the substitute that morning as she'd promised them yesterday? What would they think when she didn't return tomorrow? Or the next day? She could see all their faces clearly in her mind's eye. She'd enjoyed instructing primary grades when she'd started teaching at the age of thirteen. But when she began instructing intermediate and upper grades seven years ago, the bright and inquisitive minds of those ten- to fourteen-year-old boys and girls took her own passion for educating to new heights.

Already, she missed them, and hoped the teacher who assumed her class would nurture the older girls' education as much as the boys', same as she'd done herself. Many of her fellow teachers focused the boys' studies on arithmetic and civics, while steering the girls toward home economics and literature. Josephine taught them both equally—though she admittedly downplayed home economics—and clung to the hope that her leaving Atlanta would be temporary. That the day would come when she could return both to her students and her life. But right now she couldn't see past the moment at hand.

The rhythmic *thump* of steel wheels and rails lulled her eyes closed. *Some of the men saw him draggin' you back here. They'll figure it's you who did it, and figurin' will be proof enough, whether they have real proof or not.*

Her eyes popped open, Sarah's warning stoking her fear. Not even distancing herself from Atlanta brought comfort. Because they knew who she was. And if Mayor Darden would so brutally mistreat suffragists for merely picketing, what would he do to the woman who had killed his son?

She shifted on the cushioned bench seat, the world a blur outside the window, nothing but passing fields and an occasional farmhouse as the terrain gradually ascended. The heavily forested hills in the distance drew her gaze, wisps of clouds trailing off their highest peaks like tufts of cotton strewn in the wind.

The train hugged a hillside and the sun shone through her window, acting almost like a mirror, and Josephine gasped, hardly recognizing her own reflection. A welt, swollen and discolored, the exact width of a leather belt, marred her left cheek, and her left eye appeared puffy and bruised. She wiped away tears, her fingers gritty. Traces of dried blood still stained her right hand.

She reached into her coat pocket for her handkerchief, then remembered she'd traded garments with Sarah. She checked the other pocket and pulled out Sarah's sash. Wadding it up so as to hide the lettering, she wet a corner of the cloth with her saliva and scrubbed off the blood as best she could, giving special attention to the thin silver wedding band on her right ring finger.

Since slipping the ring on her finger the day after her mother died—the same day she'd discovered the inscription on the inner circle—she'd rarely taken it off. This ring was all that tangibly remained of the family she'd once had. But looking at it now, recalling how the ticket clerk—and even the woman a few rows up—had eyed her, she glanced from her right hand to her left, then slowly removed the band and placed it on her left ring finger.

A little loose. But if she was going to look like a battered wife, she might as well play the part. Besides, Mayor Darden would be searching for a single suffragist schoolteacher, not a wife running from an abusive husband.

Nearly three hours later, the train pulled into Chattanooga's Union Station and as several fellow passengers disembarked, she sat in the very last seat, gaze glued to her lap and angled away from the terminal-facing window, her head aching and throat parched. Only after most of the passengers had exited did she sneak a look toward the terminal. And her senses shot to alert.

Policemen. Stationed everywhere. At entrances and exits. By newspaper stands. Even by the ticket office. Was that normal? Or had news of what happened back home already reached Chattanooga?

The train whistle blew two sharp blasts as a porter boarded the car.

Josephine ducked and lay flat on the bench, uncertain whether or not he'd seen her. Able to see only a portion of the aisle, she struggled to listen over the rushing in her ears. The porter made light conversation as he tore ticket stubs, and all the while she hoped and *prayed* he wouldn't walk back here. But footsteps approached, then dark slacks and boots came into view—and stopped right beside her bench.

"Josephine Dunham," the porter said softly, more caution than question in his resonant voice.

Josephine's body flushed hot then cold. Knowing she was had, she started to sit up.

"No, ma'am, you stay right there. Let me come to you."

As he knelt, she dared look up. An older man, a pained expression passing over his face.

"I don't know what it is you've done, ma'am, but every uniform in this city showed up about an hour ago. And your name is what's on their lips."

"I promise, sir, it was self-defense. He was beating me and I—"

He held up a hand. "What I should have said just as quickly is, I don't care to know what you've done either, ma'am. Don't mean to make light of it. *No, ma'am.*" A kind expression relieved the statement of any sting. "Just can't afford to be privy to it, that's all. In case anyone goes to asking me. But from where I'm looking, whoever did this to you? Deserved all they got and more."

The compassion in his tone tugged hard at her emotions.

"Do you have a ticket, Mrs. Dunham?"

She handed it to him, the wedding band on her left hand weighing heavy and false.

"Tullahoma," he said softly, tearing her ticket. "You got people there?"

She shook her head. "The man in the ticket booth said it was a tiny town, not much to it. And considering everything, that sounded better than Chattanooga."

He nodded. "You stay put right here. Don't get up. Don't sit up. Not even after the train moves out. Not until I come back for you. You just stay still and keep down. You understand, ma'am?"

"I understand," she whispered. "I don't know why you're helping me, but *thank you.*"

"Well, you're not out of the woods yet. No way of telling what's waiting in Tullahoma. Takes about an hour to get there, so won't be long." He paused. "And the main reason I'm doing this? Because a woman I know got off this car a few minutes ago. She heard the police talking about looking for a white woman who might be on the train from Atlanta. So she came and found me."

Josephine pictured the woman from earlier and was beholden to her, whoever she was.

"And the other reason?" the porter added softly, his gaze sweeping her face. "I know what it's like to get beaten with a strap."

Fresh tears came, stinging the wound on her cheek, and Josephine reached out a hand.

He gently clasped hers and gave a soft laugh. "First time for everything, I guess."

She gave him a questioning look.

"Shaking hands with a white woman." He rose and walked back up the aisle.

Josephine lay still, clutching the cushioned bench, as the train lurched forward and began to gain steam. The emotion she managed to stem earlier spilled over, and she let it. She attempted to remain alert, but the rhythmic rocking and steady hum of the rails kept coaxing her eyelids shut, despite the chill in the air.

She awakened with a start some time later and sensed the train slowing. Staying down as promised, she worked to stretch sore muscles, the wounds on her hands and face aching. The car gradually came to a stop as the station came into view. A clapboard building with a tin roof, far more modest than Atlanta's or Chattanooga's Union Stations. But *modest* boded well for the size of the town and her circumstances.

Somewhere off the beaten path. A place to hide, at least until she could prove her innocence. *If* given that opportunity. Because one fact she couldn't escape: Men would be her sole judge and jury. So was a fair trial even possible?

As the other passengers disembarked, noises drifted in from outside—voices mingling with the shuffle of heavy foot traffic and the squeak of luggage carts. A delicious aroma prodded her hunger, something sweet with a trace of cinnamon, and her mouth watered. Curiosity nudged her to take a peek, but she stayed hidden—until a brass band started playing a rousing rendition of "I'm a Yankee Doodle Dandy" which drew enthusiastic applause.

Curiosity finally winning out, she cautiously peered out the window.

People everywhere. From her vantage point at the back of the train, the platform appeared to be standing room only, and above the station entryway hung an enormous banner—*Welcome Municipalities of Tennessee to Bottle Spring Spas*—complete with colorful streamers and ribbons. Panic tightened her chest and she quickly lay back down.

So much for Tullahoma being off the beaten path. What if the authorities here had also been alerted? And were waiting for her?

Struggling to keep the barrage of "what ifs" from careening out of control, she listened for the porter to return, beginning to fear he'd forgotten about her. Or worse, that he'd decided to turn her in. Where would she go and what would—

The door to the passenger car opened and footsteps hastened down the aisle.

"I'm sorry, ma'am." The porter knelt. "I had to help unload and transfer trunks. We picked up a slew of passengers in Chattanooga and every car was full up. Everybody seems to be getting off here for some kind of celebration."

"I know. I heard the commotion outside and took a quick look." Seeing his frown, she hurried to continue. "But I don't think anyone saw me."

The look he gave her said he hoped not. "I wish I had a better story to tell you, ma'am. But either way, we don't have much time. They're looking for you here, same as before. Asking for you by name."

Dread coiled inside her.

"But the good news," he continued, "is that this town's so small it's only got one sheriff and two deputies."

"But if they're looking for me and know who I am, how can I stay in Tullahoma?"

"Oh, you can't. But you can't stay on the train either. Deputies are checking all the cars right now, which is why we've got to hurry. They started looking up front first, so I figure we've got a little time yet. But the sheriff is somewhere close too, so we'll have to keep watch."

We. The fact he'd spoken in the plural made her feel as though she wasn't completely on her own. "But even if I make it past the station, where do I go?"

"I don't rightly know, Mrs. Dunham. But sometimes all we have is the choice staring straight at us. And the only one you've got right now . . . Choose to get off this train, or choose to stay on and get found."

"I definitely choose the former."

"All right then." He nodded. "Stay close once we're outside. Don't get separated."

He headed down the aisle toward the very back of the train, and she hurried to catch up, her lower back stiff. He paused briefly on the outside platform, and she trailed his gaze to see the two deputies entering the fifth passenger car. Only three cars separated them. They were moving fast.

"Let's go," the porter whispered back.

"Wait . . . What is your name, sir?"

He looked back, a faint smile coming. "Slim Poyner, ma'am."

"It's nice to meet you, Mr. Poyner. And thank you again. I'm indebted to you."

"No, ma'am, you're not. God has met me in my need far more times than I can count, and this is my way of thanking him. So if you owe anyone, it's the good Lord." He joined the fray of passengers on the platform, and she followed, feeling somehow smaller in light of his statement.

As the brass band launched into "The Stars and Stripes Forever," she stuck close, her head down, intent on not being discovered by the authorities while also wishing to avoid eye contact with passersby. Though of far lesser concern, the attention her injuries drew and the way some people looked at her now—with such distaste and disgust, almost as though *she* had done something to deserve the marks on her face—filled her with shame. And for something that was neither her fault nor her choice.

They pushed through the crowd and headed around the side of the station. Twice, other passengers managed to cut between them. In desperation, Josephine finally grabbed the back of Mr. Poyner's suit coat and held tight. If he minded or found it shocking, he didn't show it.

As sunlight broke through the gray cloud cover, the band played on, the crowd clapping and laughing at the upbeat melody, children dancing and clutching striped paper cones filled with sugary strands of fairy floss, their faces a blur of sticky grins.

Mr. Poyner came to an abrupt stop. "Turn around. Quick!"

Josephine instinctively looked up—and locked eyes with a man whose gaze seemed to home in on hers. Warning shot through her, and she spun and headed in the opposite direction.

"Josephine Dunham!" a man's voice boomed.

A chill skittered up her spine. But she didn't dare look back.

Just inside the door of the train station, Mr. Poyner shoved a suitcase into her hand. "A woman traveling without a bag doesn't look natural."

"But it's not mine. I can't—"

"I'll find you and get it back. Just make it outside. Find a place to hide. And keep watch for me."

Josephine pushed through the throng. "Excuse me, please. *Excuse me.*" She set her sights on the exit doors ahead when her senses shot to full alert.

Men were stationed at each of the exits. None uniformed or wearing badges that she could see. But they were scanning the crowd just the same. Was that normal? Instinct told her no.

Forcing deep breaths, she saw a family with four young girls only feet in front of her and quickly maneuvered toward them. She followed closely, but not too closely, hoping anyone watching would assume her to be their nanny. The queue narrowed and slowed as they approached the exit. Fear knotted her throat.

Josephine fixed her attention on the two younger girls as though intent on keeping them corralled with their parents. Not until she cleared the doors and had exited the station did her pulse begin to return to—

"You there, ma'am. Stop! *Ma'am!*"

Tempted to run, she quickened her stride until a firm touch on her shoulder brought her up short.

4

A MAN TOWERED OVER HER and the keenness in his eyes siphoned the air from her lungs.

"You sure seem anxious to get out of there, ma'am. Did you not hear me calling after you?"

Josephine tried to respond, but nothing came out at first. "I-I'm sorry. I'm not overly fond of crowds."

"Then I guess you're in the wrong place today, aren't you?"

Her mouth went dry. They had her, and she knew it. Sarah was right. Mayor Darden would sentence her to prison and she'd never get out.

The man held something out. "I'm pretty sure one of your charges dropped this back there. My guess is she'll be missing it soon enough."

In his hand was a little rag doll, and Josephine's breath left in a rush. "*Yes.* Yes, she certainly will. Thank you, sir."

"You bet, ma'am. You take care of yourself now."

The unmistakable sympathy in his tone might have touched her if he hadn't just frightened her out of her wits. Not looking back, she stuffed the rag doll in her coat pocket and put distance between herself and the station. On the street, she searched for the family but they were gone.

Gray clouds conspired to mask the sun again as a chilly wind knifed through her thin coat. She tugged her collar higher, thinking of Sarah and hoping she was safe.

Suitcase in hand, Josephine scanned the busy thoroughfare for a place to hide while still watching the train station. A haberdashery and general mercantile stood directly across the street, both crowded, as was a bakery whose warm bread made her long even for stale saltines from a cracker barrel. Then she spotted the tack shop near the livery.

When she stepped inside, familiar scents of oiled leather, woodsmoke, and sawdust met her. Thankfully, the shop was empty. Voices drifted toward her from the back room, one female, the other clearly male.

"Your husband does fine work," the man said.

"Yes, sir, he does. This is crafted of the finest leather, as you requested, and should last her for years to come. She's a very lucky girl."

"She's a very *special* girl," the man responded. "And I want her to know that . . . what with all she's been through." His voice dropped so low the rest of what he said was lost to her.

Josephine stepped behind a display of saddles and kept watch for Mr. Poyner through the front window. People hurried past—men in suits and bowler hats, women in woolen coats tugging children along—racing to keep pace with life while a razor-edged loneliness widened inside her.

If she didn't find a way out of this town . . .

Her gaze snagged on her reflection in the window—pale, bruised, unfamiliar. She pulled out her hairpins and tucked wayward curls back into place before letting one fall forward to hide the tender flesh on her cheek. No tears came this time. Only anger.

She could still feel Clay Darden's weight on her, see the hatred in his eyes as he straddled her and reached for his belt. Her strength had been nothing against his. Even as she was grateful for what hadn't happened, rage filled her. What possessed a man to think he had the right to lay hold of a woman in such a manner? In *any* manner. The law should protect her. But it wouldn't. Not in Atlanta anyway. Not when the attacker was the mayor's son.

Was the mayor's son.

A shudder ran through her. She had killed a man. Not intentionally, of course. In self-defense. But would that matter? Perhaps the other suffragists were right: most men were so insecure in their own standing that they had to cow every woman around them, even with violence. She hadn't wanted to believe it, but now . . .

A familiar figure outside caught her eye. Mr. Poyner hurried from the station, scanning the street.

Josephine grabbed the suitcase and stepped just outside the door of the tack shop. The instant he saw her, relief flooded his expression. He motioned for her to join him at the corner.

"I'm sorry it took me so long, ma'am. All this hoopla and so many people. Here, let me take that." He relieved her of the case. "Come with me. We don't have much time."

No sooner had he said the words than a train whistle blasted.

She followed him inside the livery where he briefly spoke to a couple of workers. They passed rows of stables and finally paused by the large open doors.

He looked around and shook his head. "I'm sorry, Mrs. Dunham. I was hoping to find a delivery wagon headed out of town. A handful per day service the surrounding communities and—"

Just then a loaded freight wagon drawn by mules rounded the corner. The driver, mostly hidden beneath a heavy beard and dark Stetson, wore a leather rain cape. A compact, muscular dog with a mottled blue-gray coat with black speckling crouched beside him on the seat, mirroring the man's disgruntled expression.

"Wait right here, ma'am." Mr. Poyner waved as he approached the wagon. "Dodge! Good to see you again, my friend."

The driver tugged the reins. "Same to you, Slim. But got no time to spare today. I'm doing my best to beat the weather."

"Who said I wanted anything?"

"Charlie totes that same grin every time he comes asking for something."

Mr. Poyner chuckled. "How is my young nephew? Still working hard, I hope. Doing a good job for the man?"

"Last I heard, Uncle Jack was pleased."

"Well that's good to know. Listen, Dodge—"

"Again, Slim, I can't be hauling anything back for you today. I'm full up with a heavy load. And it's weathering up good and fast. If these skies make good on their threat, it'll be rough going."

"No, no, I don't have any freight to haul. But I do have a favor to ask." Mr. Poyner stepped closer to the wagon, shifting the suitcase in his grip, and though Josephine could no longer hear what he was saying, his glance back in her direction said enough. But should she join him now—or wait?

Just then, the driver shot a skeptical look in her direction and his dark expression kept her rooted in place.

"I wish I could offer some help to you, Slim. But like I said, I'm full up. Besides, she's got no business going up there. And what am I supposed to do with her once we get—"

"I wouldn't ask if it wasn't important, Dodge. You know that."

His scowl deepened, and his quick once-over told Josephine he was about to refuse—ending any chance she had. His Southern drawl carried an Appalachian lilt, rustic yet dignified, its music roughened by displeasure.

Mr. Poyner must have seen some hint of agreement, because he motioned her over.

Yet the closer she came, the less sure she was how well Mr. Poyner actually knew the man. *Rough* didn't begin to describe him—an overgrown beard, mud-caked dungarees, collar-length hair long overdue for cutting, and a broad frame filling most of the seat. But it was the way he glanced at her, then quickly looked away, that drove shame like a spike through what remained of her pride.

"Mrs. Josephine Dunham, meet Dodge Coburn. He's agreed to take you on to Lynchburg."

Lynchburg . . . The name sounded vaguely familiar, yet she knew nothing about this area. She also knew she was in no position to negotiate. Although she did wish Mr. Poyner hadn't shared her real name. "Thank you, Mr. Coburn. I appreciate your willingness to—"

"Best climb on up. Need to be on our way before the skies split wide open."

A shadow flitted across Mr. Poyner's face but Josephine chose not to acknowledge it. She spoke softly so only he would hear. "Mr. Poyner, your kindness is something I will never forget. Much like yourself, sir."

"I wish you only the very best, Mrs. Dunham. I'll be praying for you, ma'am. God go with you." He glanced back at the wagon. "With you both."

His afterthought only stoked her uncertainty, and as she rounded the freight wagon and was about to "climb on up" as Dodge Coburn so chivalrously suggested, she spotted a rock about the size of her fist. Without hesitation, she discreetly scooped it up and shoved it into her coat pocket holding the rag doll. No man would ever gain the upper hand on her again.

She climbed up to the seat, not waiting for assistance. Good thing, considering Dodge Coburn offered none. But now that she was up here, she would've sworn the seat had shrunk by half. And judging by the way the dog eyed her, the animal, some sort of cattle-herding dog, she thought, appeared to be as amiable as its owner.

"Jessie," he said softly. "Come on, girl." With a jerk of his head the dog edged closer to his side.

Josephine barely got seated before he flicked the reins and the wagon jolted forward. She held on, the conveyance rough and complaining over the rain-rutted roads. But she didn't mind. Every rotation of the wheels put more distance between her and the authorities at the train station. And Mayor Darden and prison.

Hand in her coat pocket, she drew courage from the rock and kept her attention confined to her lap as they drove through town. Hunger gnawed her insides and her throat felt like gravel. Hopefully Lynchburg wasn't too far away.

The occasional *clink clink* from the wagon bed told her the cargo was likely glass—delicate, and plenty of it judging by the stacked, tarp-covered crates. She hadn't noticed any company name on the wagon, and the freight was strapped down tight.

Not until the outskirts of town did she lift her head, a cold breeze kicking up once again. They turned onto a dirt road lined by winter-paled fields, the waist-high grasses bending in the wind while barely budded oaks, poplars, and maples hinted at spring. Woodsmoke and pine drifted on the air. The gentle sweep of the hills—rolling for miles—tempted her with a peace she didn't dare trust.

Fatigue washed over her, and she steadied herself on the seat, stiffening her back. How long until Lynchburg? And what help, if any, waited there?

Dodge Coburn hadn't looked at her since they'd left the livery, much less said anything. Which was fine by her. She already felt self-conscious about her appearance, and his initial response upon seeing her hadn't helped. She cast a discreet glance his way, highly doubting conversational skills were his strength, but hard work clearly was. His muscular forearms and thighs said as much, and his hands, calloused and rough, told a similar—

"So do you plan on doing me in somewhere along this lonely stretch, ma'am? Or will you wait till we're up in those hills?"

Josephine glanced over. "I-I beg your pardon?"

"That rock you tucked in your pocket." His gaze slid to hers. "Or did you just take a sudden shining to it back there at the last."

Embarrassed that he'd seen her pick it up and wondering now if he knew something about her, maybe even what she'd done to the mayor's son, she faced forward, flustered by his accusation. And the startling blue of his eyes. "I . . . I was simply—"

"You have no cause to be afraid of me, Mrs. Dunham. I'll do you no harm, ma'am."

"I am *not* afraid of you, Mr. Coburn. And I'll have you know I can take care of myself."

Those eyes met hers again, and she knew he heard the false bravado in her voice as well as she did. But it was the fact that her countenance so clearly bore the evidence of her ability to "take care of herself" that completed her humiliation.

She stared ahead, absentmindedly urging her hair forward on one side until she became aware of what she was doing. And stopped.

They rounded a curve and a creek bed lay ahead, its entry fairly steep and its depths swollen from recent rains. The dog whined, ears pricking, and Josephine held tight to the seat again, bracing for the crossing. What she wouldn't do for a sip of that water. But not if it meant being more beholden to this man than she already was.

Dodge Coburn expertly guided the wagon down the descent and through the swift current, the wheels creaking and slipping in the rocky bed. He took it slow and steady, speaking soothingly to the team of mules as he did. Once they cleared the creek, he brought the wagon to a stop, set the brake, and climbed down. A sharp whistle, and Jessie bolted to join him.

Josephine turned on the seat, wondering what he was doing and if there was time for her to get a drink.

"No, ma'am. You stay put."

It was not a request, which only made her want to climb right down and prove herself a self-sufficient, independent woman. Yet, weak as she felt, she doubted she would make it back up without assistance. And the very thought of having to ask him for—

He reappeared, canteen in hand, water dripping from the sides, and held it up to her. Her throat convulsed at the mere promise. She drank and drank and drank, the water cold and crisp. Finally, she paused and dabbed at the corners of her mouth, the left side tender, her breath coming hard.

"Thank you," she managed, wanting more, but thinking better of it. She held out the canteen.

"Finish it up, if you can."

So she did, draining the contents until the water sloshed in her belly. It wasn't exactly sustenance, but it was something.

"More?" he asked.

She shook her head.

A minute later, Jessie bounded back up to the seat, water dripping from her mouth, fairly smiling if that were possible for a dog. Mr. Coburn followed, wiping his mouth with his sleeve, his beard damp.

"Thank you again," Josephine said, meaning it.

"No trouble." He urged the team onward. "How long's it been since you've eaten?"

"Last night," she finally admitted, not looking at him.

He reached into his shirt pocket and pulled out a strip of dried beef. Or what was left of it. "It's not much, but it's yours if you want it."

She accepted without hesitation, her mouth watering. "Thank you." While beef jerky had never been a favorite, too salty for her taste, she attempted to tear off a piece by hand.

"I'm afraid that's the kind you got to sink your teeth into, ma'am."

She did, and bit off a thick chunk. Flavors exploded in her mouth. Pepper, garlic, onion, and . . . another ingredient she couldn't identify. She briefly closed her eyes. *Delicious.* Smooth and smoky. Her stomach flinched, not quite a spasm, but definitely unpleasant, and no doubt stemming from lack of food. But knowing even this little amount would help, she chewed all the more.

Still savoring, she shielded her mouth. "This is very good."

"Glad you like it. But seeing as there's nothing but water in your belly, you might want to take it easy. See how it sits first."

"I'll be fine." She tore off another piece with her teeth, eager to regain her strength and unable to remember anything tasting so good. After a minute, she grew very aware of the dog's attention. "Is it all right to give her a bite?"

He gave a nod.

Josephine held out a small piece.

"Easy, Jessie," he whispered, but the dog was extremely gentle when taking the piece of jerky from her grasp.

Only when Jessie started growling and the wagon stopped did Josephine look up to see two men on horseback stopped in the middle of the road ahead—rifles aimed.

"Whatever happens," Dodge Coburn whispered, cocking the revolver now in his grip. "Don't say a word."

"But what do they—"

"Not . . . *a word.*"

5

"How can I help you gentlemen?" Dodge called out, already knowing Jessie would follow his command, but doubting the woman would. Not based on the fire in her expression seconds earlier.

The man on the right nudged his mount forward, the thickness of his beard unable to mask his sunken cheeks. The recent winter had been hard. "Teamsters ain't drivin' the wagon today."

"You're a mighty astute man." Dodge scanned either side of the heavily wooded dirt road. "But again, what can I do for you?"

"It be more 'bout what we can be doin' for you." The second man edged closer. "Let's see what you got in that there wagon, then we'll see if it's anything we're wantin'."

"That's nonnegotiable, my friend. The delivery of this freight has been entrusted to my care, and I intend to see it to fruition."

The two men looked at each other then slowly back again.

Dodge bit back a sigh. "I aim to get this load where it's going. So you're not taking what's in the wagon. Best you move on."

They hesitated for a beat then responded with high-pitched laughter, the first man gesturing. "Y'seems to be missin' somethin' here—like it's two guns agin' one. Reckon me and Rufus here's the ones who's gonna be settin' the way of things, don'tcha think?" His gaze slid to Mrs. Dunham who noticeably stiffened. "So after we take us a gander to what's in yer wagon, reckon we'll take a look at yer woman, too. Her face ain't too comely just now, seems like you done seen to that." He let out a low chuckle. "But the rest o' her . . . she's more'n lookin' like she's wantin' for a good—"

Dodge raised the revolver, took aim, and fired. The man's worn, low-crown Confederate hat went flying as he ducked, eyes wide. His partner cocked his rifle and took aim just as Dodge got off another shot, considerably lower this time, and the man's horse reared, nearly throwing him off. His rifle fell to the ground.

Dodge retrained his focus. "Now toss that Springfield down or next time I'm taking flesh." When the man didn't comply, Dodge feather closed his left eye. "Right ear or left? It's all the same to me."

Cursing, the man finally threw his rifle to the dirt. "You don't got no idea who yer messin' with, boy. If ya did, you wouldn'ta gone and done that."

"You're the one who picked the fight." Dodge jerked his chin. "Now get on down the road. Come back later for your rifles. I'll leave them in the brush."

A sharp tug on his sleeve. "Mr. Coburn, I strongly object to that—"

"Quiet." Dodge cowed her with a look, not about to give the men cause to pursue this. A contentious, mouthy woman could trigger a man from the hills faster than a hot brand to a bear's backside. Dodge held their stares as they passed, while Mrs. Dunham's indignation burned a hole clean through him.

Once the pair disappeared around the curve, he hopped down, removed the cartridges from the rifles and scattered everything in the brush, then got the wagon moving again. He wanted to clear the pass sooner rather than later, especially now, and still had to negotiate the narrow switchback trail ahead.

He could feel Mrs. Dunham's attention, but hoped she would just let it drop. The altercation was done and over. No bloodshed, nothing and nobody hurt, other than manly pride, which usually healed up sooner or later, given time. Now to get this load—and her—delivered. But the next time he saw Slim Poyner, he was going to give the man a piece of his mind for—

"You *truly* believe that was a wise choice, Mr. Coburn?"

Dodge tightened his grip on the reins.

"I mean, really," she continued. "Leaving rifles for men like that where they can come back and get them? And then do who knows what to us or anyone else?"

"Mrs. Dunham, I realize you're—"

"I, for one, believe those men *lost* the right to those firearms when they pointed them directly at us and threatened us."

"Out here, ma'am, a firearm can mean the difference between life and death. It's been an especially harsh winter, and the code among people in these hills is—"

"The code?" She gave a disbelieving huff. "I believe what *we* just experienced borders on something between life and death, so I think—"

Dodge pulled hard on the reins, ready to grab hold of her if need be. But to her credit, she maintained her seating.

He nudged up the brim of his hat and looked her square on, pained again by the wounds on her face. "Listen to me, Mrs. Dunham. You're not in Nashville or Chattanooga or Raleigh or wherever else it was you came from anymore. It'll come as no surprise that I didn't want to take you with me today, and there's a reason for that. This is no place for a woman like you, and you'll do well to get back to wherever you came from lickety-split."

Her mouth slipped open. "A woman like me? And just what do you mean by that, Mr. Coburn?"

Not at all swayed in his opinion, nor in his desire to take a whip to whoever had done this to her—presumably the husband she was running from—he looked pointedly down at the embroidered sash hanging out of her coat pocket, having noticed it shortly after she'd climbed onto the wagon. Only able to see the partial phrase *Votes for W—* he knew what declaration the sash bore. He was no stranger to that movement. A familiar bitterness filled him.

Mrs. Dunham followed his line of sight, and she quickly stuffed the sash back into her pocket, her chin lifting. "You have no right to judge me. Or to think you can even begin to understand what it means to—"

"I know all about your cause, ma'am, and what you stand for and what it is you want. And I'm not saying it's all for naught. What I *am* saying is that folks in these parts, hill-folk especially, don't take kindly to a woman claiming to be the same as a man. And back there when you were about to give me what for?" He gestured behind them. "You could've gotten us both killed."

To her credit, she didn't respond immediately. "So, Mr. Coburn, you're of the mind that women are not equal to men?"

He briefly looked away, wondering if she'd even been listening. "I'm of the mind, *ma'am,* that you need to understand that no one much cares about suffrage in these parts. Or whether women can vote or what they get paid. Most women here do good just to survive, to get enough to eat, enough to wear. Enough for their children." He paused. "Do you have any idea what those men would have done to you if given the opportunity?"

Her gaze flickered and in that instant he read understanding. And fear.

"With all respect—" He looked at the angry red welts on her face. "*This* is nothing compared to the brutality of some of the men in these hills. That is what I'm trying to say to you. You're in unfamiliar country now, Mrs. Dunham, and foreign to your sensibilities too, I'd wager. Best hold your cards a little closer to the vest . . . and keep your mouth shut with men like that."

Emotion welled in her expression, and she quickly looked away.

He did the same, steeling himself against the vulnerability he knew she hadn't wanted him to see. He pulled his hat low, slapped the reins, and Flossie and Betty responded. Blissful silence settled in as the road passed beneath them, the plod of the mules and sway of the wagon as familiar as the sigh of the breeze. He welcomed the stay of conversation, especially with the hairpin turn ahead.

It wasn't suffragists filling a woman's head with all manner of nonsensical ideas that angered him. Their notions weren't *all* nonsensical. But the few that did bear legitimacy proved far too dangerous and costly in the end. The woman sitting beside him was living proof of that, even if she couldn't see it.

Thunder rumbled in the distance and large droplets of rain splattered and plopped in the dirt as clouds loosened their purse strings. The swath of valley to the right, carved deeper and wider than any other in these hills, was a treasured view and stomping ground since childhood. But today, with one eye on the road behind him and the other on the threatening steely gray clouds, he scarcely paid it any mind.

Uncertain whether or not Mrs. Dunham was accustomed to navigating mountainous terrain, his gut told him the latter. "Best keep your eyes on the road, ma'am. Not on the drop-off. There's no turning back once we start the climb."

She didn't respond, but her white-knuckled grip said plenty.

"Let's go, gals," he coaxed as the mules started up the hill, braying and straining beneath the load. "Get on up there. *Move!*" He could drive this road in the dark and had, on occasion, with the help of a full moon.

But as they rounded the curve, the wheels failed to grip, and he felt the back of the wagon slipping toward the drop-off.

"Move on, Flossie," he called, standing to better see the wagon's position. "Come on, Betty. Just a little more. Come on, girls!"

The animals strained, pulling strong and true, and as they rounded the final curve and hit steady grade again, Dodge breathed easier. "Well that was worth the price of the ticket, wasn't it?" He laughed.

But when he looked over at Mrs. Dunham, her complexion was an odd shade. Her hand went to her mouth, and he stopped the rig. She quickly scrambled down and scarcely reached the road before emptying the contents of her stomach. He winced, wishing she hadn't insisted on eating that jerky so fast. Her pride would pay a steep price for such lack of propriety. As if it meant a hill of beans to him. Maybe if he offered her an out.

"Don't feel too badly, ma'am. That switchback has caused many a flatlander to lose their lunch."

He tossed her the cleanest rag he had, even more eager to get this woman off his hands, though not quite sure what to do with her.

She climbed back up rather unsteadily but he wasn't keen on offering assistance. Not just to get it thrown back in his face. He knew the suffragists' mantras—*Independence is happiness. Men, their rights and nothing more; women, their rights and nothing less. There will never be a new world order until women are a part of it.*

No, if this woman wanted to be treated equally, he'd oblige her. At least as much as his upbringing and common sense would allow. He offered her the canteen and, to her credit, she drank in small sips. Eager to get home, he urged the mules on.

Not a mile down the road, the light sprinkle stepped up its game. Dodge shrugged off the oiled rain cape and held it out to her. She managed a quiet, "No, thank you." But a minute later when the sky unleashed its storehouses, he offered again and she accepted, pulling the tarp up over her head.

Jessie whined and looked up at him longingly.

"Mrs. Dunham, would you mind letting Jessie get under there with you? She's a mite skittish of the rain."

Looking none too sure, she held open the cape and Jessie nudged close to her, looking equally uncertain. Quite the pair.

"How much longer?" Mrs. Dunham asked after a while.

"Another hour or two, depending on the roads."

Disbelief shone in her features, as did dread. But she kept any complaint to herself. He honestly didn't know how she still remained upright after what she'd been through. The wounds on her face were fresh. His guess? After the beating, she'd just up and left, blind with fear and fed up with it all. Again, give him a whip and five minutes with the man who'd done this to her.

Nearly two hours later with the rain ceased and the hills draped in darkness, they pulled into Lynchburg. Despite having been raised here, having buried his parents and then younger sister Kathleen in the cemetery a hefty stone's throw beyond the church, despite knowing every nook and cranny of this town and the lives of most everyone in it, Lynchburg didn't feel like home. Not anymore. Not since that trip last spring.

He still appreciated this place and these people, but nothing here matched the soul-deep pull he'd felt riding the vast stretches of wide-open plains out west last year. Rich grasslands dotted with sagebrush and wildflowers. Rolling plains jutting into mountains so steep he wondered if their heights had ever been trod by anything but angels, then those soaring peaks falling away into breathtaking plunges, giving way to valleys so deep and wide only the hand of God himself could have carved them.

All that beauty, so wild and untamed, had reached deep inside him, grabbed hold of a long-held dream, and refused to let go. Then Kathleen had taken ill, and everything changed. His promise to her on her deathbed came first, and he would guard the treasure she'd entrusted to him. Or die trying.

Just seven months since his sister's passing, yet the pain still felt brutally fresh at times. For both him and her daughter, Bethie. The reality that he was solely responsible for Bethie now still put the fear of God in him. Being an uncle? He wasn't too terrible bad at that. But being the only parent to a nine-year-old girl? Especially one so feisty and stubborn, and the spitting image of her mom—so much so it was like looking back through time at his sister? That was something else.

Yet that wild, open Wyoming land with its fertile fields and crystal rivers rushing with winter melt still had a hook in him, stuck hard and fast. And the purchase of ranch land he'd made before Kathleen took ill was his life's savings. Almost everything he'd had.

He knew he needed to let it go, return the documents to the broker in Cheyenne, and get the land up for sale. But how did a man let go of what he knew he'd been born to do? What he'd spent his life preparing and saving for . . .

But that's what had to happen. No way could he take Bethie out there. It was no place for a young girl. Then again, raising her around a distillery wasn't the best answer either. But in a town of scarcely four hundred people, options were few, and none paid as well as Jack Daniel. He valued his position as foreman of the cattle farm and was good at it. But when he'd started working at the distillery at age twelve, doing odd jobs, whatever needed to be done, there hadn't been any cattle. He'd stumbled across that idea later, and had spent the bulk of his adult life raising someone else's cattle and pigs, growing their farm, making them richer—and that's what he would have to keep on doing.

Not that Uncle Jack wasn't generous with his employees. He was. Generous was the man's middle name.

Dodge held back a sigh as he guided the wagon down the shadowed street, working to shake off the melancholy while determining, yet again, to reframe his situation in a better light. Most men would kill for his position with Jack Daniel Distillery, for his pay, his life. So he just needed to let go of that Wyoming dream—and whatever money he would lose in the sale of it—and just accept it. But as happened every time he told himself that, the hook inside him just sank deeper.

But one thing he *had* figured out—where he was taking the woman beside him. Just thinking about it brought a slice of pleasure. Because Mrs. Josephine Dunham was about to meet her match.

6

Shivering with cold and damp, Josephine squinted as she read the wooden shingle in the flickering glow of the single kerosene streetlamp planted by the walkway. "Miss Mary Bobo's . . . *Boarding House*?"

"That's right. Used to be old Doc Salmon's house. He practiced from here until he retired and sold it." Mr. Coburn jumped down from the wagon and removed his hat. He ran a hand through his still-damp, wavy, collar-length hair, hardly looking worse for wear.

Meanwhile, she could well imagine her own haggard appearance.

Earlier on when he'd stared her down, maintaining his gaze had all but drained her pride, yet shame still poured through her as she climbed down, legs wobbly, stomach aching with hunger. "While I appreciate the ride, Mr. Coburn, I . . . don't possess the means for a boarding house."

"Well, that's not a problem. Because Miss Mary's full up right now. Last I knew, anyway."

Gripping a spoke of the wagon wheel for support, she stared, not understanding.

"This is the only inn in town, Mrs. Dunham. But Miss Mary's not an altogether unfeeling woman. Most days, anyway. So I'm betting she'll work out something with you. Least for a night or two."

Whether in his tone or appraising glance, she caught the reprisal of his earlier stated opinion, *This is no place for a woman like you.* As though she had a choice in whether to be here.

Dodge Coburn wasn't as unlearned a man as she'd initially pegged him to be, despite his vernacular. Whether that would ultimately be a good thing or bad, it had certainly played in her favor earlier that day. It made her skin crawl remembering the way those two men had looked at her like she was a slab of meat on a plate, their vulgar intent unmistakable.

Like it or not, she owed Dodge Coburn a debt, and for far more than just passage.

He strode past the white picket fence with no gate and down the wide brick walkway, not bothering to knock on the double front doors before entering.

She followed at a slower pace, the simple but stately white, two-story clapboard building demanding admiration in a subtle, humble sort of way. Square white columns rose to support an upper balcony, and black rocking chairs flanked the entrance. Even in the cold and damp, the house issued a warm welcome.

Josephine could well imagine *Miss Mary*, its proprietress—a dour, persnickety old spinster resolute on condemning everything and everyone. Especially those daring to challenge the status quo. She knew those women only too well. After confirming her suffragist sash was tucked securely in her coat pocket, she followed Mr. Coburn inside, smoothing a hand over her damp skirt and arranging her mess of hair as best she could without benefit of brush or comb.

As soon as she crossed the threshold, aromas so delicious, so promising, caused her stomach to spasm in anticipation, and emotion sprang to her eyes, as did hunger pangs for home and family long gone. And for Sarah—and their tiny, shared boarding house room.

"It's late, so supper's probably long over." Mr. Coburn glanced back. "But I'm sure one of Miss Mary's cooks will be able to rustle up something for you."

Willing to eat almost anything, she whispered a throaty, "Thank you," then quickly looked away, uncomfortable beneath her vulnerability.

To her left, an open door revealed a dimly lit but nicely appointed den, one wall filled with bookshelves. To her right stood two closed doors she assumed to be bedrooms for boarders who, hopefully, had already retired for the night.

A staircase leading to the shadowed second-floor landing drew her gaze, and the steepness of the stairs reminded her of her childhood home. She could still recall every nook and cranny of that house. After her parents died, the proceeds from the sale had barely covered their outstanding debt, leaving next to nothing. They'd spent nearly all they had championing freedom and rights for the formerly enslaved. A tempered bitterness rose inside her. If only her parents had considered the rights of women—of their own daughter—to be equally as worthy, then perhaps her current circumstances would be different. How could two people so devoted to equal rights not have seen that she needed a champion too?

"Mrs. Dunham?"

Pulled back by the gentle whisper, she swallowed against the knot in her throat and joined Mr. Coburn at the far end of the shadowy hall. But seeing the odd look he cast back in her direction, then hearing the din of conversation, she slowed her steps. Too late, she spotted a half dozen men and three women still gathered around a dining room table, and it took everything in her not to bolt.

At that same moment, an older woman clearing the table looked in their direction. "Well, look what the cat done dragged in."

Josephine took a swift step back, thinking the comment directed at her. But the woman's grin, clearly intended for Mr. Coburn, corrected her misassumption. Meanwhile, conversation around the table continued unabated.

Mr. Coburn removed his hat and gestured to one of the serving dishes she carried. "Don't tell me you're out of those candied apples I love."

"If you're late to this table, son, then you get what you deserve. Come here and give us a hug."

Mr. Coburn obliged and, with a forefinger, sneaked a swipe in one of the bowls and licked off the remnants. She swatted his arm, her laughter playful—until her gaze moved past him.

"And just who might you be, young miss?" she asked, her humor fading, as did the table conversation.

Heat rose to Josephine's face, all eyes on her.

Mr. Coburn looked back. "Oh, my apologies. This is Mrs. Josephine Dunham of . . . Tullahoma, most recently. Charlie Poyner's uncle, Slim, asked me to give her a ride. I told her I thought y'all might be able to help her for a night or two."

The woman raised a brow.

He motioned for Josephine to join them.

She didn't move.

"Dodge . . ." The woman cocked her head. "Why don't you take Mrs. Dunham on out back to the kitchen while I finish up in here."

Grateful for the woman's astuteness and compassion, Josephine thanked her with a nod and followed Mr. Coburn outside to the porch, grateful she'd been proven wrong about the proprietress. Miss Mary, expectedly older, seemed far more understanding than dour and judgmental.

Shadows draped the porch, which actually appeared to be a deck, judging by the plank boards beneath her feet. Darkness obscured the path, the only illumination a pale silver moon and the warm glow from a window a few feet ahead. Josephine looked to her right and down the street as far as she could see, but could scarcely distinguish the shadowed outlines of darkened buildings and houses. Then she realized . . .

No electricity. Anywhere. That's why the interior of the house had seemed darker.

She wasn't unfamiliar with oil lamps, but electricity had been installed in their family home some years back. And parts of Atlanta, thriving city it was, had been powered by electricity for over two decades. But not Lynchburg, Tennessee, which felt another world away. A very good thing, in one sense. But very lonely and unfamiliar in another.

In the kitchen, they found two women standing by a massive cast-iron stove in the center of the room, their backs to them. And they were having words.

"All I'm saying, Calla, is it simply doesn't taste as good as usual. It's still worth eating, mind you. It's simply not your best. And it's important we always give our best, no matter who's sitting at the table."

"I'm hearing you, ma'am, but I made it just how I always do. I don't know what's making the difference."

"Maybe the eggs weren't as fresh."

"I gathered them eggs myself this morning, so it wasn't—"

"Well—" The woman, presumably the head cook judging by her authoritative tone, gave a succinct nod, clearly ending the discussion. "Let's make it again later this week and see if it doesn't come out better."

"Yes, ma'am, I'll do it, and with a skip in my step. But I'm telling you, I—"

Mr. Coburn cleared his throat, announcing their presence, and the women turned.

Surprisingly, the head cook was much younger than Josephine had assumed from seeing her only from behind. Calla, her coworker with warm brown skin and steady eyes, looked to be a few years older. Both women shifted their attention from Dodge to her—and their smiles faded. Concern washed over Calla's face, while guarded suspicion settled on the younger woman's.

"Mr. Coburn . . ." Suspicion seeped from the woman's tone as well. "You're much later than expected. And toting a stranger to boot."

"Yes, ma'am. Got held up in Tullahoma, then hit some hard rain on our way back. Heavy load didn't help either. We slipped and slid our way up and over Lynchburg Hill. But allow me to introduce—"

The young woman held up a hand, and in that simple gesture, commanded the room. She approached Josephine, her gaze assessing. "Welcome to Lynchburg, Miss . . . ?"

"It's M-Mrs. actually," Josephine managed, regretting the stammer and trying not to squirm beneath the lie. "Mrs. Josephine Dunham."

The woman's gaze darted to her left hand, as though she doubted Josephine's claim. Only then did Josephine realize, with sickening regret—her *wedding* ring was gone.

"My ring!" She clutched her left hand, searching the floor for her mother's thin silver band. "It was on my hand just a—" When was she last aware of it? She couldn't remember. Regret hardened her gut. The thought of having lost that ring too, on top of all else, felt like the final blow. "It has to be here somewhere, I—"

Aware of the sudden silence, she looked up.

The young woman's gaze had turned downright appraising. "I'm right sorry about your ring . . . *Mrs.* Dunham. That's more bad luck on top of what already looks to be none too good. I'm Mrs. Jackson Bobo. But everybody around here just calls me Miss Mary."

7

Josephine blinked, thrown even more off-balance. *This* was Miss Mary? The dour, persnickety old spinster she'd imagined? This woman couldn't be more than ten years her senior, if that. Yet she exuded authority—and unmistakable skepticism. She had an old soul quality about her, too. The faded blue of her eyes, perhaps, or the way her light brown hair was plaited and coiled in a knot at the nape of her neck. Whatever the case, Josephine knew instinctively not to underestimate her—or get on her bad side.

"Miss Mary," she responded and tried to produce a smile. Her lower lip felt like it might split open again from the effort. "It's a pleasure to meet you . . . *ma'am*," she added, unable not to, despite their closeness in age. Her stomach rumbled, and she hurried to cover the sound. "You have a lovely boarding house. It's very welcoming. Especially on such a dark and rainy night."

Miss Mary gave a slow nod, the silence lengthening. Thankfully, Dodge Coburn filled it.

"Mrs. Dunham's in need of lodging for the night, Miss Mary. And I was wondering if you might put her up. If it's not too much of a bother."

A smile, tepid at best, tipped the woman's mouth. "No bother at all. You're welcome to stay the night here, Mrs. Dunham." She glanced about. "But I'm not seeing your bags."

Josephine winced. "I had to leave hurriedly, so—"

"Leave from where, if that's not prying overmuch?"

"Chattanooga," Josephine answered quickly, working to form a story that would hold water.

"I thought I heard some city in your voice. You're a long way from home, aren't you?" Miss Mary's gaze moved over Josephine's face, pained empathy softening her features. "Just so we're both tugging on the same end of the rope . . . I don't kin to a man raising his hand to a woman. Ever. But neither can I abide you bringing trouble to my doorstep. To my tenants, and into my home. So don't think me unfeeling for asking, but . . . are you running from your man?"

Taken aback by so direct a question, Josephine simply nodded.

"Any reason of thinking he knows you're here? In Lynchburg?" Miss Mary continued. "And that he'll come banging on my door in the dark of night?"

Josephine shook her head, keenly aware of everyone's attention, especially Dodge Coburn's. "No, ma'am. He doesn't know where I am. I promise."

Miss Mary eyed her. "Dodge says he picked you up in Tullahoma. You got people there?"

"I've got no people. Not anymore. It—" Her voice broke. "It's just me now."

Miss Mary held her gaze, then eventually looked back at Calla. "Fetch Mrs. Dunham some supper, please, Calla. Then get some quilts. We'll make her a pallet here in the kitchen by the stove. I'm sorry, Mrs. Dunham, but all my rooms are let."

"She can stay with me in my room, ma'am," Calla offered softly.

"All right then. That's done. Go on and rest yourself before your legs give way beneath you." Miss Mary gestured to a small table in the corner of the kitchen. "And take off that damp coat or you'll catch your death for sure."

Josephine obeyed, her knees ready to buckle.

Not a minute later, Calla placed a large dinner plate piled high with fried chicken, mashed potatoes smothered with gravy, fried okra, cooked apples, and a crusty biscuit slathered in melted butter before her. "Here you go, young missus. And I'm sorry about that ring," she whispered.

Eyes filling with emotion, Josephine looked up and mouthed the words *Thank you.* But no sound came. It occurred to her then that a wedding ring from an abusive husband wouldn't be near so tender a loss, so she downplayed the grief, rather than let it show.

"Drink a swallow or two of this milk first." Calla set a glass by the plate. "Then start in slow with the taters. The candied apples with cinnamon should sit well too. The rest'll be there when you're ready."

Calla gently touched her shoulder and moved away, and Josephine stared at her own empty left hand, wondering if somehow God had played a role in her losing her mother's ring. Maybe this was his way of punishing her for lying about her current situation. Or for killing Clay Darden. Or maybe for not thinking as highly of him as she once did. But how did you think highly of someone who had the power to change your circumstances for the better, and yet didn't?

She took a long swig of milk, the cool working its way down inside her. It tasted better than anything she could remember, despite the tenderness of her swollen lip. She sipped slowly, waiting, not wanting a reprisal of what had happened with the jerky.

"Well," Dodge said behind her. "Think I'll go find Bethie."

Josephine perked up at the name. *Bethie?* Was the man married? Was that his wife, or did he have a daughter? She would've pegged him as a loner.

"Not before you have supper, you don't." Miss Mary's tone brooked no argument. "Now sit on down. We've got plenty, as usual."

"Thank you, Miss Mary. I won't decline your hospitality, but I need to get going. See my load secured for the night, and Bethie home and to bed. I hope she didn't put y'all out much."

"No way that girl could put us out," Miss Mary responded. "Ever."

"Though, land sakes . . ." Calla chuckled. "She totes a poke full of questions 'round with her. Pulls them out almost faster than I can give answer."

Dodge laughed and the sound was so genuine, so inviting, Josephine had to look back, mashed potatoes and gravy melting in her mouth. The difference in the man was striking. She'd experienced his surprising decency firsthand. But his smile hinted at a layer of kindheartedness that, on first impression, she would've doubted existed.

Miss Mary gave his shoulder a motherly pat. "Sweet Bethie takes after her mama in that way, for sure. A generous dose of sweetness cut through with some downright ornery—and a mouth that never stops." Her smile softened. "But you're doing good, Dodge. Never doubt that. You both are."

Tenderness swept Dodge Coburn's expression, and while Josephine knew it wasn't polite to stare—especially at another woman's husband—she couldn't not. Despite his formerly gritty demeanor and rough exterior, those blue eyes and the emotion in them tugged at something inside her. He fingered the Stetson in his hands as though uncomfortable beneath the praise, which made him considerably more attractive than Josephine cared to acknowledge.

He chose that moment to glance her way, and she busied herself with smoothing the cloth napkin in her lap, embarrassed at having been caught staring, while also painfully aware of how rough *she* must look right now.

"Here you go, son," she heard Calla say, then watched the woman push a cloth-covered tin into his grip. "I'd say there's enough for two meals, but I done seen you eat too many times. And don't you worry about feeding Bethie. She ate with us earlier."

He looked down at the tin. "Thank you kindly, both of you ladies, for helping me like you do. I'm much obliged."

Miss Mary waved off the comment. "Go on now. You'll find Bethie in the library. Sound familiar?"

"Yes, ma'am, it does," he answered.

"After supper," Miss Mary continued, "I told her to go stick her nose in a book. She can borrow whatever she takes a hankering to, as usual."

Dodge slipped his hat on and redirected his gaze to Josephine again. This time she didn't look away.

"Mrs. Dunham, you take care. I hope things go better for you here on out, ma'am."

"Thank you, Mr. Coburn. Both for the ride and . . . for your kindness."

He tugged the brim of his hat and left, presumably to retrieve his daughter and head home to his wife. The realization that he was married brought a slight, surprising disappointment, which Josephine quickly dismissed. Best she concentrate on getting her story straight before Miss Mary's next cross-examination.

To her relief, Miss Mary took her leave as well, but her voice carried as she visited with tenants in the dining room. She addressed each by name and conversed as though they were family. Her keen wit drew laughter more than once, and Josephine wondered which of the men she'd glimpsed at the table was Mr. Jackson Bobo.

The door to the dining room opened and the woman Josephine had seen clearing the table when they first arrived entered carrying stacks of dirty dishes. Josephine tried to catch her eye, unsuccessfully so.

"Mrs. Gibbs—" Calla looked up from where she kneaded a wad of dough on the worktable. "This here's our newest guest. Meet Mrs. Dunham from over Chattanooga way."

Mrs. Gibbs deposited the dishes by the washbasin. "Yes, I done met Mrs. Dunham on her way in."

Josephine formed a half smile and paid for the effort. "It's nice to meet you, Mrs. Gibbs. I'd like to thank you for your sensitivity earlier. In asking Mr. Coburn to bring me to the kitchen the back way instead of traipsing me through the dining room."

"Oh, it were my pleasure," the woman responded, yet her cool expression conveyed otherwise. "Just how long you planning on being in town . . . Mrs. Dunham?"

Josephine glanced at Calla to see if she noticed anything odd about the woman's behavior, but Calla was focused on her task. "I . . . don't know exactly. A few days at least."

"Well, you boasting from the big city and all, I doubt you be finding much here to your liking. Probably be aching to leave quicker than you think."

Certain now that she wasn't imagining it, Josephine studied the woman. In turn, Mrs. Gibbs gave her a look like she was yesterday's trash—or worse. Josephine didn't know how to respond.

"Well . . ." Mrs. Gibbs opened a cupboard and retrieved a purse. "I best be getting on home, Calla. I done cleared the table of dishes and people, then wiped it all down. I can't be here tomorrow night, and done told Miss Mary. But I'll be back the day after to help. Hope y'all have a good night."

Calla waved a floured hand. "'Night, Mrs. Gibbs. You be careful going home now."

"Oh ain't nobody gonna dare mess with me, Calla. You know that."

The women laughed, but as Mrs. Gibbs left, she shot a parting look at Josephine that held nothing short of warning.

Staring after her at the closed door, Josephine fought to make sense of the exchange, and couldn't. A possibility occurred to her, but she immediately dismissed it. She'd only just met the woman. Impossible that Mrs. Gibbs would know about what she'd done back in Atlanta. Perhaps the woman found her haggard appearance distasteful. After all, numerous passengers on the train had given her disapproving looks. And with Mrs. Gibbs working for Miss Mary, the woman was no doubt protective of her employer.

Deciding that had to be it, Josephine returned to her meal and ate until she could hold no more, then watched as Calla scraped the remnants of her plate into the compost bucket. She'd gone so long without food, the act felt wasteful, especially with food this good. Yet she said nothing, her full belly conspiring with exhaustion to keep her silent.

Dodge had mentioned something about this being the only inn in town, so she had to find a way to stay here. At least for a while, until she knew what to do next. Would it ever be safe to return to Atlanta? The image of Clay Darden on top of her filled her mind again—the rage in his eyes, him removing his belt as terror coiled in her gut, then how she'd struck him in the head and his lifeless body falling limp. She kept reminding herself she'd done it in self-defense. That she'd had no choice. Either that or be beaten to death. But as Sarah said, that wouldn't matter.

She squeezed her eyes tight to dispel the memory but all she could see was the blood pooling beneath his temple. Would a jury of men be able to see the truth if it was laid before them? Or in killing Clay Darden, however unintentionally, had she issued—and signed—her own death warrant?

8

"WHY, LOOK AT YOU, MRS. DUNHAM," Calla said a minute later, pulling Josephine back to the present. "So plumb tuckered you can hardly keep them eyes open. Let's get you where you can rest."

Josephine gave herself a mental shake, the disturbing images gradually fading. "Please, call me Josephine. And I insist on helping you with the dishes first. The one who cooks should never have to clean up alone."

"Now that's a kitchen rule I like . . . Josephine. I'm Calla Jenkins, but you call me Calla. I always welcome an extra set of hands."

Water heated quickly on the cast-iron stove, heat emanating from its intricately patterned sides and doors, and they set to work.

"Thank you again for dinner, Calla. I haven't had food that delicious since I don't know when."

Calla winked. "I'm thinking you were just hungry."

"I was that, but the truth remains."

"And just so you know, I don't know how y'all do it where you hail from, but here at Miss Mary's? We call the noon meal dinner. And this here meal is supper."

Josephine nodded. "Then thank you, Calla, for *supper*."

When they finished a while later, Josephine stretched the drying cloths over hooks along the wall while Calla retrieved bedding from upstairs. Josephine peered after her through the open doorway leading into the dining room. The door to the foyer beyond stood open as well.

Treading quietly, she found the foyer dark and still. Distant snatches of muted conversations floated toward her from behind closed doors, the only light issuing from an oil lamp burning low on a table in the corner. She felt like she'd stepped back in time.

While oil lamps weren't foreign to her, she was simply accustomed to more modern amenities. Electric streetlamps and streetcars were commonplace in Atlanta and considered indispensable by most. Electricity powered many of the homes, her family's home among them. Occasionally, power interruptions in the evening plunged parts of the city into darkness. But within two or three moments, backup gas-powered generators would send light flooding back across the city in a golden haze.

She crossed to the front doors and peered into the night. Rain fell in soft sheets, moisture gathering on the windowpanes until the world beyond turned murky and blurred. Dodge Coburn's wagon was gone, and the single kerosene streetlamp at the end of the walkway struggled to push back the darkness.

Thoughts of Sarah tugged hard, as did the desire for something familiar. But at least the mounting panic inside her had quieted by a degree. Lynchburg felt another world away. And for good reason. But being a world away from the world she'd known wasn't a bad thing. For now.

She glanced at her left hand, grieving the loss of her mother's ring. Where had it slipped off? On the road somewhere between here and Tullahoma? Or maybe when she'd scampered down from the wagon about to be sick. It could be anywhere.

She'd seen the doubt in Miss Mary's eyes when the woman had glanced at her empty left hand. The absence of the wedding ring definitely did not play in her favor.

The glass on the door was cool to the touch and, grateful no one was around, she briefly pressed her injured cheek against it. She glanced up the stairs to the second-floor landing, watching for signs of Calla. Seeing none, she peered into the den to the left of the hallway and found her gaze drawn to the large bookcase on the opposite wall.

Even in the dim light of the oil lamp, she saw books of all sizes and widths filling the shelves, and wondered which book Dodge Coburn's daughter had chosen. Was the girl old enough to read? Or perhaps Miss Mary had a collection of picture books for the very young.

Comforting scents of binding glue and ink dried on paper lured her closer, reminding her of the library in her family home—when she caught the image of an older woman in a portrait on the wall. Only, the portrait moved, and she realized with numbing sobriety that she was looking at her own reflection.

She stepped closer, the empty eyes looking back almost ghostly. She angled her face from side to side. The bruising on her cheek, jawline, and around her eye had grown more pronounced, as had the swelling. But even with the mirror's chipped and faded silver backing, the reflection did not lie.

Only that morning, though it seemed far more distant, Miss Anthony had issued a solemn warning in her speech, challenging fellow suffragists to prepare to pay a high price for freedom and equality. *Like countless women before you, many of you will be called upon to bear the marks of this struggle, both inwardly and out. So stay strong, my sisters. Arm yourselves with courage, and lean into the eternal strength that far exceeds your own. Because you will need it.*

With the fire of Miss Anthony's delivery still resonating inside her, Josephine swallowed hard, the truth of her situation bearing down. "I just never thought it would happen to me," she whispered, her voice familiar yet the face staring back anything but. "Or that the price would be so dear."

She gently fingered the deepest cuts, the blood long dried, the flesh still tender. The scarring on her face should have been the least of her concerns, she knew. But despite everything, the heartbeat of vanity still fluttered down deep.

She turned away from the mirror and crossed to the shadowed bookcase, and ran a hand along the spines of the books, wishing she could make out the various titles to know if any were ones she'd—

"Looking for something specific, ma'am?"

She whirled around at the voice behind her. A man, seated in a chair in the darkened corner, book in hand, stared, a small oil lamp casting its anemic glow on the table beside him.

"Begging your pardon, ma'am, if I startled you. T'weren't my intention."

Her pulse still pounding in her ears, Josephine attempted to speak normally. "I didn't realize anyone was in here. I'm sorry for intruding."

His outstretched hand slowed her hasty retreat. "First off, you didn't. Intrude, I mean. I was just drinking in the quiet of the night and letting my supper settle. Me and Mr. Ben-Hur—" He held up the book. "We meet here in Miss Mary's front parlor from time to time to confer and . . . ruminate together. And considering I just learned today about his creator's demise, I thought a visit tonight was appropriate."

Seeing the half-empty glass on the table beside him, she wondered if the man had been drinking in more than just the quiet. Yet she felt a touch of sadness. "You're saying Lew Wallace has died? The author?"

The man, mid-to-late fifties, she guessed, nodded, his salt and pepper goatee nearly touching his vest. "Nigh onto a month ago, it seems. Funny how you can grieve the passing of someone you never met yet still feel like you knew, simply through the words they put to paper."

He took a long drink, a mantel clock she hadn't noticed before slowly ticking off the seconds. His waxed mustache nearly eclipsed his upper lip, and his finely tailored suit revealed a man attentive to detail. One who valued the importance of making a good impression. Which begged the thought . . . What must he make of her? And had he heard her speaking to herself a moment ago? Discomforted by the thought, she hoped not.

"Well . . . I'm sorry to have disturbed you, sir. I'll leave you to your visit."

"You ever read him?"

Nearly to the door, Josephine paused. "Have I ever read the novel *Ben-Hur*?" she asked, the teacher within her reacting to the abbreviated fashion in which these people spoke. Not altogether lacking appeal, the dialect did lack the finished quality she attempted to instill in her students.

His slow smile gave the impression he knew exactly what she was thinking. "That is precisely what I am inquiring of you, Mrs. Dunham . . . most recently of Tullahoma."

Josephine eyed him, already having gathered from his comment about supper that he'd been at the table when Dodge Coburn first brought her in. He'd obviously caught Dodge's introduction. The man had a mischievous quality about him. Flirtatious, in a way, though not inappropriately so. More like charming, in a backwoods Tennessee sort of way. And his accent. Definitely of the hills and hollers but sprinkled with a sophistication he seemed to command at will.

"Yes, I have read *Ben-Hur*. Several times, in fact."

He leaned forward. "So it was to your liking?"

She didn't have to reach far for one of her favorite quotes from the novel, memorization being another habit her parents had instilled in both her and her brother. That, and she routinely assigned the novel for reading and discussion with her older students. "*To begin a reform, go not into the places of the great and rich; go rather to those whose cups of happiness are empty—to the poor and humble.* Chapter five, I believe, if memory serves."

"Well, well . . . I have, indeed, met my match." He rose, and, to her surprise, stood a good three or four inches shorter than she, though his knee-length black frock suit coat lent him a taller air. "I am impressed, Mrs. Dunham, if you don't mind me saying." He made a show of clearing his throat. *"Every age has its plenty of sorrows; heaven help where there are no pleasures."*

Finding it an odd quote but nonetheless remembering the thought in the novel, she gave a nod. "Well done to you, sir."

He drained his glass, set the book aside, and retrieved a wide-brimmed ivory country squire hat from the back of the chair. "We don't get us many visitors through these parts, ma'am. I surely hope our paths cross again while you're here."

"Thank you, sir. That's most kind of you."

"Kind got nothing to do with it. Pure selfishness on my part." He offered a bow. "Jasper Newton Daniel at your service, madam." He held her gaze. "You need anything while you're visiting our fine little town, you let me know."

Seeing the sparkle in his almond-shaped eyes, Josephine edited her previous assumption. *Smooth* in addition to charming, and with a definite penchant for flirtation. Not that she had to worry about unwanted advances in her current state. No, the man seemed harmless enough. "Thank you, Mr. Daniel."

Without looking back, he exited the front door, closing it behind him with familiarity in the gesture as though he'd done it a thousand times, then he disappeared into the night.

The lingering damp of the cold night air brought a chill, and she ran her hands over her arms, the cuffs of her blouse filthy with dust and dirt. She didn't even have a change of clothing, and only fifteen cents remained from the money Sarah had so generously given her.

Unbidden, images of the floods of women with children who had come to Atlanta's office of the American Woman Suffrage Association seeking help crowded her mind, and she blinked, suddenly viewing their plight in a much starker light.

She was just herself, alone. No child, or children, depending on her for shelter, nourishment, and safety. She closed her eyes tight, hearing the echo of her own now glib-sounding counsel to them. She'd encouraged them to have enough bravery to leave their abusive husbands, saying they could find shelter in one of the women's centers until they could locate another situation. But what other situation did they have waiting? Where would help for them come from? How shamefully casual her words of counsel seemed now, however well-meant at the time.

Staring out into the night, she better understood now why women in such circumstances stayed.

She turned and let her gaze trail the lobby, the furnishings simple compared to Atlanta hotels, but still tasteful with small-town appeal. She simply had to find a way to win Miss Mary over so she could stay here. At least for a while, until she could make contact with Sarah again and figure out what to do next. *What to do next . . .*

The words sounded so simple. But what did a woman do after she'd killed a man? One thing was for certain, she could not return to Atlanta, at least for now. Not with Mayor Darden. Not with the corruption in the police department and lack of rights for women. As numbing as her new reality was, she realized Sarah had been right. If she wanted to live, she had to run. And keep running. The question was . . . to where?

As she waited for Calla to return, a rustic wooden box on the foyer table caught her eye. It was similar in size and shape to one that might hold cigars. She ran a finger over the top, admiring the rugged mountain ridge the artist had carved. Jagged peaks rose in varying heights with one in particular soaring above the others. The edges of the lid bore markings resembling wildflowers.

Curious, she lifted the hinged lid, its slight squeak scarcely audible, then stared, wide-eyed. Coins. A lot of them. The shallow box was nearly full. Ashamed at the thought that sprang to mind, she immediately closed the lid just as footsteps sounded behind her.

She turned, expecting to see Calla. But there stood Miss Mary in her night robe instead, hands on hips.

"Can I help you with something, Mrs. Dunham?"

"No, I'm—" Aware of what it might look like, Josephine took a hasty step back. "I'm just waiting for Calla. She's getting bedding from upstairs." She glanced at the table. "I was simply admiring the box. That's all."

The silence lengthened, as did Miss Mary's doubt-filled stare, and a vivid image of being cast out into the cold and rain brought a suffocating dread.

Finally, Miss Mary sighed and shifted her weight. "Can you do more than fair to middling around a cookstove, Mrs. Dunham?"

Josephine hesitated. "I'm not sure what you—"

"I'm asking do you know how to cook? 'Cause I got a sneaking suspicion you're looking for a place to stay. And for more than just a night or two. Am I right?"

Not prepared to have this discussion yet, Josephine could only nod.

"My door is always open to the truly needy, Mrs. Dunham. But I do not abide folks taking charity when they're fit to work." Her gaze drifted to the box. "And I sure don't take kindly to someone stealing the cook's tips."

"Oh no, ma'am, I would never—"

"If you're wanting shelter only for the night, you and me are fine, and I'll see to it you get safe passage back to Tullahoma tomorrow. But if you've a hankering to stay longer, then you're going to have to work. So I'm asking you again . . . Can you cook?"

Josephine's mind raced. "What about housekeeping? I'm very good at cleaning and I can wash clothes, too. I'm also good with numbers. I could keep your books and—"

"I keep my own books. And I already got a good cleaning woman and washer woman, too. What I *need* is help in my kitchen. My other cook quit me two weeks back and it's too much for one alone. I only hire the best, and the pay is good. But hearing you running every whichaway around that question is answer enough. I'll ask Dodge in the morning if he can tote you on back down the—"

"No, please," Josephine said quickly, attempting to sound confident. "I can cook! In fact, I'm . . . very good at it."

Miss Mary started to respond when footsteps sounded on the stairs.

"Sorry for taking so long," Calla whispered, arms ladened with bedding. "One of the tenants needed something."

"Mr. Motlow?" Miss Mary asked.

"Who else." Calla rolled her eyes then winked. "Needed help with his hearth. That flue's getting a little gummed up, I think. I'll get Charlie out to look at it."

"Thank you, Calla. Well, it's late." Miss Mary gestured. "Good night to you both. And Mrs. Dunham . . . I aim for everyone who comes to my table a stranger to leave as a friend. Don't make that difficult this time. Come morning, we'll have us that interview."

"Interview?" Calla asked before Josephine could. "Are you trying out for job of second cook, ma'am?"

Josephine nodded, looking back at Miss Mary. "But what do you mean by interview?"

"Well, I've got to know what you can do before you get the job!" Miss Mary exhaled. "Won't be anything hard. Just making some biscuits with sausage gravy, or maybe some fried hand pies. Any cook worth her salt can handle that."

Seeing the dare in Miss Mary's expression, Josephine worked to keep the panic from her own. "Of course," she replied, trying for a casual tone.

"Oh, 'fore I forget . . ." Calla fished something from the bedding. "Mr. Motlow still had it up in his room. Said he done forgot the rule."

It was Miss Mary's turn to roll her eyes. "How many times do we have to tell that dear man to bring the newspapers back to the lobby?"

Seeing the folded newspaper in Miss Mary's grip, Josephine felt a flush of warning.

Bidding a "good night" over her shoulder, Miss Mary disappeared into the last room on the right and closed the door behind her.

"Lynchburg has a newspaper?" Josephine asked, her chest tightening as the distance between Lynchburg and Atlanta shrank by the second.

"Oh gracious, no. No newspaper. And no telegraph either. That'd be *The Chattanooga Times* I just gave to Miss Mary. Rich man in town gets it posted to him, then shares it with Miss Mary and her tenants after he's done. It's sometimes nigh onto a week old by the time we get it, but least we know what's been going on out in the world. Come on now . . ." She gestured to the door at the end of the hallway. "I live in the cabin out back. Let's get your bed made so you can fall headlong into it."

The Chattanooga Times? Delivered to Lynchburg? As Josephine followed, the dreaded *tick tick tick* began drumming inside her again. Only one week until what she'd done in Atlanta could become the talk of these Tennessee backwoods.

Was there anywhere she could go to outrun this?

9

Dawn edged over the heavily forested hills in a glowing blaze of gold and indigo, colors that would forever remind Dodge of his sister—and of a similar sunrise some ten years ago. Steam rose from his coffee cup and ghosted a pane of the front window that overlooked the lower pasture. How blind he'd been to the plans Kathleen had been hatching. He should have seen it coming. Should have figured that Kathleen—all of sixteen at the time, independent, stubborn as a mule with an adventuresome spirit to match, and eager to see the world—would trust far too easily. Would believe enticing lies cloaked in citified charm and dripping with promises of all that could be.

That morning had been a chilly one, much like today, and it hadn't taken him long to realize she'd sneaked off during the night with that slick-tongued devil of a man who lured her to Nashville, took what he wanted, then abandoned her there.

Dodge winced. He'd never wanted to kill a man so badly in his life. And he would have, too. If he could've found him.

He tossed the remaining corn cakes into the skillet with the scrambled eggs, then heard a gentle whine. Jessie stared up at him, her head cocked to one side, ears pricked. Her cattle-dog coloring—the customary blue-gray hide shot through with black specks and the warm tan markings on her cheeks, chest, and legs—fairly glowed in the twilight hours. But his favorite was the black marking that haloed her right eye and trailed to her ear. Looked like she was wearing an eye patch.

He tossed her a bite of eggs then leaned down and rubbed her behind the ears. "You're a beauty, you know that? Now go on, sweet girl, and eat the food I already put out for you."

Jessie eyed him as though making sure he meant business, then trotted obediently to the tin in the corner and did as asked.

Dodge cleaned the breakfast dishes, then quietly peered into Bethie's bedroom. She was still asleep, her blonde hair spilled across the pillow all wild and free like the mane of her sorrel mare when Bethie loosened the reins and gave Ginger Snap the lead. That horse could fly. And the girl could ride, too. Better than most of his farmhands. She was a natural.

In moments like this the thought that he needed to be not just an uncle to her, his niece, but a father now, threatened to overwhelm him. "God, help me do right by her," he whispered more in his heart than aloud. *Don't let me fail her like I did my little sister.* He would *not* make that same mistake again. He'd keep closer rein on Bethie. Wouldn't allow her head to be filled with foolishness and nonsensical ideas that would only lead to heartache and ruin.

Of course, that was easier said than done. The girl read everything within arm's reach and had a thirst for learning that couldn't be slaked. But she came by it naturally. He'd forever be grateful to Dr. Salmon for letting him grow up in that library of his. The same library that now belonged to Miss Mary in the boarding house. Dr. Salmon's wide variety of books had held such fascination for a boy of eight—and still provided enjoyment for a man of thirty-four.

The Wonderful Wizard of Oz lay open on Bethie's bedside table. Beneath that, *The Time Machine* and *The Little Mermaid.* She'd already read those novels, same as him—the latter at her request so they could discuss it—and the stories had sparked some lively back-and-forth, especially when Kathleen was still alive.

He stared at the books, then at Bethie, aware of the common thread running through those stories. Excitement. Adventure. Discovering different worlds and faraway lands. She was so much like her mother, possessing that same indomitable spirit. He could still hear the excitement in Kathleen's voice when he'd first told his sister about Wyoming.

"Are you kidding me, Dodge?" Kathleen had grasped his upper arm and squeezed tight. "Of course, I want to go. I want a fresh start. A place where people have no memory of what I did. A place where my daughter can grow up outside the shadow of my mistakes. Where I can help Bethie forge her own path and where she can be anything she wants to be."

Then Kathleen had fallen ill, scarlet fever finally taking her, God rest her sweet spirit, and the dream of Wyoming had died with her. She'd known it, too. He'd felt it in the last gentle squeeze of her hand. Had seen it in her tear-filled eyes before she'd slipped away. He hoped she'd heard his strained, repeated whispers of assurance there at the last. He hadn't wanted her entering eternity with that regret. Because he could never view Bethie as anything but a blessing. A remarkable, unexpected gift he'd spend his life providing for and protecting.

He noiselessly closed the door, then paused. Bethie had already lost the most important person in the world to her. How did he take this dream away from her as well? Yet, it was time he told her the change in plans. No matter how much it hurt him to do it. Maybe the gift he'd had special made for her would help make up for it in some small way. The leatherworker at the tack shop in Tullahoma had sure given it his best.

He shrugged into his coat and grabbed his hat from the hook by the door, then carefully slid open the top left drawer of his desk. He reached to the very back—knowing Bethie's tendency to snoop—and withdrew the envelope, its contents having robbed him of sleep for days now.

He unfolded the document and read the title across the top. *The United States of America, Department of the Interior.*

He scanned the legal verbiage again, having reviewed it thoroughly two nights earlier once Bethie was asleep. His gaze slid to the signature of the land agent on the bottom left, then to the empty line adjacent to it on the right . . . that awaited his own pen. Every one of those four hundred and twenty acres in Wyoming were his, for now. Until he sold them. Which, according to the land agent in Cheyenne who brokered deals, could happen lightning fast or drag out for months. All depended on price and interested buyers.

The thought of selling still made his stomach churn. He'd saved for that land for nearly fifteen years. Had put aside near everything he'd earned, after caring for Kathleen and Bethie's needs, for that purchase. But he knew it was the right thing to do, even if it meant possibly losing most of what he'd worked for all his adult life.

He retrieved his fountain pen, signed the document, and tucked the envelope into his coat pocket. Before mailing it, he'd talk to Uncle Jack to make sure they were on the same page, then he'd make it official.

The air outside hit him crisp and cool, and he latched the cabin door behind him and headed for the stables, Jessie trotting beside him.

How to break it to Bethie was the question. Probably best to just state it outright. That's how he'd want it done, if it was him. Quick and to the point. Don't make him guess. Yet he'd learned long ago that females were a different breed, and he'd all but given up on trying to figure them out.

But life was full of unforeseen switchbacks. He'd learned that young, and, unfortunately, Bethie was learning that too.

Angry shouts drifted toward him, and he slowed his steps. Curses punctuated the argument, and he turned in the direction of the distillery downhill. A gunshot rang out, and he broke into a run, Jessie easily outpacing him.

As Dodge drew closer, he thought he recognized one of the voices. He commanded Jessie to stay and didn't hesitate as he burst through the side door.

10

Dodge skidded to a halt as Gideon Cartwright leveled his Colt .45 dead center on Micah Hackett's chest. "I told you before, you lying son of a—"

"Cartwright!" Dodge yelled.

The man turned, a wild look in his eyes.

"Lower the gun," Dodge commanded. *"Now."*

"But, sir, you got no idea what he done to—"

"Doesn't matter right now what he did, Cartwright. You're standing smack in the middle of a distillery!" Dodge glanced at the handful of workers backing off to one side. "You get off another shot, and this whole place could go up in a fireball. Us along with it! So lower the gun and stand down. Then we'll talk through things. Get to the bottom of it together."

His face ruddy with rage, Cartwright begrudgingly complied, still glaring at Micah Hackett. "You're a lying, cheating snake of a coward for doing what you did."

"I ain't done nothing she didn't want me to do. Just ask her!"

Cursing, Cartwright raised the gun again.

"Hackett!" Dodge stepped forward. "Shut your stupid trap, you fool! 'Less you want your chest blown open. Now Cartwright, give me the gun. And we'll talk it through like I said."

"But I—"

"Now!"

With a desperate look that said he hoped Dodge would make good on his promise, Cartwright finally did as asked. Dodge released the hammer on the single-action revolver and checked the cylinder. Five bullets left. Cartwright had come to do business.

Dodge tucked the gun in his back waistband and gestured toward the door. "Outside, gentlemen."

Hackett shot Cartwright a smirk as he passed, and Dodge was tempted to clock the idiot upside the head himself. The Hacketts were a surly bunch with egos to match. Micah worked on the line in the distillery and had a way of getting under a person's skin, and enjoyed doing it, too. Two of his five brothers were farmhands, herding cattle and helping with the pigs. Hard workers, for the most part, but all three had mouths that wouldn't quit and a loyalty to family that cut across all else. Wrong one of them, and you'd wronged them all. Still, whatever Micah had done, Cartwright wasn't one to pick a fight without cause.

A bear of a man, Cartwright, once justifiably riled, didn't forget. Some called him simpleminded, and he did have a peculiar innocence about him for a man full grown. But Dodge would take that over hotheaded pride any day.

He slammed the door behind them, tossing Jessie a firm look that said to stay where she was, while curious employees gathered to check out the ruckus. He held up a hand. "Everything's under control, folks. Get on about your business." The crowd slowly dispersed, though some hung on the fringe to see what would happen next. Dodge turned back. "Neither of you men are to speak until I ask you a direct question. Do, and you'll regret it. You hear me?"

Gideon Cartwright nodded. Micah just stared.

"Now Cartwright . . ." Dodge faced him. "Tell me what's going on."

"I'll tell you what's going on," Micah started in. "This big ol' goon's all fired up 'cause he heard that me and Mollie Jean been—"

Dodge planted his fist square in Micah's gut. The younger man—almost a foot shorter but a good twenty pounds heavier, all of it lean muscle—doubled over and staggered back. But did not go down. Dodge knew if the man chose to fight, he'd have his hands full.

"Hackett, I said not to speak until I asked you a question. Do it again, and that'll be one week off the job."

Eyes hot, Micah glared but said nothing.

"Let's try this a second time." Dodge resisted the urge to shake off the sting in his right hand. "Cartwright, why'd you take a shot at him?"

"Hackett's been dogging my Mollie Jean, sir. Won't leave her be. She and me, we been promised since we was kids. Both our families say so."

"Yeah, well, what does Mollie Jean say?" Micah laughed beneath his breath, and Cartwright plowed into him.

Despite Cartwright's enormous bulk, Micah fought hard and dirty. Dodge finally drew the revolver and fired a warning shot into the cloudless blue overhead. Both men stilled, then gradually came to their feet.

"One week off the job for you, Hackett." The man opened his mouth, but Dodge beat him to it. "One more word, and I'll make it a month. And you know Uncle Jack will back me. Now get off the premises. I don't want to see your face on these grounds for a week."

Micah trudged off, fight still oozing from him.

"And that'll be two weeks off the job for you, Cartwright."

"But sir, he's the one who—"

"I know he's chasing after Mollie Jean. But that's between you and her. You cannot bring a gun into the distillery. You know that. Much less fire on another employee. And right by one of the stills?" Dodge shook his head. "Frankly, I'll have to run this by Uncle Jack. He may say to do more than two weeks."

Cartwright's brow wrinkled. "Meaning I could lose my job?"

Dodge nodded.

"Don't it matter a'tall that I ain't done wrong first? That Hackett did?"

Dodge held his stare. "The order of things doesn't matter. Hackett doing wrong doesn't make the wrong *you* did right. You see that, don't you?"

Cartwright finally nodded. He glanced in the direction Hackett had gone, his jaw muscles working with emotion. "Why is it some women take to men such as Hackett like bees on a honey hive? His sort is rotten to the core, sir. How come they don't see that?"

Thinking again of Kathleen, Dodge experienced the same searing pain he'd felt that morning. Yet he knew even though Cartwright had grown up with his sister—and was aware of what had happened to her—he wasn't insinuating anything. While a plumb line of justice ran deep through Gideon Cartwright, not a hint of cruelty or meanness weeded his character. If only Mollie Jean could see and value *that*.

"I don't know, Gideon," Dodge said softly. "You best ask someone else on that count. I'm a farmer, a cattleman, and a crack shot. I know how to raise livestock, I can live off the land, and I know a fair amount about making good whiskey. But females . . . They're a foreign study to me, and will likely remain as such."

Gideon smiled. "Oh I don't know, sir. I seen the way Rowena Gibbs been looking at you. Everybody in town sees it. They're talking on it, too. 'Bout how she might be the one to keep you from heading west to Wyo-*ming*," Gideon said, giving the last syllable more than its due.

Dodge shook his head. "Don't give heed to that kind of talk. Rowena's a child yet."

"She don't look like no child, sir. Not no more. And she done turned seventeen of late. Talk is, her mama's all up on you and her daughter being paired up and hitched by summer. And you know Mrs. Gibbs." Gideon's eyes went wide. "She don't take no from folks very kindly. Truth is . . ." He leaned in. "That woman scares me a little."

Dodge couldn't help but laugh, yet was eager to change the subject. "I think I can handle Mrs. Gibbs. What I can't handle, Cartwright, is you, with a gun, on these grounds. Understood?"

The man nodded.

"But far more . . . I can't abide the thought of this distillery without you being part of it. You've been working here almost as long as me."

"Slopped hogs for you way back in the day, sir. Then you moved me up to overseeing hog killing time. Now look at me." Gideon's broad chest grew more so. "Seeing after vats of whiskey belonging to Uncle Jack himself. Who'd've thought it?"

Reaching up, Dodge laid a hand on his shoulder. "Take the next two weeks and settle things between you and Mollie Jean, whatever that comes to. Then unless you hear otherwise from me, report back."

He returned Cartwright's revolver, holding on to it until the man nodded in silent understanding. Cartwright shoved the pistol into his waistband and strode toward town.

Jessie gave a little whine from where she sat, and Dodge signaled. She trotted over to him, and he knelt down and gave her a good rub. "You're the one female I *do* understand, girl."

She licked his chin, and he kissed her on the head, eyeing the graying around her muzzle. Six years wasn't old for an Australian cattle dog. They could live up to fifteen years or more. But as he rubbed her, he found himself hoping she would live much longer.

He spent the next half hour discussing both men's absences with their supervisors, then addressed employee concerns. Opinions were divided. Some sided with Cartwright, never having liked the Hackett brothers. Others thought the man to be a fool who deserved to be fired outright.

With Jessie at his side, Dodge headed to the little white house that served as the distillery's office to get a final reading on his decision from Uncle Jack, but heard the man yelling even before he opened the door.

"Confounded, stupid safe!" Jack took a step back as though he might haul off and actually kick the floor safe a good one.

"You do that, sir, and I'm pretty sure the safe's going to win."

Jack stopped mid-stride. "I hate this dad-blamed thing. Can't ever get it to open."

"Did you try the combination?"

Jack looked first at Jessie then at him. "Morning, sweet girl. And Dodge, don't make me cuss you this early in the morning. I'll do it."

Smiling, Dodge crossed to the safe and carefully turned the dial, feeling the almost imperceptible click of tumblers give way within the steel door. The handle complied without resistance. "There you go."

Jack muttered something beneath his breath. "I'm gonna haul off and shoot this thing one day."

"Best stand back a fair piece, if you do. She's likely to give it right back."

That drew a laugh. "Safes are a lot like women, aren't they? All-fired hard to get them to open up to you, but when they do . . . *Mmmph,* what treasures await. Unless of course, they won't shut up!"

Dodge ignored the mischievous gleam in Jack's eyes, as well as his musings on women, which the man shared often. He was known for the wide company of women he kept and, much as Cartwright had just said, they flocked to Jack Daniel like bees to honey. And no wonder. Rich as King Solomon, always dapperly dressed in a vested suit with tails and customary white hat, Jasper Newton Daniel was quite the catch—who fully intended never to be caught. But did any of the women chasing after him realize that, Dodge wondered.

"We just had an incident, sir. Up at the stillhouse."

"Stop calling me *sir.* Not when it's just the two of us, anyway. I've known you since you were twelve, and was there when you earned the name Dodge, don't forget. Oh do I remember that afternoon. Darn near got yourself killed!" He chuckled. "I still don't see how you got out of that one." He leaned down and patted Jessie, and the dog promptly dropped to the floor and presented her belly. Jack laughed, rubbed her good, then reached into the safe and withdrew an envelope. "I've already heard the gist of what happened. But let me hear it from you."

Dodge filled him in, leaving out nothing. "So my question is, do you agree with my decision for both men? If not, I can—"

"Course, I agree. I taught you everything you know, right?" Jack grinned, striking a match to light a cigar.

He offered one to Dodge, who was tempted, but declined. Another last promise to his sister.

Jack puffed on the end until plumes of smoke rose. "Micah Hackett is the nasty end of a jackass, but he's a good worker. There'll be hell to pay from his brothers."

"As well I know. I'll watch them."

"Good man. As for Cartwright—" Jack sat down behind his desk and frowned at the chaos of papers, bills, and receipts before him. "That kind of behavior can't be tolerated. Two weeks is a long time, especially with his folks being older and down in their health, and him being the only breadwinner. But any less than that and others would have seen it as going too easy. How many family members are living at the Cartwright place now?"

Dodge thought for a minute. "Seventeen, if I'm remembering all the spouses and children right. No, wait. Eighteen. Cartwright's youngest sister just got married. She and her husband are living with the family until they get their own place finished this fall. They're building nearby to help with the farm."

"Such as that farm is. Their piece of land ain't exactly the cream of the crop."

"No, sir, it's—"

Jack eyed him.

"No, Uncle Jack, it's not. They've always struggled."

"Get one of the hogs out to them, if you would. Maybe go by the mercantile and pick up some other staples. Whatever's needed. And do it—"

"Quietly, I know. As always."

Jack shuffled papers from one pile to another, scowling, then finally stopped and propped his feet on the edge of the desk, his black boots polished to a shine. "I hate the business side of business!"

"You actually feed off the business side of business. And you're good at it. It's all the paperwork you hate. You ought to hire someone to come in and straighten out all this for you."

"Give me a name, and I'll do it! I thought my nephew Lem was gonna step in, but he's got too much on his plate right now."

"Miss Mary's the only one I know of with a mind sharpened for business enough to wade into all this. But she's got her hands full up."

"Don't I know it." Jack shot him a look. "And with more than just running that inn."

Dodge nodded but said nothing, aware of Miss Mary's *home* situation, mainly due to her and Kathleen having been thick as thieves, the two of them, in recent years. He doubted things had changed much for Miss Mary over the past seven months since Kathleen's passing. Jackson Bobo, Mary's husband, wasn't a bad sort, by any means. He just never seemed quite able to settle down and put his hand to any one thing long enough to make a go of it.

Wanderlust was a dangerous indulgence, and a person didn't have to wander far to fall prey to it. Always chasing greener pastures or quick riches was its own kind of curse.

"Cattle ready for market?"

Dodge nodded again. "The road to Tullahoma's muddy but passable. I'll help load them on the train myself."

"I bet you will. Seeing as they're all yours this time."

Dodge smiled. Having sunk his savings into the land out west, it would feel good to have a little cushion again.

"That was a good deal you made with me all those years ago when you suggested I start a cattle farm."

"If memory serves, and it does, you were the one who offered the deal."

"Let's not muddy the memory with facts, Dodge. Let's just say it was a good deal for us both. You starting my cattle farm with your family's herd, then gradually cutting me in for half." Uncle Jack winked. "I trained you right."

They laughed, and Uncle Jack looked down at the mess of paperwork on his desk. "Now if I could only find someone to help me with all this."

"Maybe in the evenings, I could—"

"You've got more than you can handle already, Dodge. Especially with young Bethie now. I'll just buckle down and get it done. But thank you."

"One last thing, Uncle Jack." Dodge withdrew the envelope from his pocket. "After a lot of thought . . . and a fair amount of prayer, I've decided—"

"You're selling your Wyoming land," Jack said, disbelief in his tone.

Dodge hesitated. "It's the right thing to do. I just need to make sure before mailing this that you're good with me . . . staying on."

Jack snuffed out the cigar in an ashtray and rounded the desk. He gripped Dodge around the back of the neck like a father might have done, and looked up. "You know how I feel about you, son. I swear, I see so much of me in you. Always have," he whispered, his voice going raspy.

Dodge swallowed, not having expected this exchange to be so hard.

"I'm sorry things worked out this way for you. And for little Bethie. Your ranch in Wyoming would have been the best there was and your cattle the finest. But in the same breath, you know how grateful I am that you're staying. You will always have a job at my distillery, Dodge Coburn. Because you're the best at what you do, no matter what you put your hand to. Kind of like me." Winking, he clapped Dodge on the back. "But you know the Hackett brothers will take this extra personal. Cole, the oldest, has already been sniffing around here, gunning for your job."

"I know that, too. I can talk to him."

"No. Leave that to me. He'll take it better that way, I think. And if not, I'll just fire the arrogant ass."

Jack laughed, and Dodge followed suit, doing his best to cover the profound sadness he felt.

He turned back at the door. "Would you give me a couple of days before making this public? I still need to tell Bethie."

11

Fighting a sense of doom, Josephine lifted the cast-iron skillet, unprepared for its weight. Exhausted, she'd slept little and had risen before dawn to scour the kitchen and library for recipes.

Miss Mary's book collection was extensive—law, science, arithmetic, languages, Greek mythology, shelves of classics and Shakespearean works. Dickens, Brontë, Whitman, Henry James. But the volumes on animal husbandry, farming tools, and agricultural methods were entirely new to her.

And still—not a single recipe anywhere.

She'd hoped Calla or some former cook had left a clipped newspaper recipe, notes scribbled on the back of an envelope. Something. How many "women's columns" had she skimmed past to reach the local, national, and international news? What she wouldn't give now for one of those simple lists of ingredients and measurements.

She set the skillet on the massive stove, which now resembled a fiery, red-eyed beast ready to devour her. She could almost feel her teeth rattling as Dodge Coburn's wagon carried her over rain-rutted roads back to Tullahoma—and to certain arrest. Or worse.

She bowed her head, wanting to pray but unsure God was listening—or even cared anymore. A whisper, steely and insistent, threaded her thoughts. Perhaps he truly had written her off, and she really was on her own.

"Oh, don't you go getting scaredy now, Josephine." Calla came up behind her, working an apron over her head. "Miss Mary's a hard judge, but she's fair. Just give her your best."

Josephine looked at her. "What if my best isn't good enough?"

"Don't you worry about that. You'll do fine."

"Thank you again for tending to my face last night. Whatever you put on it helped."

Calla's gaze moved over Josephine's countenance. "You keep slathering on that liniment at night and those places should heal up right good." Tenderness moved into her eyes. "You might come away with a scar or two, but that's not the worst thing."

Josephine forced a smile.

Calla finished tying her apron. "Use whatever you want from the larder. We keep the dried fruit toward the back. Peaches and apples, maybe some apricots. Miss Mary likes them all, but favors apple most," she whispered. "Or if you're thinking biscuits and sausage gravy, the sausage is in the springhouse I showed you out back last night. Same for the buttermilk."

"Buttermilk?"

"For the biscuits." Calla paused. "You still ain't decided which one to make?"

Josephine hesitated, an idea forming. "Which one would you do? If you were me."

"I'd do the one I'm best at."

"Which is?"

"Now there you go trying to make me boast. And me a God-fearing woman." Calla grinned. "But I do make about the best fried apple pies you ever put in your mouth."

"Then I'm definitely making biscuits with sausage gravy."

"All right then. Best get to it."

Calla reached for the teakettle, and Josephine noticed a tremor in her hand.

"Are you all right, Calla? You're shaking."

Calla laughed, clasping her hands. "Oh, I'm fine. Just getting older is all. My hands shake, my hair's thinning, and my eyes don't work like they once did. But at least I still got my mind. Or what's left of it."

Josephine smiled, her plan moving into clearer focus. She only hoped her tone wouldn't betray her. "I guess I'll head out back then and get the sausage and buttermilk. Anything else I should grab?"

"Nope. But mind your step in the springhouse. Those stairs can be slick."

Satisfied those were the only items needed from cold storage, Josephine counted that as one solved piece of the puzzle.

The springhouse door was heavy, but a hard shove opened it. Calla had been right about the steps, and Josephine tread carefully. After a quick search, she found a package labeled *sausage* and a bottle of buttermilk.

As she returned to the kitchen, the teakettle whistled. Calla was pouring something from a small blue bottle into a mug.

"I found the sausage and buttermilk."

Calla jumped and quickly screwed the lid back on. "Good for you. And you minded the steps?"

"Yes, thanks for the warning. They were slick."

"You want a cup of mint tea with honey?" Calla held up the bottle. "Happy to make you one."

"No, I think I'll wait for coffee. But thank you."

"Already got it brewing. Be ready shortly." Calla began cracking eggs into a large bowl.

Josephine watched. "You do that one-handed?"

"Just like my mama taught me. How'd your mama teach you?"

Josephine was hesitant to admit that her mother hadn't known anything about cooking either. That they'd employed a cook for as long as she could remember. "I've always used both hands, but I'll have to try it your way sometime." *When I have an hour to dig shards of broken shells out of a mess of eggs,* she wanted to add, but didn't.

Feeling guilty about trying to trick Calla into helping her, she continued nonetheless, the threat of being sent back to Atlanta all too real. "So you said the rest of what I need is in the larder? Would you mind showing me where everything is?"

"I would, but I need to get these eggs on the stove. Tenants'll be down soon. Besides, everything's labeled."

Already knowing that from her earlier search, Josephine stepped into the larder. Biscuits weren't a complete mystery, so she grabbed the flour tin and tried to recall how Lannie, their family's cook, had made them. Flour, certainly. Buttermilk. What else?

She pictured Lannie kneading the dough, cutting biscuit with practiced ease. As a little girl, Josephine had stood at the table's edge, watching every move. Sometimes Lannie would "accidentally" leave a scrap of dough within reach, and Josephine had gobbled it up, believing it a secret gift.

She hadn't thought of Miss Lannie in years—or appreciated her skill nearly enough.

Dragging her thoughts back, she dumped flour into a bowl. It didn't look like enough, so she added more.

"Oh, you're making *lots* of biscuits!" Calla said. "That's good, our tenants love to eat."

Taking that at face value, Josephine poured in plenty of buttermilk, stirred, frowned, added more flour, and stirred again. Still a thick, soupy mess. Grateful Calla wasn't watching, she added yet more flour until it finally resembled dough.

She dumped it onto the worktable and tried to knead. The dough stuck to everything. Then she remembered standing close to the table's edge, watching Miss Lannie work, and ending up with flour on her nose. She dusted the table with flour, hoping to hide her mistake. After a few minutes, she almost convinced herself this wasn't so difficult.

"You gonna use that skillet?" Calla asked.

"I can use whatever you'd like."

"No, that one's fine. Cast iron gives biscuits a nice crust."

"You're welcome to check what I'm doing, if you want."

"Oh I'm afraid I can't help when it comes to a cook's interview. Miss Mary's strict on that. She wants to see what a cook can do on her lonesome."

Josephine crammed as many biscuits into the skillet as would fit, then slid the extras on a baking sheet. Not wanting to think about how long it would take Miss Mary to toss her to the curb if the woman discovered she'd lied to her, she turned to the sausage.

"You already got your biscuits in?" Calla asked.

"Sure do. Now I'm making the gravy."

"Milk or water?"

Josephine froze, not sure what she was asking. But the gravy Lannie used to make was a creamy white. "I use milk. What about you?"

"Same. And Miss Mary likes both. She just loves gravy!"

Calla chuckled and turned back to the eggs while Josephine broke up the sausage with a wooden spoon. As it cooked, hot grease popped and splattered, burning her hands and forearms.

Calla gestured. "You can close the damper a little if the stove's cooking too hot."

Josephine reached for the cover.

"No, ma'am!" Calla said sharply. "Not with your bare hand!"

Josephine jumped back, embarrassed.

"Gracious, woman, what are you thinking?"

Josephine shrugged. "I-I guess I wasn't. I'm a little nervous."

"Here, let me do it for you." Calla grabbed a cloth and adjusted the cover. "I need to fetch a fresh tablecloth. Milk's in the icebox."

Josephine pulled the sausage off the heat and poured in the milk. But no matter how long she mixed, the grease and milk wouldn't come together. Then she smelled it.

Her biscuits!

She grabbed the oven door handle then sucked in a sharp breath, muttering a word she'd heard Sarah use too often. Snatching a drying cloth, she tried again. Smoke billowed out. The biscuits in the skillet had fused into a hard, lumpy mass. The ones on the baking sheet had spilled over the edges and dripped into piles onto the bottom of the oven. Two were in flames.

She doused the flames with water, and it hissed and crackled, sending up more smoke. She flung open the back door just as footsteps sounded behind her.

Calla stopped short. "What in land's sake—"

"*What* is going on in here!" Miss Mary's voice cut like a knife.

12

"I'm sorry," Josephine whispered. "I-I'm so sorry. To you both."

Miss Mary looked from the stove to the oven, then back to her. "*This* is your attempt at biscuits and gravy?"

"I can explain, Miss Mary. I—"

"You lied to me, Mrs. Dunham. Straight to my face, in my home, under my shelter last night, you lied."

Fighting back tears, Josephine couldn't bring herself to look either woman in the eye.

Miss Mary huffed. "What a mess. And with tenants sitting at my table waiting to be fed."

"I can explain," Josephine said again. "It's true, I don't know how to cook. But I do have other—"

"You should've been honest with me. From the very start, *Mrs.* Dunham, something told me not to trust you. But since you arrived in Dodge Coburn's company—and anyone could see you were in a hard way—I decided to give you a chance." Miss Mary shook her head. "But I see now that my gut was right."

Her gaze moved to Josephine's left hand. Josephine knew what she was thinking, and couldn't argue. Wearing her mother's ring had been a lie, too.

"I'd ask you to pack your bags," Miss Mary continued. "But seeing as you don't have any, I'll just send for Dodge and have him tote you on back down to Tullahoma."

"*No,* Miss Mary. *Please.*" Josephine's voice broke. "I cannot go back to—" About to say Atlanta, she caught herself. "To him. If I go back, it will be the end of me." Tears spilled freely now. "I can work. I'm a teacher. Or I was. I know how to—"

"Got no need for a teacher."

"Maybe there's a school—"

"We've already got *honest* people teaching our young."

Josephine hiccuped a breath. The image of Clay Darden, rage in his eyes, filled her mind, followed by that of his father, Mayor Darden, and she began to shake.

"You could've been honest from the start," Miss Mary said, her voice tightening. "Then maybe we'd be on better footing. But you made your own bed when you took to lying."

"I had no choice," Josephine whispered.

"We *always* have a choice," Miss Mary snapped, her own voice catching. "No matter how hard the road is. It's what makes a person who they are!"

Miss Mary's eyes glistened, and Calla blinked back tears.

Miss Mary drew herself up. "You're saying if you go back, your man will kill you?"

"Yes. Him or his father, one." Josephine wiped her cheeks and stood straighter. "If you'll allow me to stay, just for a little while, I'll do whatever work you give me. And I won't cause trouble."

"Why do I have trouble believing that?" Miss Mary glanced back at the stove.

"I'll clean this mess. All of it. Just please, allow me to—" Maybe it was the dire need of her circumstances, the pleading in her own voice, or realizing how far—and quickly—she'd fallen, but Josephine felt something break down deep inside her. "I don't know how I got here," she whispered. "Or why all this happened. All I know is . . . I need your help. Because I have nowhere else to go."

Miss Mary studied her, and Josephine—standing in yesterday's clothes, near penniless—was reminded of the freedmen who had come to her parents' door, their families huddled behind them, weariness etched across their faces. Only now did she truly begin to understand that look.

"You said you're good with numbers." Miss Mary eyed her. "Was that truth? Or another lie?"

"It's the truth. I'm very good with numbers, and with keeping books. I'd be honored to help you—"

"I already told you, I keep my own books. But there's a man in town who needs help with orders, receipts, and the like. I heard him talking again last night at the table. His business is growing faster than he can manage." Miss Mary's gaze hardened. "But if I put my good name behind yours and you fail to—"

"I won't. I promise you. I'll do a good job and will not tarnish your name."

Miss Mary glanced at Calla. "You okay with this?"

Calla nodded without hesitation.

"All right then." Miss Mary laid out her terms. "You'll clean this mess, staying out of Calla's way while *she* gets breakfast for my tenants, then clean yourself up." Miss Mary gave her a once-over. "I'm a mite taller than you, and thicker 'round the middle but I think I've got something that'll fit you. I'll make loan of a skirt and blouse, and you get into town this very day and see that man about the job. I'll write everything down, even send him a note."

Josephine blinked back a flood of relief. "Thank you, Miss Mary."

"Don't go thanking me just yet. You don't get the job, that means you can't pay room and board. And an able body works and pays their way. I know you're down on your luck, and I feel for you. But everybody's got something. No matter if you can see it outright or not. So you get that job, and you can stay here." She glanced at Calla, who again nodded. "And Calla here, good-hearted woman she is, will let you share her space. You'll take your meals here in the kitchen with her. Table in the dining room is for tenants or guests only. And you'll attend church every Sunday. Either the Methodist church with me or where Calla goes. Doesn't matter to me. What matters is getting the Word inside you. You good with all that?"

Josephine didn't hesitate, even though it meant sitting through sermons she knew wouldn't be to her liking. "Yes, ma'am, I am."

"All right then. Get to it."

With that, Miss Mary swept back through the door to greet her tenants.

Josephine gripped the back of a kitchen chair, still struggling with emotion. "I'm sorry about your kitchen, Calla."

Calla covered Josephine's hand. "Things that can be cleaned up so easy ain't worth spilling tears over. It's the things we do to each other that we can't undo that deserve mourning." She drained her honeyed mint tea. "More than we usually do."

13

"Move on, Angel." Dodge nudged the mare's flank and guided her back through the herd, watching for signs of illness. After discovering two sickly cows that morning, he'd sent for Doc Wyatt. Despite his unease, he told himself the dread pressing in his chest came from knowing he still had to break the news to Bethie after school—and nothing else.

"Seein' anything over there, boss?" Jake hollered from across the pasture.

Dodge shook his head. "You?"

"No, sir. Not a one."

"Maybe it's just the two we found."

"You think they're gonna make it?"

"We'll see what Doc says. I'm heading in. Come find me if anything else turns up." Dodge spurred Angel into a canter toward the lower barn, Jessie racing alongside.

Sawyer, the newest—and youngest—farmhand, ran out to meet him, eager as ever. At twelve, the boy reminded Dodge of himself. Maybe that was why he'd hired him two weeks earlier when Sawyer came asking for work, saying he'd do anything if he could just learn to be a cattleman.

"Let me take Angel for you, sir!"

"Thanks, Sawyer. Rub her down good."

"You bet I will. Maybe give her extra oats?"

The boy's exuberance coaxed a smile. "A little won't hurt. Doc inside?"

"Yes, sir. With them sickly ones."

Dodge found Doc Wyatt kneeling in a stall, glasses riding low on his nose. "What's the verdict, Doc?"

"Afraid it doesn't look good. I'm glad you culled these two when you did."

"What do you think it is?"

"While I'm not certain, my best guess would be—"

"Texas fever," Dodge said quietly.

Doc glanced back. "You already knew . . ."

"More like suspected." Dodge removed his hat and raked a hand through his hair. "Any cattleman worth his salt has heard of it." He studied the cows collapsed in the hay. "Weakness in the limbs. Blood in the urine. They were stumbling and groaning when I found them. But if it's Texas fever wouldn't you find—"

Doc Wyatt held up a dingy white kerchief splotched with blood—and containing numerous enlarged ticks. "These were still alive when I pulled them off."

Dread hardened Dodge's stomach. "What about the seventy-five steers ready for market? We're driving them to Tullahoma today."

Doc shook his head. "Not with this, you're not. If it *is* the fever, you'll be shut down for weeks. Maybe months."

Dodge let that sink in, hearing the money he'd hoped to earn drain away. "No sales to national markets. No local buyers either. The lost revenue will be sizable."

"I'm afraid it might be a lot worse than that, Dodge. Because the fever tick—if that's what it is—isn't your usual cattle tick. After mating, the females don't drop off after each molt like usual. They stay attached, feeding until their life cycle's nearly spent. *Then* they drop off, lay thousands of eggs, and die. The larvae live in the grass until other animals happen along and—"

"It starts all over again." Dodge glanced out the open door of the barn. "So you're telling me I not only have a pasture full of sick cows, but that a whole slew of tick eggs are in field grass ready to hatch?"

"I'm afraid that's the big and small of it. But remember, I don't know for sure yet that it *is* Texas fever."

"Don't you, though, Doc?"

The older man hesitated. "If we're right, and I hope we're not . . . the sick ones won't last long. Emaciation, fever, anemia, blood in the urine, then death follows fast. That'll pretty much answer the question. I'll send these ticks to a colleague who works for the Department of Agriculture in DC. See what he says. But I don't know of any medicine able to treat this." He started to stand, then faltered.

Dodge grabbed his arm. "You okay there, Doc?"

The older man straightened and rubbed his lower back. "I'm fine. Just old as these hills, that's all." He rubbed the bridge of his nose. "You'll need to check the entire herd. Horses too. Quarantine anything showing symptoms. And don't move the cows from that pasture."

Dodge nodded. "How long does a field stay infected?"

"Weeks. Sometimes months. All depends on the vitality of the young ticks. Dead of winter is a struggle for them. But spring . . ."

"Can people get it?" Dodge pictured Bethie riding Ginger Snap all over that field the previous afternoon.

"I don't know, but best to take precautions until we do."

They walked to Doc Wyatt's wagon.

"I appreciate you coming so fast, Doc. I'll let Uncle Jack know."

"Hopefully things won't go as bad as I've laid out."

"In all the years I've known you, Doc, I don't ever recall you being wrong."

The older man laughed. "That's because you weren't around in my early days. I made plenty of mistakes. The secret, I learned early on, is always learning from them. Never waste a hurt, as my dear Lucille used to say."

Dodge sobered. "How're you getting along, sir? I know you still miss her. It's been what? Two years?"

"Two years, two months, and four days." Doc's gaze drifted to the hills. "But we had sixty-one wonderful years together. Well, most of them were good anyway." He winked, then sighed. "I always thought I'd go first. What with my heart condition. But God had other plans."

"He often does," Dodge said softly.

"Oh to be young again like you, Dodge, with your whole life stretching out before you." He gripped Dodge's shoulder. "You and Bethie will be sorely missed. I still can't picture this distillery, this holler, without you all in it. Won't be the same. There've been Coburns here since before Lynchburg became a real town. And despite what you've always said, I still held out hope you might take my place one day once I'm gone."

"I'm a cattleman, sir. Not a doctor."

Doc laughed. "That's not what Dr. Salmon used to say. He claimed you devoured every medical book in his library, and kept coming back for more."

Dodge didn't answer immediately. "I know what I was born to do. And once a man knows that . . . nothing else compares." He glanced around, lowering his voice. "Please keep this between us for now, but . . . I've decided not to go to Wyoming. I can't take Bethie out there alone. It was different when Kathleen was alive. I've known for a while now it wasn't going to work. Just took me some time to accept it, I guess."

"I'm sorry to hear that, Dodge. Sorry as I can be. How'd Bethie take it?"

"I haven't told her yet."

Doc whistled low. "I don't envy you that talk. She's a handful, just like her mother was, God rest her." He smiled faintly. "I don't see dandelions but what I don't think of Kathleen. She made the best dandelion wine I ever had. And I've had my share." Doc Wyatt glanced in the direction of the distillery. "I know this isn't what you wanted for your life. At least, not for the rest of it."

"But it's a good life," Dodge said a little too quickly. "And Uncle Jack's been real good to me."

"As well he should. You've helped make him a very rich man. And I'm not talking about just being his cattle foreman. I heard what happened yesterday with Hackett and Cartwright. Nobody else could've handled that like you did. You're respected. Even by men hoping to take your job." Doc climbed up to the buckboard. "I'll send word the minute I hear from DC."

Dodge gathered his supervisors, ordered quarantine signs posted, then headed back down to the distillery, Jessie on his heels. School would let out soon and he wanted to be there to meet Bethie. He'd take her for candy at the mercantile then once they got home, he'd break the news.

But first, he needed to talk to Uncle Jack.

The office was empty, but Jack's suit coat still hung on the coat tree. Dodge penned a note and started to leave it atop the desk, then saw the chaos of paperwork and left it on his chair instead. He'd swing back by on their way home.

~

Josephine closed the front door of the boarding house behind her and hurried to the street, later than planned. Turning right, she followed the directions Miss Mary had left in a note on the kitchen table before heading to an afternoon appointment. The town square lay a short walk ahead and, judging by the wagons and foot traffic, business was brisk.

Calla had heated water for a bath, and Josephine had nearly cried when she sank into the soothing warmth, her aching muscles finally yielding. At Calla's urging she washed her hair, then sat out back in the sunshine, towel-drying it before sweeping the curls up with borrowed pins and a comb. For a brief moment she almost felt like a new woman—until she caught her reflection in a mirror.

She looked every inch a battered wife and would keep to that story, ring or no ring, though losing her mother's ring still stung. She could tell Miss Mary didn't fully believe her anyway. The woman had an uncanny intuition and a bluntness both admirable and unnerving.

At the square, a handsome courthouse sat in the center, and Josephine paused to reread the note.

> *Cross the square and turn right at the mercantile. Continue past the blacksmith and dry goods store. That road leads from town. After a fair piece, you'll see a white-framed house with a front porch on your right. You can't miss it. Don't worry about knocking. That's Mr. Daniel's office. Go on in and introduce yourself, and give him the envelope. Mrs. Dunham, please be mindful of the skirt and blouse I've made loan to you. They belonged to a dear friend who passed away last year. So your care is greatly appreciated.*

Josephine clutched the high-waisted cerulean skirt, keeping the hem clear of mud and puddles. The homespun ensemble was lovely, sewn by an expert hand. At first she'd taken the pattern for dots. Only later had she realized dozens of tiny cream-and-pink wildflowers were embroidered into the folds. The cream blouse, with pearl buttons and delicate lace at the collar and sleeves, was just as fine.

Still, Josephine wished she'd had time to wash and press her own clothing. Because if anything happened to this . . .

She glanced at the sealed envelope and the name written on it. *Mr. Daniel.* The same name as in Miss Mary's note. Recalling the gentleman she'd run into in the library last evening—and given Lynchburg's size—she doubted it was a coincidence. Jasper . . . *something* Daniel.

She only hoped he wouldn't fault her for anything she might have said or done. More than that, she hoped he was hiring. In a town like this, opportunity had to be scarce.

Her thoughts returned to what Miss Mary might have written about her. The envelope was sealed tight. Not that she would have read the contents, however tempted. But there was no getting around delivering the note as promised. Miss Mary would follow up, for certain.

With a full sun overhead and keeping a quick pace, she began to perspire. Townsfolk watched her pass, their expressions ranging from curiosity to open disgust. Much like the train. Vanity reared, persistent as ever, and she hoped her wounds would heal without scarring. She vowed to apply Calla's salve morning and night.

Taking the boardwalk, she passed a whitewashed brick building bearing the name Farmers Bank on the north side of the square and admired that such a small town boasted such a fine financial institution. Shops with awnings framed the square, but the White Rabbit Saloon stood out most. Was no corner of the world untouched by liquor?

A few doors down, a colorful window display slowed her steps. *Velma's Candy*, the shingle read. Hand-drawn pictures of confections made her mouth water. Inside, a woman with a large bowl tucked in the crook of her arm stirred furiously, intent on her task. Another female entrepreneur, perhaps. This town kept offering surprises.

At that moment, the woman turned, and Josephine resisted the urge to duck from view, knowing she'd already been seen. The woman smiled and waved, then pointed to the sign on the door. *Open 3pm - 6pm, Monday through Friday.* Josephine nodded as if that had been her question and gave a thumbs-up with an expression indicating she'd come back some other time.

But she'd need money first.

Nearly to the main road, a building set back from the boardwalk caught her eye, as did the man sitting out front whittling, watching her. Too far away to require conversation, thankfully, she offered a nod and kept moving past the jail, forcing herself to breathe evenly. The deputy—or sheriff—returned the gesture and continued to follow her progress.

The presence of law enforcement in this small town didn't surprise her, but neither did it lend a sense of safety as it once would have. After turning the corner and finding no one behind her, she breathed easier. Lynchburg had no telegraph, which she would have considered antiquated before. Now it felt like a saving grace. Still, from now on she would keep to the far side of the square.

The main road followed a meandering creek, and as she walked east, private residences gradually gave way to rural businesses. She passed a tannery, the sharp stink reaching her before she spotted two men bent over a stretched hide. Then a cotton mill and gristmill, and finally a cotton gin. For all its size, Lynchburg lacked no industry.

After fifteen minutes, she spotted a small, wood-framed saltbox cottage with a front porch up ahead on the right. Massive oaks arched above it, lending the place a sheltered, homey feel.

A shingle hung from the porch ceiling—

JACK DANIEL DIST.
LYNCHBURG, TENN.

Jack Daniel Distributors. Not Jasper, as he'd introduced himself last evening. A nickname, perhaps. Or maybe the owner was a relative and he ran the business.

Wondering what kind of business it was, she guessed a successful one, judging by the numerous larger outbuildings dotting the acreage. What Miss Mary hadn't told her was that the house was situated by a cave. Hearing the faint melody of water and feeling her throat go dry, Josephine couldn't resist.

As she neared the mouth of the cave, cool air greeted her. Lush ferns and shade-loving moss clung to stacks of damp, layered rock supporting the bluff, and the sweet scent of honeysuckle drifted toward her. Spring water spilled from the cave into a small pool before continuing in a streambed to outbuildings beyond.

Josephine leaned over the rocky ledge, cupped her hands, and drank. The water, cold and clear, revived her. She peered into the cave, but darkness swallowed the view, as though guarding secrets. If she and Todd had ventured upon such a place in their younger years, they would have explored without hesitation. So much of her life had died with him.

Unbidden, the memory rose of standing beside him in church—Todd's rich baritone lifting his favorite hymn: *Nearer, my God, to thee . . .* But she pushed it away. Both the memory, and the hymn. Yearning to be nearer to God was not foremost in her thoughts right now. But it had been in Todd's, especially near the end. He'd often spoken of feeling God's direct nudges, moments of unmistakable guidance. She'd never fully understood it, nor experienced anything so certain.

Now she wished she'd asked him more, and wondered if she'd missed something that might have shed light on his death. His *murder*.

She regretted not hugging him goodbye that last night as he'd rushed out to a meeting, troubled by something that had happened. How many times had she urged him to meet at the house, where she could at least know the men he worked with—his partners in crime, as she'd teasingly called them. But he had always insisted on meeting elsewhere.

In moments like this, she still felt like half of herself was missing, reaching for someone who wasn't there anymore. And never would be again. Would it always be this way?

The sharp clang of iron on iron carried toward her from an outbuilding and reverberated in the cave. Sensing the clock ticking . . .

She hurried back to the little white house and stepped up to the porch. Hand on the doorknob, she hesitated. Miss Mary had said knocking wasn't necessary, but propriety—and the need to make a good first impression—argued otherwise.

After checking her hair in the front window, she squared her shoulders, summoned the confidence she'd once worn with ease, and knocked.

14

HEARING A MUFFLED RESPONSE FROM INSIDE, Josephine entered, unsurprised to find the man behind the desk was, indeed, the same gentleman she'd met in the library the night before.

"Good day, Mr. Daniel . . ." She closed the door behind her, her attention drawn to the utter derangement of ledgers and paperwork stacked precariously on his desk and a nearby farm table. She quickly returned her gaze to his, careful to mask any hint of disapproval. Miss Mary had been right—his office was a mess. And yet the man himself was, once again, immaculately dressed.

"I wager you did not expect to see me again so soon, sir."

Already on his feet, he rounded the desk and offered a brief bow. "The pleasure only dared linger at the edge of my sincerest wishes, Mrs. Dunham."

He remembered my name. Whether that would work in her favor remained to be seen.

"Please, have a seat." He indicated one of the straight-backed chairs facing his desk, and she gratefully accepted, still sore from yesterday. "Pray tell, madam, do reveal what brings you to my office on this fine Thursday morning."

She fingered the envelope in her lap, aware of his gaze flitting to it as he reclaimed his seat. Yet she felt the need to speak first before giving Miss Mary the floor. Especially not knowing what the note held. "As you've likely assumed, Mr. Daniel, given the state in which I arrived at the inn last evening—" She briefly touched the side of her face. "My current situation is . . . precarious at best and—"

"Let's tug on those reins for just a minute, Mrs. Dunham, if you would."

Her stomach sank.

"While some folks race like the dickens to form first impressions," he continued, "I am not one of them." A slow smile curved his mouth, one that seemed very much at home on his face. "It will come as a great surprise to you, I'm sure, that throughout my life, certain people, upon first meeting me, have formed swift and—may I daresay—*faulty* opinions based on what they see." His eyes narrowed with a glint of wicked humor. "Must be my five-foot-two strappin' good looks and commanding appearance that skew their reasoning."

Josephine couldn't help but smile. "That misstep is to their utmost detriment, I would imagine. And even hope," she added in a stage whisper and appreciated the warmth in his expression.

"Now that we have shown a bit more of our hand to each other, Mrs. Dunham, please . . ." He gestured for her to proceed.

More at ease, Josephine still chose her words carefully. "My situation here in Lynchburg, Mr. Daniel, while temporary, still demands that I seek employment. You see, I was forced to leave my home after a most . . . unexpected altercation. That unplanned departure, costly in more ways than financial, has left me near destitute."

"I'm so sorry, Mrs. Dunham." His voice softened. "Did your husband follow you?"

Her brow lifted.

"It's not hard puttin' two and two together, Mrs. Dunham. Even for someone from these hills and hollers." He winked, then his demeanor sobered. "Especially once you've been shown what's truly in a man. Or *some* men. Certainly not all."

The compassion in his gaze made it difficult for her to speak. "No one followed me. I'm certain." Looking down, she again saw the envelope in her lap. "Mr. Daniel, I am here at Miss Mary's urging. This note is from her." Rising slightly, she handed it to him, then hurried to speak before he opened it. She told him the truth. All of it. Including the kitchen disaster.

By the time she finished, his eyes danced with amusement.

"Oh, my dear woman, if there is one person in this town you do *not* want to lie to, it's Mrs. Mary Evans Bobo." He leaned back, laughing. "What I wouldn't give to have seen that play out. And in *her* kitchen, of all things. But as you've told it, I almost feel like I was there."

Josephine winced. "It was disastrous. And humiliating. And I deserved every bit of what she gave me. What I didn't deserve was her kindness in sending me to see you . . . for a job." She glanced at the unopened envelope. "So, since I obviously will not be getting the job of second cook . . . she suggested you *might* have need of a bookkeeper."

He slapped his hand on the desk, and Josephine jumped.

"Might?" He laughed hard. "Come now, Mrs. Dunham, if we are to work together, then I insist you be more plainspoken. I do not pussyfoot around the truth. I value plain talk. Especially from my employees."

She blinked. "Do you mean—"

"The job is yours, if you want it."

"Well, yes, of course, I want it. But how do you know I'm capable of—"

"Because I know Miss Mary. She wouldn't send you if she didn't believe you could do the job, short and simple. So . . . do you want it or not?"

"Don't you need to read her note first?"

"My, my . . . You are one for the rule books, aren't you? Oh, I'll read it all right." He slipped the envelope into his coat pocket. "But again, she'd have sent you packing if she hadn't seen something promising in you. Especially after biscuits like rocks and fires in the oven . . ." He grinned. "At the risk of sounding high and mighty, I have a fairly good sense of reading people as well."

"So the bookkeeper position is mine?" She could hardly believe it.

"You bet it is. We still need to talk pay." He reached for a pen. "How does—"

The door to the office opened.

"Hey Jack, I really need to talk to you about—"

Josephine turned, and sat bolt upright.

"Dodge!" Mr. Daniel waved him in. "Come on in and meet my new bookkeeper! Miss Mary sent her my way. Though come to think of it, you two already know each other, don't you?"

Dodge Coburn's scowl answered for him. "Mrs. Dunham," he said quietly, his gaze slowly taking her in. So thoroughly, in fact, she felt a tinge of discomfort.

"Good day to you, Mr. Coburn."

He removed his hat. "Pleasure's mine, ma'am," he answered, sounding anything but pleased.

"I got your note, Dodge." Mr. Daniel exhaled. "We need to talk, I know. But hang on a second. Me and Mrs. Dunham here are still working out some last details." He scribbled on a slip of paper and handed it to her.

Josephine stared at the figure, doing her best not to show her surprise.

"That amount sit okay with you, ma'am?" Mr. Daniel asked. "I do payroll every week. Or, you will, from now on."

"Y-yes, this amount is very generous."

"Generous nothing." He stood. "You've got your work cut out for you. Speakin' of, when can you start?"

"Today. *Now*, if you'd like." She rose, a little dizzy with relief and gratitude. She glanced at his desk then eyed him playfully. "But I think it would be helpful to know something about your company first. Your shingle out front reads Jack Daniel Distributors. What exactly do you *distribute*?"

She didn't miss the glance that passed between the two men. But it was the look on Dodge Coburn's face she couldn't decipher.

"Jack Daniel *Distributors*?" Mr. Daniel repeated, that glint sliding into his eyes again. "My dear Mrs. Dunham, we simply ran out of room on that shingle." He reached into his desk drawer and produced a bottle. "This is Jack Daniel *Distillery*, home of good Old No. 7 itself. Sour mash sipping corn whiskey, charcoal mellowed, drop by drop!"

15

Josephine stared at the bottle in Mr. Daniel's grip, then out the window at the buildings beyond his office, and finally back to the desktop. Receipts, bills, and order slips lay scattered. She picked them up. All were stamped with *Jack Daniel Distillery*.

"You make *whiskey*?" she asked, her voice as hollow as she felt.

"Not just whiskey, Mrs. Dunham." Mr. Daniel beamed. "World's *Best* Whiskey. That's the title the World's Fair in St. Louis gave it last year, and we came home toting a gold medal to prove it."

He looked past her, and she turned to see a framed gold medal on the wall behind her.

"If I weren't so secure a man, Mrs. Dunham," he went on, "I might be a tad offended you've never heard of my little company. But as Dodge already knows"—he glanced at Mr. Coburn in the doorway—"neither had anyone at the World's Fair. We walked in just a nothing-of-a-distiller from a town nobody knew." His grin widened. "So I'll forgive you this once. But we're growing fast. Soon everybody will know about Jack Daniel's whiskey. So if you're going to work here—"

He opened a drawer and pulled out a shot glass.

Despite his jesting tone, Josephine could only shake her head. And though she didn't dare look at Dodge Coburn to confirm it, she could well imagine the humor he was finding at her own expense, knowing what he already knew about her. "I'm sorry, Mr. Daniel, but there's been a terrible misunderstanding. I cannot accept this job, after all. I—"

Rapid footsteps thumped on the porch, and a young girl burst in, breathless. "Uncle Dodge! Mr. Carver gave me extra jelly beans. Said to share with you. But I told him—" The girl's attention skidded to Josephine. "Who are you? And what happened to your face?"

"Bethie!" Mr. Coburn laid a gentle hand on the girl's shoulder.

Fighting instinct, Josephine met the girl's gaze, remembering the name and not missing that she'd addressed Mr. Coburn as *uncle*. "I'm Mrs. Josephine Dunham. I was in an accident, but I'm going to be fine."

"Well, you look like you got the tar beat right out of you!"

"Bethie!" Mr. Coburn's tone sharpened. "Head on up to the cabin. I'll be there directly."

He attempted to steer her toward the door, but she resisted, eyes narrowing as she stepped closer.

She was a striking child—golden hair, blue eyes, athletic build, and the indigo dress set off her features. She had an almost tangible exuberance about her, a keenness hinting at intelligence just waiting to be nurtured. The kind of student every teacher longed for, but that came along only rarely.

Then in a blink, the girl's excitement dimmed. Her eyes went dark. "Where'd you get that skirt? And that blouse? Those belonged to *my mama*! You oughtn't be wearing them!"

"Bethie Grace." Mr. Coburn took her by the hand. "Now is not the—"

"But Uncle Dodge, she got no right. She didn't even know Mama!" She turned on Josephine. "I bet you're staying at the boarding house. I bet you *stole* them from Miss Mary when she wasn't looking!"

Heat rushed to Josephine's face, made worse when she caught the flicker of doubt in Mr. Coburn's expression. Embarrassed and ashamed, she couldn't get the words out fast enough. "I promise I didn't take them. Miss Mary allowed me to borrow them so I could come here today. But I'm returning them immediately. In fact, why don't I take my leave, and I'll—"

She moved for the door, but the child blocked her. Josephine half expected her to grab at the skirt, but tears filled the girl's eyes and spilled down her cheeks. Only then did Josephine recall what Miss Mary had said about the garments. *They belonged to a dear friend who passed away last year. So your care is greatly appreciated.*

This precious child's *mother* . . .

The girl's grief—and the raw pain on Dodge Coburn's face—threatened to unravel what little composure Josephine had left. "I'm *so* sorry," she whispered. "If I'd known, I would never have—"

"Don't you ever wear those again," Bethie sobbed. "You got no right. You just got no right . . ."

Mr. Coburn scooped her up, and she clung to his neck, face buried in his shoulder.

"She got no right," Bethie whispered.

"Y'all excuse us, please," Mr. Coburn said, voice tight. "Jack, I'll be back in a few minutes." He looked at Josephine. "Mrs. Dunham . . ."

Josephine struggled to think of what else she could possibly say or do to make things right.

"Take your time, Dodge." Mr. Daniel came around the desk. "And Bethie, you stop by the house later, darlin'. I got pineapple shipped in special, and Clara's making her upside-down cake tonight."

Bethie didn't respond until Mr. Coburn whispered in her ear.

"Thank you, Uncle Jack," she managed, the brokenness in her voice wounding Josephine all over again.

Josephine watched Mr. Coburn carry her out. The door stood open and she saw her path to escape, but couldn't move, her vision blurred with tears.

"Mrs. Dunham . . ." Mr. Daniel's voice filled the silence. "You've no reason to feel badly about what just happened. It was plain bad luck, that's all. Just sorry, rotten timing."

Josephine shook her head. "I never should have come here today. I shouldn't even be in this place," she finished in a whisper, astonished again at how swiftly her world had come undone. "I'm sorry to have wasted your time, Mr. Daniel."

"You didn't waste my time, ma'am. In fact, far as I'm concerned, I'm still looking at my new bookkeeper. Although I got to say, I'm a mite confounded as to why she hadn't already gotten to work. I mean, it's not like she can't see what needs doing clear as day, right in front of her. Unless she's holding out for a pay raise, which—" He fingered his goatee as though having to think hard on the subject. "I guess I could bump it up a little. I mean, seeing as she can start immediately, and she was obviously so *very* impressed with my gold medal. As every woman has been thus far, and rightly so."

Perhaps it was his outlandish suggestions or quick-witted humor—or maybe the way he cocked his head to one side, looking at her expectantly—but Josephine felt the hint of a smile. This man possessed a dangerous amount of charm, and knew how to wield it.

"Thank you, Mr. Daniel, for that most gallant attempt to help me save face, and to change my mind, but—"

"How about I throw in a free bottle of good Old No. 7 every last Friday of the month, just for kindness sake?"

She gave a half-hearted laugh. "That would *not* qualify as an incentive from my viewpoint. You see, I'm a—"

"Teetotaler," he said, snapping his fingers. "Just like our good Miss Mary."

Josephine hesitated.

"Oh yes." He wagged a finger. "Miss Mary Bobo doesn't allow alcohol under her roof. Not a drop. And if she catches you imbibing?" He slashed a finger across his throat. "You're gone and done for. Tossed into the street with everything you own. No, ma'am, don't cross Miss Mary in that regard. She has no tolerance for it."

"And yet, you have a seat at her table. In her home."

He frowned. "Miss Mary and I may not see eye to eye on every little thing—"

"That's a pretty big thing."

He seemed to weigh that comment. "Not particularly. I respect her boundaries and she respects mine."

"So . . ." She recalled their initial meeting in the library. "You weren't enjoying a little Old No. 7, as you call it, last night? During your visit with Ben-Hur?"

His frown deepened, then awareness moved into his eyes. "No, ma'am, I was not. When I am in Miss Mary's home, I abide by her wishes. But interesting that you jumped to that conclusion."

Josephine winced. "I didn't mean to insinuate that—"

"Oh, I think you did." His smile returned. "As I said, Mrs. Dunham, I prize bluntness. I loathe trying to figure out what someone's thinking. Which is one reason why I esteem Miss Mary like I do. And not to toot my own horn, but I believe she holds a similar opinion of me. Hence, why she sent you here today. She knows you need a job, and she knows I need a bookkeeper. Which brings us full circle again, doesn't it?"

Feeling put in her place, yet knowing she was in the right on the alcohol issue, Josephine offered a slight nod. "It does, Mr. Daniel. And while I sincerely appreciate your offer, I cannot work for you. Or more rightly, for your *distillery*. Because to state it bluntly—" She knew this would sever any future ties with the man, but preferred to go ahead and tell him herself rather than have him hear the truth from Dodge Coburn. What a laugh they would share together later. "I'm not only a teetotaler, I am a suffragist. I've vowed to champion temperance, abolition, the rights of labor, and equal pay for equal work. I believe everyone is equal under God. Men *and* women."

He leaned back against his desk, arms crossed, smiling. "I had you pegged, didn't I? You *are* one for the rule books."

She lifted her chin. "It was *we, the people*—not we, the male citizens, nor we, the *white* male citizens—but we, the *whole* people, who formed this Union. And we formed it, not to give the blessings of liberty, but to *secure* them. And not to the half of ourselves and the half of our posterity, but to the whole people—women as well as men."

To her surprise, he began to clap.

"Well done, Mrs. Dunham. Is that your own speech? Or someone else's?"

Josephine briefly looked away. "I've long admired Miss Susan B. Anthony's courage and dedication, and have heard her speak on occasion."

"Ah, yes . . . Miss Anthony. I've read about her. Quite a stiff debater, I hear, even so advanced in years. But the problem is, Mrs. Dunham . . . I agree with everything you've just said. Men, women, equality, black, white. I'm right there with you."

Josephine stared. "But how that can be? You run a distillery."

"Do you know the definition of temperance, ma'am?"

She resisted the urge to roll her eyes. "Of course, I do, Mr. Daniel. Abstinence from alcohol."

"No, no." He raised a forefinger. "That's the definition taken on by the American Woman Suffrage Association, or the like. Let's consult Merriam Webster." He retrieved a thick volume from a lower bookshelf and made a show of blowing off the dust, smiling as he did. He flipped through the pages. "Ah, here we are. Temperance . . ." He cleared his throat. *"Moderation in action, thought, or feeling. An avoidance of extremes. Restraint."* He emphasized the last word then closed the dictionary with a thud. "My whiskey can be safely enjoyed in moderation.

Yes, it demands restraint. As do many culinary pleasures. All of that lies within individual choice."

Meeting his self-satisfied stare, Josephine grabbed the dictionary and thumbed through the pages. Then looked pointedly at him before reading. *"Preposterous: Contrary to nature, reason, or common sense. Absurd."* She closed the volume with a similar thud and tossed it on the desk.

A gleam slid into his eyes. "Mrs. Josephine Dunham, you must absolutely accept this job. Think of the discussions we would have! And I give you my word, you won't have to fend off unwanted advances from me. No doubt you've heard, or soon will, about my reputation . . ." He shrugged. "I do enjoy the company of women, and I freely admit to having several . . . female friends."

Josephine had no trouble believing that.

"But to put it delicately, ma'am, you're not really the type of woman I'm attracted to. No offense. You're just a mite tall for my liking." He winked. "And even if you weren't already married, I'm quite sure I'm not what you'd be looking for."

"Good day, Mr. Daniel." Josephine headed for the door, his laughter following.

"You won't find another job in this town that suits you as well. Or comes close to paying what I will."

She paused on the threshold. "While that may be true, I prefer to hold to my convictions."

He grinned. "Your rule book, you mean."

Josephine gestured. "Door open or closed, sir?"

He bowed slightly. "For you, Mrs. Dunham, I'll keep it open."

She closed the door firmly behind her.

16

No sooner had Josephine left the distillery office than she collided with Dodge Coburn barreling around the corner, his expression a tangle of concern and frustration. He stopped short and caught her arm to steady her.

"Beg your pardon, ma'am." He stepped back, granting quick release, and removed his Stetson.

His gaze swept the length of her again—appraising, yes, but not for any untoward reason, she knew now. Still uncomfortable and eager to change from these clothes, she forced herself to look up. "Mr. Coburn, please accept my apologies again for—"

"It's not your fault, Mrs. Dunham." He held up a hand. "And I'm sorry for the way Bethie spoke to you. That wasn't right. I talked with her and—"

"Your niece had every reason to react as she did. To see a complete stranger wearing her *mother's clothes*?" Josephine winced. "I venture to say I would have reacted much the same way at her age."

"Your allowance is kindly taken, ma'am. It *was* a hard thing for her." His jaw tightened. "But Bethie shouldn't have gone off half-cocked like that. And certainly not to someone her senior. My niece, she's a passionate thing, just like her mama, God rest her." He exhaled. "Still, she's got to learn you can't just go around saying whatever comes to mind."

Touched by his affection for the child, she glanced toward the office. "That's a difficult lesson. One even some adults have yet to master."

A slow smile tugged one side of his mouth. "Jack Daniel always speaks his mind. You never have to guess where you stand with him. He lets you know straight up."

"Much like Miss Mary."

"Yes, ma'am. They're akin that way."

It struck Josephine then how familiar Dodge Coburn had been with Mr. Daniel, how he'd walked in as if the place belonged to him. And she'd heard the telltale *tink* of glass in the wagon bed on the way from Tullahoma. A distillery needed bottles. Perhaps Mr. Coburn was a supplier, a partner in crime, and probably getting rich by association—while also worsening the situation for untold women and children in this town and far beyond the reach of Lynchburg, too, if what Mr. Daniel had said was true about his distillery's growth. Gold medal for World's Best Whiskey, indeed.

A breeze rustled the branches overhead, sunlight sluicing through, and Josephine looked away, painfully aware of the wounds on her face—and of those discerning blue eyes.

"Well, if you'll excuse me, Mr. Coburn, I'd best be on my way."

"You could do a lot worse than working for Jack Daniel, you know. Folks in this town would crawl over cut glass for the offer you just got. *If* they had the know-how to do the job, which they don't."

Josephine searched his expression for any hint of humor. But he was serious. "Mr. Coburn, you know very well that I cannot, nor would I ever choose to, work for such an establishment. My beliefs forbid it. Though I'm sure you found amusement watching that scene unfold, despite my current circumstances."

His eyes held hers. "I'd have to be a fairly base man to find amusement in the situation you now find yourself in. And I assure you, ma'am, I am not."

Taken aback and a little ashamed at her hasty judgment, Josephine inclined her head. "Thank you, Mr. Coburn. That's . . . most kind."

"But while you're holding tight to those beliefs, I'd ask you to consider something . . . Not everyone in the world is out to get you, ma'am. Some folks actually want to help. Maybe even lighten your load. Good people, too. Different from you, for sure. But different doesn't mean they're against you." He slipped his hat back on. "As my father used to say . . . *That's all for free, but free don't always mean dreck.*"

Josephine studied him. His demeanor seemed genuine enough but experience had taught her caution. Rare was the man who considered a woman his equal, and when the topic turned to women's rights, most tried to placate their *inferiors* with a smile or proverbial pat on the head. Like her father had done. The worst sought to cow women into submission.

Intuition told her Dodge Coburn wasn't in that latter category. But he likely fell into the first.

Best she set him straight right now. "Mr. Coburn, while holding to such convictions may seem frivolous to someone like you—"

"I didn't say that, ma'am—"

"I have witnessed what alcohol does to a man and what pain it inflicts on his family. Innocent women and children suffer. Wages meant for food and clothing go to bar tabs and barrels. So while others might *crawl over cut glass* for that job, I am not one of them. I'll find gainful work elsewhere."

"Elsewhere," he echoed, brows lifting. "In Lynchburg."

"Yes. This town may be small, but surely there are other opportunities. I taught school back in—" She caught herself. "*Chattanooga* . . . So bookkeeping is not the only skill I possess."

Humor slow-brewed in his eyes. "I'd wager that's a right true statement." He gestured toward the square. "Folks hiring usually let the word walk until it finds its mark. Some tack notices on the board inside the mercantile. Mr. and Mrs. Carver keep a good ear on what's what."

"Thank you, Mr. Coburn. I'll visit there now. Good day to you."

She turned to go, catching his slow smile again.

"And a fine day to you, too, Mrs. Dunham." He tipped his hat. "And . . . good luck."

"Xparianxt hawg haend," Josephine read softly, scanning the scraps of paper pinned to the mercantile's "community board," as an older couple, Mr. and Mrs. Carver—the proprietors—had called the rough-hewn plank hanging slightly askew near the front door.

She sounded out words phonetically, after deciphering the poorly written script. Nothing she wasn't accustomed to as a teacher. But it was a characteristic typically seen in younger students, not adults. Then again, each step changes the view, as Todd used to say to her.

Thinking of her brother stirred the melancholy crouched at the fringes, ready to pounce. *Remember, you didn't always know what you know now. Give others the chance others gave you.* Taking his advice to heart, she read on with a more generous eye . . .

Mill werker at Mckays.

Blacksmith with tuuls se Big Jed.

Many listings had curled edges, evidence of longevity. *Farmhand needed. Includes room and board. See Mitchamore Farm.* Room and board would help, but the fact she knew nothing about farming or tending livestock could prove problematic.

Carpenter for barn razin. Hot meals and room for pay. While she had to smile at that one, she felt less skilled with every line read.

Distillery Laborers Needed.

Her brow rose.

Men of good character sought . . . mash tubs, stills . . . experience welcome, training provided . . . good wages.

The ad was well written, the lettering precise. Jack Daniel was certainly educated. Not a single misspelling. The teacher within her gave him excellent marks, though "men of good character" for a distillery gave her pause.

Her gaze slid to another notice overlapping older ones. *Excellent cook needed for boarding house . . . inquire to Mrs. Bobo.*

Josephine inwardly groaned and forced herself to look again, until a notice near the bottom caught her eye.

Schoolteacher Needed. Position open for a lady or gentleman . . . modest salary . . . lodging arranged . . .

Hope rising, she unpinned the notice and hurried back to the counter.

"Excuse me, Mr. and Mrs. Carver. This ad—" She held out the piece of paper. "Do you know when it was posted? And whether the position has been filled?"

Mrs. Carver read the ad. "Why yes, ma'am. A teacher was hired a few months back. Ain't that right, Harold?"

His confirming nod sent Josephine's hopes crashing.

"Fellow named Weston," Mr. Carver said. "Come down from Fayetteville way. Lives just up the hill if you need him."

"No, that won't be necessary, but thank you." Josephine tried to phrase her next question without sounding condescending. "Do the ads posted on the board stay up for a certain period of time . . . or indefinitely?"

Mr. Carver set aside the cloth in his hand and offered a patient smile—one she imagined he reserved for confused children. "That there's a *community* board, Miss—"

"Dunham. And it's *Mrs.*," she corrected.

"*Mrs.* Dunham," he continued. "Folks post what they need or got to sell—jobs, crops, sewing, building. It's where they see what's going on in town, too. So we don't rightly track it when news goes up or is hauled down. We leave that to the one doing the posting. That's part of what makes it community."

"I see . . ." Josephine found the notion somewhat charming, though highly inefficient. She noticed Mrs. Carver eyeing her skirt and blouse and hastened to conclude her business. "I'll return this advertisement to the board. But would you happen to know of any opportunities in town that *aren't* posted?"

Mr. Carver shook his head. "Not for womenfolk."

He returned to his work, while his wife discreetly gestured Josephine to the side.

"There's things womenfolk only tell me, Mrs. Dunham," Mrs. Carver said softly, leaning close. "Ol' Miss Ruby's down with the arthritis again. She can't keep pace with her sewing, so she's needing help. Only, her daughter-in-law can't be knowing of it. So you'd have to come and go when Erma Dale ain't home."

Josephine hesitated. "I'm afraid I don't sew well, Mrs. Carver. I can mend, but it's none too pretty. I'm a teacher by training."

"Well . . ." Mrs. Carver sighed wistfully. "That teaching job would've fixed you right up then, wouldn't it?"

"Yes, ma'am, it would have."

"Can you cook good?" the woman asked, then must have read the answer in Josephine's face. "*Hmmm* . . . No cooking either."

Josephine attempted a pleasant countenance, feeling small and foolish in this woman's eyes.

"Well Mrs. Dunham, I been through about everything I know. 'Ceptin'. . ." She leaned in again. "Can you wet-nurse?"

Josephine's eyes widened. "*Wet-nurse?*"

Mrs. Carver laid a gentle hand on her arm. "That's when a woman who ain't done the birthing—"

"I *know* what it is, Mrs. Carver," Josephine said quickly. "And no, that is also something I cannot do."

Mrs. Carver's voice softened. "So there ain't been no children yet?"

The simple question sparked emotion Josephine couldn't name. "No, ma'am, no children."

"It were the same for me and Harold. Four times I carried, but I couldn't ever get them to the birthing." Her voice wavered, and she briefly squeezed Josephine's hand. "But you're young yet. And strong looking. You got plenty of years ahead for that." Her gaze shifted to Josephine's bruised face. "Your man . . . He the one done this?"

Josephine gave a small nod, as if a gesture didn't constitute a lie the same as speaking the words aloud.

"I take it he don't know you're here?"

"No, ma'am."

"And you ain't wanting to go back if'n he does come lookin'?"

Josephine shook her head.

"You still got your folks? Family to help?"

Again, she shook her head.

Mrs. Carver seemed to weigh that. "If he comes aiming to tote you back and you need somebody, you head on here. Harold and me, we live in the back rooms. I'm usually here, 'ceptin' on Sunday mornings for prayer meeting. Don't know what I can do, but I'll do what I can." Her eyes sharpened. "Just don't say nothing to Harold. He don't hold to gettin' mussed up in such things."

Josephine swallowed against the knot forming in her throat. "Why would you offer to help me? You don't even know me."

In a gesture that looked as natural as breathing, Mrs. Carver brushed the hair back from Josephine's temple. "'Cause we womenfolk got to stick together," she said softly.

Josephine smiled.

"Only a blink ago, Mrs. Dunham, I was you. Young, full of hopes and fancy dreams." Her delicate eyelids fluttered closed. "My mama, she warned me, but . . . I still weren't ready for it." She finally looked up. "Took me time to learn what set him off . . . but I did. And you will too, with your man. *If* you choose to go back."

Josephine went still inside. She glanced at Mr. Carver as he stacked crates filled with canned goods. Time and age had stooped his frame, but his broad chest and shoulders revealed the man he'd been in younger years. She looked back at Mrs. Carver, anger and compassion filling her. "Does he still do it?" she whispered.

"Oh no, that was some time ago. Most men mellow in their back years, and he has." Mrs. Carver's voice stayed hushed. "I'm only saying that the worst of it, what you're gettin' now, ain't something forever. It's only for a season."

"Only for a season?" Josephine repeated, forcing a hushed tone. "Mrs. Carver, there is never *any* justifiable reason for a man to strike a woman. Much less a husband to strike his—"

Mrs. Carver shushed her with a look, and Josephine saw Mr. Carver approaching. He set down a crate and began shelving bottles—Jack Daniel whiskey—right by the register.

"I know you're new to town, ma'am," he said, holding up a bottle. "But I'm assuming you've heard about our world-famous whiskey."

"Not until I arrived, but . . . I'm familiar with it now."

He beamed. "Mark my words. This here stuff is gonna put Lynchburg on the map!"

The bell over the front door jangled. A man in mud-streaked overalls and a slouch hat entered. His beard masked his precise age, but the strained buttons at the waist did not hide his girth. He nodded to them, but gave Josephine a hard look, then moved off.

She felt a light touch on her arm.

Mrs. Carver's gaze dropped to the blouse and skirt. "That's our dear Kathleen Coburn's handiwork, God bless her sweet soul. I reckon that means you're kin to Dodge and Bethie?"

"No, ma'am, I'm not." Josephine smoothed a hand over the blue skirt. "Miss Mary loaned them to me for an appointment. I'm staying . . . temporarily, at the boarding house."

"Oh, Miss Mary and Kitty Kat," Mr. Carver chimed in, stacking bottles just so. "Those girls were thick as thieves. Good friends if ever there was such."

"Kitty Kat is what Harold used to call Kathleen," Mrs. Carver explained. "As a little girl, she'd sweet-talk him out of candy, and Bethie's even better at it." She fingered one of the pearl buttons on Josephine's sleeves. "I remember the day Kathleen ordered these. *I want some right special buttons, Miss Celia,* she told me. We pored over catalogs till we found these." Tears tinged her eyes. "She was a good girl, even if she took a wrong turn for a bit. Harold and I knowed her afore she was born. Augustus and Madge Coburn, they was fine people. Don't seem right sometimes . . . how the old stay behind while the young are taken. But the Lord's got his ways," she said softly. "And we're to trust them."

Josephine gave an obliging nod.

The bell over the door jangled again, and they turned. A young woman—or girl, really, upon closer look—entered, basket in hand. Upon seeing Josephine, she stopped, recognition sharpening her features. Josephine, too, felt a stir of familiarity, yet was certain they'd never met.

"Good day to you, Miss Rowena," Mrs. Carver offered.

The young woman's attention shifted from Josephine, and she joined them at the counter. "Good day. Mama said she left an order yesterday."

"She surely did, and we got it about ready. The Mitchamore's hens ain't been layin' good of late, so let me see if they got their eggs delivered." Mrs. Carver started toward the back, then paused. "Rowena, this here's Mrs. Dunham from—" She arched a brow at Josephine. "Where you hail from, dear?"

"Chattanooga," Josephine answered.

"From Chattanooga," Mrs. Carver repeated. "She's staying at the boarding house. You might've met Rowena's mama, Mrs. Gibbs. She works the dining room for Miss Mary. Mrs. Dunham, this here's Miss Rowena Gibbs."

So this was the daughter of Mrs. Gibbs, the woman who'd acted so strangely toward her. Josephine offered a smile. "Good to meet you Miss Gibbs. And, indeed, I've made your mother's . . . acquaintance."

"Yes. She told me she met you."

The man who'd come in earlier reappeared at the counter, plunked down some goods, and pointed. "Gimme a couple of bottles of that, too, Carver."

Josephine caught the odor and realized what she'd taken for mud was manure—and that he'd tracked it across the floor. Already, Mrs. Carver had placed Miss Gibbs's order on the counter and was quietly sweeping behind him as if it were the most ordinary thing in the world.

Mr. Carver packed the man's purchases in a box, wedging the bottles in. "Careful with them last two things, Jed. And enjoy!"

The man grunted and left.

Mr. Carver tallied Rowena's order while the girl suddenly found her voice—chatting easily, smiling. She was lovely, perhaps sixteen or a bit older, and nature had blessed her in all the right places. She knew it, too.

"Rowena . . ." Mrs. Carver asked. "You know any womenfolk needin' help? Mrs. Dunham could use some work."

Rowena's gaze slid to Josephine. "I thought you was only here for a few days. Now you got a hankering to stay?"

What she'd done to get on the wrong side of the Gibbs women, Josephine didn't know. But Mrs. Carver's eyes revealed surprise as well. "I have no intention of staying indefinitely, Miss Gibbs. But while I'm here, I must provide for myself. So any ideas would be appreciated."

"I ain't got none." Rowena gave a shrug. "'Less you know how to slop hogs. But I'm guessing you ain't no better at that than you are at cooking."

Rowena Gibbs had excellent aim for one so young, and her arrow hit its mark.

Josephine forced a self-deprecating laugh. "I see my efforts in Miss Mary's kitchen this morning have sprouted legs." She didn't have to wonder who had repeated the tale. Mrs. Gibbs would've pleasured in it. "But you're right, I'm not a very good cook. However, I am a good teacher. So if you know of any children needing instruction in reading, writing, arithmetic, or even manners, I'd be happy to oblige."

Rowena's face flushed red. The girl grabbed the basket and turned, then pulled out the bottle of whiskey. "Mama didn't order this."

"No," Mr. Carver said. "Your papa sent word by one of your brothers. So you make sure he gets it."

Rowena shoved it back inside, but Josephine caught the shadow of disapproval—or was it dread—in the girl's features before she slammed the door behind her. Josephine watched her through the mercantile window, regretting how she'd responded to her.

"Don't you mind Rowena." Mrs. Carver's voice cut through her thoughts. "She's strongheaded, like her mama." Her attention darted about the empty store. "But I guess that's a good thing, considerin' Gus

Gibbs turns meaner than a rattler when he drinks. Even them boys know to steer clear till the next day."

Josephine's stomach knotted. Her gaze moved to the neat stack of whiskey by the register, and she wished she could smash every last bottle. She weighed her options, but there were none. She could not return to Miss Mary's without a job, not after the woman had all but handed her one. She could already picture Miss Mary waiting for her on the porch, hands on hips, with Dodge Coburn summoned and ready to take her back to Tullahoma.

She could not let that happen. There had to be another way.

"Can I get you anything, Mrs. Dunham? I got some fresh eggs left, and Mrs. Tolley brought some of her good 'country loaf bread,' as we call it. It's good with butter."

Josephine's mouth watered, but she shook her head. "No, thank you. But I appreciate your kindness." She turned to go, then paused. "Where I'm from . . . there are women who have banded together for the sole purpose of bringing change for women. Change for—"

"You one of them suffragists?" Mrs. Carver whispered, glancing toward her husband. "The ones we get wind of from newspapers now and again?"

Josephine hesitated. Dodge Coburn and Jack Daniel knew, but no use broadcasting it. "Other women have helped me, so if I can help another woman—especially with what we talked about—I want to. So please, let me know."

Caution flitted across Celia Carver's face. "You mean well, Mrs. Dunham, and no doubt. But you're new to town. You don't know our ways. Be careful what burdens you take on, even in kindness."

Mrs. Carver returned to her work and as Josephine left, something inside her turned hard and fast, like a lock long stuck finally giving way. She closed the door to the mercantile, vowing that before she left this town, she would do as much damage to Jack Daniel's distillery as she could.

But first . . . she had to accept that job.

17

"So did you get the job or not, Mrs. Dunham?"

Miss Mary pinned Josephine with that look as Calla lifted golden fried chicken from the cast-iron skillet and piled it high on a platter.

Unable to admit she'd flat-out refused Jack Daniel's offer earlier that day, Josephine glanced through the open doorway to the dining room where tenants would arrive any minute for supper. No sign of Jack Daniel yet, and with any sliver of luck, he wouldn't show. When she'd returned to his office that afternoon to say she'd changed her mind and would accept the position, he'd been nowhere to be found. So she planned to be there first thing in the morning.

She was relatively certain his offer would still be open. But if she told Miss Mary she'd gotten the job, then he showed up tonight saying otherwise . . . Josephine wiped damp palms on her skirt.

"Mr. Daniel offered me the position, ma'am, but I—"

Miss Mary turned. "But you *what*?"

"Well, I . . . I—"

"Lying is not one of your gifts, Mrs. Dunham. But your determination to hone that talent only makes matters worse. So I'm going to ask you one more time—"

Josephine cringed. "I refused the offer because I didn't realize he owned a distillery. I thought it was . . . another sort of business."

Miss Mary stilled. "And you object to working in a distillery because . . ."

"Because I am opposed to drinking, ma'am. I've seen the misery it brings. Especially to women and children."

Miss Mary studied her. "And I reckon you know my stance on it?"

"Yes, ma'am. Mr. Daniel made me aware of that fact."

"And I reckon you're wondering why I'd send you there."

"I might have," Josephine admitted. "If I hadn't learned how scarce jobs are in Lynchburg. At least for someone like me." She lowered her gaze. "You knew I needed work, and you knew he needed a bookkeeper."

"That's *precisely* why I sent you, Mrs. Dunham. You have skills Jack Daniel sorely needs. And his business, while not to my personal taste, provides for dozens of families. Folks take pride in their work there, and the place is growing, which means Lynchburg will be the better for it." She frowned. "Didn't you see the shingle hanging out front on the porch?"

"Yes, but it says Jack Daniel D-I-S-T." Embarrassed, Josephine looked away. "I took that to mean distributors."

Miss Mary snorted then laughed outright. "Jack Daniel *Distributors*? Oh glory be . . ." She nudged Calla. "Our dear Uncle Jack for sure *distributes*, doesn't he?"

Calla smiled faintly, eyes on the chicken, not a trace of burnt on it. "Yes, ma'am, he sure do. Now that's the last of the meat. The mashed taters are ready, too. I'll get the apples and fried okra dished up."

"Hands down, Calla Lilly, you're the best cook in Moore County," Miss Mary added matter-of-factly. "And I'm blessed to have you."

Calla's smile softened, and the name Miss Mary had used—*Calla Lilly*—didn't go unnoticed. About to comment on the beauty of it, Josephine felt Miss Mary's gaze.

"So," Miss Mary continued. "What's your plan to secure that job?"

"I'll be there first thing in the morning to ask Mr. Daniel to reconsider."

Miss Mary nodded. "My guess is Uncle Jack'll be tickled to see you coming. Though he's likely to have a bit of fun with you on the front end."

"After our meeting this morning, that's not hard to imagine."

Miss Mary yanked the rope on the bell and the already-familiar *clang* echoed throughout the house, announcing to tenants and any guests waiting on the front porch that supper was about to be served.

Miss Mary glanced at the bowl of steaming potatoes mounded high, a generous dollop of butter pooling in the center. "Mrs. Gibbs isn't able to help us tonight. Would you carry those potatoes in? No serving. Just set them down and—"

"Quickly back away before destroying anything else?" Josephine finished for her.

Miss Mary's eyes lit. "I wasn't going to say that, but yes. Exactly."

Josephine followed Miss Mary's lead and placed the potatoes on the table then turned to go.

"I don't believe I've seen you here before, madam," a gentleman seated at the end said, his attention moving over Josephine's face. His accent pegged him as a Northerner. "Are you new to town?"

"This is Mrs. Dunham," Miss Mary cut in. "She's helping us out for a while." Miss Mary's fleeting look in Josephine's direction held a world of private meaning. "Mr. Prince is one of our favorite tax revenuers who stays with us pretty regular. The revenuers make sure our dear Uncle Jack is keeping things on the right side of the law."

"So far." Mr. Prince paused overlong as he looked around the table. "The man has never given us cause to question. But we're watching close as a hawk on a bunny in case he ever does."

Everyone laughed at his joke, Josephine included, and Mr. Prince beamed with somewhat awkward pleasure at their response. She couldn't say what, but something in his demeanor struck her as a little odd. Not threatening. Just a little off-center, perhaps. "It's nice to meet you, Mr. Prince."

"Welcome to Miss Mary's," a middle-aged gentleman sitting down beside Mr. Prince chimed in. "I'm Mr. Tom Motlow, president of Farmers Bank here in Lynchburg."

Josephine gave a tilt of her head. "I admired that building today, sir, as I passed through town."

"Why thank you kindly, ma'am. If we can be of service in any way with your financial dealings, please let me know."

Josephine just nodded.

"It's nice to have another female in our midst," an older woman added as she took her seat. "I'm Miss Thelma Livvy, a teacher at a local school."

"Nice to meet you, Miss Livvy," Josephine answered. "I was a teacher, too."

Miss Livvy's expression brightened. "What ages did you teach?"

"The younger ones at first, then gradually moved to the upper grades."

"The *upper* grades? I'm impressed. You're still quite young."

Josephine smiled, appreciating the comment but feeling a homesickness when thinking of her students. And Sarah..

"The fine gentleman at the end," Miss Mary continued, "is Mr. Roughton Waggoner. He owns a store on the square where you can find everything you need, no matter if you knew you needed it or not."

More laughter, and the man nodded silently in her direction. Josephine sensed his quiet nature.

Miss Mary continued the introductions—each sharp, warm, and perfectly fitting. The woman had a gift for hospitality and wit, and Josephine resolved to stay on her good side.

Another gentleman entered and conversation ebbed as he took the last seat, casting Mr. Motlow a dismissive glance before tucking his napkin in his lap.

"Mrs. Dunham, this is Mr. Will Parks." Miss Mary's tone took on the guarded calm of a teacher heading off a squabble. "Mr. Parks has pledged to open Lynchburg's first automobile store—once Mr. Henry Ford has his newfangled Model T ready. Haven't you, Mr. Parks?"

"I sure am, Miss Mary. Might be another two or three years, but mark my words, Ford's Model T will change the world. And I'm going to do my part to help it along."

"Hear, hear!" Mr. Prince said a little too loudly.

Mr. Motlow cleared his throat. "I just hope the Model T is a better contraption than Ford's *Quadricycle*." He laughed under his breath. "Some horseless carriage that turned out to be. And for two hundred dollars? Why, I wouldn't do anybody in this town the disservice of loaning them the money for such a bucket of bolts."

Mr. Parks flushed crimson. "Don't start with me tonight, Tom Motlow. I am not in the mood for your tomfoolery!"

Mr. Motlow smiled, his gaze sweeping the table. "I recently heard of a fellow who named his Ford after his wife. He said he did so because he can't control either one."

Laughter erupted, and though Josephine was tempted, she didn't join in. Not seeing Mr. Parks's reaction. Nor Miss Mary's, who appeared none too pleased.

"However," Mr. Motlow continued, "I will say that Ford really is a *family* car. There's a hood for Mama, a tank for Papa . . . and a rattle for Baby!"

More laughter, and Mr. Parks shoved his chair back. Miss Mary was behind him in a flash.

"Calla, our wonderful cook, has prepared all of your favorites tonight. Especially yours, Mr. Parks. Chicken fried up golden brown and those candied apples you love so much. We've got fried okra and pinto beans with smoked ham hock, mashed potatoes fairly floating in butter, and rolls coming hot from the oven. And for dessert, fudge pie for everybody who cleans their plates." She winked. "Now let me say the blessing, thank God for the friendships in this house—"

Josephine caught the look she gave Mr. Motlow.

"—then we'll dig in and eat while it's still hot."

Josephine bowed her head. All followed suit except for Mr. Motlow, whose grin lingered beneath closed eyes.

She counted twelve tenants in all. And no sign of Mr. Bobo. Five mismatched dining room chairs lined the far wall, and she got the impression that if more people showed up, Miss Mary would simply squeeze them in.

She had no idea how many rooms were in this house or how many beds each accommodated. But as she headed back into the kitchen, she caught the friendly interactions between tenants, heard the *tink* of utensils as people ladled sumptuous food onto their plates, and it occurred to her that Miss Mary Bobo's Boarding House was far more than meals and beds. It was community. Friendship. A place of belonging. And even a place for *friendly* rivalry, it would seem.

And while the warmth of that settled deep inside her, it also sharpened the ache of standing on the outside looking in.

Later that night, she lay awake on her cot in Calla's small quarters in the old cabin out back, staring through the window beside her bed into the dark night sky. No stars. No moon. Only blackness. Her heartbeat felt heavy and sluggish in her chest.

The salve Calla had smoothed over her face was pungent and not yet dry, so she kept her cheek angled away from the thin pillow stuffed with cotton batting.

She'd eaten supper with Calla in the kitchen, every bite better than the last. When she'd said so, Calla had waved off the compliment. "Cooking's about all I know, Josephine. That and cleaning and sewing. I know gardening too, I reckon. I'm fair to middling at growing things."

While Calla's humility was admirable, Josephine doubted anything the woman did was merely *fair to middling*. The custard in her fudge pie melted on the tongue, the pastry absolute perfection. Atlanta restaurants would have lined up to hire her.

But Josephine knew the truth, even with all the education she'd amassed through her life, Calla and likely everyone in this town possessed more practical skills than she did. So much for being "the youngest but most mature candidate" the Atlanta Educational School Board had ever interviewed. A lot of good that did her now.

Behind her, Calla moved about the room preparing for bed. Josephine shifted on the cot, careful not to reveal she was still awake. Grateful for Calla's loan of a nightgown, she tugged at the too-short sleeves and tried to get comfortable. Her belly was full, but the hollowness inside her felt cavernous.

After supper, she'd brushed the dust from the skirt and blouse sewn by Dodge Coburn's late sister and returned them to Miss Mary—relieved to have them out of her care. Then she'd soaked and scrubbed her own clothes and hung them by the fire to dry.

"Josephine," Calla whispered after a minute. "If you're still awake, you want some tea? Got some chamomile that might help you sleep."

Josephine sniffed, willing her voice steady. "No thanks. But I appreciate it."

Soft footsteps approached, but she didn't turn, not trusting the ache in her throat. A gentle hand smoothed her hair, and her resolve nearly crumbled.

"You're going to be okay, young miss," Calla said softly. "I know you're affrighted, being so far from home and on your lonesome. Or leastwise, it feels that way. But you're not alone. Not hardly. Wherever we go, the good Lord sees. He knows. And he's got grace—" Her fragile voice broke. "—even when we got none for ourselves."

Josephine drew in a shuddered breath. At last, she turned. "Thank you . . . Calla Lilly," she whispered.

Calla laughed softly. "You heard Miss Mary earlier."

"It's a beautiful name."

"My mama gave it to me. She said it comes from stories her mama told her about the most beautiful flowers growing back home, right along the riverbanks. White, pink, yellow, purple, even a dark red-brown. Big old trumpet-looking blooms with leaves shaped like Indian arrowheads." She sighed. "Mama wanted me to remember where my people came from. So she gave me this name."

Josephine's chest ached at what Calla said, and didn't say. She reached from beneath the covers and clasped Calla's hand. "It's wrong," she whispered. "People owning people."

Calla held her gaze for a long moment, the distant night song of crickets moving closer in the silence. "It sure is. And it's wrong, too . . . a man beating a woman."

Josephine swallowed. "It sure is."

Giving her hand a final squeeze, Calla moved away.

Minutes later came the soft whistle of the kettle, the slosh of water, and the faint clink of a spoon. Josephine glanced back to see Calla rocking gently, stirring honey into her cup from the little blue bottle. The chair creaked in steady rhythm as she sipped.

At last, Calla crawled into bed. The ropes beneath the hay-stuffed mattress groaned softly, then the lamp went dark. Josephine pulled the thin blanket to her chin, the night air cool and damp. But sleep wouldn't come.

Sometime later, the mantel clock chimed twice on the hour, worry keeping rest at arm's length. What if Jack Daniel changed his mind? At the same time, accepting the job felt traitorous. If given the opportunity to explain herself to fellow suffragists, she hoped they would understand. But if the roles were reversed . . . would she?

Without that job, Miss Mary would send her straight back to Tullahoma—where authorities waited.

18

"ARE THEY *ALL* GONNA DIE, UNCLE DODGE?" Bethie asked, dread threading her voice.

Dodge latched the cabin door and watched his niece lean against the porch railing, staring out at the cattle scattered across the fields. Jessie lay at her feet, head on her paws, keeping watch just as closely.

For a moment his mind betrayed him, and Bethie was a toddler again—chubby hands gripping those same spindles as she pulled herself upright for the first time. He and Kathleen had clapped and cheered, later sipping dandelion wine while he rocked Bethie to sleep in the porch swing.

Then the memory faded, leaving him in a world without his sister, and Bethie without her mama.

She was growing too fast. Nine years old and nearly grown, and he had no earthly idea how to navigate the years ahead. Truth was, he'd been in deep water for a while now.

"I don't think we'll lose all of them, honey," he said gently. "But a good many *will* die."

"And there's nothing to stop it?"

He slipped an arm around her shoulders, but she edged away slightly, apparently still riled over him correcting her misbehavior yesterday. Bethie could hold a grudge with the best of them. Same as Kathleen at that age.

He wished he could shield Bethie from everything hard. But that wasn't life, and losing cattle would pale in comparison to learning they weren't going west. He couldn't even give her the gift he'd had specially made for her in Tullahoma, not after forbidding her to ride Ginger Snap until they had answers.

"Doc Wyatt thinks it's Texas fever."

Her eyes searched his. "That sounds bad."

"Straight shooter?" he asked softly, thinking of the fourteen steers following the same course as the two from yesterday—all formerly headed for market.

She nodded without hesitation. "Straight shooter."

"It's bad, Bethie. Doc's written a man he knows in Washington, DC, who works for the Department of Agriculture. We're hoping for answers. But right now, there's no cure we know of."

She turned back toward the fields. "Will they hurt before they die?"

Her question took him straight back to Kathleen's bedside, Bethie there with him toward the end, Kathleen's breath labored and raspy. He tightened his grip around Bethie's shoulders, and this time she leaned into him. And something deep inside, like a cord anchored fast, tugged hard.

"I promise," he said softly. "I'll do everything I can to keep them from suffering."

She nodded.

In the silence following, he recognized the moment he'd both been waiting for—and dreading. "Bethie, I've got something I need to talk to you about—"

"I decided I want Mama's clothes back," she blurted. "The ones that woman was wearing yesterday. I been thinking hard on it, and I want them back!"

Dodge hesitated, intent to stay the course but knowing this mattered too. "You know your mama gave those clothes to Miss Mary before she died. The two of them were close, and your mama wanted her to have them, knowing how Miss Mary always admired them."

"That's what I'm saying." Bethie scoffed. "Mama wanted Miss Mary to have them. Not some hoople-headed—"

She must have read the warning in his eyes.

"—some . . . level-landed nobody we don't even know. And who didn't know Mama at all." Her voice cracked, and she bowed her head.

The image of Josephine Dunham wearing his sister's skirt and blouse had unsettled him, too. But the woman's remorse had been genuine. He couldn't say how he knew—only that he did.

Bethie lifted her chin. "I'm gonna ask Miss Mary if I can have them back. For safekeeping."

Dodge knelt. "Tell you what . . . I want you to think on it for a few days first. Will you do that for me?"

"I won't change my mind."

"All I'm asking . . . is you ask the Almighty what he thinks about that first, and listen to what he says. Then we'll talk again. If you still want them, we'll go together. Deal?"

He held out his hand, waiting. Prayer hadn't always come easy to him, but lately he found himself leaning on it more. Especially in moments like this. And hoped she would, too.

Her handshake felt firm as a pledge.

"Is Uncle Jack mad at you?" she asked. "With all the cows sick and us leaving?"

"No, he understands. But that's part of what I need to talk to you about, honey. And it's not an easy thing to—"

"Mornin', boss!" a couple of farmhands called out as they passed the cabin. "Mornin', Miss Bethie!"

"Morning, Hank," she called back, waving. "You too, Duffy! It's Friday, best mind the barrel check today. Make sure those bungs are holding tight. That's part of fine whiskey making!"

The farmhands laughed. "Yes, ma'am, Miss Bethie!"

Dodge nodded a greeting, vaguely unsettled by the exchange. Bethie knew the rhythms of this place as well as Kathleen had. And while Wyoming was no longer an option, raising a young girl around a distillery carried its own weight. She had that same independent streak as her mama—*You tell me I can't, and I'll show you I can.* The thought dug in, and grew talons.

"Come on, Bethie girl," he said. "Let's walk. Don't want you late for school."

He took the porch steps in twos and whistled for Jessie. The dog bounded down as Bethie grabbed her pack off the rocker and fell into step beside them.

"You remember how your mama and I talked about how we were going west to—"

"Wyoming," she filled in, smiling up at him. "Mama said it was her dream. And a gift for me."

His gut knotted. "Life out there is hard, Bethie. Harder than you think. And—"

"Hey, Bethie!" a high-pitched voice called out. "Hey, Mr. Dodge!"

They turned to see little Moriah Green racing up the road, her smile big as ever.

The girl skidded to a stop, panting. "Wanna walk the rest of the way together, Bethie? But we gonna have to hightail it. Else we'll be late and have to write sentences after."

Bethie peered up. "Can I, Uncle Dodge?"

"*May* I," Dodge corrected, then seeing the moment gone, kissed Bethie on the crown of her head. "Run on. We'll talk more at supper. And no stopping at the Carvers."

As the girls raced down the road, he wondered, as he sometimes did, if the veil of heaven ever lifted, even a little, allowing what happened here to be glimpsed from there. Not that everything on this side was worth seeing. Not hardly. But this life shaped the next, so it figured that some who'd gone on might take a gander back.

"Our girls are like two peas in a pod."

Dodge turned to see George Green, Moriah's father, approaching. "Morning, George. I'd say two very *silly* peas." They shook hands and fell into comfortable stride together, Jessie sticking close.

"You should've come to Uncle Jack's last night, Dodge. *Mmmm* . . . That fancy pineapple cake was some kind of good."

"I appreciate you and your family coming by for Bethie. She enjoyed it. She needed some time away from me, I think, and I needed to tend the stock."

"Sorry about the cattle, Dodge. Word's traveling fast."

"Good. Folks need warning. Doc's hoping to know something more next week."

George hesitated. "Bethie was in rare form last night. She told everybody about the woman wearing Kathleen's clothes. She said you *thumped her a good one* for telling the woman off."

"I didn't thump her a—"

George laughed. "We know. That Miss Bethie . . . she's her mama made over. Fit for the stage, both of them. But you're doing good with her, Dodge. Lottie says the same."

Dodge shook his head. "Some days I wonder."

"Being a papa is hard. 'Specially the way you came about it. And on your lonesome."

"But that's just it, I'm not her papa. I'm her uncle. But this . . ."

"Just know you're doing fine by her. Kathleen would be proud."

"Thanks, my friend."

They walked on, silence a part of their friendship as much as conversation. He'd worked with George and several members of his family at the distillery for years, and though George was a few years older, they'd shared a bond from the beginning.

Dodge fondly remembered Nearest Green, George's father and Uncle Jack's first head distiller. Enslaved at the time, Nearest—along with the late Lutheran preacher Dan Call—had taught young Jack the craft of whiskey making. The business of it, however, Jack had taken to on his own. Natural-born entrepreneur if ever there was one.

They passed a field thick with wildflowers—black-eyed Susans, butterfly weed, wild bergamot, and his late mother's favorite, purple coneflowers—and Dodge remembered Kathleen's habit of keeping a pitcher of wildflowers on the kitchen table. How had that slipped his mind? He hadn't seen that blue metal pitcher in months.

As they neared the distillery, its distinctive smell—a pungent, yeasty tang with a sour edge, an acquired appreciation—wafted toward them. And while part of him knew he'd carry a yearning for Wyoming until his dying day, he would have missed all of this, too. It was in his blood.

"You know this place won't be the same without you two, Dodge. Uncle Jack won't be either. What's he gonna do without you?"

Dodge slowed. "Keep a secret for me? Just until I've told Bethie?"

George frowned.

"I've decided not to go. I can't take her all the way out there. Not just the two of us."

George sighed then slowly nodded. "I wondered about that. What about your land? All those acres you bought?"

"I'm trying to sell them. Mailed the papers to a land agent yesterday. I've spent months trying to make it work, but that's just selfishness on my part. Staying's the right thing. I've just got to tell her."

George shook his head. "I don't envy you that."

Dodge gave a dry laugh. "That's what Doc said. I've told him and Uncle Jack, but no one else."

"And nobody'll hear it from me. Not even Lottie. And while I'm sorry for you—you've wanted this for a long time—I'll say this much . . . I ain't disappointed you're staying. You're part of this place. This town. And Uncle Jack losing you would be like losing his right arm."

"Same could be said for you. You've been around this place longer than I have. What with your father having been such a part of things."

George smiled. "We seen a lot, haven't we?"

"We have." Dodge looked ahead. "But Uncle Jack'll be fine, no matter what happens. He always is. You know as well as I do, Jack Daniel doesn't give up for anything or anyone."

"Ain't that the truth." George's gaze drifted toward the stillhouse. "Sometimes I think what he's building here's gonna outlast us all."

The words sank in as Dodge took in the early-morning bustle of the distillery. A new barrel house was going up. Sugar maple was being stacked in five-foot cords for charcoal, doused in raw whiskey, and set to burn in the rickyard. Production had doubled just to keep up with demand. Another crew hauled cold limestone spring water from Cave Spring Hollow, which Jack swore was part of the secret to his whiskey.

George's voice softened. "I wish my daddy could've seen all this. Would've made him so proud."

"Your daddy was a good man. I miss him, too."

Dan Call's farm lay just over the rise, and Dodge often walked those hills and hollers, picturing a young preacher, an eight-year-old Jack, and Nearest Green working side-by-side, unknowingly building something that stood to outlast them all. What was *he* building that would endure like that?

For the second time that day, something shifted inside him and left him feeling unmoored. An odd sensation given he'd decided to stay put.

Sensing George's attention, Dodge gathered himself. "I do miss your daddy's stories. The way he and Uncle Jack would sit on the front porch late into the night, laughing and talking about old times. And your daddy playing that fiddle of his like nobody else could." He smiled faintly. "Those were good days. You know your laugh still reminds me of his."

George glanced over. "Really?"

Dodge nodded and clapped his shoulder. "And rest assured, my friend, your father *is* proud. Proud of what he helped build here, but even prouder of you and your brothers and sisters. Of all his family. He talked about y'all every chance he got. And who knows?" Dodge shrugged. "Maybe he *can* see. Maybe he and Kathleen both can."

They walked on until the path split.

"Hey," George said. "Don't go telling Miss Bethie it was me said you thumped her."

Dodge smiled. "I won't. But I appreciate you letting me know."

"Us papas . . . and uncles . . . we gotta stick together." George gave his customary parting salute, then paused. "You know anything about that woman? The one wearing your sister's clothes?"

"Mrs. Dunham? Not much. Why?"

"It's just that . . . there's a rumor going 'round about her. Ain't my business, but Bethie's been stirring things up. Mind you, I ain't even laid eyes on this woman. But folks were saying last night they think she's lying about being married." George briefly looked away. "Some say she might be . . . in the family way. That her daddy beat her and turned her out. And that she came here to hide."

Images flashed in Dodge's mind—Mrs. Dunham's bruised face, the way she'd bent down to pick up that rock before climbing into the wagon, her sickness on the road, the panic over the missing ring. Try as he might, he couldn't remember if she'd been wearing a ring when she climbed into the wagon.

"All I know," Dodge finally said, "is Slim Poyner asked me to give her a ride when I was pulling out of Tullahoma. So I did. As for the rest . . . people talk. Especially in this town. But Bethie seeing her in Kathleen's clothes was just bad timing. Mrs. Dunham didn't do it on purpose. She didn't even know. Miss Mary loaned her those clothes for an appointment."

"Oh, folks know all about that appointment, too. Jack was talking last night, saying he tried to hire somebody for the office." George gave him a look. "Wasn't hard piecing those two things together. But hear tell, she turned him down. That didn't sit well with some folks, them taking offense on Uncle Jack's part."

Dodge felt heat climb his neck. "But if she'd said yes to Jack's offer, those same people would be angry that an outsider got it. I swear, we'd all be better off if people would just mind their own business!"

Hearing the anger in his own voice—and seeing George's uncertainty—Dodge blew out a breath. "I'm sorry, I don't know why I reacted that way."

George's look was steady, compassionate.

Dodge lowered his head, clarity coming. "Kathleen," he said quietly. "You remember how folks talked about her behind her back? Even years after, and even after the kindness she'd showed them. I still see it sometimes when they look at Bethie." He swallowed. "I want better for her."

"And she'll have it, my friend. From the people who matter."

Dodge nodded. "That's something Uncle Nearest would have said to me."

"Did I mention I'm glad you're staying?" George smiled, then took the path toward the barrel house.

Dodge returned his salute and headed for the office, wondering if the pull of Wyoming—and all he was determined to let go of—would ever let go of him.

19

Josephine paused just shy of the distillery's front porch to catch her breath. She'd helped clear the table after breakfast earlier, then washed the dishes and left them to dry before rushing out the door.

Though she and Miss Mary hadn't formalized her duties at the boarding house yet—she figured that would come after confirming she had a job—she simply couldn't leave all that to Calla. Not when she was enjoying all of Calla's fine cooking, and not while knowing Miss Mary still hoped to hire a second cook to ease Calla's load.

Ascending the stairs to the front porch of the white clapboard building, she heard the trickle of water again and looked toward the cave at the base of the rocky bluff a short distance away. Such a tranquil setting, and so opposite what she was feeling now.

She simply could not return to the boarding house without securing this—

The office door suddenly swung open.

"Well, good morning, Mrs. Dunham!" Jack Daniel's wry smile said everything. "What might bring you to my door on this lovely March day? And so early? I'm barely into the office myself."

Reading the playful sparkle in his eyes, she took a deep breath.

"I always find it difficult," he continued before she could even start her readied speech, "to have to eat crow so early in the day. Just kind of chokes you a good one, right about here, don't you think, ma'am?" He gripped his throat just above his bow tie and made a show of not being able to swallow. "Just doesn't . . . want to . . . go down."

Josephine laughed out loud. She couldn't help it.

Mr. Daniel paused, his expression lighting. "Now that right there might be one of the prettiest sounds I've ever heard." He looked at her with a steadiness that might have unnerved her had he not already told her she wasn't his type. "Yes, ma'am, you should do that more often. And please, in my presence."

Gaining her composure, she gave him a smart nod. "Allow me to clear my throat of said crow, sir, and perhaps I will."

Laughing, he moved to one side. "Please, Mrs. Dunham, grant me the pleasure of your company in my office."

Josephine stepped inside and started to take her seat in one of the two chairs facing his desk.

"Oh no, no." He gently took hold of her elbow and led her around the desk. "*This* is where the distillery's bookkeeper sits."

He pulled out his office chair, but she didn't sit. "Mr. Daniel, first, I must apologize to you for—"

"Mrs. Dunham, when your boot gained my porch a second ago, and I saw you standing there? You said everything to me that needed saying. I know how strongly you feel about distilleries and whiskey making. And yet here you are." His tone softened. "Coming back today took courage, and likely gnawed a fairly good hole in your pride through the night. Which makes this reprisal even more meaningful. For us both." He glanced at the desk. "Because when I closed my eyes last night, I wondered what on earth I was going to do with all this. So, please . . . Everything has been said between us. Agreed?"

She held his gaze, marveling at his kindness, and not at all certain she could carry out her still-forming plan to sabotage the distillery's production. "Thank you, Mr. Daniel. And agreed."

"Now, if you'll sit, we can start reviewing all of this paperwork and—"

"Do we need, perhaps, to discuss again the various aspects of the position?" she asked carefully. "Have . . . any of the conditions changed?"

His brow furrowed, then understanding dawned. "Ah . . . You mean has the salary changed? Due to you dressing me down so squarely yesterday and giving me your honest opinion of what I've chosen to do with the whole of my life?"

Merriment lit his eyes, but she could not laugh.

"Ma'am, not many people have attempted to do that to me in recent decades. And certainly none have done it with such style and grace, and on my own turf, to boot. So again, you and me? We are more than fine. I admire a woman with grit and backbone. Someone who'll speak her mind straight out. So, to answer your question . . . The salary I quoted stands firm. But I *am* thinking of taking back the offer of the free bottle of Jack every month. So if that's a deal breaker then—"

Josephine claimed his office chair and began sorting papers. "Are you going to keep jabbering on, sir, or shall we get started?"

He chuckled and pulled up another chair beside hers.

For the next several minutes, she listened patiently as he presented document after document, explaining each as though she couldn't determine its purpose at a glance.

"Now this one here"—he held up an order from a bottle supplier out of Kentucky—"is for bottles, so you need to make a file for—"

"Mr. Daniel." Josephine placed her hands on the stacks of paper. "While I appreciate your instruction, I am more than capable of sorting through all of this on my own."

"But this is important stuff, ma'am. I've got to make sure you understand who my suppliers are and what they routinely ship—"

"For inventory purposes and on what schedule," she finished for him. "Yes, I know. Because timing is important, and you must keep adequate stock on hand. I assure you, I am quite clear on those points."

"You know, Mrs. Dunham . . . You're a fair mite bossier than I thought you'd be." A slow grin spread across his face. "I like it."

Josephine rose. "Then you'll be absolutely enchanted when I ask you to kindly take your leave—"

"Of *my* office?" he interjected.

"Yes, sir, precisely." She gestured toward the door.

"Perhaps it would be advantageous if I were to sit quietly in the corner and just observe in the event that—"

"Should I have questions, Mr. Daniel, I'll keep track of them." She shooed him toward the door.

He grinned. "This is gonna be fun, Mrs. Dunham."

"Doubtful, Mr. Daniel." She worked to school her smile.

He retrieved his hat from the coat tree. "I'll be around if you need me. Door open or closed, ma'am?"

She caught the humor in his tone—and the subtle echo of what she'd asked him upon leaving his office just yesterday. "Closed, please, Mr. Daniel. Thank you."

She watched him through the office window until he rounded the corner, actually wishing she could dislike him, at least a little. But he was an amiable, even charismatic man. Generous, too. The salary he'd agreed to pay her—fifteen dollars a week—was nearly double what she'd earned as a teacher in Atlanta, which meant she could send a portion to Sarah once it was safe to correspond.

She glanced at the calendar hanging from a nail on the wall. Friday, the tenth of March. Mr. Daniel said payroll was issued every Wednesday, which meant five days before she'd be paid. First order of business would be to somehow purchase another skirt and blouse, or perhaps a dress.

The mercantile sold cloth off the bolt but no ready-made clothing, and yards of fabric did her little good personally. Maybe she'd have to slip into Ol' Miss Ruby's when her daughter-in-law wasn't looking. She'd also need to give Miss Mary something for room and board. But at least she had the promise of money coming in.

She exhaled as the moment settled around her. Here she was standing in the office of a distillery—employed as its bookkeeper. What would Sarah say? And her fellow suffragists? More than that, Miss Anthony?

But no disappointment they could express would equal the bruising already left by her own conscience.

Jack Daniel's coveted gold medal on the opposite wall caught her eye, and she stared it down, sensing challenge. As guilty as she felt about working at a distillery, another guilt chided her—the motivation that had changed her mind about taking the job. To do the distillery harm. Yet she needed only to think of the battered women and children she'd tried to help through the years—innocents who'd suffered grievously at the hands of alcohol—and that particular guilt eased its grip.

She moved behind Mr. Daniel's desk and, choosing to stand, pushed aside the leather office chair. It rolled easily on casters as she surveyed the work before her. "If you know the enemy and know yourself," she spoke softly, "you need not fear the result of a hundred battles."

It was a quote from *The Art of War* by Sun Tzu, a book her father had encouraged her brother to read. And so, of course, she had read it, too.

She wasn't at war with Jack Daniel personally. From all appearances, he was quite wealthy, so whatever she might manage to do would hardly cause him irreparable harm. No, it was whiskey making itself that drew her aim.

She intended only to impair the distillery's ability to produce it, for however long she could. Industry payback, some might call it. But before she could act, she needed to understand how this burgeoning enterprise truly worked.

She set to work organizing the stacks of paper, finding little pattern in their present arrangement. Even within a single pile, dates jumped erratically, some documents separated by months, others out of sequence altogether.

But after a while of skimming and combing, dividing and stacking, natural categories began to emerge—inventory management, orders and invoicing, payroll and employee records, correspondence, shipping and logistics, sales records, and general accounting for office supplies and sundries.

One thing became apparent almost immediately—Jack Daniel enjoyed food. And, at times, a great deal of it. The man clearly liked to entertain. Orders from the mercantile revealed quantities that would have fed a family of ten for a week or more, and not modestly. He also favored finer fare, with certain delicacies shipped in from considerable distances.

Reading about the food made her hungry, and she pulled out the cloth sack holding a leftover biscuit and thick slice of ham. Calla had insisted on packing her lunch, fully confident she'd secure the position. Josephine ate it like a sandwich, but halfway through found it difficult to swallow. Yet she hadn't thought to bring anything to drink.

She searched the office for a glass or cup and finally unearthed an old mug. Carrying it outside, she walked the short distance to the spring at the base of the bluff, the cool air from the cave greeting her before she stepped into the shade.

She rinsed the mug, then filled it once, twice, and a third time, draining each one. She couldn't remember tasting water so cold and invigorating. Refreshed, she returned to her work.

Using the dusty stack of file folders Mr. Daniel had located for her in a cabinet from the back room, she labeled each one in turn, the simple act of setting things aright bringing a quiet satisfaction. She had always valued order and neatness. Everything in its place.

Which stood in stark contrast to her life at present.

How she wished she could go back to that suffragist rally only *two* days ago. As satisfying as it had been to put Clay Darden in his place in that moment, the cost had been too great. To her. And far more to *him*.

The image of him lying sprawled on the ground, blood pooling, the brick still in her hand, rushed forward. She had *killed* a man. In self-defense, yes. But the truth remained unchanged, and no amount of washing had fully erased the stain of his blood from her blouse.

Part of her wished she could apologize again to young Bethie about the clothing. The greater part, however, dreaded their paths crossing at all. She didn't want to cause the girl any further pain. And the thought of facing Dodge Coburn again filled her with a dread she could scarcely name.

Turning back to her work, she quickly found a rhythm, recognizing repeat names on bills and receipts, the stacks growing more orderly by the minute—until her gaze snagged on a document bearing the words *United States Bureau of Tax Revenue* across the top.

Immediately, Mr. Prince, the revenuer staying at Miss Mary's, came to mind.

She paused, leaning against the desk, and read through the lengthy verbiage of the official-looking document. From her work with the suffrage movement, she knew whiskey production was heavily taxed and tightly regulated by the federal government, and that strict compliance was a top priority for distillery owners. Failure to comply carried serious consequences. A distillery could be shut down for weeks—if not months, or longer.

As the implications settled, something else began to stir. Possibilities.

She pulled a fresh file folder from the stack and wrote *Tax Revenue* on the outer edge, retribution wrestling with remorse. But the shutdown would only be temporary. Nothing permanent. *If* she could even manage it. Because as of yet, she had no idea what steps would be required. It wasn't like she would be burning down a building or taking an ax to the stills in a fit of—

Boot steps sounded on the porch.

Pulse jumping, she hastily tucked the tax documents into the folder and slid it onto a side table, guilt quickening her movements. As the door opened, she straightened and schooled her features into calm—then froze.

Dodge Coburn paused on the threshold, doorknob still in hand. *"Mrs. Dunham?"*

20

Reacting to the shock in Mr. Coburn's expression, Josephine squared her shoulders, standing as tall as she could. Her conscience alone was punishment enough, but seeing herself reflected in his eyes stung. Her convictions—so fiercely declared only yesterday—now chafed like an ill-worn robe of self-righteousness. If only she hadn't been so forceful with him, so absolute. *I would never take such a job.* And yet here she stood.

She gave a crisp nod. "Mr. Coburn. Good morning. How may I help you?"

The slight narrowing of his gaze told her that greeting alone would not suffice.

Already self-conscious about the slow-healing marks on her face, she was doubly aware of them in his presence, but refused to show it. "I realize this must come as a surprise."

He let out a measured breath. "Ah . . . yes, ma'am. That's one way to put it." He removed his hat and closed the door behind him, his gaze never leaving hers. "I was under the impression you turned this job down. In fact, I'm quite certain you told me as much yesterday."

"That is true." She clasped her hands. "I did refuse Mr. Daniel's offer. At first. But after giving it more careful thought, I realized it was hasty of me to cast aside such an opportunity, given my current circumstances." She hesitated, then pressed on. "And since Miss Mary was the one who sent me to speak with Mr. Daniel, and since I *am* staying under her roof . . . Well, refusing him felt increasingly untenable. I did not wish to offend her."

The explanation felt thin even to her own ears. And his expression confirmed it.

"So," he said quietly. "A female suffragist working in a distillery. What about the convictions you spoke of yesterday? With such certainty."

Tempted to look away, she resisted, not wanting to appear weak to this man. "You said yourself, Mr. Coburn, that many people would welcome such an opportunity."

"Yes, ma'am. I—"

"*Would crawl over cut glass* is, I believe, the phrase you used," she continued, lifting her chin, knowing her anger was partially fueled by her own guilt and disappointment in herself.

His stare held. "That's exactly what I said. It just never occurred to me you were the type of woman who would listen."

Heat flared in her chest. She knew when she was being baited. "I can't imagine how I've survived this long without a man telling me how to think, especially one as humble as yourself. How fortunate our paths crossed." The brittleness of her smile matched her tone. "I am quite busy, Mr. Coburn. So I will ask again . . . What is it you need?"

He didn't say anything. And didn't have to. The suspicion in his eyes said it all. He didn't believe her. Which parts, she didn't know. But she hadn't counted on this. She hadn't counted on *him*.

"Mr. Coburn—" Fighting desperation, she lowered her head, a courtroom tactic coming to mind. One she'd learned from watching her father practice his masterful closing arguments. She and Todd had swiftly adopted the gesture when debating issues in front of their parents. Todd had nicknamed it "the humble, deliberating pause" and had mastered it far better than she ever had.

But she needed it now.

Slowly lifting her gaze, she attempted as contrite a tone as she could muster. "As you advised me yesterday, Mr. Coburn, I checked the community board in the mercantile. And unless I wished to slop pigs, hire on at the mill, raise a barn, blacksmith, or assist Ol' Miss Ruby with sewing while carefully avoiding her daughter-in-law—"

A flicker of humor touched his eyes.

"—then bookkeeping at a *distillery* proved to be the only position in Lynchburg for which I possess a useful skill. As a former schoolteacher, that was a most humbling discovery. But a true one. And with little money left to my name, I had no real choice. Pride notwithstanding."

He seemed to weigh this then, to her surprise, took a seat.

She followed suit, settling into Mr. Daniel's office chair.

"You have to admit, Mrs. Dunham. It's quite a reversal. And in so short a time."

"I cannot argue with that. But I trust you now understand the reasons behind my decision."

He didn't answer at first, his stare appraising. "I think I have a right fair understanding, yes, ma'am."

His disappointment was undeniable, as was the doubt framing it. "Well . . . I need to get back to work. Mr. Daniel isn't paying me to sit and converse." She started to rise.

"Actually, ma'am, I came on business. I was hoping to see Uncle Jack, but I expect you can help me."

"*Uncle* Jack?" She sat back down.

"No relation. I've known Jack Daniel all my life. I was born and raised here in Lynchburg and have worked for him for years. In fact, most people in town call him that."

Priding herself on having guessed correctly about Mr. Coburn's association with the distillery, she retrieved a pen and paper. "Are you here regarding another shipment of bottles?"

He frowned. "Bottles?"

"Yes. Aren't you a supplier for the distillery?"

The frown creased further, until understanding swept it away. "Ah, you're talking about the wagonload I had when you hitched a ride. No, ma'am, I work with the livestock. That wagon from Tullahoma was just a favor."

"So you're a farmhand then."

A slow smile curved his mouth and its effect was downright disarming. Warmth swept through her, and she found it difficult to maintain his gaze—yet impossible to look away.

She swallowed. "S-so, Mr.—" Her mind went blank.

"Coburn," he supplied softly.

"Yes! I know your name, Mr. Coburn." She exhaled. "So what is it exactly that you require?"

He leaned forward. "I was doing some reading on Texas fever last night—"

"Texas fever?"

"The cattle on the distillery's farm just uphill are failing, ma'am, and we believe it's Texas fever. I think I've found something that'll help and came by to tell Uncle Jack I'm sending a telegram to Tullahoma to request supplies."

She penned a quick note for Mr. Daniel, pausing as she wrote. "And do you have authority for this expense without prior approval?"

Again, that patient smile. "Yes, ma'am. That won't be a problem."

"Very well then. I'll make certain Mr. Daniel is aware." She rose, hoping he would take the hint. She set the note atop a small floor safe near the desk. "Will there be anything else?"

"I think that's it for now." He stood, hat in hand, his attention moving to the stacks of paper and folders covering the desk. "Something tells me you're going to whip this place into shape. And maybe even Uncle Jack along with it, if he stands still too long."

Though his tone was pleasant enough, he didn't smile when he said it.

"I was hired to pay the bills and keep the office running smoothly. That's my intention, Mr. Coburn." She crossed to the door and opened it, welcoming the cool breeze if not the sunshine on her face.

He slipped his hat on. "Well, I hope this proves to be a . . . better situation for you, Mrs. Dunham. Uncle Jack's a good man, and a lot of people in this town are right partial to him. Look up to him. Not to mention are employed by him. Regardless that you don't see eye to eye with him on the subject of whiskey."

And there it was again. Suspicion. Clear as day.

"Good day, Mr. Coburn. I'll make certain Mr. Daniel gets your message."

He didn't move. "What I said before, about you being the type of woman to listen. I didn't mean it exactly the way it came out. It's just with you being part of the suffrage movement and knowing how you all feel about things . . . Seeing you here caught me off guard, is all."

Josephine just stared, letting the silence answer for her.

He finally tugged the brim of his hat. "Good day to you, Mrs. Dunham." Almost out the door, he paused. "For what it's worth, ma'am," he said quietly, his gaze taking in her face, "whoever did this to you should be whipped. And I will gladly do the honors should he ever show his face in this town."

"But you promised!" Bethie cried. "You promised Mama *and* me!"

Dodge reached for her arm, but she jerked away, nearly sending her supper plate crashing to the floor. "I know that, honey. I do. But things have changed. I wish we could still go, too. But—"

"We *can* go!" Tears welled and spilled. "Just you and me. That's what Mama wanted. For us to go like we planned. I know it!"

"Bethie . . ." He pulled his chair closer so he could face her square on. "I'm convinced your mama knew before she died that Wyoming wasn't a possibility anymore. Not with her having to leave us."

Bethie set her jaw, whether to keep from crying or to hold back words she knew better than to say, he couldn't tell.

"Wyoming is hard country," he went on gently. "Wild and treacherous. A person has to *carve* a life out of land like that. It's dangerous, sometimes downright hostile. And it's no place for a little girl."

"I'm not a little girl! I'm near grown, Uncle Dodge. And I can do this. I'm not scared." She drew in a thin, hitching breath. "I can help with the cattle. Drive the herd. I ride better than half your hands, you've said so yourself. I can drive the wagon, too. You and me . . . we can do it. *Please*."

The pleading in her voice cut him clean through. But it was the accusation in her eyes—the betrayal—that twisted the knife.

"Bethie, with everything in me, I wish we could still go. But I've had to accept that we can't. And I'm so sorry, but somehow you're going to have to find a way to accept that, too."

She opened her mouth, but he pressed on.

"I've put the land up for sale, honey. I signed the papers. It's only a matter of time now before someone buys it."

That time frame was hopeful fiction and he knew it. Four hundred and twenty acres wouldn't sell quickly—not at a fair price—but he couldn't leave even the smallest door ajar.

Bethie wiped her cheeks with the heel of her hand, fists clenched tight. "Mama still wanted us to go," she said, voice flat. "Just you and me. She told me that before she died."

All pleading was gone now. Something harder had taken its place. But it was the shadowed anger in her eyes that confirmed the lie.

"Bethie girl," Dodge whispered, sinking to one knee so they were eye to eye. "Your mama wouldn't want you to lie, sweetheart. She didn't say that . . . did she."

Her face crumpled. Her breath broke loose into sobs, and Dodge drew her to his chest. For a moment, she went slack against him, weeping the way she had as a little girl after a fall or scraped knee. Then she shoved him away.

"I don't want to live with you anymore."

The words struck like a blow.

"Honey . . . this is your home. You and me, we have to stick together now that—"

"I said I don't want to live with you!" She shoved her chair back. "I don't want to live *here* either. I'm gonna go live with Moriah and her family." She bolted for her bedroom and slammed the door.

Dodge rose, starting to go after her, then stopped. He couldn't say why, other than he knew he'd only make things worse. He cleared the table, stacked the dishes by the washbasin, then reached for his hat.

Jessie trotted after him.

"Not tonight, girl." He knelt and rubbed her ears. "You stay here. Watch over Bethie."

Jessie whined softly, then settled down facing the front door.

"Good girl."

Dodge reached above the doorframe, took down the .45 caliber Remington, and headed for the lower barn, hoping Doc Wyatt might still be there.

21

THE COOL EVENING BREEZE carried the sweetness of honeysuckle countered by a whiff of musk from a hopefully distant skunk, and Dodge decided to walk for a bit instead of going straight to the barn. Maybe he was only putting off a job he dreaded, but it felt good to stretch his legs—and his thoughts.

Bethie's words replayed, over and over, and he wondered if he could have handled things better. But despite feeling bad about it all, he knew the truth. Nothing he'd said, or how he'd said it, would have changed her reaction.

At least it was done. No more circling the matter. They could get back to focusing on life here, as much as the prospect of spending future years in Lynchburg still left him hollow. That feeling would ease with time, he trusted. And Bethie had good friends here. That would help her in coming days.

He passed the darkened distillery office and thought again of Josephine Dunham standing behind Uncle Jack's desk. He didn't often feel as though he'd had the rug pulled out from under him, but that had done it. Clearly, she'd been just as surprised to see him, and more than a little ashamed, if he'd read her right. She'd been so adamant about refusing the job. But desperate people did desperate things.

And while he knew her situation was dire—alone, no money, nowhere to stay long-term—the last place he would have expected her to land was at the distillery.

Running from an abusive husband.

That's what she claimed. But the phrase snagged, refusing to fit, and her behavior in the office sharpened in his mind. What she'd said . . . *I can't imagine how I've survived this long without a man telling me how to think.* A husband who would raise his hand to his wife wouldn't think twice about giving her what for. Then there was the way she'd looked at him. And the moment she'd blanked on his name.

He was no Jack Daniel with women, nor did he aspire to be. But he knew when a woman looked at him in that way. And she had. It had surprised him then. Now it felt downright revealing. Josephine Dunham struck him as a woman of intellect and conviction. Well-spoken, articulate, a formidable sparring partner. Her remorse over Kathleen's clothes had been genuine. So had her passion for her beliefs. He'd seen her tell the truth. And the story she told about having a husband didn't quite measure up.

She was running from something, that much he didn't doubt. The wounds on her face said as much. But his gut said she wasn't married. His gut also told him she found him attractive, which made for a tricky situation. Because truth was, he was drawn to her as well. A suffragist . . . The irony brought a reluctant smile.

Suffragists were nothing if not passionate. Some pursued change with discipline and restraint. Others with fire and fury. Newspapers reported women suffragists chaining themselves to posts, picketing saloons, smashing windows. All of it justified, they claimed, in the war against liquor.

He couldn't tell yet which kind of suffragist Josephine Dunham was. But if first impressions counted—she was a fighter. He smiled again, remembering how she'd picked up that rock before climbing into his wagon, thinking he hadn't noticed. Then his smile faded. A woman that afraid of a man didn't take chances without reason.

George's mention of the rumors circling town didn't help matters. Outsiders were always suspect—especially those from the city. He'd meant to speak to Bethie about her part in fueling those whispers, but supper had derailed that plan entirely.

Reaching the far side of the square, he caught sight of Miss Mary's house and turned back. Whatever Josephine Dunham's truth was, she was lying about something. And she was scared. Although word about the distillery was spreading, she was likely safe enough. At least for a while. Lynchburg wasn't a place a person just stumbled into. You had to mean to find it.

The thought that the rumor about her might be true—that she was unmarried and in the family way—tightened his chest. And no guess as to why. But if she'd come here seeking refuge for herself and a child,

Lynchburg would not be kind. Better she'd never gotten off that train in Tullahoma.

As he neared the barn, the cattle's ragged breathing reached him. Their low moans, the crush of hay as they struggled to stand before weakened legs gave way. The sickness was spreading fast. Lantern light glowed from the second stall on the left.

"Hey Doc," Dodge said, not wishing to startle him. "How we doing?"

Doc Wyatt looked up from where he knelt beside a pregnant heifer. "Nine more have come down with it. Including this one."

"Nine counting earlier today?"

"In addition to."

Dodge exhaled and set aside his rifle. "Did you get my note? About what I ordered?"

"I did. And while I don't think copper sulfate will cure it, it may help slow the spread. That'll help. Least until we hear back from Washington." Doc removed his gloves and spectacles, and rubbed the bridge of his nose. "Let me guess . . . You couldn't sleep last night and went digging through Doc Salmon's old handwritten notes again."

Dodge shook his head. "His old farming periodicals. Some he gave me years ago."

Doc laughed beneath his breath. "Ezekiel Salmon always said you could've filled his boots if you'd had a hankering to."

"Dr. Salmon was a kind man, and generous toward me. I appreciate all he taught me. Giving me free rein to that library of his . . . That was such a gift to this eight-year-old boy at the time." Dodge treasured the hours he'd spent reading there, back when the house served as Dr. Salmon's home, medical office, and Grand Central Hotel—years before the Bobos turned it into a boarding house. "Those books opened up so many worlds to me. Not only the medical volumes, but the books on history and science and Greek philosophy. The novels, too. I'm grateful to him. But even if I had wanted to be a doctor, I didn't have the training or medical degree."

"You learned more there than most doctors learn in school. Training only gets you so far. Experience is the best teacher. After all, there's a reason we still call it *practicing* medicine."

Dodge pulled on gloves and stroked the heifer's neck. She was already struggling for air, and he remembered his promise to Bethie, difficult though it would be. "I'm good doing what I'm doing, Doc," he said quietly. "Besides, God already had a doctor in mind to replace Ezekiel Salmon when that time came. And the Almighty chose well."

Doc Wyatt's gaze conveyed gratitude. "As I told Lucille every day of our lives together, doctoring the people and animals in these hills has been the joy of my life. And to get to do what 'feeds your soul,' as she used to say . . . That's far better than this ol' coot deserves."

What *feeds your soul* . . .

The words lodged deep, stirring an ache Dodge didn't have time for and could do nothing about. He could still have a good life here in Lynchburg. He *did* have a good life, especially compared to so many. It just wasn't the one he'd dreamed of. The one that fed his soul.

He would mend things with Bethie, too. That would take time, and patience. But she mattered more than anything now. He would make certain she understood that.

He ran a gloved hand over the heifer's distended belly. "Does she have a chance, Doc?"

"She may yet. Pregnancy can sometimes spare them the worst. But the others . . ." Doc Wyatt looked down the line of stalls. "They won't last another day. *If* they make it through the night."

Dodge retrieved his Remington.

"You want my help?" Doc asked softly.

"No, sir. It's mine to do."

Doc squeezed his shoulder. "Have you told Bethie yet? About Wyoming?"

Dodge nodded. "Tonight. At supper. Didn't go well."

"Did you expect it to? That girl's every bit the dreamer her mother was. And just as fiery. Which means she'll be fine in the end. She's strong."

Dodge said nothing, just silently vowed that no foolish dreams or fanciful imaginings would be planted in her head. No matter what—or who—he had to protect her from. He shed his gloves, wrapped burlap around the rifle barrel, and stepped into the next stall.

He made it quick and clean, then moved on. At least this was one promise he'd made to Bethie that he could keep.

Two mornings later, Josephine awakened and, for a moment, couldn't remember where she was. Then reality came crashing back. With effort, she resisted the fear rising inside and, instead, thought of Sarah and silently repeated, *This isn't forever, it's just for now*—the promise they'd made to each other before she fled Atlanta.

She sat up and stretched, having slept fitfully. Calla was already gone, and the pale pink of dawn edged through the curtained window above her bed. Her gaze fell on the rag doll perched on the sill, and she thought back to that moment of panic at the train station in Tullahoma, when the man had pursued her beyond the exit.

The doll with its golden yarn hair and embroidered smile was a cheerful little thing, likely far more so than the girl who had lost her. The finely sewn blue calico dress and white pinafore were rumpled and worn thin in places, and faint smudges dulled her happy face. Clear signs she had been well loved. Yet judging by the fine clothing of the family, Josephine suspected the doll, though once treasured, had already been replaced. Perhaps even forgotten. The thought bothered her more than it should have.

She wondered if Bethie might like it. Not that she was in any position to offer a gift to the girl. And not that Bethie would want it, coming from her.

Knowing Calla was already at work on breakfast, Josephine dressed quickly—wincing at her reflection as she left the cabin.

The house was quiet, the kitchen, too. But the aroma of coffee, the pot angled on a burner, and two loaves of bread rising on the worktable told her Calla had been up for some time. A large pot of water steamed on a back burner.

She poured a cup of coffee and had barely taken a sip when a commotion sounded from behind the house. She peered out the back window to see Calla in the chicken yard near the coop. Gathering eggs, she assumed—until Calla suddenly grabbed a chicken by the legs. The bird squawked and flapped. Calla held it upside down for a minute, and the bird grew strangely calm. Then, in one swift motion, Calla grasped the bird by the neck and—almost before Josephine realized what was happening—swung it overhead in a sharp, whipping motion. The chicken went limp, and Josephine's hand shot to her mouth.

Calla laid the bird on a stump, reached for a hatchet, and—quick as a thought—severed its head. She held the body steady as the blood drained, then caught another bird and dispatched it just as efficiently.

Thinking of the fried chicken she'd enjoyed since arriving, Josephine knew she'd never eat it again so casually. She also knew better than to underestimate this woman. Calla—and Miss Mary—were both forces of nature in their own right.

Josephine opened the back door for her. "Remind me never to get you riled."

Calla laughed. "I saw you watching. I'm guessing killing chickens ain't something you've done before."

"How could you tell?"

"Reckon it was that hand shooting up to your mouth that tipped me off. You ever plucked one?"

Josephine just looked at her.

"All right then. Time to learn." Calla nodded toward the steaming pot. "We'll just dip these two lovelies in that pot of water for a minute. That'll loosen up the feathers. Make them easier to pluck."

"I thought you said we were having pork roast for lunch today."

"We are. But Sundays are special. Miss Mary likes to serve two meats."

Calla eased the chickens into the hot water, then lifted them out a minute later, patted them dry, and handed one to Josephine by the legs.

Calla chuckled. "City girl through and through."

"Yes, but I can learn. Just tell me what to do."

Calla demonstrated, and Josephine followed suit, starting with the wing feathers, then moving to the breast, back, and legs. The sensation was strange as was the experience, but the conversation between them felt like second nature.

After a few minutes, Calla inspected her work. "Not bad for a first timer. Now let's finish these at the worktable, then put them in the springhouse till it's time for roasting."

After breakfast, Josephine washed the last of the dishes and carried the heavy wash bucket down the back steps. She dumped the dirty water into the field grass, then paused to rub her shoulders and lower back. She smoothed a hand over her abdomen. The biscuits and gravy she'd eaten a while earlier, while delicious, had left her a little queasy.

Her thoughts turned toward home, as they often did. To Sarah and her fellow suffragists. To all she'd been forced to leave behind, and to how betrayed they would feel if they knew what she was doing now.

She stared across the fields toward the heavily wooded hills a hefty stone's throw away, the soothing murmur of Mulberry Creek carrying on the air. The sweet warble of birds in the trees drew her gaze upward. The cool morning air was damp, and gray clouds gathering in the west promised yet more rain. But it was the mist rising from the hollows like torn tufts of cotton lifting on unseen wings that tugged at something inside her.

As backwoods as this place seemed, there was no denying its beauty. Despite that, the helplessness she'd fought to keep at bay crept closer. As did the unsettling sense that Dodge Coburn could see straight through her.

Whoever did this to you should be whipped.

His comment had shaken her in the moment, and it did again. He hadn't said "Your husband should be whipped," but that *whoever* had done it should be. Did he not believe she was married? If so, that could prove troublesome. She would need to be more guarded in his presence, and somehow convince him her story was true.

Just then she heard someone coughing, or gagging more like. Concerned, she scanned the field around the house and the slope toward the creek but saw no one. Feeling the minutes tick past, she emptied the last of the water in the bucket and turned back toward the house.

The salve Calla had given her to apply each morning and night still hadn't dried, and the air felt chilly on her face. The concoction, its scent unappealing, did seem to be helping. Her skin was healing. Yet in some ways the injuries looked even worse now—the wounds tightening and drying at the edges, dark crimson scabs forming over the deeper cuts.

"You decided who you're going with this morning?"

Josephine turned to see Miss Mary approaching from behind, handkerchief in hand. She hadn't noticed her leave the house. Josephine glanced again toward the creek, then back, wondering if it was Miss Mary she'd heard earlier.

"Makes no difference to me," Miss Mary continued. "Go with me and my sister Ophelia and her husband, or with Calla. Both churches teach the Word. That's what's important."

Josephine took a fortifying breath. "Miss Mary, I'm sick and tired of your coercion and have decided not to go, and you cannot force me to do otherwise" was what she wanted to say. But, of course, she couldn't. Miss Mary held the balance of power.

"I'll go with Calla this morning," she responded, though the last thing she wanted was to sit through a sermon as a man went on about God's loving plans for her life. If this was the Almighty's loving plan, she definitely thought she could improve on it.

"As I said, matters not to me."

Josephine waited for Miss Mary to catch up to her. The woman looked a little pale, tired shadows beneath her eyes. "Are you all right, ma'am?"

"Fine as rain. Now we both best hurry so we're not late." Miss Mary hastened her steps and disappeared around the house.

Josephine climbed the back steps, her mind jumping to what Miss Mary's ailment could be. If it was an *ailment* at all. She left the wash bucket to drain on the deck and found Calla at the worktable finishing up preparations for Sunday dinner.

"I'll be ready to go right after I get the flour and spices mixed. I'm glad you're going with me this morning."

"Thank you for asking me."

Calla paused. "You don't have to put on a face for me. I can tell you ain't keen on it. You only doing it 'cause of Miss Mary."

Josephine hesitated. "It has nothing to do with you, or your church." She gave a little shrug. "I'm just not . . ."

"On good speaking terms with the Almighty?"

"Something like that."

Calla's expression softened. "We've all been there, so you ain't alone. And we won't stay long after. I gotta hurry back to finish dinner."

"I wish I could help you more with the meals. It's a lot of work."

"You are helping! You doing the dishes and cleanup, that's a good slice of my work gone from me."

"I meant with preparing. We all know I can't cook, but I am capable of mixing flour and spices."

Calla smiled. "Miss Mary made me promise you wouldn't be coming near her food dishes. But give her time." She winked. "She'll soften some."

"I doubt that." Josephine lowered her voice. "She doesn't strike me as a woman who easily changes her mind once it's set."

"Oh she don't, I can promise you that. But she is fair, Josephine. I know it don't feel that way now, what with all the hurting and grieving over what you been through." Calla brushed the flour from her hands, her voice dropping. "She got her own reasons for doing things the way she does. And I ain't one to judge her for them. Same as I don't want no one judging me for mine."

Josephine heard more in Calla's words than what she'd actually said. Exactly what *reasons* of Miss Mary's was she referring to?

"And just so you know," Calla continued, looking up. "She didn't say nothing about me not being able to *teach* you to cook. On our own time, if you want."

Josephine smiled. "I very much want." Then she noticed it again, the tremor in Calla's right hand. "Are you sure you're all right, Calla?" she asked, looking down.

Calla followed her gaze, then made a quick fist and shook it loose. "Oh, I'm fine. Just overdid it. Kneaded two loaves of bread and made biscuits this morning." She drained her third cup of honeyed mint tea, snipped a couple of leaves from the potted plant on the sill, and popped one into her mouth. She offered the other to Josephine. "Might help your stomach some."

Josephine hesitated before accepting. "How did you know—"

"Saw you out back, rubbing your tummy." Calla paused, as if she might say more, then continued to the pantry. She returned a minute later. "You ain't seen a jar of pickled beets anywhere, have you?"

"Beets? No, I haven't."

"Hmmm . . ." Another pause. "Could've sworn I had one more. I always serve them with my herbed pork roast—adds a good tang. But today, we'll just have to do without."

They talked all the way to church and managed to squeeze into one of the last open pews toward the front just before the service began. To Josephine's surprise, the congregation was comprised of both colored and white people. Sitting side by side. On the same pews. Growing up, her family had worshipped with a colored congregation in Atlanta, her father staying afterward to offer legal help—always pro bono. And though she would have preferred to avoid yet another familiar sermon, sitting with Calla did much to soften her resistance.

Until she looked around. And saw Dodge Coburn.

22

As though sensing her attention, Mr. Coburn turned and looked directly at her, then gave a subtle nod. Josephine would've sworn she read distrust in the man's eyes. Perhaps it was just her guilty conscience, but she quickly faced forward.

The song leader invited the congregation to stand and sing "Blessed Assurance." Her mother's favorite. From old habit, Josephine opened her mouth to join in, but the lyrics she'd known by heart since childhood wouldn't come. Not honestly. So she chose to listen instead. Especially to Calla beside her, the woman's soprano soft yet vibrant with belief. Calla, too, knew the words without benefit of a hymnal.

"That's mighty anointed singing this morning, church."

The middle-aged man leading them lifted hands in praise as hearty *Amens* filled the gathering. He motioned for them to be seated, then stepped aside as another man took the pulpit. Josephine settled back and braced herself for the duration, grateful for the open window nearby.

She couldn't remember exactly when she'd stopped going to church. Sometime after her parents died. Though she'd continued attending for a while after Todd's death, something inside her had already withdrawn. And whatever it was, she couldn't get it back, no matter how hard she tried. Eventually, she'd stopped trying altogether.

"Our Scripture reading this morning, brothers and sisters . . . *Be not deceived; God is not mocked: for whatsoever a man soweth, that shall he also reap.* Galatians chapter six, verse seven."

Just outside the window, a tiny bluebird lit on the branch of a maple tree, its vivid plumage striking against the gray morning. Josephine watched as it flitted about.

"Some of you may ask, why are we reading from Paul's letter to the Galatian church this morning. Aren't we still studying the Gospel of John? Yes, we are. And we will return to that next week—"

The bluebird hopped along the branch, singing and peering around. Josephine recalled how her students had enjoyed studying native animals with the changing seasons, and bluebirds had always fascinated her. Perhaps because her mother had always kept nesting boxes ready for them each year.

"However, this morning, we have a guest preacher with us. A leader in the National Baptist Convention, and someone I know you will all be blessed to hear."

As the preacher continued, Josephine watched the bird and remembered racing to those nesting boxes as a girl, searching for twigs or grass that signaled new tenants. And how disheartened she'd been to learn that male bluebirds often carried nesting material only for show—it was the female who did the real work of nest building. Why did that not surprise her?

Calla shifted beside her then stood, along with everyone else in the congregation. And they were clapping. Uncertain, Josephine rose as well, not wanting to appear rude. But why on earth were they—

She glanced toward the front, then looked more closely, not trusting her eyes. A woman? In the pulpit?

Josephine scanned the room to see if anyone shared her surprise. From her peripheral vision, she sensed Mr. Coburn look her way, but she deliberately averted her gaze. "Thank you, my faithful brothers and sisters in Christ," the young woman said, her voice strong and assured, filling the one-room church. "Pastor Taylor was generous with his praise. Though I suspect he's mostly enjoying a Sunday off."

Laughter rippled through the room as she motioned for them to be seated.

"I deeply appreciate the pastor's kind introduction and the opportunity to be with you today. I was recently asked by a Southern white woman—an enthusiastic worker for votes for white women— *What can the Negro woman do with the ballot?*" She paused. "And I answered her with a question of my own: *What can she do without it?*"

Josephine's breath caught.

"When the ballot is placed in the hands of the American woman, the world is going to get a correct estimate of the power of the Negro woman. It will find her a tower of strength of which poets have never sung, orators have never spoken, and scholars have never written."

A chorus of "Amen!" and "That's right!" rose around Josephine as emotion blurred her vision.

"The ballot, wisely used, my brothers and sisters, will bring to her the respect and protection that she needs. It is her weapon of moral defense. Under present conditions, when she appears in court in defense of her virtue, she is looked upon with amused contempt. She needs the ballot to reckon with men who place no value upon her virtue, and to mold healthy public sentiment in favor of her own protection!"

The words washed over Josephine like water on parched ground.

"You may be asking yourself, *Well, Miss Burroughs, what does the ballot for women have to do with Galatians chapter six, verse seven?*" She leaned forward, hands braced on the pulpit. "This is a Scripture the Lord has not merely written on my heart, but has engraved on it. *Be not deceived; God is not mocked: for whatsoever a man*—or woman—*soweth, that shall he*—or she—*also reap*. What we do with our lives *matters*. Not only for us, but for generations to come. The seeds we sow will one day manifest themselves in either a harvest of righteousness or a crop of weeds. Which shall it be? This is not a rhetorical question. No, it is a question we must ask ourselves every day, and every day we must answer it with honesty and clarity."

Josephine leaned closer to Calla. "Who *is* this woman?"

"Someone I knew you'd want to hear," Calla whispered, her eyes bright with knowing.

"We must stop calling this land 'Christian' and the government thereof a democracy," Miss Burroughs continued. "The fact is, brotherhood and fellowship among coloreds and whites are not the practice in most American churches. Although I am overjoyed to find it *is* the practice here in Lynchburg, at least at this fine church. You may be a town far from the rest of the world, and a little difficult to find—"

More laughter followed. Curious, Josephine glanced back at Dodge Coburn, seated at the far end of a pew. His focus was fixed on the pulpit, his expression rigid. She looked for Bethie beside him, but the girl wasn't there.

"—but you are far ahead of this nation in that regard. And I thank God for you."

As Miss Burroughs spoke with boldness and clarity, Josephine found herself leaning forward, wanting more.

"Finally, in closing, my dear brothers and sisters . . ." Miss Burroughs patiently looked around the room, her gaze passing over Josephine before briefly moving back. "Let us go forth in power with the biblical—and scientific—truth that *God hath made of one blood all races of men to dwell on the face of the earth.* The New Testament reaffirms this fact when Jesus declared, *One is your master, even Christ; and all ye are brethren.*

"America could practice these teachings of Jesus Christ in human relations and brotherhood; justice and goodwill could be applied in education, labor, civil rights and religion without making the white race any blacker or the black race any whiter. As Booker T. Washington, one of the wisest men of this generation, would say it, *The races can be one as the hand, and as separate as the fingers thereon.* So let us lock arms together—black and white, men and women—and move forward boldly in the Kingdom of our Lord Jesus Christ for his glory, and his alone. May God bless you all and give you boldness as you walk in his will."

The congregation rose in applause, or most did, and none more enthusiastically than Josephine, her heart ablaze. The few people who didn't, sat quietly, staring ahead. Dodge Coburn was standing, at least, but his applause was anemic, and Josephine could well imagine what was going through his mind and how he felt about the sermon.

"Sorry I didn't tell you before," Calla whispered, bringing Josephine's attention back. "About her speaking today."

Josephine stared.

"Your pillowcase needed washing a couple of days ago so I grabbed the sheets off your cot, too, and—" Calla's voice lowered to a whisper. "That's when your voting sash slipped from beneath the mattress. I figured you wanted that kept quiet."

"So that's why you wanted me to come with you today."

Calla smiled. "That, and I've taken a liking to your company."

Josephine gently squeezed her arm. "I've taken a liking to yours, too."

After the benediction, the pastor dismissed the congregation, and Josephine looked toward the pulpit, hoping for a chance to meet Miss Burroughs.

"Auntie Calla! Let me hug your neck!"

To Josephine's surprise, Miss Burroughs slipped up behind them and wrapped her arms around Calla. The two embraced warmly, both talking at once.

Calla looked over. "Mrs. Josephine Dunham, I'd like to introduce Miss Nannie Helen Burroughs, my dear friend's daughter who is setting the world on fire! Nannie, Mrs. Dunham here is visiting Lynchburg for a while."

"Miss Burroughs, it was an absolute pleasure listening to you this morning. It's hard to find the words to tell you what your message meant to me."

Miss Burroughs's smile turned conspiratorial. "Then I suspect we are kindred spirits, Mrs. Dunham. And call me Nannie, please."

"Indeed, we are . . . Nannie. And it's Josephine, if you would."

The young woman glanced behind her. "I'm to have lunch with the pastor and some of the other members, and they're waiting. But would you mind if I come by later, Auntie Calla?"

"I'll be sorely put out if you don't. I want to hear more about this school you're hoping to start up north."

Miss Burroughs winked. "I'll come by the boarding house afterward, I promise."

As Josephine and Calla left, Calla greeted people by name as they did her. She knew everyone. Josephine met their gazes and smiled, but most people turned away. Even worse, two young women gave her downright ugly looks as they walked past.

Calla stopped short. "What on earth was that about?"

Josephine shrugged. "I don't know. But why don't you walk on ahead. I'll follow on after you."

Calla gave her a look like she'd grown a second head. "We ain't gonna play that game, Josephine. You're my friend at Miss Mary's, which means you're my friend everywhere."

Calla linked arms with her, and they continued on outside.

Josephine spotted Dodge Coburn walking toward them, still without his niece. Preferring to avoid him, that seemed impossible at the moment.

He tipped his hat. "Calla. Mrs. Dunham."

"Good morning." Josephine tilted her head.

"Morning, Dodge." Calla looked around. "Where's that sweet niece of yours?"

"She spent the night with Moriah so she's having lunch with their family." Mr. Coburn pointed across the way where the two girls stood giggling together.

Josephine didn't know Mr. Coburn well at all, but something in his manner felt off.

"Well, why don't you come on over to Miss Mary's and eat with us?" Calla gestured to him. "There's plenty, and I made that buttermilk pound cake you love."

Josephine swallowed an inward groan.

"I'm afraid Mr. Coburn's company is already spoken for!" a woman called from behind them.

Mrs. Gibbs made a beeline for Dodge Coburn, and her daughter slipped an arm through Mr. Coburn's and pulled him close. Calla's gaze flicked pointedly to the girl—Rowena—then back to Dodge, who looked far less comfortable than a moment earlier.

"Dodge is already spoken for," Rowena said, running a hand over his upper arm. "He's joining us for Sunday dinner then he's staying to look over the cattle with Pa."

Josephine caught the look Rowena sent her, sharp and possessive, though for what reason, she couldn't imagine. She had no interest in Dodge Coburn.

"Come, Rowena," Mrs. Gibbs snapped. "Mr. Coburn, you'll ride together in the wagon."

"I'm fine to walk, ma'am. But thank—"

"Nonsense. We live three miles out. This'll give y'all time to visit."

Rowena tugged him along, and Mr. Coburn tipped his hat and followed, looking for all the world like a fish on a hook. Rowena glanced back and smiled.

"That girl," Calla muttered as she and Josephine continued walking. "She's been trying to get her scheming little claws into him for a while now."

Josephine laughed. "If Mr. Coburn isn't careful, he'll find himself trussed up and being pushed—or carried—by Mrs. Gibbs down the aisle."

"Not likely. Not with him and Bethie heading for Wyoming soon."

Josephine slowed. "Wyoming?"

"He bought land out there before his sister, Kathleen, died . . . God bless her." Calla shook her head. "Hate to see them go. But if it means he gets away from that one, I'll help him pack."

Josephine smiled, but couldn't deny a small sting of disappointment. Why, she couldn't say. Dodge Coburn leaving was a good thing. She would be rid of his suspicion. Although she had no idea where else she would go, she did not plan on staying here. Yet returning to Atlanta still felt impossible.

After listening to Miss Burroughs, she wanted to believe a time would come when she could plead self-defense and have her voice heard. But that time was not now, and the clock was ticking. And in the back of her mind, buried beneath fear and uncertainty, was a voice that told her she would never go home again.

23

"Have another piece of buttermilk pound cake, Nannie. You too, Josephine." Calla didn't wait for replies but plopped second slices of dessert onto their plates.

Nannie shot Josephine a look that said arguing would be an uphill battle. Josephine smiled, enjoying their playful banter.

With a light supper served to Miss Mary's boarders and the dining room cleared—thankfully without Mrs. Gibbs who didn't work Sundays—the three of them lingered at the table, talking and laughing. Late-afternoon sun slanted through the kitchen window, glowing like firelight and bathing the room in a golden haze.

"Now finish your story, Nannie," Calla urged as she rejoined them, pouring herself another cup of tea. Always with mint and plenty of honey. "The one about your missionary friend."

Nannie nodded and leaned forward. "Well, as I was saying, she's a remarkable woman, following God's call to share the gospel in China."

Calla shook her head. "Talk about gumption!"

"Oh, she has plenty of that," Nannie said. "And she loves the Lord, which makes for a powerful combination. When she was preparing to leave, her church asked to pray over her and her ministry. But afterward, a small group pulled her aside." Nannie paused. "They wanted to give her a *special* gift."

Josephine frowned.

"A pair of men's trousers," Nannie stated evenly. "They told her to go home, hang them on her bedpost, and pray for God to fill them. Because she had no business doing such work as an unmarried woman."

Josephine stared. "They didn't!"

"They did. And they meant it."

Heat rushed to Josephine's chest. "That's absurd! As if a woman must have a husband to legitimize her calling. Men have *no right* to dictate what a woman should think or do—or who she should be!"

The kitchen went still. Only then did Josephine hear the sharpness in her own voice. She looked away, wishing she could gather the words back. Not only because of their force, but because she feared they betrayed her. She sounded like a woman without a husband.

"I-I'm sorry," she said. "That was . . . far too blunt. And out of turn."

Nannie reached across the table and covered her hand. "It's never wrong to speak honestly among friends. I hope you won't consider me impertinent if I ask you something."

Sensing what was coming, Josephine braced herself.

"After all our visiting, you've heard much of my story." Nannie gave her hand a gentle squeeze. "But I know very little of yours. And I'd like to, if you're willing to share it."

Calla's expression echoed the same quiet encouragement.

"So . . . you're asking how I came to be in Lynchburg," Josephine said softly. "And how I came to have these marks on my face."

"As much as your injuries concern me . . ." Nannie's gaze was steady and kind. "I'm far more interested in the courage of the woman bearing them. Scripture says God never wastes a tear of our earthly journey. That he collects all of them in a bottle. I find strength in that. And I sense you've traveled a hard road."

Josephine didn't answer immediately, not trusting herself to speak. Because in that moment, she wanted—desperately—to tell them the truth. About the suffragist rally. The brick. Clay Darden. Sarah. The train station. All of it. But confession carried too high a cost.

"My story isn't uncommon," she began, choosing her words carefully. "My . . . husband is a man given to anger. Recently, it turned dangerous. And this time, I believed he might kill me." The shudder that followed was real, even if the story was not. "So I fled. I left everything and . . . ran. And somehow, I ended up here. In Lynchburg. A town far from the rest of the world and a little difficult to find," she finished, borrowing Nannie's words from the sermon.

Her smile faint, Nannie nodded. Calla did too, though more slowly.

"And how does your husband earn his living?" Nannie asked.

Josephine lifted her cup to hide her hesitation. "He's an attorney."

Nannie's brows rose. "Where does he practice?"

Josephine panicked. No doubt this young woman had connections, ones she would have previously welcomed in service of women's rights and the vote. But right now those same connections could sink her. "Outside Chattanooga. A small practice." She forced a smile. "But I'd much rather hear about your plans for the school you hope to start."

Nannie studied her for a moment. "We can speak of that. But first, may I say I agree with what you said earlier—with one small adjustment." Her eyes sparked. "You said, *As if a woman must have a husband to legitimize her calling.* While a woman's calling doesn't come from a husband, but from God . . . Marriage, when rightly joined, should strengthen the callings of both. Two people yoked together pull farther than one alone. God's plans for our lives are always the most important and best. Wouldn't you agree?"

Josephine wanted to say yes, knowing that was expected. "I used to believe that," she said softly. "But lately I've been given cause to doubt."

"Because of what you've endured?" Calla asked, the question mirrored in Nannie's gaze.

"Not only that, it's—" Again, she hesitated, careful not to be too transparent. "A lot has happened in recent years. A lot of loss." She swallowed. "But truly, I'd rather talk about something—"

"Nannie's school!" Calla said, clapping her hands as she stood. "How about y'all talk while I wash dishes?"

"How about we *all* talk and work?" Nannie countered.

"I agree!" Josephine stood, grateful for the reprieve. "While y'all do that, I'll get started on tomorrow morning's biscuits!"

Calla laughed full and unguarded, and Josephine joined her, surprised at how good it felt.

Nannie looked between them. "Am I missing something?"

At Calla's urging, Josephine shared the embarrassing story—Calla supplying details as needed—and it did her heart good to tell something about herself that was wholly true, even if not flattering.

A short while later, with the kitchen put to rights, Calla invited Josephine to join her and Nannie as they walked to the preacher's house where Nannie would be staying with the family for the night. Josephine declined, wanting to give them time together.

Nannie paused on the front porch. "I hope our paths cross again, Josephine Dunham. Know that I'll be praying for you, trusting that the Lord Jesus does have a plan for your life. Even here in little ol' Lynchburg, Tennessee."

"Y'all don't be forgetting this is where I live my life," Calla shot back, a subtle smile betraying her.

"Thank you, Nannie. I'll be praying for you, too. I do still pray . . . on occasion." Josephine gave a small shrug. "I'm just not sure he's listening these days."

"I've been there," Nannie said gently. "Everyone has, if they're honest." She lifted her gaze to the dusky sky, the sinking sun painting the forested hills in a soft luster. "Never forget—even though Jesus was God's Son, he learned obedience from the things he *suffered*."

Josephine waited.

"Pain draws us closer to God, my dear sister. It helps us hear his voice . . . better than anything else." Nannie leveled her gaze. "I don't like that truth, but me not liking it doesn't change it." She took Josephine's hand. "Do me one favor, Josephine. Promise me you won't judge God by your circumstances. Not now, not ever. He works on a far larger landscape than the one we can see. And please don't judge all men by one. There *are* good men in this world. Many of them. To judge them all the same isn't fair. To them, or to yourself. God created men and women to work alongside each other in his Kingdom. We truly are better together."

Josephine held her gaze. "That's actually two favors," she answered, then seeing Nannie's sincerity, she nodded. "I promise . . . to try, at least."

"Fair enough." Nannie squeezed her hand. "And don't let what your man did to you put out your fire. God's Spirit within you is far stronger than you realize." Her eyes sparkled. "Now, give me time to get that school funded, find a location, and get it running. But sometime in the future, probably not until well into next year, if you're looking for a teaching position in Washington, DC—" She winked. "You let me know."

As Calla and Nannie walked arm in arm down the street, Josephine headed back inside.

A newspaper lay on the foyer table. Sunday, March 5, 1905. Exactly a week ago, three days *before* she'd fled Atlanta.

As it turned out, Jack Daniel was the wealthy man in town who shared newspapers with Miss Mary, which made her new job downright fortuitous. It also made her the one who now delivered the papers to the boarding house.

Calla had told her it usually took a full week for *The Chattanooga Times* to reach Lynchburg. Which meant if the incident had been reported in *The Atlanta Journal* the following day—and surely Mayor Darden had seen to that—she likely had three or four more days before someone here might read about it.

She would simply have to get to those newspapers before Jack Daniel did—and hope no one else in town subscribed.

Hearing Miss Mary speaking with someone toward the back of the house, Josephine ducked into the library, relieved to find it empty. Relishing the chance to read, she selected a novel she'd been eyeing, lit the oil lamp on the side table, and settled into the corner chair, tucking her legs beneath her.

She'd first read *Black Beauty* as a child and had loved it ever since, though certain passages still unsettled her. She smoothed a hand over the green cloth cover, the gilt-and-black embossing worn smooth with age. Then she opened it. A first edition, like the one in her family's library.

"1877," she whispered, published four years before her birth.

She knew something of the late author, Anna Sewell, having once written to the London publisher after recommending the book to her students. *Black Beauty*—Sewell's only novel—had been written later in life and over several years while the author was very ill, and published only months before her death.

Reading the opening lines felt like greeting an old friend.

"The first place that I can well remember," Josephine read softly, *"was a large pleasant meadow with a pond of clear water in it. Some shady trees leaned over it, and rushes and water-lilies grew at the deep end."* She traced the words with her finger. Brilliant, how Miss Sewell chose to write the novel through the horse's eyes. The first novelist to do so, according to her publisher.

Moments later, fully immersed, Josephine sensed movement across the room, and slowly lowered the book to see Bethie Coburn, of all people, standing by the shelves, scanning the spines.

24

Josephine had thought of Bethie countless times since that horribly embarrassing moment in the distillery office. While she'd dreaded their paths crossing again, she was grateful for the chance to finally apologize. Watching the girl scan the shelves with such focus, as though searching for something specific, Josephine wondered if this might be her opportunity to make amends.

"Hello there," she whispered, not wishing to startle her.

Bethie jumped and turned, her eyes widening before narrowing to slits—whether from the dim lighting or due to present company, Josephine couldn't be sure.

"What are *you* doing here?" Bethie asked, the question settling it.

"I was reading." She rose and held up the novel. "It's one of my favorites. Are you looking for a particular book?"

Bethie's gaze moved to the volume in Josephine's hand, lingered there a bit too long, then slid away, and Josephine knew she'd come for this very title.

She held it out. "Please, take it, if this is what you came for. I've read it many times."

"I don't want that one." Bethie lifted her chin. "I'm looking for something else."

Believing otherwise, Josephine returned the book to its place. "My name is Josephine Dunham."

"I know who you are . . . ma'am."

The accusation beneath the words stung. "And you're Bethie." Josephine forged on. "Mr. Coburn's niece. It's nice to formally meet you."

Bethie's unwavering stare conveyed confidence beyond her years, her eyes so very like her uncle's.

"I'm grateful we've met again, Bethie. Because I owe you an apology. If I had known the story behind that skirt and blouse—how special they are—I never would have worn them. Miss Mary meant it as a kindness, but the hurt it caused you was never my intention."

Bethie's expression hardened. "She's fetching them for me right now. I'm taking them home!"

"As well you should," Josephine said gently. "Things that belonged to your mother ought to be treasured. And one day, when you wear them, I hope they will help you feel close to her." She glanced down at her empty left hand, regret digging deep. "They should never have been worn by a stranger. I'm truly sorry. And I'm deeply sorry about your mother."

Nothing but that unwavering stare.

Unwilling to end there, Josephine searched for safer ground. "Calla mentioned this morning that you and your uncle are leaving for Wyoming soon. You must be so excited. It sounds like a grand adventure, and one you'll enjoy." Never mind that she preferred civilization and culture over the vast, empty prairie.

Emotions flickered across Bethie's face, too many and too quick to name, and Josephine regretted having mentioned the loss of the girl's mother.

"Well . . ." she said quickly, eager to ease the moment, "I'll bid you good night and leave you to make your choice."

"You do know what people around town are saying about you, don't you?"

Josephine stilled and turned back, the anger in the girl's tone palpable. "No . . . I-I don't. What are they saying?"

Bethie's mouth curved. "That you're a liar. And a fake. That you're not really—"

"Bethie girl, you in here? Miss Mary gave me your mama's—"

Dodge Coburn stopped in the doorway, the familiar skirt and blouse in hand. "Oh, Mrs. Dunham, I didn't realize you were . . ." His gaze moved between them. "Everything all right in here?"

Josephine could barely breathe. Bethie, however, recovered swiftly.

"Everything's fine, Uncle Dodge. Mrs. Dunham and me were just talking."

"Mrs. Dunham and I," he corrected, then frowned. "You feeling all right, Mrs. Dunham? You look a little pale."

Josephine forced a quick nod. "I'm fine. Bethie and I were just . . . talking."

The clip-clop of horses passing by out front filled the awkward silence.

"Bethie, take your mama's clothes and go wait in the wagon."

"But Uncle Dodge, I haven't picked out a—"

"Now." His tone allowed no debate. "And stop by the kitchen. Calla saved you some pound cake."

With a sharp exhale, Bethie took the clothes and marched out, the slam of the screen door on the back deck punctuating the moment.

Mr. Coburn stepped closer. "Mrs. Dunham, I'd be much obliged if you'd tell me honestly . . . Was my niece disrespectful to you just now?"

"No," Josephine answered, considering the situation. If Bethie had heard something in town though, certainly he had as well. "She's still hurt. Understandably so. But she wasn't disrespectful."

"Good, because I've—"

"But I would like to know . . . What exactly *are* people in town saying about me?"

Surprise crossed his face, followed by caution. "Ma'am, you know how people like to talk. Especially about folks new to town. I wouldn't put much stock in anything they—"

"I'd be much obliged if you'd tell me honestly . . . Mr. Coburn." Her hands started to shake, and she clasped them tightly.

He exhaled. "What did she tell you?"

A knot formed hard and cold in the pit of Josephine's stomach. "That people think I'm . . . not being truthful. That I'm a *fake*. And I'm fairly certain she was about to expound on that when you came in."

He briefly looked away. "Rumor's going around—and mind you, I did not participate in its origin or spread. But some folks are saying they don't think you're really married. That you're running from . . . some other situation."

"And just what other situation would that be?" She braced herself, wondering who could have found out so quickly. And if authorities were already on their way to arrest her.

"They're saying that—" He fingered his thick beard, looking anywhere but at her. "You're . . . in a delicate way. And that your father raised his hand to you when he found out, which explains the marks on your face."

Josephine could only stare, both shocked—and overwhelmingly relieved. Perhaps she should be insulted that people would think her so unscrupulous as to be unmarried and expecting. Instead, relief flooded her that they didn't know the truth.

She steadied herself. "That's quite a fiction, Mr. Coburn. But it is not true. I can assure you . . . I am not *unmarried and with child*."

"I never said you were. I just stated the rumor. Frankly, a person's business is their own. Leastwise, until it brings trouble to someone else's doorstep. Or . . . proves to be false."

"Do I hear doubt in your voice, Mr. Coburn? Do you believe what's being said?"

"I didn't say that."

"But you didn't dismiss it either."

He studied her. "My gut tells me you're hiding something. I don't know what. And I could be wrong." His eyes sharpened. "But I don't think I am."

25

THE THROB OF HER OWN PULSE pounded in her ears, and Josephine regretted pressing him for an answer. If meeting Dodge Coburn's gaze had been difficult before—and it had—it now took every ounce of her resolve. How did she extract herself from this conversation without digging an even deeper hole?

"Well then . . ." she said carefully. "Where does such an assessment leave us?"

A slow smile tipped one corner of his mouth. "Right where we were when I walked in, ma'am. Only maybe a little less cloudy. Good night to you, Mrs. Dunham."

He turned to leave.

"Oh, please take this with you." She drew *Black Beauty* from the shelf and held it out. "Bethie was eyeing it earlier. Only, don't tell her I asked you to take it, or it may end up in the kindling box."

He studied the cover.

"It's a novel told from the perspective of a horse," Josephine continued. "Black Beauty is his name, and he narrates the story himself. It's a wonderful book, especially if you're an animal lover. I've recommended it to my students for years."

"She's actually read this one," he said, thumbing the pages. "More times than I can count. It's a favorite."

"Do you read, Mr. Coburn?"

Something in his expression suggested he found the question amusing. "On occasion."

She debated whether to share her next thought but figured if he was raising a girl who loved to read . . . "Considering your work with livestock, you might find the novel of interest as well. It would be worth giving it a try. You have nothing to lose."

He nodded slowly. "I appreciate that recommendation, Mrs. Dunham." Then his stare turned downright appraising. "Though I might describe this novel more as a powerful portrayal of animal cruelty and the importance of treating all creatures with kindness. Not to mention the story explores themes of compassion and social injustice in relation not only to the treatment of animals but of human beings as well. But what you said is true . . . It's a wonderful book."

Josephine tried to mask her surprise. And failed. "I-I'm sorry, I did not take you for a man who reads novels written for children."

"I think what you mean is you didn't take me for a man who reads at all. Or possibly one who knows how to. And for the record, I wouldn't call this a children's book. Plenty of adults would do well to read it."

Embarrassment coursed through her, yet his quiet laughter held no rebuke. And once again, the word *underestimated* came to mind.

"I actually enjoy reading, ma'am. Surprising as that may be. And I make a point to read everything Bethie does."

"You read all the books she reads?"

"Yes, ma'am. I want to know what ideas she's taking in. What worlds she's visiting. Because sooner or later, those ideas will make their way out and shape who she becomes. I'd rather walk those roads alongside her now, help her navigate her path. And help her make the right choices that'll serve her well in life."

A spark of warning stirred inside her. "Your niece strikes me as a very bright girl. I imagine she does well in school."

"She does."

"She has a confidence about her, too, more than is customary for a girl so young."

"Again, that's Bethie. She's an independent little thing, much like her mother was." Melancholy edged his voice. "But I'm determined to give her the guidance she needs."

Perhaps she was mistaken, but something in his tone hinted that his sister's choices might not have been good ones. Still, she couldn't let the comment pass. "Guidance is always proper, of course. But caution is warranted against foisting our own choices upon children as they grow. Take your niece, for example . . ." She chose her words with care. "As she comes of age, she must be free to choose her own path. Even if it's one you might not have chosen for her."

His laugh came out hollow. "That's quite the speech, Mrs. Dunham. And no offense meant, but given what I know of you—and having seen that sash in your pocket that first day—I don't have to guess where that sentiment comes from."

The spark from moments earlier ignited. "It's not sentiment, Mr. Coburn. Women must be allowed to pursue their own callings. And that includes girls coming of age in a culture where men dominate—"

"Allow me to bid you good night, ma'am." His tone was polite, but final. "And on Bethie's behalf, thank you for the book."

Staring at his back, Josephine didn't like being so summarily dismissed. "Apparently I had you pegged as well, Mr. Coburn. A man so threatened by a woman's independence and capability that he cannot even entertain the notion she might be his equal in—"

He turned and swiftly closed the distance between them. Heart pounding, she stood her ground.

"Ma'am, you can peg me however you like. But do not presume you have leave to fill my niece's head with your suffrage ideas. I will thank you to keep your distance in that regard. Do I make myself clear?"

"Do you even understand what you're talking about when you say suffrage ideas? Because I—"

"Believe me, I know more than you think. And those ideas you champion?" His voice tightened. "They've already cost me more than I care to—" He broke off, jaw hardening. "I will not allow her head to be turned by such foolish notions."

"Foolish notions?" She stepped closer. "You would deny women the very rights you enjoy as a man, then call those same rights and freedoms *foolish*?"

"Those rights come at too high a price, Mrs. Dunham. The world is not ready for your brand of freedom."

"As long as laws are made solely by men, women will never—"

"Save your speech for one of your rallies. I've heard it all. Some of what you're after has merit, I'll grant you that. But the world doesn't change so quickly. It takes time. You're pushing so hard and fast that—"

"So fast? We've been fighting for equality for decades! You may not be aware, Mr. Coburn, living where you live, but this is not a new fight.

And it's not going away! Women *will* gain the vote. Perhaps not in my lifetime, but I will fight for those who come after me. Including girls like Bethie. Because others fought before me, and I will do no less!"

He looked at her. No, looked *into* her, and she let him.

"You have determination, Mrs. Dunham," he finally said. "You're a fighter. I saw that straightaway." His gaze briefly lowered to her mouth, then he looked away, frowning. "That can be a good thing, as long as it's tempered with wisdom. Just be careful. Folks around here don't take kindly to others meddling in their affairs. In fact, they can get downright prickly about it."

"You mean men who mistreat their wives won't take kindly to a woman being given a seat at the table—and to having a voice in the laws that govern this land."

He opened his mouth as though to respond, then sighed instead, weariness in the act. "I trust I've made my position clear. Bethie is my charge, my responsibility." He paused, then swallowed with effort. "She's all I have left of my sister. I love her with all my heart. And I will not allow her to be misled. Good night, Mrs. Dunham."

26

The next morning following her breakfast duties, Josephine hurried out the front door on her way to the distillery, and nearly collided with a gentleman on his way in. She didn't recognize him, and she'd met every boarder. Perhaps he was a new arrival.

Regaining her balance, she smiled. "Welcome to Miss Mary Bobo's Boarding House. If you're looking for Miss Mary, you'll find her in the kitchen—through the dining room on the left."

"Well that's a good thing. Because I'm her husband."

Josephine wished the porch would open up and swallow her whole. "Mr. Bobo, please accept my apologies. I've only been here a handful of days so—"

"No harm done, Miss . . . ?"

"*Mrs.* Dunham."

Though his smile remained pleasant, she sensed she'd offended him, which likely meant she'd just offended his wife. She knew there was a Mr. Bobo. She simply hadn't met him yet.

"Lacy Jackson Bobo, at your service, Mrs. Dunham. I've been away on business in Shelbyville, Tullahoma, and the surrounding area this past week."

"Well, welcome home, sir. It's good to meet you."

"Jackson!"

At Miss Mary's voice, Josephine turned.

Miss Mary stepped onto the porch. "I thought you weren't getting back until the end of the week."

"Finished my dealings earlier than planned. I hope that's not a disappointment."

Miss Mary shooed away the comment. "You know better than that."

"I don't know. Judging by the name of this place, I'm never quite sure."

Josephine thought he was kidding, yet if she read his wife right, Miss Mary didn't welcome the joke.

"But as promised—" Jackson Bobo reached into his worn satchel. "I picked up newspapers from each town I visited, like I always do. I know how you like to keep up with what's going on in the world."

An icy shiver slid down Josephine's spine.

"Thank you, Jackson. I'll read these later today. But first, let's get you some breakfast." Miss Mary turned back inside. "Have a good day, Mrs. Dunham. And again, good for you on getting that job. Don't let me down!"

The door closed, and Josephine moved down the walkway toward the street, her surroundings barely registering. Newspapers from each town? The iciness slithered into her chest, tightening her breath. She paused, tempted to go back inside, to invent some excuse to get her hands on those papers. But not with Miss Mary. That would definitely raise suspicion.

By the time she reached the distillery office—taking the longer route to avoid the jail—she'd mostly talked herself off the cliff. What were the odds that smaller town newspapers would run the story if Chattanooga hadn't? She clung to that logic, thin as it was.

Mr. Daniel had left for Nashville the day before, so the office was quiet. He'd mentioned a meeting with the owner of the Maxwell House Hotel—one of the South's most prestigious establishments—to discuss carrying his whiskey in the gentleman's bar. She'd never been there, of course, but had read about the hotel in newspaper coverage of the Tennessee Centennial Exposition seven or eight years earlier. From all accounts, the place was magnificent. No doubt, Jack Daniel would return successful in his endeavor.

She kept an eye out for Dodge Coburn, not quite ready for another encounter. She hoped he'd given Bethie the book, and had kept her name out of it. She couldn't stop stewing over his comment about suffrage ideas having already cost him.

His protectiveness of Bethie made sense. She'd felt much the same about her students. How much deeper that instinct must run for a niece—a child you were raising yourself. But it was his remark about his gut telling him she was hiding something that troubled her. He didn't strike her as a man who let go of things easily.

The office door creaked open.

Josephine looked up half expecting to see Mr. Coburn. Instead, a man stood in the doorway—not tall, but broad shouldered, his vest straining at the buttons, a badge pinned to his chest.

Her heart dropped to her stomach.

"Mrs. Dunham, I presume?" He stepped inside and removed his hat. "Sheriff Rigby. Thought I'd stop by and say hello. See who's got a hold of Jack's ear these days." His gaze swept the office. "He around?"

She had the distinct sense he already knew the answer, and that his cordiality was calculated. "It's good to meet you, Sheriff Rigby. And no, Mr. Daniel is away. In his absence, may I help you?"

"Oh, I don't need any help, really." He walked to the desk and eyed the open ledger and stacks of invoices. "I check in from time to time. Make sure he's staying on the right side of the law." A polite smile followed.

Josephine returned it, closing the supply ledger and placing it atop the paperwork. "I'll let him know you stopped by."

"As sheriff, I make it my business to know what's going on in my town. And who's new in it." He settled on the edge of the desk. "So tell me about yourself, Mrs. Dunham. Where're you from?"

She laid her pen aside, her hands steady despite the tremor inside. "The Chattanooga area. And before you ask what brought me here, I'd think one look at my face answers that plainly enough."

He seemed taken aback, but not for long. "You know, the world's turning upside down these days." He sighed. "What with women wanting to be treated like men. Taking men's jobs. Some even wanting the ballot." His smile held warning beneath the polish. "I say let's leave those weightier matters to men. That's only my opinion, of course, but I reckon the Almighty intended it that way from the start."

Perhaps it was his smug expression or the condescension in his tone, but she recalled something Miss Anthony had shared, and couldn't resist. "As a dear mentor of mine often says, *I distrust those people who know so well what God wants them to do, because I notice it always coincides with their own desires.*"

He laughed. "That's mighty clever sounding on the surface. But it's my experience, Mrs. Dunham, that some women just don't know their place." He fingered his hat in his hands. "But life has a way of reminding us where we belong. Best we listen when it does."

Heat surged in her chest, but she held her tongue.

He slipped his hat back on. "You need anything while you're here, you know where to find me." His gaze lingered. "And I know where to find *you*."

Later that afternoon, Josephine reluctantly returned to the boarding house, half expecting to find Miss Mary waiting for her, newspaper in hand, demanding an explanation for what happened in Atlanta. But when Josephine opened the front door, the lobby was empty and the house quiet, save for sounds of supper preparations drifting from the kitchen. Already, savory aromas filled the air.

Still not confident she was out of the woods, she quietly opened the kitchen door. Calla stood at the stove, pouring a generous amount of honey into a cup of tea.

"I'm back from work," she finally said when Calla didn't turn.

Calla sucked in a breath and nearly dropped the cup and saucer. "Gracious, you scared me to death! Next time make some noise when you come in." She tossed Josephine a smile, but her tone held a trace of irritation.

"I'm sorry, I didn't mean to scare you."

Calla took a long drink, then another. "No harm done. Just shaved a few years off my life, which ain't the worst thing." She gestured toward the table. "Sit yourself down and rest a minute, then we'll finish supper. Help yourself to the corn bread there if you're hungry. Miss Mary left newspapers for us. Mr. Bobo always brings them back with him."

"You've already read them?"

"Mostly." Calla glanced over her shoulder. "One goes on about President Teddy Roosevelt's niece having married her fifth cousin once removed earlier this month. Line after line given to the bride's dress and how she looked. Then bad news filled the pages. An explosion at a shoe factory in Massachusetts killed fifty-eight people. Another in a mine in West Virginia took twenty-four more." She shook her head. "Got enough sorrow right here. Don't need to borrow it from the rest of the world."

While Calla turned back to the stove, Josephine quickly scanned each newspaper. They were thinner than *The Chattanooga Times*—and none mentioned her name. Or Clay Darden's. Her nerves eased, she helped with supper, then the cleanup afterward.

When the last dish was washed and put away, Calla handed her a slip of paper. "If you're sure you're wanting to learn how to cook . . . I wrote out what's needed."

Josephine studied the list of ingredients. Simple enough. And she did want to learn. "You're certain you feel up to it tonight? You seem tired."

"I'm all right, long as it's fit to eat when you're done." Calla winked.

"You're going to stay here with me, right? Until it comes out of the oven?"

Calla huffed. "After what you did with those biscuits, you think I'd leave you alone in here? Miss Mary walks in and sees you cradling a mixing bowl, spoon in hand, she'll faint dead away on that plank floor."

Josephine laughed. "All right then. Gingerbread with lemon sauce!"

"That's one of Miss Mary's favorites. You do this without burning down her house, and it'll go a long way toward winning her over."

Josephine gathered the ingredients, then started by measuring the molasses, the thick syrup slow to pour. She glanced at the list again. "Half a cup of sugar. Do you know this recipe by heart?"

"Mmmhmm . . . But I should. Been making these recipes for years. Now mix that good so the sugar blends nice and smooth. Butter's on the table. I'll get your water boiling. You want a cup of tea? I'm making me another."

"Yes, please."

Josephine added the butter and stirred, her arm already tired. The long day at the distillery—and Sheriff Rigby's visit—still weighed on her. Authority had a way of doing that, reminding her too much of the corrupt police department in Atlanta. Not that Sheriff Rigby was crooked. Biased? Without doubt. Opinionated? Absolutely. And chauvinistic? Through and through. In her experience, some men, when faced with the suffrage movement, felt compelled to reassert their masculinity. If they could only understand—suffragists weren't seeking to strip them of their rights. They simply wanted those same rights for themselves.

"Now add the boiling water. Mix it good so it cools, then drop in that egg. But not while it's hot, else it'll curdle right up. Keep stirring."

Josephine followed instructions.

Calla set her cup of tea on the table. "I put some mint in yours, too."

"Thank you. Does this look like it should?"

Calla peered into the bowl. "Sure does. We gonna make a cook out of you yet. Think I'll sit down and watch you for a bit. My back's about to give out."

Feeling confident, Josephine cracked the egg on the side of the bowl—too hard—and the shell shattered into the mixture.

Soft laughter sounded behind her. "You ever cracked an egg before, my friend?"

"Yes."

"How many?"

Josephine averted her gaze. "A few."

"How many?" Calla asked again.

"Maybe . . . a dozen. Or less."

They laughed together as Josephine fished out the shell fragments. For reasons she didn't examine too closely, Dodge Coburn came to mind—and what he would say if he could see her now. She'd expected he might visit the office today, but he hadn't. She felt certain their exchange in the library had laid his suspicions about her to rest.

"Make sure and get all that shell out. Miss Mary ain't fond of crunchy gingerbread."

"So I've gathered."

Minutes later, Josephine slid the pan into the oven then sat and took a sip of tea. "Mmmm . . . I love the mint you put in this."

"Makes it good, don't it?"

Josephine rubbed her lower back.

"Your back bothering you?"

"Not really. I just stood a lot today. I reorganized the boxes in the back storeroom. Still trying to clean up a little."

Calla sipped her tea, seeming more relaxed, and no tremor in her hands. "How's the job? What's it like working for Uncle Jack?"

"Not as awful as I thought it would be." Josephine smiled. "He's very generous with his employees. And it feels good getting things organized." She sighed. "But I miss my students. I didn't even get to say goodbye."

Calla stirred her tea. "Miss Mary told me you were a teacher. So your husband, he don't mind you teaching? Most men won't stand for that after they're married. They want their woman home, taking care of them."

Josephine thought quickly. "It was definitely an issue. Among other things." She sneaked a look at Calla over the rim of her cup, hoping that answer would suffice.

Calla was quiet for a moment. "You and me don't know each other overwell yet . . . And I ain't asking to pry. Just to help . . ."

Calla wouldn't meet her gaze, and Josephine's unease ticked up a notch.

"I was just wondering, Josephine—" She finally looked up. "If you're with child."

Josephine breathed again.

"Reason I'm asking," Calla continued quickly, "is people in town been talking. Said your papa beat you when he found out you were—"

"My father did not beat me, Calla. And I am not with child."

Relief crossed her face. "I'm so glad to hear it. Not that children ain't a blessing from the Lord. They are. Or that running from a no-good man ain't a hard thing. It is. But being with child and running . . . That's a whole kind of harder."

Seconds passed, and Calla chuckled.

Josephine eyed her. "What's so funny?"

Calla shook her head. "First I hear that rumor, then next morning I see you rubbing your belly out back. Then my pickled beets come up missing. I just let my thoughts run wild." She chuckled. "Done made a fool of myself."

"Not at all. I probably would have thought the same thing."

The squeak of door hinges drew their attention.

Mr. Prince, the revenuer, peered into the kitchen. "Good evening, ladies."

"Evening, Mr. Prince." Calla pushed aside her teacup. "Something we can do for you, sir?"

He stepped inside, looking faintly uncomfortable. "I was wondering, Miss Calla, if you have some bicarbonate of soda? I may've had a little too much supper."

Calla smiled. "Maybe it was that second piece of buttermilk pie?"

His expression turned sheepish. "It was actually three. I ate Miss Livvy's too. That pie's about the best thing I've ever eaten. That, and your fudge one. You know we revenuers fight over who gets sent to Lynchburg. And it's not for the distilleries. It's Miss Mary's hospitality and your fine cooking."

"Well that does my heart good to hear." She headed toward the foyer. "Give me a minute and I'll fix you right up. Be right back."

"Mrs. Dunham." He bobbed his head. "How are you, ma'am?"

"I'm well, thank you, Mr. Prince. And you? Besides the unsettled stomach."

"Doing fine. I visited several of the smaller distilleries today, so that was good."

Josephine frowned. "There are other distilleries besides Jack Daniel's in this area?"

He chuckled. "Oh yes, ma'am. None as large or as fast growing, but close to twenty other family-run distilleries operate in these hills."

"Twenty?" Josephine let that sink in. The fight for prohibition suddenly loomed larger—and farther from reach—than she'd ever imagined.

"That's right," he continued. "And we check them all. Make certain they're complying with the law and paying what's due."

She leaned forward. "What exactly do you check for?"

His expression sobered. "Everything. An internal revenue agent has *very* specific and important duties. We examine stills, worm tubs, fermenters, mash tubs, hidden pipes, secret stills. Any way a distiller might siphon off whiskey without reporting it. *Every* piece of equipment has to be registered. It's the law!" He withdrew a badge from his coat pocket and held it out with a flourish.

"That's quite impressive, Mr. Prince." Josephine schooled a smile, while recognizing the opportunity for what it was. "I imagine there's considerable paperwork involved."

"Oh, yes. We audit ledger books, production logs, payments. We interview employees. Then file our reports with the Treasury."

Josephine glanced behind him, watching for Calla. "And . . . if irregularities are found?"

He straightened to his full height, all but coming to attention. "Immediate fines and seizures of equipment. Or the whiskey itself." He tapped his badge. "The Treasury doesn't take kindly to tampering."

"Oh, I imagine not. And woe to any distiller who thinks they can." Feeling both guilty and justified, Josephine tucked all that information away, realizing the line between a distillery's lawful operation and ruin was a narrow one.

Calla returned with a glass near full to the brim, and he slipped his badge back into his pocket.

"Here you go, Mr. Prince. Drink this and you'll feel better in no time."

"Much obliged. And next time, no more than two pieces of pie."

He took his leave, and Calla shook her head fondly. "That man's a character. You ever seen him pushing that one-wheeled bicycle of his around town?"

Josephine frowned. "Why only one wheel?"

"'Cause Mr. Prince likes to walk, and folks—friendly as they are around here—kept offering him a ride. He got fed up with it, so he got himself a bicycle. Then one day a wheel came off, but he just keeps pushing it along."

Josephine laughed, despite no one in town having offered *her* a ride. Well, except Dodge Coburn. And he hadn't exactly offered.

Calla sniffed and glanced back at the stove. "You happen to check the clock when you put that gingerbread in?"

"No!" Josephine grabbed a kitchen cloth and lunged for the oven. "Do you think it's burned?"

"Pull it out and see."

She did—and sighed in relief. "It doesn't look too brown."

"Stick a knife in. If it comes out clean, it's done."

The blade came out, clean, and Josephine held it up proudly, like Mr. Prince with his badge.

Calla shook her head. "Only thing you forgot . . . we ain't made the lemon sauce yet."

Josephine winced. "Maybe we could just eat it plain this time?"

"Oh, I was hoping you'd say that! I'm ready for a slice and then to bed."

They sat at the table, and Josephine cut them each a piece. Hers melted in her mouth. "I can't believe I made this," she managed, still chewing. "And it's edible!"

"It ain't just edible, honey. It's *good.*"

"Because of you!"

Calla winked. "Because of *us.*"

Josephine lifted her cup of tea in salute then drank.

"No, ma'am! That one's mine!"

Too late, the lukewarm tea burned her throat like fire all the way down. Josephine choked and coughed, eyes watering, barely managing a breath.

But one look at Calla's face told her everything.

27

Regret filled Calla's eyes until it spilled over. "Oh Josephine . . . I'm sorry. I'm so, so sorry."

Josephine looked at the cup, then back at her friend. "Whiskey?"

"I only take a little now and then." Calla buried her face in her hands. "No, that ain't true. Lord, forgive me, and help me. This time of year it's just . . . so hard." Her voice broke. When she looked up, the sorrow in her eyes made Josephine's chest ache. "I know I ain't doing right, and that I oughtn't be—"

The kitchen door opened.

"What *is* it you're cooking in here, Calla? It smells divine, and I—" Miss Mary stopped short, her gaze darting between them. "What's wrong?"

Josephine rose at once and gathered both teacups. "We were just talking, Miss Mary. I heard you call her Calla Lilly the other day, and Calla shared the touching story behind her name." She dumped the remainder of both their cups in the wash bucket then turned back. "And believe it or not, she just taught me how to make gingerbread. Why don't you join us and have a piece."

Still not looking convinced, Miss Mary pulled up a chair beside Calla. "You sure you're all right, Calla?"

"Yes, ma'am." Calla's voice went quiet. "My heart just got a little over tilted there for a minute."

"And with good reason." Miss Mary touched her shoulder. "You know, I remember, too," she whispered. "Every year. I honor your wish not to speak of it, but that doesn't mean I forget. I never will."

Calla offered a weak smile. "Thank you, ma'am." She looked as though she might cry again, then pushed herself up. "Well, you best have a piece of this cake our Josephine made. Lemon sauce or no, it's mighty good." Calla gripped Josephine's hand, gratitude clear in her eyes. "You done good, my friend. Now let me bank the stove fire and get these weary bones to bed."

"I'll take care of the stove." Miss Mary gestured. "You go on."

"Thank you, ma'am. Thank you both."

Miss Mary reached for the knife. "Calla, there's no nutmeg in this bread, is there?"

Calla turned back. "No, ma'am. No nutmeg."

"Well, good. Because I cannot stand nutmeg."

"How well I know. But if you die before me, ma'am, you know what I'm gonna do."

"You better not go sprinkling nutmeg on my casket. I'll come back and haint you good!"

Miss Mary's wry smile bookended with Calla's soft chuckle as she left felt like the brief lifting of a veil. Josephine didn't know how far back these two went together, but they had a bond. That was undeniable.

What was also undeniable was that Calla was hurting. Over what, she didn't know. Only that, sometime in the past, something painful had happened to Calla *this time of year*. She also knew now why Calla always chewed mint leaves.

Miss Mary cut a slice of gingerbread and took a bite, her color looking noticeably better. "Not bad . . . Josephine. Not bad at all."

"Thank you, ma'am." Josephine wasn't sure which meant more to her—Miss Mary's praise or that she'd called her by her first name. "Calla's a good teacher."

"You couldn't learn from a better cook." Miss Mary cut herself another piece. "I wanted to speak with you about room and board."

"I should be paid tomorrow, so—"

"Already?" Miss Mary nodded. "Good. Uncle Jack says he's pleased with your work, which pleases me." She met Josephine's gaze. "How does a dollar and a half a week sound? Provided you keep helping Calla as you have been? She's got more on her plate than usual."

"That's more than fair, ma'am, and I'll help her however I can." With Mr. Daniel paying her fifteen dollars a week, that left over thirteen dollars, plenty to send to Sarah and still be able to save some. "I truly appreciate you putting your good name on the line for me."

Thinking of her conversation with Mr. Prince just now, she imagined what Miss Mary would do if made aware of her plan to disrupt the distillery's production. She would simply have to make sure whatever she did couldn't be traced back to her.

"And you're welcome to the library. Same as the tenants." Miss Mary used the fire poker to open the side of the stove. "Still no word from your husband?"

"No, ma'am. And there's no way he knows I'm here." Josephine covered the gingerbread with a fresh dishcloth, then placed their plates and utensils in the washbasin.

Miss Mary returned the poker to its hook. "I've heard a rumor. I need to know if it's true."

Josephine didn't flinch but faced her full on. "I think I know what you're going to say. Because Mr. Coburn already confronted me about it, as did Calla earlier. And the answer is no. My father didn't beat me and I'm not pregnant."

Miss Mary slowly nodded. "Well, well . . . Calla's asking doesn't surprise me. Dodge Coburn, though—then again, that man is as True North as they come."

Josephine suspected that to be accurate. "His niece doesn't care for me very much."

"That'll pass soon enough. That sweet girl's still grieving her loss. We all are. Some days it's hard to believe Kathleen's gone. Sometimes life just doesn't turn out the way you think it will, does it?"

"*Most* times," Josephine said softly.

As they reached the hall, Miss Mary paused. "You have surprised me, Josephine. And I am not often surprised."

"Thank you for that. I—"

"Don't misunderstand my meaning. I still don't think you're telling me the truth. At least not the whole of it. But I'm trusting that in time you will. And until then, I'm also trusting that whatever you're hiding won't come back on me."

Seeing the steel in Miss Mary's eyes, Josephine nodded, feeling the warning.

"And for what it's worth, Josephine . . . heartache teaches what happiness can't. Whatever it is you've been through, take the lesson and leave the pain, if you're able."

Miss Mary bid her good night and closed her bedroom door, and Josephine was reminded again of how old a soul she was—perceptive in ways that bordered on uncanny. But what heartache shaped Miss Mary?

She couldn't say why, but Mr. Bobo wasn't what she'd expected Miss Mary's husband to be like. His remark that morning about the inn's name had struck a dissonant note. Perhaps Miss Mary's competence—or her independence—sat ill with him, as it would have with most men Josephine had known.

Taking the oil lamp from the foyer table, she slipped into the library and traced the spines of the books, just as she'd done as a child in her father's library. Passing over familiar titles—*Personal Memoirs of U. S. Grant*, *Life of Robert E. Lee*, and *History of the United States*—she decided to look for one completely unfamiliar to her. And found it.

Cattle: Their Breeds, Management, and Diseases by William Youatt.

She pulled the leather tome—the first in a series—from the shelf and opened it. *Dr. Ezekiel Young Salmon* was written in embellished script on an interior page. The copyright date read 1834 and portrayed a picture of a bull, if the prominent horns were any indication.

She thumbed through, already half inclined to return it to the shelf, when the margins, crowded with notes, caught her eye. The handwriting was clean and precise, markedly different from the ornate signature in the front.

She set the lamp on the side table and settled into the corner chair, then turned the book sideways to better read the notes.

A good stockman should be as attentive to the health and comfort of his cattle as to his own family. Their well-being is his wealth.

An intelligent observation. She read on.

It is not the quantity of food, but the quality, and the manner in which it is given, that determine the profit of feeding.

Again, insightful. A few pages later . . .

The cow is the poor man's friend. She supplies his children with food, and his garden with manure; she is the nurse of his family, and the support of his field.

She smiled. Poetic, especially for a passage about a cow.

Then she noticed page numbers penciled beside underlined sentences. She flipped to one, then another, and realized whoever had made these notes hadn't merely read this book. They had studied it.

On a whim, she pulled down the next volume. It, too, held copious margin notes in the same careful hand. As did the next. And the next.

Yawning, the day finally catching up with her, she began to close the book when heavily underlined sentences stopped her. She leaned closer to the lamp.

"Man was placed at the head of the animal creation to be its master," she read the text aloud. *"But not its tyrant. The treatment of the brute creation is one of the surest tests of the character of a people or an individual."*

She continued to the handwritten note in the margin—the same script, though smaller, more deliberate . . . *If you have to punish something into obedience, you've already failed it. Fear isn't the same as respect. And never will be.*

She read both again, hearing echoes of the stewardship Anna Sewell had woven so powerfully into *Black Beauty.* She wondered if Miss Sewell had read this very book. If not, she would surely have approved.

But more than that, Josephine wondered who in Lynchburg, Tennessee, had read it—and left these words behind.

28

"Queen Victoria?" Fountain pen in hand, Josephine peered up from her seat behind Mr. Daniel's desk, a years-old invoice in hand. She'd been waiting for this moment since she'd discovered the document two days earlier. "You sent a barrel of whiskey to the queen of England?"

With a Cheshire cat grin, Jack Daniel, immaculately dressed in his customary vested suit with tails, closed the office door behind him and hung his hat on the coat tree. "Your eyes do not deceive you, Mrs. Dunham. Note the address . . . Windsor Castle."

It was Wednesday morning, and though she wasn't about to admit it, she secretly welcomed his return. Even if she was still a little tired from her impromptu reading of animal husbandry the night before.

"It was one summer evening several years back," he continued, "when I found myself in a state of repose on my veranda and thought, *Why shouldn't the most important woman in England—perhaps the world—slow sip the world's best whiskey?*"

Josephine gave him a look. "Possibly, sir, because Queen Victoria, God rest her, didn't drink whiskey. Or perhaps because she didn't drink at all."

"Oh, my dear Mrs. Dunham, allow this humble student of life to correct you." He moved toward the desk. "This revelation may cause a suffragist such as yourself no small emotional upheaval, which will, of course, bring me enormous personal delight."

Josephine managed to keep a straight face. Barely. She had missed their sparring.

"I was reading a newspaper at the time," he went on, seating himself opposite her at the exact moment she rose to relinquish the office chair—he waved her back down. "I learned the queen often enjoyed a glass of wine with her meals. German wines, mostly, thanks to her beloved Prince Albert. But the truly intriguing detail was this . . . whenever she traveled to Balmoral Castle in Scotland, she partook of Scotch whiskey."

He waggled his brow. "And while I respect my own Scots-Irish heritage and the whiskey-making traditions coursing through my veins, I knew Old No. 7 would beat that stuff hands down! So I shipped a barrel to the ol' gal!"

Josephine shook her head. "You are quite the entrepreneur, Mr. Daniel."

"I will take that as a compliment, though your tone lacks the admiration I typically receive from the more delicate gender."

"Which I imagine surprises you not at all."

"Goodness, no. That's partly why I hired you." He leaned back, boots finding the corner of his desk. "I knew you'd be a challenge! But mark my words, madam. Little by little, I will win you over."

Josephine gave him a droll look, but the mischievous sparkle in his eyes said he wasn't fooled.

"Did you know," he continued, "that Queen Victoria lived another forty years after her beloved Prince Albert died? She wore black for the rest of her life. What a great love they must have shared."

"Don't tell me you're a romantic, Mr. Daniel."

"Could there be any doubt, Mrs. Dunham? After all, I do adore women. The pursuit, the wooing . . ."

She turned to file the receipt in a folder. "Being a romantic and adoring women *in general* are not the same thing. How can a man and woman share a great love when one of them is continually infatuated with the pursuing and wooing, as you put it?"

Silence followed.

She looked up. The sparkle in his eyes had dimmed.

"Mr. Daniel, I didn't mean to—"

"No, no, Mrs. Dunham, you spoke truth," he said quietly. "And truth, as I've learned in my fifty-five years, is often barbed. Even when unintended." Memory swept his features. "There was a woman once. Frances Elizabeth Blythe. Fannie, everyone called her." He paused. "I asked her father for her hand but . . . He told me I was a little too old for such a young woman. I've long wondered whether my occupation factored into his refusal. After all, distillers are not always held in the highest regard." His focus shifted back, his smile wry. "Difficult as that may be to believe."

Not even tempted to smile, Josephine realized genuine regret when she saw it, and she struggled with what to say next. "I don't know why her father refused you, sir. But I am sorry it turned out that way. It seems you cared for her deeply."

He shrugged. "I haven't spoken of her in years. And don't know why I did now. She played the piano at gatherings I hosted in my home. I'd send my carriage to collect her and her mother. She could play anything—classical pieces, popular ditties. She was a gifted musician. And a genuine soul." He hesitated. "It seems neither of us have found our great love story yet . . . have we?"

When Josephine didn't answer, he abruptly straightened.

"Please forgive me, ma'am. I spoke out of turn. I did not aim to imply that your marriage, despite its apparent difficulties, is not—"

"Please." She met his gaze. "Any man capable of doing *this* to a woman is not capable of a *great love story.* So no, I haven't found one yet either. Nor is it likely that I will," she added softly.

The last comment outmaneuvered her better judgment, but was true nonetheless.

He leaned forward. "My dear woman, you are young yet. You have time. Assuming you can find a man equal to your ideals. Which, indeed, may prove challenging."

"I am not looking for a man, Mr. Daniel. Or *another* man," she added quickly, knowing he must be aware of the rumors about her.

She rose, eager to change the subject. "Several invoices arrived in your absence. They'll require your approval before payment."

He joined her at the desk.

"Also, sir . . ." She kept her tone even, her conscience stirring even before she got the words out. "Mr. Prince with the Department of the Treasury was waiting on the porch this morning. I tried to help him, but he said he prefers to meet with you personally. He'll be back later."

"Ah. Mr. Prince." He nodded. "Our favorite revenuer. And a stickler for details. I'm assuming you've met him? He always stays with Miss Mary. They all do."

"Yes, sir, I've met him." She stared unseeing at the invoices in her hand. "If I can help you get ready for your meeting with him, I'm happy to."

"He'll want to start with the gauger's book in the safe."

"The gauger's book?"

He looked at her. "You're working for one of the fastest-growing distilleries in the world and don't know what a gauger's book is?"

"I do not. And I'm rather proud of it."

He chuckled. "Gauger's books record daily production—how much whiskey is made, stored, and barreled. Every barrel is measured, sealed, then stamped with a tax strip."

"I *do* know tax strips. My father always enjoyed a cigar in the evenings, and those boxes came sealed with tax strips."

"Enjoyed?" he asked, his voice softening.

Only then did she realize what she'd said. A bit more of her personal life revealed. She had to keep up her guard. "Yes . . . My father passed away almost two years ago."

Compassion lined his features. "I'm sorry for your loss, Mrs. Dunham."

His sincerity landed a solid blow to her conscience. "Thank you, Mr. Daniel. Now . . . where were we?"

"I believe we were discussing how revenuers stamp anything a man might start enjoying too much."

She smiled. "Let's just hope that doesn't include Calla's fudge pie."

He winced. "Did she make it while I was gone?"

She nodded. "And you weren't there, so I ate your piece."

"You are a cruel woman, Mrs. Josephine Dunham."

"You don't know the half of it."

"No, but I'm betting I'd like to. *If* you were my type," he quickly added. "Which, of course, we've already established you're not."

She glanced over, half expecting a flirtatious look. But he wasn't looking at her at all. Then again, why would he? What man would be attracted to this?

"You know, it just occurred to me," he continued, "you haven't had your tour yet. The warehouses, the distillery, the charcoal works. We'll remedy that immediately and—"

"No, thank you, sir. I don't require a tour. If you'll just confirm these invoices, I'll get them paid then you can go on about your day."

"Mrs. Dunham, everyone who works here gets the tour. And the story."

She paused. "The *story*?"

"It's something I started after returning from the St. Louis World's Fair with the—"

"Gold Medal for World's Best Whiskey," she finished for him. "Yes. I'm well aware."

He gave her a slow grin and glanced at the framed award. "It's growing on you, isn't it? Sitting there, beholding it day after day? I daresay it's nearly speaking to you!"

"My world would no longer be complete without it, sir."

He laughed. "Mark my words . . . little by little, ma'am. And you should start calling me Uncle Jack. Everyone else does."

"I'll take that under advisement . . . Mr. Daniel."

A minute passed then she remembered. "The sheriff stopped by while you were gone."

He looked over. "What did he want?"

"He claimed he was jesting, but said he was checking to make sure you were still abiding by the law. But I believe he mainly wanted me to know that *he* knows I'm here."

He shook his head. "That's Sheriff Rigby. He makes it his business to know everybody coming and going, whether it's his business or not."

That comment eased her concern more than she cared to admit.

"You know he arrested me back in '81 for carrying a pistol in town."

She laughed. "He did not."

"He most certainly did. I was acquitted, of course. But Rigby takes his job seriously. A mite too seriously, if you ask me."

Boot steps sounded on the front porch, and they both looked up.

A heartbeat before the door opened, Josephine wondered if it would be Dodge Coburn. She hadn't seen him since their spirited exchange on Sunday evening in the library, though another encounter felt inevitable. If he'd been avoiding her, he should know that wasn't necessary. She could handle another round with him. Any chance to chip away at stilted patriarchy and blind tradition, as Miss Anthony liked to say. He was a worthy debating partner.

Squaring her shoulders, she prepared herself.

29

A man in overalls walked in with a little girl in tow, and Josephine felt a stab of disappointment, which she swiftly brushed aside.

The man offered no smile, yet his countenance was kind. Whatever warmth he lacked, the girl more than made up for. Mischief lingered in the vivacious gleam of her eyes, and Josephine felt an instant fondness for her. Especially when the girl smiled at her still-healing face without so much as a flicker of discomfort.

"Good day, Uncle Jack." The man extended a large, calloused hand, as the squeak of wagon wheels drifted in through the open door.

Jack Daniel shook it heartily. "Ballard Preston! Good to see you. I was just about to hunt down Dodge and ask him to send word we need more mules."

"Dodge must've read your mind, sir, 'cause he's already been to see me. Me and Agnes brought down six."

Only then did the man look Josephine's way.

"Ballard," Mr. Daniel said, gesturing. "Allow me to introduce my new bookkeeper, Mrs. Josephine Dunham. She's recently moved to town and needed employment, and—"

"The Almighty knew you needed help, sir," Mr. Preston drawled, his dry humor never touching his features, which somehow made it even funnier. "Good to meet you, Mrs. Dunham. Welcome to town."

"Thank you, Mr. Preston."

He glanced down. "This here's my daughter Agnes."

Josephine smiled. "Nice to meet you, Agnes."

Agnes dipped a little curtsey. "Howdy-doo, ma'am."

"Let's get you paid, Ballard." Mr. Daniel bent down to open the safe.

Josephine felt Agnes watching her and sneaked a quick wink. The girl winked right back, adding a tiny shoulder shrug as if they shared a secret.

Mr. Daniel straightened, face reddening. "I never can get this dad-blame thing open." He tried again, then looked as though he might actually kick the safe.

"Mr. Daniel," Josephine intervened. "What can I do to help?"

He dug through his coat pockets, vest pockets, then sighed. "Of all the—"

Footsteps sounded on the front porch a second time.

When Josephine met Dodge Coburn's gaze, something shot clean through her, stealing her breath for a beat. He paused, too, then looked away, as if nothing had happened.

"Morning, folks." Mr. Coburn shook Mr. Preston's hand. "Ballard, good to see you. Morning, Agnes." He chucked the girl under the chin. "Bethie was just talking about you at breakfast. She's got a book she wants to share."

"Dodge!" Frustration roughened Mr. Daniel's voice. "This blasted safe is giving me fits! Would you try it?"

Within seconds, Dodge Coburn opened the door, and Mr. Daniel muttered something Josephine hoped Agnes didn't hear.

"Just leave the blasted thing open," Mr. Daniel grumbled. "Payroll's at noon."

Grateful to hear she'd be paid today, Josephine watched as Mr. Daniel counted out a generous stack of bills.

"Here you go, Ballard. And thank you for coming down so quick. I know that's a haul from up in the hills."

"Railroad still ignoring your ask for a closer stop, Uncle Jack?" Mr. Preston asked.

"They are. Dodge and I keep proposing new track closer to town, and to Fayetteville, but they refuse. So for now, we'll keep you busy breeding and breaking those Jacks and Jennys."

"Fine by me, sir." A bona fide smile finally crossed Mr. Preston's face.

Mr. Daniel clapped his shoulder. "And don't go letting George Dickel, Wooten, Nutt and Renegar, or Brinkley and Patterson—any of those other distilleries—pick you off. You're the best around, and we aim to keep you. Busy and well paid."

They shook again—less like a farewell than a contract.

"Hold up there, Ballard." Mr. Daniel reached into his pocket and crouched to Agnes's height. "You help your papa get those mules to town?"

"Sure did, Uncle Jack. I mucked the stalls and helped with all the feeding, too. Raisin' mules for Jack Daniel is an honor for us Prestons."

The girl recited it with practiced pride, as though she'd heard it said a hundred times.

Mr. Daniel pressed a coin into her hand. "This here's for you and you alone. Go to the mercantile and get you some candy. And eat it before you get home so those brothers of yours don't gobble it up!"

Agnes beamed. "Thank you, sir. But . . . might it be agreeable if I spent it on a story instead? If I find one to my liking?"

"Darlin', you earned this money. It's yours to spend as you please. With your papa's say, of course."

Mr. Preston's hand settled on her slender shoulder. "Books are better than candy any day. But who knows—" Pride filled his gaze. "Maybe we can get both."

As father and daughter walked away—Agnes hustling to match his stride—Josephine caught a glimmer of emotion on Mr. Daniel's face. Whatever else he was, he cared about people. He had a gift for finding common ground, too. A trait he and Miss Mary shared.

"Uncle Jack, I need a word." Mr. Coburn closed the door, direness in his voice.

"The cattle?" Mr. Daniel asked.

He nodded, then hesitated, glancing at Josephine.

"Go on," Mr. Daniel urged. "Mrs. Dunham's made of tougher stuff."

"We lost another twenty-four since yesterday afternoon. Same symptoms, all of them."

Mr. Daniel's features tightened. Josephine's did, too. When Texas fever was mentioned the other day, she hadn't understood how serious it was.

"How many are we down since this started?"

Mr. Coburn exhaled. "Fifty-one. Most of them the steers meant for market."

"Don't let them suffer, Dodge. You know how I feel about that."

"I feel the same, sir. And I'm not." A heaviness settled in the lines around Dodge Coburn's eyes. "I'm doing it quick and clean, like you taught me. Doc sent another telegram from Tullahoma, trying to hurry Washington along."

"Washington moves slow, Dodge."

"Don't I know it. I'm sorry, Uncle Jack. We've done all we know to do."

"No need to be sorry to me, son." Mr. Daniel ran a hand through his thinning hair. "You've always treated my cattle like your own, and I won't forget it. I'd head to DC myself and raise a ruckus if it would help."

"I doubt it would. Doc thinks we'll hear back soon."

"Still no spread to people?" Mr. Daniel asked.

That got Josephine's attention, as did the flicker of uncertainty in Mr. Coburn's eyes.

"No, sir. Not yet."

"Then do what you need to do. Whatever Doc says, too. And Dodge . . ." Mr. Daniel's voice gentled. "However this turns out, I'm grateful you've decided to stay here."

Hope warmed Mr. Daniel's features. The opposite settled in Mr. Coburn's.

"You and Bethie aren't going to Wyoming?" Josephine blurted before she could stop herself.

Dodge Coburn finally looked at her. "No, ma'am. We're staying put."

"And Lynchburg is the better for it." Jack Daniel turned to Josephine. "Anything Dodge needs, Mrs. Dunham, already has my approval."

"I understand, sir." What she didn't understand was the small spark of pleasure she felt at learning Dodge Coburn wasn't leaving.

Mr. Daniel checked his pocket watch. "Tom Motlow asked me to stop by the bank this morning. Dodge, would you stay and help Mrs. Dunham with payroll? Just get her started."

"Will do, sir."

"My meeting won't take long. I'll head up to the farm after."

He left the door open, and Dodge Coburn knelt and withdrew a thick leather pouch from the safe. "Has he gone over payroll details with you?"

"Some. I've prepared the ledger and addressed the envelopes with each employee's name." Josephine removed the stack from the desk drawer. "But I don't know what each employee earns."

He thumbed through the envelopes, whistling low. "Alphabetical. We usually just scribble names as they come in."

"I like order, and things being in their proper place."

He huffed a quiet laugh. "I'm sure you do."

She felt a prickle of defensiveness. "Mr. Daniel is paying me to organize this office, Mr. Coburn, which means—"

"I meant no disrespect, ma'am." He lifted a hand. "Truth is, I'm impressed. Uncle Jack is, too." He looked around. "This place hasn't looked this good since . . . well. Ever. He says you're doing a fine job. And I appreciate it."

She let out a breath. "And I apologize for misreading you."

His gaze held hers. "Friends again?"

She made a show of weighing her options. "Perhaps . . . if you'll tell me where to get the jerky you gave me that day in the wagon."

He studied her. "From memory, that didn't sit too well."

"That's because I hadn't eaten and was not in a good way. I usually don't like jerky, but that was . . . delicious."

"Thank you. I'll take that compliment."

"No." She shook her head. "*You* made it?"

His brow furrowed. "Now *that* I think I should definitely take offense at."

"Probably," she admitted, grinning. "But I'm surprised, that's all. And—fine—a little impressed. What do you put in it that makes it taste so good?"

A shadow crossed his expression.

Then she understood. "Ah . . . An old family recipe you don't share."

"No, ma'am, it's not that. I just—"

A group of men passed by the window outside, headed for the office.

"Payroll time." Mr. Coburn reached for the pouch. "How about I stay with you today. And next week you're on your own."

"Sounds fair."

He introduced her to each man, but the line moved so fast she barely managed to stuff envelopes with the bills Dodge handed her. She'd never match names to faces—except the three Hacketts. Brothers, surely, judging by their similar arrogance.

The shortest sauntered up with a grin that told Josephine everything she needed to know about him.

"And just who might you be, sweet little missy?"

Mr. Coburn stepped forward. "Micah, take your pay and move on."

"I'm just being friendly." Micah's gaze slid to Josephine. "*Mrs.* Josephine Dunham, ain't it?" He laughed and his three brothers joined in. The implication was clear—they'd heard the rumor.

Mr. Coburn looked ready to come around the desk, but Josephine beat him to it.

"Yes, Mr. Hackett," she said evenly, checking his name in the ledger and handing him the envelope. She was tempted to ask him if he needed help counting, but when she met his eyes she saw Clay Darden's instead—and a chill went through her.

She looked past him. "Next."

The last of the men cleared, then another group arrived, followed by women—young as late teens to older women, all from the bottling house. Conversation came more easily with them.

What didn't escape Josephine was how nearly every one of them—regardless of age—looked at Dodge Coburn with open admiration, some even with a touch of longing. Either he didn't notice, or he chose not to. "True North," Miss Mary had said, and Josephine was beginning to see it.

With only two envelopes left—his and hers—Mr. Coburn closed the door, his expression somber.

"Thank you for not engaging with Micah Hackett."

"I considered it."

"I could tell. The Hacketts are a hotheaded lot. Cross one and you've crossed them all."

"Men like that are walking advertisements for why God made women—and gave them more discernment."

"Don't hold back now," he said, his tone dry. "Say what you mean."

She smiled. "Perhaps I should have held *that* back."

"No, ma'am. Always say what you think with me. Whether you think I'll like it or not."

She tilted her head. "Well, you'd better brace yourself. I do have opinions."

"That," he said, counting bills into her envelope, "I have never doubted." He handed it to her. "Congratulations on your first official earnings."

She stared at the money, an odd sourness rising knowing her earnings were tied to the successful sale of liquor.

Mr. Coburn tucked a thick wad of bills into his own envelope, returned the pouch to the safe, and locked it. Through the window, Josephine spotted Mr. Daniel coming back.

Dodge must have seen him, too. He grabbed his hat from the coatrack. "Have a good day, Mrs. Dunham." And went out to meet him.

They rounded the office building and headed uphill toward the outbuildings, their easy camaraderie obvious, as was their mutual respect.

Josephine returned to the invoices.

The mail arrived soon after, including *two* letters from new vendors—one in Nashville, the other Chattanooga—now carrying Jack Daniel whiskey. Both expressed an earnest desire to come to Lynchburg to see the distillery and to meet "the esteemed Mr. Jack Daniel himself."

She stared at the letters, unsettled. The distillery was making a name for itself, exactly what she didn't need. And she was helping it happen.

Her mind went to the tax revenue file she'd tucked in the back of a drawer. She would have to be careful. And timing was everything. But regardless of how kind a distiller might seem, didn't she owe something to the countless women and children who had suffered so terribly at the hand of alcohol? How could she be this close to a distillery, to its inner workings, and do nothing?

By midafternoon, the office looked night-and-day different from when she'd first walked in a week ago. She unearthed a bottle of linseed oil from the back room and set to polishing the desk and adjoining table, then oiled the springs in Mr. Daniel's squeaky leather chair.

When four thirty came and went, she closed up the office and started toward the boarding house—then caught a whiff of something foul. She slowed, frowning, but as quickly as it came, the smell lifted on the breeze.

She continued on, aware of the looks from passersby. They thought they knew her story. She hoped they never learned the truth. Once again, she wondered who had started the rumor. And why.

Calla would be nearly finished with supper for the tenants by now. Sensible as it was to return to Miss Mary's, she found herself tempted to head to the cattle farm to see how things were faring. But her presence would likely not be welcomed by Dodge Coburn, and for sure not by Bethie, if the girl was around.

Best to go back to the boarding house.

Repeating the thought like a mantra, reminding herself that distance from Dodge Coburn was the wiser choice, she made it two blocks before turning around and heading uphill instead.

30

Slightly out of breath from the climb, Josephine paused at the crest, surprised by the sweep of gently rolling fields stretching all the way to the foothills beyond. Split-rail fences stitched the land into corrals and pasture, and from where she stood, she could make out two large barns and several smaller outbuildings. A snug log cabin sat tucked among the stalwart pines and newly leafed oak, its porch swing—suspended by thick ropes—drifting lazily in the breeze.

It looked like a picture. Earthy greens against a cloudless blue sky, the whole scene peaceful enough to mask the trade that thrived a stone's throw away.

A bunkhouse stood beyond the barns, set well away from the cabin, and judging by the number of farmhands moving about, it was likely full—and presumably where Dodge Coburn lived.

Then again, no. He wouldn't live in such an unsuitable environment for Bethie.

The breeze shifted and the same foul odor she'd caught wind of earlier—sharp and metallic— permeated the air. She covered her mouth and nose as her gaze trailed to the far end of one of the fields. Thick plumes of smoke curled upward from a smoldering mound, and farmhands—their faces half-covered with kerchiefs—loaded burlap-wrapped cargo into waiting wagons.

She looked closer, and her stomach clenched.

Taking measured breaths, she searched for Dodge Coburn among the men, but didn't see him. Or Mr. Daniel.

She ventured into the nearest barn, the air heavy with hay and dust. The smell of death lingered, diminished only slightly, mingled with labored breathing and low, pitiful moans that twisted her gut tight.

She paused to let her eyes adjust, and voices drifted toward her. One she recognized.

"Doc, you've got to tell him to give her more time. She's due to drop her calf any day now."

"Child, I don't tell your uncle what to do," a man replied gently. "I tell him the condition of each animal as best I know it, then he decides."

"But this is Maple. She's special. I raised her. Bottle-fed her. I was going to take her with us. Uncle Jack said I could."

The man's voice dropped too low for Josephine to hear.

She couldn't see Bethie or the doctor the girl was speaking with, but guessed they were just beyond the stalls lining the corridor. Being in a barn again stirred memories of her early years teaching—taking her students to a dairy farm outside Atlanta so they could glimpse a life beyond brick and streetcars, most having been raised in the city as she had. Eventually, those visits had been deemed impractical, and finally unnecessary, by the school board.

Standing here now, and considering her lack of skills relevant to such a setting, she questioned that decision more than ever.

She moved quietly down the corridor just as someone entered from the opposite end. Instinctively, she stepped back out of sight, but not before recognizing the girl immediately.

Rowena Gibbs. And the basket on her arm likely contained something to entice a certain someone the girl was after.

"What are *you* doing here?" Bethie snapped.

"I'm here to see your uncle, girl. Do you know where he is?"

"Wherever he is he's too busy to talk to you."

Josephine bit back a smile. Bethie's protectiveness was fierce—and understandable.

"Tell him I'm leaving something for him on the porch. I'll come back tomorrow."

"He'll be busy then, too."

"Just tell him, Bethie!"

Bethie mumbled something Josephine couldn't hear, but could easily imagine.

She admired Bethie's spunk. Her clarity. And not for the first time, she wished she'd possessed such certainty at that age. Wished she'd known sooner that women didn't have to make themselves small. That they could be strong, capable, independent—

And what? End up getting beaten senseless in an alley. Forced to run. To hide. To land in backwoods Tennessee, where much of what she'd spent her life learning seemed to count for very little. Except bookkeeping for a distillery.

It might have been amusing had it been someone else's story.

Maybe what we're fightin' for is too much, Sarah had whispered to her in the alley. *Maybe it's never goin' to happen, Finny.* Josephine mouthed the words she'd answered with then, willing them to give her fresh courage. "Failure is impossible."

Because didn't they owe it to girls like Bethie to keep fighting for equality? Even if, perhaps, a certain girl's uncle warned her off? She had no plans to turn Bethie into a young suffragist. Because, whether Dodge Coburn knew it or not, he already had the makings of one on his hands. If Bethie was this strong-minded at nine years old, heaven help the man when the girl came of age.

"No, Uncle Dodge! You can't. I won't let you!"

The urgency in Bethie's voice snapped her back.

Josephine edged forward just enough to see Dodge Coburn standing in the stall, rifle in hand, looking as though the weight of the world was on his shoulders.

"One more day, Uncle Dodge. Just one more!"

"That's what you said two days ago, Bethie. I'm just keeping my promise not to let Maple suffer, remember? And she's suffering plenty right now."

"But Doc said—"

"Bethie," he said gently, but firmly. "There's a good chance the calf will have it too. Then we'd have to put it down too. So please, go on home. I'll be there directly."

Bethie ran from the barn, her sobs heart-wrenching.

Feeling every inch the intruder, Josephine decided it best to leave. She turned—and knocked a pail from its hook. It clanged, struck another, and both crashed to the dirt floor.

She cringed, then looked up to see Dodge Coburn striding toward her.

"May I help you, Mrs. Dunham?"

She rehung the pails on their hooks. "No, I'm sorry. I— I shouldn't be here. I just came to see how things were." She gave a small shrug. "To see if I could help."

A faint smile touched his mouth. "I appreciate that. But I think we've got it covered."

She turned to go.

"Dodge! You best come quick! It's Maple!"

Dodge Coburn rushed back to the stall, and Josephine could only follow.

31

Josephine wasn't prepared for the grim sight that met her when she peered into the stall.

The young heifer, barely more than a calf herself, lay on her side, her reddish-brown hide dull and slick with sweat. The young mother-to-be shuddered and strained in feces-stained hay, her taut, bloated belly rippling as she labored.

"Dodge, her calf's coming!"

"It can't be." Mr. Coburn stared. "She's all but dead, Doc."

"She may be, but the calf isn't. And she's trying to push it out."

Mr. Coburn knelt and ran a hand along the heifer's belly. "How can she have the strength left?"

"She doesn't," the doctor said, tone somber. "But motherhood has a power not of this world. One I've learned never to question."

Mr. Coburn set his rifle aside. "Mrs. Dunham, you best take your leave. Or at least wait out by the corral."

Watching the young heifer writhe, her emaciated body heaving, Josephine ached for her. And for Bethie, knowing what the animal meant to her. "What can I do to help?"

The doctor, an older gentleman, looked up. "You ever assisted with a calving, Mrs. Dunham?"

She shook her head, only mildly surprised that he knew her name.

"I'm Doc Wyatt. Newcomers are few around here, so I have the advantage." He nodded toward the far wall. "If you want to help, fetch some fresh straw."

"I'll do that," Mr. Coburn said, already moving. "But would you run and get Bethie? She'll want to be here."

"You sure about that, Dodge?" Doc Wyatt eyed him. "You may end up losing both Maple and the calf."

"And what will I tell Bethie if Maple dies and I didn't give her the chance to be here? However this goes."

Doc Wyatt nodded. "You're right. That girl's a Coburn, after all."

"Where can I find her?" Josephine asked.

"Try the cabin across the field." Mr. Coburn pushed aside the soiled hay with a gloved hand. "Then the other barn. And get back as fast as you can."

Josephine ran the entire way, surprised to see the sun dipping low . . . and wondering why a farmhand would live in a cabin.

She burst in through the front door. "Bethie? Are you here?"

No answer.

She tried the first door. A bedroom—likely his, judging by its masculine feel. The next room carried a stillness that told her who it had belonged to, and she closed the door without a sound. The third room had to be Bethie's. But the girl wasn't there.

She raced out back. "Bethie!"

Mr. Coburn's dog, eyes already on her, sat at the base of a wide-limbed oak, then its eyes tracked upward.

"Bethie, if you're up there, *please* come down. It's Maple!"

Branches rustled. Slender legs appeared. Then Bethie dropped lightly to the ground.

Her posture was defiant, but her red-rimmed eyes told the truth. "I already know she's gone! I don't need *you* telling me."

"She's not gone, Bethie. She's giving birth. Your uncle wants you there!"

Bethie took off running, the dog with her. Josephine followed.

Bethie rushed into the stall and dropped down beside the heifer, stroking her head and speaking to her in a soft voice.

"That's a good girl," Doc Wyatt encouraged quietly, lighting lanterns. "That's what she needs, Bethie."

Mr. Coburn positioned himself and ran a hand across Maple's belly, pressing intermittently. The heifer kicked, but quick reflexes spared him any damage.

Standing outside the stall with the dog, Josephine wanted to help but didn't know what to do. So she gathered more fresh straw and scattered it as he'd done earlier.

He glanced up, gratitude in his gaze. "Near the front of the barn, where you came in, there's a wooden box. I need the rope in it."

Josephine returned with it. "What do you want me to do?"

"Help me pull. When the time comes."

"Help you pull," she repeated confidently, as though she understood what he meant. Which she did—in theory.

"First," he continued, "we check presentation. Make sure this little one's set to come as it should."

Josephine winced as he reached inside the birthing canal. The heifer bellowed, its breathing labored, and Mr. Coburn grimaced, sucking in a breath.

"Contractions," Doc Wyatt said softly, looking at Josephine.

Understanding dawned.

"You've never done this before?" Bethie asked, disbelief sharpening her features. "I thought you were a teacher."

"Bethie . . ." Mr. Coburn straightened and reached for a towel. "There are many kinds of learning. Each has its place."

"Some more than others," the girl responded beneath her breath.

"You're right, Bethie," Josephine admitted. "While I know a lot about many different subjects, I know very little, if anything, about this one. But I'm willing to learn."

"And that"—Mr. Coburn looked at Bethie—"is half the lesson taught."

Bethie lowered her head without comment.

"Maple's presenting well, forelegs extended," he continued, sounding more like a doctor than a farmhand.

"You're doing so good, girl," Bethie whispered. "You're gonna love your little one, Maple. You're gonna be such a good mama."

"Bethie . . ." Mr. Coburn whispered.

The girl slowly lifted her gaze.

"Straight shooter?" he asked softly.

"S-Straight shooter," she repeated, voice trembling.

"Maple will likely die giving birth to her calf. But if she doesn't, we'll do our best to let her see it before she goes."

Bethie nodded, tears streaming down her face.

"I'm not feeling any more contractions," Mr. Coburn said after a moment. "We need to hurry. I'm going to try and get the loop around the hooves."

Straining, he apparently managed it, then pulled tight.

He handed Josephine the rope. "Doc's going to stay up there on that end. He knows where to push. You and me, we'll pull together from down here. When I say pull, pull. And when I say stop—"

"I'll stop," Josephine said succinctly, gripping the rope behind him and positioning herself on her haunches as he'd done.

"Come on, Maple, girl," Bethie whispered. "Stay just a little longer."

"Pull!"

Josephine pulled as hard as she could, her strength a fraction of his. Her body began to shake from the exertion, and just when she thought she couldn't pull any longer—the calf's hooves appeared, followed in a slippery rush by what looked like its nose. But it was covered by some sort of milky white—

"Stop!"

Josephine let go and fell back into the hay, the agonizing cries of the mother causing tears to knot in her throat.

"You all right?" Mr. Coburn asked, glancing back.

"I'm fine." Her breath came heavy.

Seconds passed.

"Let's go again! Everybody ready?"

Josephine rose into position. Doc Wyatt nodded.

"Pull!"

Josephine gritted her teeth, straining with everything she had, wanting Maple to see her calf before she died. But more, wanting that for Bethie.

A rush of fluid, and the forelegs and full head appeared, then the abdomen.

"Stop!"

Catching herself this time, Josephine moved to rest on her knees, gaining her breath as Mr. Coburn gently tore a hole in the white film covering the calf's body.

"One last time should do it," he said, removing the rope. "But this time, we each hold a leg. Right about here. You ready?"

Close beside him, Josephine tightened her grip. "Ready."

"Pull!"

After a moment, the body of the calf slid free, and Josephine watched in exhausted amazement as the calf's belly moved up and down, its eyes open and alert.

"Help me rub it down, then I'll carry it to Maple."

Realizing Mr. Coburn was talking to her, Josephine followed his lead and grabbed straw and began rubbing the calf's slick body. He tickled the calf's nostrils with straw until it moved its head and snorted, its coat the same deep honeyed brown as its mother's.

"Usually the mama will turn and start licking it," he said, leaning closer. "She'll nudge it, trying to get it to move. But Maple's not able to do that, so we're helping her out."

Josephine rubbed the calf's neck, its belly, then moved back to its head. Despite the straw, her hands grew slippery with afterbirth. But she didn't mind. This was . . . *a miracle.*

"Bull or heifer?" Bethie asked as she watched from where she sat, cradling Maple's head.

Dodge looked. "Heifer."

"You had a heifer, girl," Bethie whispered. "A pretty thing just like you."

Josephine looked beside her, keeping her voice low. "Does it have the disease?" she whispered, wiping her hands on the cloth he gave her.

"Hard to tell yet. But it looks mighty healthy compared to three others born in recent days."

She frowned. "Those calves all died?"

He held her gaze, and she bowed her head, unable to imagine having to do what he'd done.

"Dodge." A hint of warning laced Doc Wyatt's tone.

Mr. Coburn cradled the calf in his arms. "Come on, sweet thing. Let's meet your mama." He laid the calf down by Maple, and the dying mother struggled to lift her head, but couldn't.

"Look at your sweet daughter," Bethie whispered, rubbing the new calf behind its still-wet ears. "She's so pretty. Just like—" Her voice broke. "Just like you. Don't you worry . . . I'll take good care of her for you," Bethie said between sobs.

Josephine watched, her heart aching, but in awe of the girl's strength.

A moment passed, and Doc Wyatt slipped a hand beneath Maple's neck. He shook his head.

Mr. Coburn leaned down. "Bethie, let's get you and this new little one to another stall. We need to get her some milk."

Bethie looked up. "You have to promise me she won't die, too."

"Honey, you know I can't do that."

"Then I don't want her." Bethie stood up, hands fisted at her sides.

Mr. Coburn moved closer. "She needs you, Bethie. And besides, you just promised Maple you'd take care of her."

Josephine stared, finding that a rather cruel reminder at the moment. Especially for one so young. About to come to the girl's defense, she held back when Bethie picked up the newborn calf.

"Excuse me, sir. You need anything else before we call it a day?"

Josephine turned to see a group of farmhands standing in the entrance to the barn—all of them looking to Dodge Coburn.

"Are the carcasses taken care of?"

"Yes, sir. Burning as we speak. We got teams set up to watch the fire all night like you asked, and we'll take turns watching over the sick ones."

"Sounds good. A couple of final things . . ."

As Josephine watched Dodge Coburn interact with the other men, unmistakably in the role of their superior, the word *underestimated* came to mind yet again.

But this time, with the word *greatly*.

32

"WHY DIDN'T YOU TELL ME you weren't a farmhand?"

Dodge looked down beside himself as he and Mrs. Dunham walked from the barn, lantern light casting a soft glow over her features. It was a sight he could too easily grow used to—though the thought was inappropriate, her being another man's wife. *If* she was. His gaze drifted to her bare left hand. He couldn't pinpoint why, but the more he was around her, the less certain of that he became.

"I suppose because you never asked," he finally said.

She huffed. "You could have corrected me."

"Yes, ma'am, I could have."

"But?"

Her expression held challenge, and he smiled at the I'd-like-to-nail-you-to-the-wall look she gave him. "A man who has to make sure everybody knows what he does for a living doesn't rank high in my book. A job might tell you something about a person, but it doesn't tell you who they are. That takes time. And experience." He paused. "And for what it's worth, I *was* a farmhand here for years."

"Before you became foreman. Is that even your correct title?"

"You'll find I'm not much for titles either, Mrs. Dunham. But yes, I oversee the distillery's cattle farm, and I'm grateful for the work."

He set the lantern and a piece of soap on the rock ledge of the well, lowered the bucket, then hauled it up, water sloshing over the rim. He poured the fresh, cool water into a second bucket for her to wash in.

"You did good back there, ma'am. *Real* good. I was proud of you."

She scrubbed her hands and arms briskly, then laughed. A sound he liked. A lot.

"Could you tell I didn't know what I was doing?"

"There might've been a clue or two."

She rolled her eyes. "Bethie's an astute little thing, isn't she?"

"She doesn't miss much, that's for sure." He sent the bucket down again, hauled it up and started washing.

"I admire how forthright she is."

"Why does that not surprise me?"

She laughed again, softer this time, her movements efficient and precise—and decidedly feminine. In the lantern light, the wounds on her face were barely visible, though he noticed how she sometimes turned away or dipped her head, as if self-conscious about them.

Then again, he could be at fault for looking overlong. Wounds or not, she was a beautiful woman. And though he didn't agree with all her stances and causes, he admired her strength and confidence. Whoever had done this to her . . . Just five minutes. That's all he'd need.

"Does Bethie come by that naturally?" she asked.

His thoughts wandering, Dodge quickly backtracked. "The forthrightness, you mean?"

She nodded, then splashed her face with water and gently patted it dry with the freshest towel he'd been able to find.

"She absolutely does. Her mama, my sister Kathleen, was the same way."

She paused. "I'm sorry about your sister, Mr. Coburn. That must still be so terribly hard. On you both."

The sincerity in her voice caught him off guard. Maybe it was the strain of past weeks, the loss of cattle—and of dreams—or the grief he'd tried to outrun, but something shook loose inside him. "Thank you, Mrs. Dunham. I appreciate that."

She hesitated. "I know it's not within the boundaries of proper etiquette for us to . . ."

He arched a brow. "I'm going to need you to finish that sentence, ma'am."

She laughed again, color creeping into her cheeks. "What I was going to say is that I know some might find it improper for us to be . . . more informal. But given that we're working together, and considering what we just went through . . ."

"You're suggesting we bend the rules a little? Go by first names?"

She stood a tad straighter. "Yes. I am . . . Dodge. And I would appreciate it if you would call me Josephine."

She offered her hand. He wiped his own and accepted—briefly. Too briefly. Appreciating the feel of her skin against his a little too much.

"How long have you been foreman here?"

"A good ten years. I began working here when I was twelve. Helped in the barn after school. I watched and learned. Our homestead was a couple miles from town."

"So you've never been anywhere else?"

"I didn't say that." He smiled. "I've traveled some. Mainly for Uncle Jack on business. New York City, Chicago, Washington, DC."

Her eyes widened. "You've been to all those places?"

"None of them had what I wanted."

"Really?" Her gaze held surprise. "I'd love to travel, to see those cities. The buildings, the architecture. Think of the history you'd experience in a place like Washington, DC. Before coming here, I'd never traveled outside of At—" She stopped short. "Outside of a twenty-mile radius surrounding Chattanooga," she finished, her smile downright stiff compared to those previous.

Dodge nodded, knowing the woman no more hailed from Chattanooga, Tennessee, than he did. But the question was, did he call her on it now? Or wait. Instinct told him to bide his time.

"You must have an inkling of wanderlust in you," she continued. "You were planning on going to Wyoming, after all."

He went along with the shift in subject. "I wouldn't call that wanderlust so much as the pursuit of a dream."

She stared for a moment, and he would have given much to know her thoughts.

"And may I ask what that dream is? Or . . . was?"

"To own my own ranch."

She frowned. "But can't you do that here? Surely there's land and—"

He shook his head. "It's not just owning cattle or land. It was the opportunity to build something special and to own a piece of that wild, breathtaking place before it's all settled and changed forever."

"And you decided not to go . . . because of Kathleen's passing."

"It was going to be the three of us. But it's a hard land—beautiful, but not at all forgiving—and while Kathleen never backed down from anything and wanted to go with everything in her . . . Me taking Bethie out there, just the two of us? That wouldn't be fair to her and would be completely selfish and wrong of me." He finished washing and tossed both of their towels into the bucket. "The acreage has a river flowing through it so cold and crystal clear, with water coming straight down from snowcapped mountains, you can see all the way to the bottom. And mountains so high they look like cathedrals. When the sun hits them, they sparkle like diamonds."

"So . . . you have land. You've been out there."

"Yes, ma'am. Last summer. The mountains and rivers, the rolling prairies, and the blue sky that stretches out forever get inside you. It's like a living, breathing thing that—" He caught himself, and laughed.

"What is it?" she asked gently.

"I don't know why I'm going on like this. My apologies . . . Josephine."

"No. No apology needed. I'm enjoying hearing about it. Is Bethie disappointed you're not going?"

He sighed. "That was the worst of it, having to tell her. She was heartbroken, and is still holding a grudge. If she had her druthers, we'd already be on our way."

"Uncle Dodge?" Bethie called as she walked from the barn.

He gave Josephine a look. "Please don't say anything to her about—"

"I won't. To anyone. I give you my word."

Despite his doubts about her, he fully believed her to keep her word about this. "Thank you," he whispered, then turned at Bethie's approach. "How's the calf doing? Still taking to the bottle all right?"

Bethie nodded, yawning as Dodge sent the bucket down again.

"Jake says he and the boys will watch her for me until morning. I can already tell she's going to be sweet just like Maple."

Bethie gave them a full report as she washed up, and Dodge appreciated the questions Josephine asked her, not a hint of pretense among them. And Bethie—apparently so tired she forgot she didn't like this woman—answered at length.

"Give me ten minutes to get Bethie situated, and I'll walk you back to the boarding house."

"That's not necessary, Dodge. I can—"

"It's nonnegotiable. Come and wait on the porch. *Please.*"

By the time he got Bethie tucked into bed with Jessie lying by her door, it was closer to fifteen minutes than ten, so he was both pleased and relieved to find Josephine still sitting on the top step, waiting as agreed.

She rose and pointed. "Don't forget your basket over there."

He turned, not having seen it in the dark.

"Miss Gibbs delivered it earlier. She came looking for you."

Hearing the teasing in her voice, he decided to ignore it—and the basket. Especially when remembering the looks she and Calla had given him when Rowena and her mother cornered him for lunch last Sunday. Even in the dark, he could tell she was waiting for more.

"So tell me," he said as he picked up the lantern he'd left with her and started down the porch steps. "How are things at Miss Mary's? Have y'all reached a truce yet?"

Same as he'd done with her, she went along with the change in subject, and they talked all the way back to Miss Mary's.

She opened the front door of the boarding house. "Thank you again for walking with me, and for letting me help tonight. It was—"

"Scarring for life?"

She laughed softly. "Special in a way I could never have imagined. I'm sorry you lost Maple though."

"It's never easy, but it's all part of raising animals. But seeing new life come into the world? That never gets old. Every time's a miracle."

"I can see that," she said softly, holding his gaze.

"Well, good night, Josephine, and thank you again for helping."

"Good night, Dodge."

Almost to the street, he heard her call his name and turned back.

"I meant to ask you . . . You said *straight shooter* to Bethie tonight, and she said it back . . ."

Her question hung in the silence.

"That's something we started years ago. Even as a little thing, Bethie never wanted to be treated like a child, didn't want anything honey coated. *Tell me straight,* she used to say, unless it turned out to be something she didn't want to hear, then she'd be mad as a hornet for days. So, when there's something I think she needs to know, yet I know it's going to cause her a lot of hurt, I give her the choice."

"Interesting . . ." Her voice floated toward him in the dark. "Has she ever chosen not to hear what you had to say?"

"A handful of times, but that was a while back."

"Brave girl."

"She is that. But—" He only hesitated for a second. "I think it's more because she's learned that it's not so much a choice of her knowing the truth as it is her choosing *when* she knows it. Because truth will always make itself known. It's usually just a matter of time."

The brief distance between the street and porch seemed to expand in the silence, and her barely audible whisper, "Good night, Dodge," stayed with him long after he'd crawled into bed.

33

"DISTILLERY TOUR TIME!" Jack Daniel announced as he breezed into the office two mornings later.

Josephine didn't look up from the ledger. "Mr. Daniel, I'm organizing next week's orders, and I still have a stack of inquiries to respond to—"

"Which you'll do better after the tour." He motioned her up. "Dodge will be here any minute. I'll walk with you awhile, then head to Tullahoma. I have an appointment in Nashville."

"A lady friend?"

A waggle of his brow confirmed it.

"The same one as last time?"

Another waggle denied it.

"Mr. Daniel, your . . . love of the ladies, for lack of a better term, is going to get you in trouble one of these days."

"I'm nearly fifty-six years old, Mrs. Dunham. If I haven't earned the right to enjoy pleasant company, just put me in the grave. Women and whiskey are my greatest joys." He made a grand gesture. "As Thoreau said—'Live in each season as it passes; *breathe* the air, *drink* the drink, *taste* the fruit!'"

"You're quoting a man who embraced simplicity and reflection. I seriously doubt Henry David Thoreau meant whiskey. Or women."

Mr. Daniel waved that away. "Had he conferred with me, he'd have understood life far better. So much for living alone in a cabin in the woods."

Josephine worked to keep her smile in check. "*The purpose of life is not to be happy. It is to be useful, to be honorable, to be compassionate, to have it make some difference that you have lived and lived well.* Ralph Waldo Emerson."

"Spoken like a man who never enjoyed himself." Mr. Daniel peered out the window. "Dodge is coming. *How vain it is to sit down to write when you haven't stood up to live.*"

She tossed her pen aside. "What is it with you and Thoreau?"

"I have a lot of time to read on trains."

Dodge walked in. "Sorry I'm late. Ready?"

Mr. Daniel headed out, clearly pleased with himself. "Under mild coercion, but yes."

Josephine slowly rose, her attention riveted. Dodge looked markedly different, and the change was . . . heady. "You trimmed your beard."

"More like had to trim it." He rubbed his jaw. "Bethie and I had a little food fight this morning over who got the last of the molasses. I *think* you could say I won?"

She narrowed her eyes. "Details, please."

"She spooned the last of it from the jar when I challenged her. We went back and forth, and then . . ." He mimicked the flicking of a spoon. "She . . . finally let me have it."

She laughed. "Right in your beard?"

"She got me good." His grin deepened. "But I slathered her face pretty well too, so I guess we're even. Ready to go?"

"As I'll ever be, I guess."

The ends of his hair were still damp, curling at the collar. But it was the intensity in his blue eyes that seemed to pull her in and tempt her to forget the wounds on her face. What she couldn't forget was what he'd said about truth—that it was only a matter of time before it made itself known.

Tick tick tick.

He paused on the porch. "Between you and me, I can guess how excited you are about seeing how we make Old No. 7. So once Uncle Jack heads to Tullahoma, we'll cut the tour short."

"And you won't tell him?"

He pretended to lock his lips and throw away the key. "Not a word."

"So how's Bethie's calf?"

"So far, so good. She's named her Honey. Because, as Bethie says, she's sweet like Maple was."

They joined Mr. Daniel and conversation came easily as they approached the first outbuilding. Dodge slipped into what was clearly a well-rehearsed tour—buildings, uses, dates. And while a distillery tour held no interest for Josephine, she enjoyed the chance to walk with him more than she should have.

"Our whiskey starts with a sour mash of corn and rye mixed with spring water from Cave Spring Hollow," Dodge continued. "The limestone naturally filters out iron."

"And that matters why?" she asked.

"Why?" Mr. Daniel threw her a look. "Because iron *ruins* whiskey. The flavor, the look—everything! That spring is one of our secrets."

"And the others?" she teased.

"Nothing we're discussing today," Dodge said to Mr. Daniel's delight.

"One thing Dodge won't tell you"—Mr. Daniel's eyes narrowed—"is that feeding the cattle the spent sour mash was his idea several years back. It tenderizes the meat something wonderful, and increases the value, to boot."

Dodge shook his head. "I only got the notion because the cows started licking the slop off my shirt. After I read some of Doc Salmon's books, it confirmed it."

Josephine slowed. "Wait. The books at Miss Mary's? In the library?"

"The very ones." Dodge nodded. "Doc Salmon let me read anything I wanted. Opened the world to me."

"So those notes in the margins . . . Those are yours?" Her disbelief slipped out before she could temper it.

Mr. Daniel chuckled. Dodge raised a brow as if to say he'd heard it, too.

Her face warmed. "I didn't mean—"

"Dodge has left his mark on every shelf in that library, Mrs. Dunham. I'd come see Doc Salmon and find Dodge—young boy he was—soaking up knowledge."

"But first I had to learn to read," Dodge said, winking.

Mr. Daniel motioned. "Let's get moving. I've got a train to catch."

Even before stepping into the stillhouse, Josephine smelled the warm sourness of yeast—earthy and tangy, not altogether unpleasant. But once inside, the scent thickened and burned the back of her throat. She coughed much as she had when she mistakenly drank Calla's tea.

Dodge's eyes glimmered. "That's the fermented grain and the char. But can you smell the vanilla? Maybe a bit of toffee?"

Wishing for water, she shook her head. "No vanilla. No toffee."

Mr. Daniel waved her closer to a copper still. "You've seen one of these before?"

"In pictures," she managed, clearing her throat.

Each still—six or seven feet tall—rested on a stone-and-brick furnace with a fire burning low and steady in its blackened hearth, smoke curling around the brickwork. The massive bulbous copper pot narrowed as it rose, tapering into a swanlike neck before curving down into another copper vessel—round, cylindrical—with a nozzle protruding.

"We use copper stills." Pride accented Mr. Daniel's voice. "And we always age our whiskey in charred oak barrels, which gives Old No. 7 that distinctive, smooth finish."

Soft light from the high windows made the hand-forged copper glow. And though she wouldn't admit it, the riveted pots, though oddly shaped and made for sordid purpose, were beautiful in their worn patina.

Once outside again, Mr. Daniel turned. "I'd best be off. But Dodge, be sure to show her the charcoal-leaching process. That's important. And give her a good view of the vats." A look flickered over his face. "Mrs. Dunham, though I respect your feelings toward whiskey, a better understanding on your part will prove useful in our upcoming visits with vendors."

"Upcoming visits with vendors?" Josephine repeated, catching the gleam in his eyes.

"Oh yes. I've placed advertisements in all the major papers inviting potential vendors to come see Lynchburg and taste Old No. 7 where it's made. We'll do tours and tastings. I'm contemplating hosting dinner parties at my home when they're here. A nice meal, perhaps some dancing." He bowed. "Naturally, I'd want you there."

She smiled. "And naturally, I will decline in advance."

"No need to decide now, Mrs. Dunham." With a Cheshire grin, he turned. "We'll revisit this later." He headed toward the office, then looked back. "Oh, and Dodge. If you get word from Washington, move forward as you see fit. Don't delay. I'll be back in a couple of days."

"Will do, sir."

Josephine watched him stride off in his knee-length black frock coat, vest, and wide-brimmed country squire hat. "That man never stops thinking about whiskey, does he?"

"No, he does not." He gestured toward the next building. "Ready for the charcoal-leaching process? Then I'll let you slip out the side door."

"Is the charcoal leaching what makes the whiskey taste so horrid?"

He laughed. "It's what makes it taste so *good*. It mellows it. You've seen the men burning piles of sugar maple three times a week?"

"The first time I smelled it, I thought a building was on fire."

As they walked to the building, he described the *mellowing* process, then opened the door. She stepped inside and the sharp mix of charcoal and whiskey stung her nose and throat, same as in the stillhouse. Dodge seemed unbothered.

The building appeared empty but for the two of them, and an almost reverent *drip, drip, drip* filled the silence. Sunlight slipped through slats in the wooden walls, illuminating dust motes that rose like mist in the hollow. Eight or ten large round wooden vats—each at least four feet across—sat in holes in the floor.

She moved closer and peered down through the side opening. The vat continued below the floor for some distance. "How tall are these things?"

"Twelve feet deep and five feet wide, filled with sugar maple charcoal and raw whiskey. Every drop spends from three to five days in one of these vats."

"Then where does it go?" She lifted a hand. "Not that I'm interested. I'm only asking so I can answer questions when the vendors come."

He nodded, but she could tell he didn't believe her.

"Near the bottom of each vat is a metal spigot. Several times a day the men draw off what's passed through. The whiskey comes out clear as pure water, then gets poured into the charred white oak barrels."

"And that charring really makes a difference?"

"If we're doing it, it's at Uncle Jack's bidding, and it's because it makes a difference."

"I'll take your word for it." She could still taste the burn of Calla's tea on her throat. Nothing mellow about it, in her opinion.

She'd seen Calla since, but hadn't spoken of it. More truthfully, she hadn't taken the chance. It was Calla's business. And she wasn't about to tell Miss Mary. She simply cared about her friend . . . and wondered what pain had driven Calla to drink.

"And that concludes our tour," Dodge said a little too loudly.

Josephine looked up. "Really? We're done?"

"No, but I sense you are."

She returned his smile. "Why don't you give me a condensed version of the rest. In case Mr. Daniel quizzes me."

Dodge obliged, continuing with details she'd never remember. "After the barrels are filled, they're rolled into barrel houses to mature. Summer heat expands the wood and whiskey seeps into the charred oak. Winter cool contracts it and pushes it back. That's what ages and colors it. About four years, give or take."

"Four years?"

"Good whiskey can't be hurried."

That earned him a look. "So after four years, you bottle it?"

"Not exactly. Each barrel's similar, and unique. We don't depend only on time, but taste and color. Aroma and flavor, too. And not all of what goes in comes out." Warmth lit his eyes. "Some evaporates. We call that the angel's share."

"I beg your pardon?"

"The portion lost to the air." He shrugged as if it were a simple fact. "A gift, as distillers like to say. Offered up to heaven."

"I seriously doubt heaven wants that *gift*."

"Probably not." He laughed. "Uncle Jack tastes barrels nearly every day to know when they're ready. Then we have a team of tasters who gather on Fridays."

She paused. "And are you one of them?"

"If I say yes, will you think less of me?"

"Only if you say you enjoy it."

He held her gaze. "Then I'll pass on answering." Humor layered his tone, then faded. "I know it likely pains you to see how the distillery is growing."

"It does," she admitted, and he didn't push. "Because I've seen what alcohol does to families." She offered a truce smile. "And don't worry, I'm not giving you another speech. But I would like to ask you something."

He nodded, patient.

"The other night you said suffrage ideas had cost you dearly. What did you mean?"

He hesitated as though weighing how much to share. "I'm a little surprised you haven't already heard. This town's rumor mill has a long memory, and seems to take pleasure in a person's downfall."

"Nothing I'd know about personally," she said, looking up.

His gaze softened. "My sister Kathleen, Bethie's mother, was younger than me. When our parents were dying, I promised I'd keep watch over her. I was seventeen. She was about Bethie's age. A spitfire. Wanted to see the world." He looked away. "When she was sixteen, a traveling salesman came through. Turned women's heads—especially hers. He fed her every line she wanted to hear. I should've seen it coming." His voice roughened. "One morning I woke to find a note. She'd run off to marry him and see the world." A bitter laugh escaped. "He showed her the world all right."

Josephine winced. "Did you know where they went?"

"No. And no one remembered him saying where he was from. I went to Tullahoma, talked to ticket clerks, porters, shop owners—anyone who might have seen them. It's like they'd just disappeared."

"How did you find her?"

"I didn't." His jaw went rigid. "She wrote me four months later. Said she was with child. He'd left her in Nashville a month earlier. She'd lived on the streets until a widows-and-orphans home took her in." He swallowed. "She said she was too ashamed to come home. But she was scared. And she had nowhere else."

"Oh, Dodge . . ." Her voice broke. "I'm so sorry."

"So am I. Still." He stared at the vat as if he could will the past into order. "I was working sunup to sundown, trying to prove myself to Uncle Jack and anyone else looking. If I'd been paying attention, if my focus had been where it should've been, Kathleen wouldn't have slipped away. I would've stopped her." He exhaled. "Don't misunderstand me. I would *never* wish Bethie away. I cannot imagine my world without her."

"No, of course not." Josephine's throat tightened. "You only wish you could've spared your sister that pain."

He nodded, eyes lowered.

"But I still don't understand what you meant about suffrage ideas costing you dearly."

He looked back. "Ever heard of Lucy Stone and *The Woman's Journal*?"

The bitterness in his tone made her flinch. "Of course. She's a hero of the movement."

"Kathleen read that journal almost like Scripture. I didn't know what it was—I thought it was like *Godey's Lady's Book.* But more and more, she talked about voting rights, education, labor, marriage reform. Then along came a man who agreed with everything she said. Told her everything she wanted to hear. In order to get everything *he* wanted." His voice went rough. "And he did."

Josephine's heart squeezed. "Which explains why you read everything Bethie reads."

"And why I won't let her young mind be filled with ideas that could cause her enormous heartache." He paused. "It'll come as a surprise to you, Josephine, but I do agree with many of the suffrage ideals. But the cost has to be weighed. And in my opinion, it's too great a price to pay. At least for Bethie. For now."

She wanted to challenge him. But from her own experience, she couldn't. "I understand," she said softly.

A faint murmur rose from beneath the floor.

Dodge pointed down. "They're drawing whiskey. Want to see?"

"I think I've seen enough. You showed me the vats, so Mr. Daniel's requirements are met—for the most part."

A faint smile. "Not quite." He tapped the rim of the vat. "Uncle Jack insists every guest gets a good whiff of Old No. 7 in the making."

"You're kidding."

"I'm afraid not." He gripped the edge of the lid. "You ready?"

"Should I hold my breath?"

"No, but maybe step back a little."

She did. He lifted the lid and let it drop.

The smell punched her square in the chest. She staggered. "Again—how does anyone drink that?"

"In a glass, on a porch, with a friend," he said, grinning. "That's Uncle Jack's wisdom."

She shuddered playfully. "Give me sweet tea, the porch and a friend, and I'll be happy."

He nodded toward the door. "Your exit—and fresh air—awaits, madam."

"Lead on, kind sir."

"Words I never expected from a female suffragist."

"Don't push your luck." She tossed him a stoic look, but he saw right through it.

Enjoying the time with him more than she should, she turned to follow him toward the door when her foot caught on something—and she pitched forward.

Strong hands caught her by the waist and hauled her upright.

"Whoa there," he said, steadying her until she found her footing. "You all right?"

She faced him. Close enough to feel the strength in his arms, the solid breadth of his chest. His trimmed beard revealed the contours of his face—and mouth—and her gaze lowered, and lingered there, her thoughts causing her face to heat. She was just grateful he couldn't read them.

Then she lifted her eyes to his, and realized—he could.

34

Dodge knew he should let go of her, but he didn't want to. And she didn't move away.

The quickness of her breath lit a slow burn inside him, and he pulled her closer, already imagining what it would be like to—

No. Even if he didn't believe Josephine's story about being married, his life wasn't his own anymore. He had Bethie now. He'd sworn to take care of her. Had sworn to give the kind of guardianship he hadn't given Kathleen. So as drawn as he was to this woman, despite their differences, and perhaps because of them . . .

He loosened his hold. Just as the door of the building swung open.

Josephine stepped back at once, and Dodge caught the flash of regret—or was it guilt?—that crossed her face. He turned as George Green walked in.

George slowed, whether to let his eyes adjust or because he'd seen them, Dodge couldn't say. His own conscience voiced the latter.

"George," Dodge called, forcing steadiness to his voice. "Good to see you! I was just showing Mrs. Dunham the vats, explaining the charcoal process. Uncle Jack asked me to give her a tour."

If his voice sounded normal to them, it didn't to him.

"Mrs. Dunham, good to see you again, ma'am." George seemed his usual self.

"And you, Mr. Green," she replied, surprisingly composed, save for the faint color still warming her cheeks.

"So you're learning how we make Old No. 7?" George asked.

"Yes. And it's far more . . . involved than I expected."

"Well Uncle Jack's had nigh onto fifty years to get it right."

Her brow creased. "But that can't be right. That would mean he started as a *boy*."

"Well, not the distillery part." George smiled. "He and my papa started making whiskey after Uncle Jack came to live with Dan Call and his wife, Mary Jane. Uncle Jack couldn't have been more than eight or nine."

"Your father taught him how to make whiskey?" Josephine asked.

"Yes, ma'am. Years back, my papa was a slave for Dan Call. He ran Dan's still. Young Jack told Dan he wanted to learn how to make whiskey, and Dan took him to meet my papa . . . Nearest. *Uncle* Nearest, folks called him."

Josephine listened intently.

Dodge never tired of hearing George tell this story. He hoped he'd keep telling it, so no one ever forgot how it all began. A preacher, a boy, and a slave.

"Dan Call told Jack," George continued, his voice taking on the echo of his father's, "*Uncle Nearest is the best whiskey maker that I know of. He is George's daddy, and he will show you exactly what he is doing.* Dan tacked on, *I'll show you what I know, too.* And Mrs. Dunham, something you've got to know is that young Jack did a real good turn for the Call family. As Dan once told my papa, *Uncle Nearest, the young fellow here saved our baby from trouble when she was caught under the house, and he saved my life from a rattlesnake less than an hour ago, with that stick.*" Memory deepened George's smile. "Dan said, *I want him to become the world's best whiskey distiller—if he wants to be. You help me teach him.* To which my papa said back, *I'll teach him everything I know, Marse Dan.* And that they did."

Josephine exhaled softly. "I would love to meet your father, Mr. Green."

"I wish you could, ma'am. He passed on a few years back. Mama followed not long after."

"They were good people," Dodge said. "You would've liked them."

"I'm sure of it." She smoothed her skirt. "Thank you, Mr. Green, for sharing that story."

"My pleasure, ma'am. I get joy in the retelling. Every time."

She turned to Dodge. "Thank you for the tour, Mr. Coburn. I need to get back to work."

"Would you like me to walk you back?"

"No, thank you. I know the way."

She left without another glance, and Dodge wished he could follow her. To apologize, to explain. To somehow undo what had almost happened.

The door closed.

"So . . . what's going on, my friend?" George asked quietly.

"Nothing," Dodge said, hearing the gentle reprimand. "Nothing is going on, George. And nothing *will.* She tripped on a board. I caught her. That's all." Dodge shook his head. "I just . . . lost my head there for a minute."

George nodded. "Hurt draws hurt sometimes. And she is a pretty woman. But—"

"She's married."

"So she says."

"Believe me, it won't happen again."

George didn't speak immediately. "Lottie says you need a woman, especially now that you got Bethie."

"Don't even mention Rowena Gibbs. She's a child."

George laughed. "That's what my Lottie said, too. That you need a *woman,* not a girl."

Dodge raked a hand over his beard. "What I need is news from Washington. And a cure. Before Texas fever takes the rest of the herd."

35

Every day at the distillery office, Josephine watched for the postal carrier—and with him, the latest edition of *The Chattanooga Times*. Today was no different, except for the steady rain that had fallen for four nights running—and the sense of dread she couldn't shake.

No mail had arrived yesterday, which meant two newspapers should come today. She needed to get to them before Mr. Daniel returned from his meeting with Tom Motlow at the bank.

So far, none of the papers had mentioned her or what had happened. Headlines favored prohibition and temperance news from New York or Chicago, legislative updates, railroad expansions, President Roosevelt's inauguration, and Japan's stunning victory over Russia.

Still, she felt like she was living on borrowed time.

She checked the mantel clock. Half past one.

To her knowledge, Dodge still hadn't heard back from Washington about the cattle. She'd seen him a handful of times since the tour, always with others present. Their exchanges had been polite, distant. And with as little eye contact as possible.

But that distance did nothing to stop her pulse from quickening when she saw him. Or her memory of being in his arms. The desire unsettled her, but equal was her resolve to move past it. She knew better than to let emotion steer her. She should've guarded her feelings more closely. Should've kept the mantras of her other single suffragist sisters closer to heart.

Votes, not vows.

Liberty wears no ring.

Even Miss Anthony, while addressing the suffragists privately before the rally had said, *I never felt I could give up my life of freedom to become a man's housekeeper.*

And neither would she.

She'd watched too many childhood friends marry and, one by one, their lives had become consumed with husbands and households, while she had pursued education and teaching without regret. So why was she experiencing these feelings now? And why Dodge Coburn? He was kind, intelligent, respected, yes. But not part of her plan.

Still, her heart had ached for him when he'd spoken of Kathleen. And Bethie. Through that lens, she understood his caution about suffrage. What he didn't see—couldn't yet—was that he already had a suffragist in the making.

She checked the clock again. Quarter till two.

Rain had no doubt turned the road from Tullahoma into a soggy mess. So far, she'd beaten Mr. Daniel to the newspaper every day but once. The day he'd intercepted Bart in the street before she could. She'd taken the mail from him under the pretense of sorting it. But she wouldn't make that mistake again.

She'd remembered how Lannie, their family cook, used to hand-press *The Atlanta Journal* before her father came to breakfast. So she had adopted the same habit. The first time she'd presented the paper to Mr. Daniel—pages perfectly aligned, edges smoothed—he'd looked up and said, "Mrs. Dunham, you can never leave."

But that was just it. She *would* leave. At her first chance.

She wanted her life back. Sarah, her students, her classroom. Yet the question lingered like a bruise: Would Mayor Darden ever allow that?

Rivulets of rain traced the window as she kept watch.

She'd written to Sarah but hadn't mailed the letter. It was too risky. The postal clerk she handed it to would then know she had ties to Atlanta. She also couldn't be certain the address to be used in such situations was still safe. It changed often, for good reason. And she couldn't risk causing Sarah more trouble.

At last, Bart appeared, slogging through the street.

She met him on the porch. "Good afternoon, Bart."

"Fine day, ain't it?" he said cheerfully, soaked through.

"If you favor rain, I guess it is." She smiled, grateful he treated her with such courtesy. Either he hadn't heard the rumors yet, or paid them no heed.

He pulled a large bundle of mail from his pouch. "It's a soaker, for sure. But won't the flowers and trees all look so purty once the rain is past?"

Wishing she shared his optimism, she thanked him and hurried back inside. Sure enough, two editions of *The Chattanooga Times.* Wednesday, March 15, and Thursday, March 16. Not quite a week ago.

Nerves taut, she sat at the desk and read through the first, looking up occasionally to watch for Mr. Daniel, then finally turned the last page with a measure of relief.

She opened the second and her heart lurched.

Women in Revolt: Suffragist Lawlessness

Scarcely able to breathe, she struggled to focus much less read past the headline. She scanned the article looking for any mention of Atlanta, her name, Darden's. But nothing.

She drew in a slow breath and read back through more carefully.

The article, reprinted from the *New York Times*, dripped with bias, and her chest ached as the journalist reported that suffragists marching after a rally on Fifth Avenue *received due punishment for their actions of reckless disorder.* Twelve women had been arrested and imprisoned, no doubt on fraudulent charges. Other women had been assaulted by police and male bystanders in the crowd, some having been beaten about the head and their hair torn out. One woman had even been stripped to the waist. Dozens had been injured, two women dying from their injuries.

Hot tears slipped down her cheeks. "God, where *are* you in all of this?"

She couldn't remember the last time she'd prayed, not with the mixture of vitriol and anger inside her. Was God even listening? If he was, surely he would do something.

Promise me you won't judge God by your circumstances . . . He works on a far larger landscape than the one we can see. Nannie's words rose unbidden, and Josephine wiped her cheeks, reminded, too, of what she'd said about God collecting tears in a bottle.

Josephine knew the Bible well enough, yet couldn't place the verse. And while God caring enough to collect tears sounded nice, she doubted the Creator of the universe truly did such a thing. Because if he cared enough to collect tears, why not simply prevent them in the first place? Along with inequality, injustice, hatred, prejudice, and cruelty.

She checked the remainder of the newspaper, grateful to find no mention of her name, then set to hand pressing and aligning all the pages, then left both papers stacked on the edge of the desk for Mr. Daniel.

The chirrup of a bird outside the window lifted her gaze. The rain had stopped, but the cloudy skies still held promise of more.

She sorted the mail. More requests for distillery visits. Mr. Daniel's advertisements were working. Too well. She set them aside to deal with later.

Without a knock, the office door opened. Expecting Mr. Daniel, she looked up.

A young woman, head bowed, quickly closed the door behind her and glanced toward the window.

Josephine stood. "Good afternoon, ma'am. How may I—"

"Mrs. Carver said you might could help me." The woman lifted her face. Bruising darkened her cheek and jaw, just beginning to bloom. "If you can't, tell me now and I'll go."

36

"Yes, I'll help you. Any way I can."

"Uncle Jack ain't here, is he?" the young woman asked.

"No, but he could return anytime."

She turned for the door.

"No, please, *wait*!" Josephine hurried after her. "Come with me to the back room. Mr. Daniel rarely goes there. If he comes in, I'll intercept him."

The woman hesitated, fear warring with need. At last, she nodded.

Josephine closed the door behind them and motioned to a chair tucked between shelves and boxes. "Sit here. We can talk."

Dappled sunlight filtered through the small window. Josephine drew the curtains and perched on a wooden crate, instinctively slipping into the calm, steady posture she'd learned at the American Woman Suffrage Association in Atlanta. "You said Mrs. Carver sent you?"

"Yes, ma'am. I went to the mercantile for food, but Mr. Carver says Henry ain't paid the last bills. No more credit." Her voice dropped. "We got no food left. We do got cows, and I give my babies some milk 'fore I walked to town. I done nursed all my younguns, but with Pearl . . . my milk ain't coming in like it did before."

"Are you eating regularly?"

The pause answered.

Josephine's gaze moved to the bruises blooming along the young woman's cheek and jaw, aware the woman was looking at her, too. "My name's Josephine—"

"I know who you are, Mrs. Dunham. Everybody does."

Josephine let that pass. "And your name is?"

"Clara." She bowed her head. "Clara Hackett."

Recognition clicked, and Josephine pictured the brothers she'd seen at payroll last week. "Your husband works here."

"For Mr. Coburn. With the livestock."

Wishing she had iodine and clean cloths, Josephine continued. "What ages are your children, Clara? And are they safe right now?"

"Yes, ma'am. They's at home. Ruthie's five and plumb smart as they come. Virgil and Eugene, twins, they's four. Otis is two. Pearl'll be one soon. And I'm grateful to have them all."

Five children, and Clara looked scarcely more than a child herself. "How long have you been married?"

"Six years. Got hitched when I's fifteen. Babies come easy to me." Her smile held pride. "You got any, Mrs. Dunham?"

"No, I haven't."

Clara frowned. "How old you be, ma'am?"

"I'm twenty-four."

"Twenty-four and *no babies*?" Clara shook her head. "Mrs. Gibbs got a potion for that kind of thing. Course, with you hiding from your man, baby potion likely ain't what you hankering for . . ."

Ignoring the question, Josephine rose. "If you'll wait here, I'll go to the mercantile and purchase some iodine and clean cloths, as well as food for you and your children. Then I'll be back shortly."

Clara nodded, pressing back into the chair as if to make herself as small as possible.

Fifteen minutes later, Josephine piled her items on the counter in the mercantile, and Mrs. Carver tallied her bill. Josephine counted out the money, grateful for the pay her bookkeeping job provided.

"Thank you for sending Clara to see—"

Mrs. Carver gave her a sharp look, then glanced at her husband across the store and gave a shake of her head. "These things," she whispered, her voice barely audible, "we keep amongst the womenfolk. Best for husbands to be kept ignorant."

Josephine nodded, struck at the dichotomy of the situation. A man created the problem by drinking, then the problem was resolved by women—behind his back. She stared at the money on the counter and saw the irony there, too. Profits from selling whiskey were being used to feed and care for those whose sustenance had been thieved by the same. A cruel irony.

"I understand," Josephine whispered back.

Her arms aching beneath the weight of the box, Josephine hurried back, trying not to act as conspicuous as she felt. Thankfully, the office was empty. She placed the second bottle of iodine and the cloths on the desk, then entered the back room.

"Clara?" she called softly.

No answer. Had the woman left? Then Clara stepped from the shadows.

"Wasn't sure you'd come back. Thought maybe you done changed your mind."

"No, it just took a few minutes." Josephine set the box on the floor. "Sit back down, if you would, and I'll tend your face. The iodine will help the cuts from getting infected. This will sting a little."

Clara didn't even wince as Josephine dabbed the brownish liquid on her wounds.

"Did this happen this morning?" Josephine asked softly.

Clara nodded. "My fault, though. I shouldn't've asked him about food money. I know better. Just forgot the day, is all."

"Forgot the day?"

Clara looked at her askance. "This being Tuesday, the money jar's long spent. But Henry gets paid tomorrow, then next week is the last week of the month. That always helps."

Josephine put the cap back on the iodine bottle. "Why does that help?"

Clara's brown eyes widened. "'Cause last Friday of the month, Uncle Jack gives everybody a free bottle. You work here and you don't know that?"

Josephine swallowed. "I bought bread, eggs, milk, and flour. There's a bottle of oil and some yeast. And a few other things I thought your children might enjoy."

Clara stared at the food. "Just like that, you giving me all this?" Her eyes narrowed. "You and me working a trade I ain't privy to?"

"No, there's no trade, Clara. You and your children are in need, and I'm grateful I can help." If she were at the women's center back in Atlanta, she could have offered Clara and her children a place to stay for a few nights, could have provided clothing and medicine. But this was the best she could do.

"Why you doing all this for me, Mrs. Dunham? We ain't kin. We don't even know each other."

"Because I know what it's like to be in need. To have nothing and to be hungry and tired, not knowing where to turn." How different her answer was now from the rehearsed response she'd given so many times before. "And also because . . ." Did she dare broach the subject? "Clara, I think it's important you know that it's not right for your husband to hit you. *Ever.* And it's certainly not your fault. Your husband—or any man—raising a hand to you is not something you should have to expect or grow accustomed to. You deserve to be treated with respect."

Clara's gaze took in Josephine's face. "Was your husband respectin' you when he did all that?"

Seeing herself through Clara's eyes, Josephine felt foolish. "No . . . he was not."

"I know you left him, ma'am, which took gumption I ain't got. But you also ain't got no babies, no mouths to feed. And even though Henry can get good and riled, 'specially after a night of drinking . . ." She gave a shrug, tears pooling in her eyes. "I love him, and he's pa to my younguns."

Josephine simply nodded and handed her the box.

"And don't you worry none, Mrs. Dunham. I got a good hidey-hole for all this. Henry won't know."

Josephine opened the storage room door—just as someone entered the office.

Clara gasped, but Josephine held up a hand. "Whoever it is," she whispered, "I'll either send them on their way or take them out front to the porch, then you leave out the back. You know where that door is?"

Clara nodded. "God bless you, ma'am," she mouthed.

Josephine walked back into the office to find Dodge writing a note at the desk. He looked up and when their eyes met, she would've sworn a current of electricity shot straight through her.

37

"Dodge . . ."

"Josephine . . ." He laid aside the pen and paper, grateful to find her here. And finally alone. Even now, just standing here, he felt the pull of her. Her beauty. Her strength. And, God help him, her stubbornness. "I was leaving you a note. I'd hoped to speak with you privately about what happened the other—"

"Why don't we step outside?" She opened the front door and motioned for him to join her, her features tense. "It's so nice out."

He glanced at the gray sky heavy with rain. "In all candor, I think this conversation is best held in private, considering—"

"Dodge, please," she whispered.

Uneasy, he followed. She closed the door behind them.

"Hey Dodge!" Peterson called as his freight wagon rolled up. "Got the salt blocks and barbed wire you ordered, sir. Want it unloaded here?"

"Take it on up to the first barn. Have one of the fellows help you."

Aware of passersby looking their way, Dodge turned back. "Josephine, I really think we should take this inside."

She glanced past him, her expression easing. "You're right. We can go back in."

Wary, he glanced in the direction she'd looked, but saw nothing out of the ordinary. Once inside, he spotted a bottle of iodine and cloths on the desk. "What's that for? Are you hurt?"

"No, I'm fine."

"Then why—"

"I thought it wise to keep some supplies on hand. For emergencies."

Hearing the lie in her voice, Dodge glanced around. Through the window, he spotted Clara Hackett hurrying down the street, clutching a box, coming from the back of the office.

He fixed Josephine in his gaze. "Remember what I told you about meddling in other people's affairs. Folks around here don't take kindly to it."

"I'm not meddling, Dodge. I'm helping."

"Same thing in their eyes."

"Not to Clara. She and her children have nothing to eat, so I—"

"So you took it upon yourself to remedy that?"

"Yes, I did. Is that such a terrible thing?"

"No, it's not. It's extremely kind. Until Henry finds out. Then there'll be the devil to pay, and you'll be the one he comes after."

"Dodge, he *beat* her this morning! All because she asked for money to buy food. She and the children have nothing to eat, because he drank it away!"

"Which, while despicable and wrong, is none of your business."

"None of my—" Her eyes flashed. "It is precisely my business. I have made it my life's goal to liberate women from the tyranny of men."

"So all men are tyrants now. Is that it?"

She hesitated. "I didn't say that."

"I think you just did."

She opened her mouth, then closed it again, her jaw firming. "Drunkenness is a crime to be punished! No woman should be bound to a man who starves his children. The vice of intemperance is—"

"Who are you quoting now? Miss Anthony? Mrs. Stanton? Mrs. Stone? I know all of them, Josephine. Kathleen quoted them, too. And look where it got her. And where else do you think Clara Hackett has to go? Her parents still have four children at home and can barely feed them. They can't take her and her children in."

"Dodge . . ." She put up a hand, her voice softening. "I'm so sorry about what happened to Kathleen. But you can't blame everything that happened in that situation on suffrage. Your sister made choices that—"

"Choices like you're making. And just like Kathleen, you have *no* idea what those choices will cost you. I'm trying to protect you, Josephine."

"I don't need protection, Dodge. I can protect myself!"

"Is that right?" He laughed beneath his breath, and she stiffened, obviously riled. "You think you can protect yourself when the Hackett brothers pay you a visit? Maybe one evening when you're walking back to Miss Mary's alone? They drag you into the woods and teach an outsider—and, in their opinion, a loudmouth, sassin' woman—a lesson in the only way men like that know how to."

Fleeting dread, even fear, flitted across her features, and Dodge almost regretted speaking so plainly. But he'd already lost his sister due, at least in part, to the illogical courage the suffrage movement nurtured in women's minds. As if women alone could change the world. There was a reason God had created men *and* women.

"I'm not trying to frighten you, Josephine. I'm just asking you to be careful. You have a good heart, and I know you mean well—"

"But you think you know best."

"In this situation? With these people? In this town? Which I've lived in my whole life? Without question, yes, I do."

"I will not turn away any woman who walks through that door needing help."

He searched her gaze, then sighed. "No, you won't. And that's what scares me. And that's not an emotion I'm accustomed to."

She looked at him good and long, much as he'd done her, and he would've sworn he felt the wall between them coming down. A softness moved into her eyes that triggered something inside him. But it was the rise and fall of her chest, and her gaze trailing to his mouth then slowly to his eyes again, that somehow dissolved the distance between them.

He took her in his arms and kissed her, tenderly at first, until she wove her arms around his neck and pulled him closer.

Her response lit a fire in him and he deepened the kiss, aware of every part of her body touching his, and of how well she fit him. He slowly traced the curve of her waist and a soft sigh escaped her that all but demolished his restraint. With determination, he finally broke the kiss and gently pulled back, his own breath coming hard.

She slowly opened her eyes, the fullness of her lips doing nothing to cool his desire.

"I'm sorry, Josephine. I—" He put distance between them. "I had no right to do that."

She lowered her gaze. "And I shouldn't have—" She made a little gesture with her hand, her meaning unmistakable. And if the liberties he'd taken hadn't been so wrong, he might've found humor in it. But as it was . . . .

"It won't happen again," he said softly. "I give you my word."

Reluctantly, she met his gaze. "No, of course not," she whispered.

He crossed to the door. "Promise me . . . you'll be careful."

Emotion pooled in her eyes, and guilt carved out another layer of his conscience.

She gave a succinct nod. "Clara said she had a good 'hidey-hole' where she could put the food where her husband won't find it."

"Let's hope she does. Because if he gets wind of it . . ."

He closed the door behind him and strode back uphill. God help him, if any man brought harm to her, he'd answer for it. She had a good heart but her courage scared him. And fear, tangled with want, was a dangerous thing.

38

THE NEXT EVENING, Josephine hurried from the distillery office toward the boarding house, hoping to arrive in time to help with pre-supper preparations—one of her duties assigned by Miss Mary. She'd stayed later at the office than planned, partly to finish ordering additional supplies for the distillery, but also because Clara Hackett had sent a friend to her.

Midday, a timid knock had sounded at the front door. The woman who stood there, little more than a shadow, was the wife of another distillery worker, desperate for food for her three children. No bruises marked her face, but her eyes bore a weight of brokenness all the same. When Josephine returned from the mercantile with the box of provisions, the woman had wept, scarcely able to meet her gaze. But watching her walk away with the food had felt like a small victory.

Another victory—one she acknowledged with far less ease—was discovering a way to halt production at the distillery. A few moments' access to the gauger's ledger would do it. The hurdle was gaining that access. Even so, she had a plan.

She held no illusion that stopping production at one distillery would spark sweeping change. But even if it forced even a handful of people to reconsider their stance on liquor, it would be worth it. Her suffragist sisters would agree.

The creak of a wagon descending from the cattle farm quickened her steps. She glanced back, hoping it wasn't Dodge—or any of the Hackett brothers. Dodge's warning had taken firm root. She would help Clara Hackett again without hesitation, but she had no desire to encounter her husband—or his kin.

Not recognizing the man driving the wagon, she rounded the corner and pressed on.

She hadn't seen Dodge since yesterday. Well, that wasn't entirely true. She'd caught a glimpse of him that morning and had vanished into the back room while he spoke with Mr. Daniel about the cattle. Still no word from Washington, and nearly half the herd gone. She'd heard the strain in his voice and felt for him. But she hadn't been ready to face him.

Embarrassed didn't begin to describe what she felt.

What had she been thinking? But that was just it, she hadn't thought. She'd simply reacted. One minute they'd been arguing, the next she'd imagined brushing her lips against his, tasting his kiss. Then she'd been in his arms, without the slightest protest.

What must he think of her? A *married* woman behaving so? And that soft sigh she'd let escape. Where had that come from? Heat flooded her body again just thinking about it.

He had to know how moved she was by him, and him having that knowledge felt like she'd somehow relinquished some unspoken balance of control between them, which was flat unnerving. Yet when he'd sworn it would never happen again, she'd felt a sense of disappointment at that prospect.

Because it wasn't only physical attraction that drew her to Dodge Coburn. It wasn't just his blue eyes or tender strength. He was a kind, caring, and intelligent man. Respected by men and women alike. Mr. Daniel regarded him almost as a son. And Bethie adored him.

Wise or not, she'd searched the library again last night, scanning books for his marginal notes. And she'd found them. The man was well-read, perceptive—far more than he let on. He'd admitted some suffrage reforms were reasonable, even if he questioned the timing. He'd called her a fighter—and meant it as praise.

But none of that changed the truth. She'd killed a man.

In self-defense, yes. But would a jury of men see it that way? Would they acquit her? She knew better. And while this quiet little town hidden in the backwoods of Tennessee was a place to hide, at least for now, she couldn't shake the feeling that even Lynchburg wasn't far enough away to evade Mayor Darden's reach.

The supper bell clanged just as she stepped inside the boarding house. She grimaced, knowing Miss Mary's stance on tardiness. She stashed her reticule—a simple handsewn wrist bag she'd purchased from Miss Ruby along with a new skirt and blouse—in the library and made a beeline for the kitchen.

"Miss Mary, I'm so sorry I'm—"

"You're *late*, Josephine. Grab the fried okra, please, then come back for the apples. Everything else should be out there. But mind yourself, those dishes have been in the oven."

"Yes, ma'am."

"Well, well now . . ." Mrs. Gibbs walked from the pantry, a jar of molasses in her hands. "Reckon punctuality ain't held in high regard where you come from. But 'round here, it still means something. Not to mention you being late adds a burden to me and Calla."

"As I said, Mrs. Gibbs, I'm sorry. The time just got away from me." Growing accustomed to the woman's occasional jabs, Josephine attempted to catch Calla's attention and failed.

A week had passed since the tea incident, and she and Calla had yet to speak of it. Meanwhile, Calla retreated more and more into herself. Concerned, Josephine wondered if being discovered was causing her to drink even more. She hoped not. She missed the ease of their friendship and playful banter in the kitchen.

But far more, she saw the evidence of Calla's pain in her eyes and in her silence.

She grabbed a cloth and carried the fried okra to the dining room, feeling the heat of Mrs. Gibbs's stare on her back. Tenants were filtering into the front hallway from their rooms, and no guests from town that she could see. She greeted each one by name and exchanged pleasantries, then returned to the kitchen.

"So you're sure you're all right, Calla?" Miss Mary asked softly. "Nothing ailing you? Other than the sadness, which I know still hurts."

Mrs. Gibbs huffed. "That, and having to do more than her share of the work because Mrs. Dunham here—"

"You've already pounded that stake into the ground, Mrs. Gibbs." Miss Mary aimed a look worthy of an old schoolmarm. "Please start filling up the tea glasses in the other room."

Brushing past Josephine, Mrs. Gibbs gave her a look that would sour milk.

"No, ma'am, I ain't ailing," Calla finally answered, her attention firmly fixed on the steaming pot atop the stove. "I'm just a bit tuckered is all."

"Well I'm still advertising for another cook." Miss Mary gave Calla's back a quick pat. "Even put an ad in the Tullahoma paper a few days back. I'll hire someone soon as I can, I promise."

"Yes, ma'am, I know. Don't you worry, I don't mind all the cooking. I can do it."

"And I'll do better at helping as well," Josephine said softly, guilt chiding her. "In fact, I'll do the dishes tonight, Calla. The pots and pans, all of it. After you eat, you go on to bed and get some rest."

Calla turned, and though it could have been the steam from the pot, Josephine would have sworn tears filled her eyes, which brought emotion to hers.

The recent distance between them had been difficult, but the hardest part of the day by far was at night when she and Calla were together in the quarters out back. Josephine had taken to turning in as soon as possible, then lying as still as she could, feigning sleep, while listening to the slow brew and whistle of the teakettle, then the telltale mixing of what she assumed to still be whiskey into Calla's tea—all the time feeling like an intruder, and knowing Calla wished she'd never offered to share her room.

Eager for this day to end, Josephine picked up the hot dish of candied apples, careful to keep a firm grip with the cloth, when the backdoor burst open.

"Miss Mary! Calla Lilly!" Bethie ran full force into the kitchen and gave each woman a hug. The girl wore loose-fitting denim overalls with a blue blouse that complemented her eyes. "What are we having for dessert tonight?"

Miss Mary brushed the blonde hair back from Bethie's face. "Calla's fixed her buttermilk pound cake with chocolate sauce."

"That's Uncle Dodge's favorite!"

Josephine looked past Bethie, hoping against hope that Dodge wasn't following, but she didn't stay to find out. She escaped into the dining room where Mr. Motlow and Mr. Parks were seated, stoic, on opposite sides of the table, Miss Livvy and Mrs. Gibbs holding the balance of conversation.

Ignoring the dark glance from Mrs. Gibbs, she listened for Dodge's voice coming from the kitchen. But, thankfully, didn't hear him.

Mr. Prince entered the dining room and took his usual seat, nodding to his fellow tenants. "How are you this fine evening, Mrs. Dunham?"

"I'm well, Mr. Prince," she managed. "How was your day, sir?"

"Most productive, madam. I'm finally wrapping up my inspection of another local distillery, which went longer than expected. I thought I discovered a possible infraction." His brows rose. "In the end, there was none, mind you. But I took the opportunity to reinforce the firm and swift arm of justice of the United States Department of the Treasury, should one have been discovered."

"As is your duty, Mr. Prince," Mrs. Gibbs chimed in, her tone stiff. "Distilleries are not above the law, after all."

"No, Mrs. Gibbs, they certainly are not. No matter how successful." With customary fastidiousness, he draped his cloth napkin on his lap. "Or how much they contribute to the federal government's coffers."

An image flashed through Josephine's mind of the reaction from Mrs. Gibbs's daughter Rowena when finding that bottle of whiskey in her order that day in the mercantile. The girl had not been pleased. Josephine had never met Mr. Gibbs, but her imagination filled in the blanks. Plus, the revenuer's comment about wrapping up another inspection explained why she hadn't seen him at the distillery since he'd stopped by a few days ago to visit with Mr. Daniel. Mr. Daniel had given him a tour of some of the buildings, but they'd never returned to the office, which all meant the review of the gauger's ledgers hadn't taken place yet.

"To that end," Mr. Prince continued, "I'll be returning to Jack Daniel's Distillery next week. Mrs. Dunham, Mr. Daniel tells me you've organized that office from top to bottom, so I assume all the paperwork will be in tip-top shape!"

The comment stabbed her conscience, and the discomfort only deepened when Mr. Daniel walked in.

"Good evening, my illustrious friends." Mr. Daniel tipped his hat to her, then placed it on a chair in the corner. "Mr. Prince, I overheard what you were saying and nothing could be closer to the truth. I daresay that office could almost run itself without me now. Mrs. Dunham has whipped it—and *me*, in particular—quite into shape."

Laughter rose as he claimed a seat, even from Josephine, but hers felt hollow inside.

"Hey Dodge!"

She froze when Mr. Daniel looked past her, and she didn't dare turn around.

"Come on in and join us for supper."

"Thanks, Uncle Jack, but I'll take my meal in the kitchen tonight. That way you can't hassle me about seconds or thirds."

More laughter, then Mr. Motlow turned in his chair. "Dodge, I haven't seen you since hearing the news about you and Bethie staying here. In a way, I was awful sorry to get wind of it. I know what the prospect of that move meant to you. To your sister, too, God rest her," he added softly. "On the other hand, I'm glad you're staying. There've been Coburns in these hills and hollers almost since the very beginning. Wouldn't be the same without you, son."

"That's kind of you to say, sir. Thank you."

"I'm assuming you're selling your land out there?" Mr. Motlow continued.

"Yes, sir. Already have it listed with an agent. But he said it could take a while."

"Well, if there's anything the bank can do to help with that, you give me a holler. I'll handle it personally."

She wondered if anyone else heard the underlying sadness in Dodge's voice, then noticed Mr. Daniel watching her. His eyes narrowed the slightest bit, then slid to Dodge before landing back on her. Josephine averted her gaze, wondering if her feelings about Dodge were so easily read.

"Dodge . . ." Mrs. Gibbs adopted a motherly demeanor. "I'd be obliged if you'd stop by in the next day or two and see to a couple of our cows. They ain't been giving milk like they ought."

"I'd be happy to, ma'am. But I just saw your husband yesterday and he made no mention of it."

"Well, that's probably 'cause he ain't been doing the milking lately. Back's been giving him trouble come morning. Or so he says." Mrs. Gibbs's laughter sounded a little too high-pitched. "I hope you liked that jar of muscadine jelly my Rowena toted over the other day. She put it up herself last fall. Don't you be in a hurry when you come, and she'll cook you up some supper 'fore you leave."

"That's not necessary, ma'am. I appreciate the offer and am happy to come out, but I won't be able to—"

"Ain't no trouble for her at all. My girl knows her way 'round a kitchen, sure as sunrise. Which is more than *some* women can say these days . . ."

As Mrs. Gibbs went on, Josephine sneaked a look at Dodge and the tightness in his expression was telling. She grabbed the opportunity to slip back into the kitchen, closing the door behind her, only to come face to face with Bethie standing by the stove as Miss Mary filled her plate.

"Are *you* eating in here, too?" A scowl replaced Bethie's earlier smile.

"Bethie." Miss Mary frowned. "You don't have to hitch your wagon to every mule, but there's no cause to start kicking at them either. Besides, Mrs. Dunham here is your senior. What would your uncle say if he heard you speaking like that?"

Bethie briefly bowed her head, but Josephine caught the side-eyed look the girl gave her—and secretly admired her honesty and spunk.

"Hello, Bethie. It's good to see you again, and no, I'm not eating in here tonight. In fact, I'm not too hungry this evening. I think I'll just—"

"You have to eat, Josephine." Miss Mary handed Bethie her food and shooed the girl toward the table, then nodded toward a stack of empty plates. "Dodge'll be joining us, too. So if everything is served out there, I'll go on in and offer thanks and get supper underway. Now fix yourself a plate, and make it a good one. You're lookin' a little peaked."

Sensing someone's attention, Josephine caught Calla looking her way. Calla held her gaze overlong before turning back to the stove, but Josephine counted that as an improvement.

Miss Mary held out a plate. "First Mrs. Gibbs, then Bethie . . . You're just making all sorts of friends in this town, aren't you?"

"It sure seems that way, doesn't it."

"Well, don't you pay it much mind." Miss Mary leaned closer. "We all know which bee is still in Miss Bethie's bonnet, and as for Mrs. Gibbs . . ." She sighed. "Lord forgive me, but I think that woman could find fault in our Lord Jesus Christ himself. Truth be known, I doubt she likes me much either. But I pay her good, so she has to act like it!"

Miss Mary gently bumped shoulders with her and the gesture was so surprising, so unexpected, that Josephine didn't know how to respond.

In recent days, Miss Mary's mood had been undeniably lighter, and it occurred to Josephine that Mr. Bobo had left three days ago on out-of-town business. Then again, the few times she'd seen them together, the snippets of conversation she'd overheard from the couple had been anything but contentious. She'd even caught them laughing together more than once.

"Thank you, Miss Mary," she finally whispered.

"For what exactly?"

Josephine looked around. "For all of this. I don't know where I'd be if you hadn't said yes to me staying here that first night."

Miss Mary's expression grew thoughtful. "We all got our story, don't we? Chapters we don't want read aloud, and other parts we pray to God nobody ever reads at all. But the thing is . . . he reads them, every page, every word, and loves us anyway. Whatever it is you're carrying, Josephine, remember that." Her features sobered. "While also remembering you gave me your solemn word you wouldn't bring trouble to my doorstep. I aim to hold you to that."

Both goodwill and tempered steel shone in the woman's gaze. "I know," Josephine whispered again. "And I aim to keep that promise. No matter what."

Miss Mary nodded as if the deal were done, then pressed a hand to her midsection, a shadow flitting across her face. "That bit of okra I sneaked earlier isn't setting too well." She exhaled. "But I best get out there and tend to our guests. Make sure Mr. Motlow and Mr. Parks aren't about to come to blows."

Josephine dished a spoonful of candied apples, fried okra, and pinto beans from the pots and pans on the stove onto her plate, but passed over the roasted pork, carrots, and potatoes. She pulled a warm yeast roll from the pan, the butter Calla had slathered on the top slicking her fingertips.

"If you call that supper, I might need to teach you a thing or two about eating here at Miss Mary's."

She briefly clenched her eyes before turning to face the inevitable. Dodge's smile held humor, kindness, and a trace of something else. Apology, perhaps?

"I'm just not that hungry tonight, I guess. I think I'll take my plate back to Calla's room."

"We're going to have to see each other, Josephine," he said softly. "Might as well stop avoiding the unavoidable. Namely . . . me."

"I'm not avoiding you, I—"

A sense of knowing moved into his gaze. "The backroom? This morning?"

Her mouth slipped open. "You saw me?"

"Through the window. You're going to have to move faster than that next time. Either that or keep the curtains in the office closed."

She briefly bowed her head, then decided if he could face it directly then so could she. "If I keep the curtains closed then I won't be able to see you coming."

He laughed. "Well played."

"Dodge . . ." She paused, her gaze fixed on the stove. "I don't know what possessed me to—"

"I take full responsibility, Josephine." The words, so softly spoken, held such certainty, such conviction and, for some unexplained reason, swept her back to that moment yesterday. While he was right in one sense—she would never have acted on what she'd been imagining—she also knew he didn't bear sole responsibility.

"It wasn't your fault alone," she whispered, still not looking at him, unable to. Already suspecting he didn't believe she was married, she guessed her actions yesterday pretty much confirmed it in his mind. Still, she determined to keep up the pretense.

Seconds ticked past, and he finally reached for a plate. "So . . . let an expert show you what eating at Miss Mary's really looks like." He started piling food onto his plate, and she couldn't help but smile.

He motioned to the table where Calla and Bethie sat eating. "After you."

She shook her head. "I think it might be best for me to eat elsewhere. Bethie's still upset at me, and I can't say that I blame her."

"Nonsense. She'll be fine."

"Dodge, I—"

"Kathleen always taught her to face things head-on, and she made me promise to teach her the same. So—" He nodded toward the table. "Please, after you."

Josephine carried her plate to the table and sat by Calla, across from Bethie.

Bethie looked up. "Thought you said you weren't going to eat in here."

Josephine saw Dodge about to respond. "I changed my mind," she said quickly, the memory of a woman she'd never met, but that Dodge had made a promise to, giving her gumption she lacked on her own at the moment. "Besides, Calla and I usually eat in here together. It's one of the highlights of my day." She caught Calla's gaze and smiled.

Calla's eyes returned it even if the rest of her features didn't. But again, progress.

"So are you planning to stay here forever?"

"Bethie." Dodge looked beside him at his niece. "Respectful and appropriate questions are always fine, but you need to rephrase that one. And address her properly, as Mrs. Dunham."

Josephine was fairly certain the girl held back an eye roll, settling for a droll look instead.

"Mrs. Dunham . . ." Bethie's tone sounded faintly like that of someone thrice her age. "Do you plan on staying here in Lynchburg for an extended period of time?"

"Thank you for the question, Bethie. And no, actually, I don't." Dodge didn't look at her, but she sensed a reaction from him anyway. It occurred to her then—especially considering how attracted she was to him—that Dodge believing not only that she was married, but that she would be leaving soon, actually worked in her favor. "I don't know when I'll be leaving yet exactly, I only know that I will be. Probably sooner rather than later."

Bethie finished chewing then swallowed. "Do you think you're going to have scars?"

Dodge paused from eating. "Bethie, some questions aren't—"

"No, that's all right. I don't mind answering. Yes, Bethie, I think I will. However, Calla's salve is helping a lot." She started to say "working wonders" but feared Bethie would disagree, then Dodge would have to interject again. "So maybe the scars won't be as bad as I was anticipating."

Bethie took the last bite of her apples, and Josephine could all but feel the girl's wheels spinning. How she wished she could have had Bethie Coburn in class. How rewarding to have had a hand in helping to shape such a bold, courageous spirit. And she would have liked to have known Kathleen Coburn as well. She was certain they would have been friends.

"Sure am sorry about your cattle, Dodge," Calla said after a moment. "Heard people talking about it when I was in town a few days back. Sounds real bad."

"Thanks, Calla, it is. We stand to lose them all if we don't hear something from DC soon."

The hum of conversation from the next room drifted in to help fill the silence.

"Calla . . ." Dodge held up a forkful of candied apples and admired them. "These are delicious."

Her eyes warmed. "You always say that."

"That's because it's true." He elbowed Bethie. "I just have to get back over there for seconds before Bethie does."

Apparently taking that as her cue, Bethie tried to stand. But Dodge, his attention on his plate and still eating as if paying her no mind, firmly held the back of her overalls. A smile touched the girl's mouth as she struggled all the more to stand.

"Uncle Dodge!"

"What?" He looked over, letting go as he did. "Oh, were your straps caught on the back of the chair again?"

She eyed him. "They were caught in your fist again is what they were."

He held up his hands. "Couldn't have been me. My hands are right here."

With a grin, she shook her head, got seconds on apples and returned. "So are we still going shooting on Sunday?"

Dodge nodded. "You bet we are."

"And you'll bring the Winchester this time?" Bethie asked, doubt in her voice.

"I said I would, and I will."

"Shooting?" Josephine looked between them. "You're taking your nine-year-old niece shooting?"

Dodge and Bethie both paused mid-chew. Josephine even felt Calla looking her way.

"Yes, ma'am." Dodge got a look on his face that she was beginning to recognize—one that said he was both aware of her disapproval and also wholeheartedly welcomed whatever was coming next.

39

Bethie's eyes, so much like her uncle's, narrowed. "You *do* know how to shoot, don't you, Mrs. Dunham?"

Josephine looked down at her plate. Her first inclination was to say she was born and raised in Atlanta, Georgia, not the wild, wild west. But she couldn't say that without revealing more than desired. "No. In fact, I do not know how to shoot. I've never had opportunity to learn, so have not acquired that particular skill."

"But Uncle Dodge says all women ought to know how to shoot. Ain't that right, Uncle Dodge?"

"*Isn't* that right." He nodded. "And yes, that is what I say. I believe every woman should know how to defend herself . . . should the situation arise."

Keenly aware of the lingering physical reminders of Clay Darden, Josephine knew what Dodge was thinking—that she'd already been in just such a situation and hadn't been able to defend herself. Likely, Bethie and Calla were thinking the same. "I'm not saying that using a gun for self-defense is wrong, Dodge. I simply—"

"So you've never shot a gun before?" Bethie asked, an almost hopeful quality slipping into her voice.

Reading a similar question in Dodge's expression, Josephine placed her fork by her plate. "No, I have never shot a gun."

Bethie stared. "No birthing cows? No shooting a gun? For being a teacher, you sure seem to have a lot left to learn, Mrs. Dunham." Not a trace of sarcasm laced the girl's voice.

Bethie leaned over and whispered something to Dodge, and the edges of his mouth pushed into a reluctant smile. Josephine was certain the child was finding pleasure in her lack of experience.

When Bethie straightened, a mischievous gleam lit her eyes. "Mrs. Dunham, I'm inviting you to go shooting with me and my Uncle Dodge this Sunday afternoon."

Caught off guard by the girl's invitation, Josephine clearly saw it for what it was. A chance to show her up. To put her in her place, as it were. And yet . . .

Before the suffragist rally, before her life had changed so drastically, she had tried—despite her doubts—to embrace the virtues of peaceful protest over aggression while citing Miss Anthony's unwavering "Firm, not forceful" stance. She'd read all about Miss Anthony famously voting illegally in 1872 then being arrested for it, found guilty, and yet refusing to pay the fine. Miss Anthony's act of civil disobedience had been intentional, peaceful, and designed to challenge the absurdity of unjust laws through public scrutiny, not through force.

But remembering Clay Darden dragging her into the alley and recalling what she'd done, Josephine knew that if that brick had been a gun, she would have used it. If she'd known how.

"I appreciate the invitation, Bethie. And gladly accept." She read pleasure in the girl's expression. "But I'm counting on you to teach me. To show me how it's done."

Bethie grinned. "Oh don't you worry, Mrs. Dunham. I will."

The next morning, Josephine awakened before dawn to the sound of crying. She'd gone to bed late after washing and drying all the dishes, pots and pans, and putting everything away. By the time she had fallen into bed, Calla had been asleep. But clearly wasn't anymore.

Josephine slipped from her cot and padded across the cool wooden floor to where Calla lay facing the wall. Moonlight shone pale and silvery through the thin curtain covering the window.

"Calla," she whispered, gently touching her shoulder. "Can we please talk about what happened?"

Calla's hand covered hers. "I'm gonna tell her," she said quickly. "I promise I will. I just need time to find another place, 'cause she gonna throw me out for sure."

"That's not what I meant. I was going to say that I'm so sorry for whatever happened that caused you to start drinking. And I won't tell Miss Mary, I promise. But please, I want to help you if I can."

Calla gradually turned over, wiping her eyes, the faint scent of soured whiskey on her breath. "You a kind woman, Josephine. But there ain't nothing you or anybody else can do. 'Less you can bring back the dead."

Josephine's heart squeezed tight, having wondered if that was it. "Who was it you lost, Calla?"

"Oh they aren't lost. I know right where my husband and son are, both of them. They're with Jesus, but that almost makes it worse. That the Lord just stood by and let it happen when he could've stopped that wagon from going over."

Josephine held tightly to Calla's hand as her own chest ached. "How long ago did it happen?" she whispered.

"Four years back now. The world just went right on spinning but every day, especially at night when the darkness moves in close like, I'm back in that field, trying with everything in me to pull them both from underneath that wagon. But I can't. Just like I couldn't that day four years ago." She covered her face with her hands. "They say the axle snapped clean through, then the mules must've spooked. Wagon, loaded full, rolled on top of them both. By the time I found them, there weren't no life left in either of their bodies. Trouble is, they took my life with them, Josephine. I'd give anything if I could've died that day, too. I've asked the Lord Jesus to take me. But he won't. I've even had the thought to—" She shook her head. "I can't even say the words."

But she didn't have to. And Josephine wept with her. She laid her head beside Calla's on the pillow, and for the longest time, neither of them spoke.

Finally, Calla sighed. "I tried everything I know to stop the drinking and ain't nothing worked. I'm gonna lose my place here 'long with the only shred of family I got left in this world."

Josephine squeezed her hand. "You're not going to lose your place here, Calla. Miss Mary loves you, that's plain to see."

"You ain't seen her when she finds out a tenant been drinking in her home. She takes their belongings and casts it all to the street! Only day she allows a touch of liquor is on Christmas. In the eggnog. But every other day—" She made a slashing gesture in the air with her hand. "You gone in no time."

Josephine wanted to reassure Calla that Miss Mary wouldn't cast her out. That she would give her another chance. But she honestly didn't know. Just like she didn't know whether Miss Mary would send her packing once she discovered the chapter Josephine hoped no one would ever read.

40

The cow didn't try to rise when Dodge stepped into the stall. Her labored breathing, sunken eyes, and fever-twitching body told him all he needed to know. He knelt beside her, Remington in hand.

"It's not your fault, girl. I'm sorry it's come to this." He smoothed a gloved hand over her forehead and down her nose. Though she'd calved twice, there was still youth to her face, as if she hadn't yet learned the weight of the world. "But you feel it now, don't you? Down deep."

She shuddered, and he exhaled, hating this part of the life he'd chosen. But every life carried moments like this—maybe not with a rifle in hand, but with decisions that clawed at a man's gut. Crossroads you wished had never landed at your door.

He was learning those reckonings weren't rare interruptions. They were woven clean through a man's days. Part of the fabric. And it took both joy and pain to make a full life.

Kathleen had been right. The more you care, the more you hurt. No way around it.

"When you give your heart to someone like I've given mine to Bethie," she'd said on her deathbed, "it feels like part of you starts living inside them." Tears had slipped down her temples. "You want to protect them, but you can't. Not from everything. And that wanting to shield them from the bad things, without the power to stop the hurt . . . it rips at something inside you." She'd managed a ghost of that sassy smile she'd given him almost before she could walk. "You'll do good by her, Dodge. I *know* you will. But you're going to have to trust her to God. I wished I'd learned that earlier on. You won't always be able to be there. But he will. Just like he was for me, even when I did wrong. And just like he still is." She'd breathed her last a few hours later.

Dodge rose, blinking hard, grateful for the memory and weary of how it still cut so deep.

He looked at the suffering animal and wished—foolishly—for a cure. Some way to stop this. His father's counsel returned from across the years. *Animals are a gift, son. They feed us, work beside us, help us provide for our families, then one day they'll help carry us to our resting place. Treat them with respect, like God himself placed them in your care. Because he did.*

Holding that treasured guidance foremost in his mind, he took careful aim—and a single shot rang out. As he left the barn, farmhands entered, no words exchanged. He'd done his difficult job, now they would do theirs.

As he walked back to the cabin, patches of blue sky peeked through tufts of gray clouds, and he figured rain was coming, probably later rather than sooner. Either way, they'd likely get a good downpour before they got back from shooting this afternoon.

He'd seen Josephine briefly at church—and had done a fairly good job of not staring at her from two rows back. While he wouldn't say she'd seemed excited about going shooting with them this afternoon, she hadn't backed out. Which would have saddened Bethie. But only because Bethie wanted to show a *citified woman* a thing or two about real life, as Bethie had said. Even if the shooting didn't pan out, the afternoon promised to hold fireworks.

He spotted Bethie seated on the front steps of the cabin, arms wrapped around her knees. Jessie lay close beside her. The cattle dog's ears perked up when she saw him, but she stayed right by Bethie as he'd commanded a while earlier. At least one female in his life heeded what he said.

As he drew closer, Bethie's gaze dropped to the rifle in his hand. "Don't bring that one today."

Hearing what she wasn't saying, he shook his head. "I won't."

He could tell she'd been crying but knew better than to ask. She, like her mama, would tell him when she was good and ready. Until then, he just laid the rifle on the porch and sat down beside her, like he'd done with his sister so many times through the years. And in this very same spot.

A long moment passed.

Bethie sniffed, sat a little straighter. "You ever think about Mama?"

"All the time."

"Yeah, me too. But—" Her voice caught. She swallowed hard, her little jaw working hard as she held back the sadness. "Straight shooter?" she whispered.

"Straight shooter," he answered, loving this girl with a fierceness he couldn't find words for. He only knew that if anyone ever tried to hurt her, he'd use full force to stop them. Either that, or take her place if it came to it.

"I wish we were still leaving here, Uncle Dodge."

"Honey, I know you do. And so do I. But I've explained why the two of us can't—"

"No, I'm not saying it because of why you're thinking. I mean, I still would've liked to have seen those mountains you talked about, and the rivers so clear you can see almost to the bottom. What I mean is . . ." She shook her head. Her face scrunched up. "It feels wrong thinking this, much less to give it voice, but . . . I still see Mama everywhere around here. No matter where I look, she's standing there, or sitting over there in the swing, or washing dishes at the sink, or walking back from the barn. Only . . . she's not. And she never will be again."

She bowed her head and—just like her mother, who never liked for people to see her cry—fought to hold it in. And did. Until he reached over and drew her close. She wrapped her arms around him and wept into his chest. He pulled her closer and kissed the crown of her head as he'd done since the day she was born.

She drew a shaky breath and leaned into him even more.

How had he missed that she'd been struggling with this, too? With seeing Kathleen everywhere. He knew she was hurting. She'd lost her mother, after all. But in his own disappointment of not going to Wyoming, it had never occurred to him that part of her grieving the loss of that move was that staying here in Lynchburg meant living with the constant reminders that the most important person in the world to her was never coming back.

Not that moving would have solved everything. Not by any means. But a change of pace would have done her good. Him, too.

Sighing, he kissed her head again. "It's not wrong for you to feel this way, Bethie. Or to have those thoughts."

"Sure feels like it. Feels like, if she could know what I'm thinking, she'd reckon I don't love her anymore."

She shuddered as fresh tears came.

"Come here, sweetie." He pulled her into his lap. A couple of workers walking by the cabin looked over then changed course, giving them a wider berth. "Honey, I don't know everything about the hereafter but I do know this . . . That Bible in there on the table beside the fireplace . . . the one she always read to you from?"

Bethie nodded even as he realized that was an area he'd fallen short in, both in his vow to Kathleen and in his care of Bethie, and he determined right then to change that. To read from it with her like his sister had done.

"God says in there that we'll be with him when we die. So your mama is with Jesus. There's no doubt about that. And I firmly believe that people who have trusted him and then have passed on into the next life . . . they see things more clearly from that side than we do from ours. So don't you worry one whit about your mama thinking you don't love her because you wish you could stop hurting from missing her so badly. She understands that, Bethie. Nobody likes to hurt, honey. And it's natural to want the pain to stop. But there's no getting around it." A sad smile came to him. "Sometimes we have to go through a storm to get to the sunshine."

She pulled away slightly and peered up. "Mama always said that."

"Yes, she did. And she was right."

Bethie didn't say anything for a minute, then leaned close again. "Do you think we'll stay here forever, Uncle Dodge?"

The sadness in her voice tugged at him and his eyes watered. He looked toward the hills in the near distance, wishing he knew the answer to that question. Because, in all honesty, he asked that same question, too. He wished the two of them could start over again somewhere. Far away from the memories. A place where Bethie wouldn't be raised smack dab in the middle of a distillery. Where she wouldn't be reminded at every turn that her mother was never coming back.

He was grateful for his job and that word was spreading about Uncle Jack's Old No. 7, and that the business was growing, but there was still a restlessness in him. And he feared there always would be.

Bethie had asked a similar question of Josephine last night, however inappropriately phrased the first time, and he thought of Josephine's answer. She hadn't hesitated to say no, that she wouldn't be staying in Lynchburg forever, as though she already had a plan in place to leave. That news saddened him.

Feeling Bethie's attention, he gave her a little hug. "I don't know if we'll stay here forever, sweetie. But would staying here be such a bad thing? I mean, we have a good life here, right?"

"Yeah, we do," she finally said, her hollow tone reflecting his own melancholy.

Hoping their outing would cheer her up, he rose. "You about ready to go? I told Mrs. Dunham we'd pick her up around now."

"Just let me grab my .22 and my satchel. And some of the jerky in case we get hungry."

"Get your jacket too. Looks like rain."

Dodge had loaded things up earlier and noticed Jessie seated on the wagon bench, panting and watching his every move. "Don't worry, girl. You're going."

She barked and wagged her tail.

Bethie hurried back out. "Okay, I'm ready!"

Dodge took the rifle, satchel, and bag of jerky from her. Then stared.

"What?"

"Your jacket?"

"I couldn't find it. But I'll be fine."

Dodge didn't move.

She huffed a sigh that—had he not known how badly she was hurting inside—he would've corrected. As it was, he let it go, and she trudged back upstairs into the cabin.

Jessie whined, her focus on the bag of jerky. Dodge gave her head a rub and pulled out a piece. He bit some off and tossed it to her. She went for it and missed—a rare occurrence—and it fell beneath the bench. Jessie started to jump down to get it but Bethie's satchel and gun blocked her way.

"Okay, girl, we don't let good jerky go to waste. Not when it's got Old No. 7 baked in." He climbed up and moved Bethie's satchel and rifle to the back bed then leaned down. He'd made a fresh batch of jerky a few days ago, and he never ate it now but what he didn't think about Josephine and that trip with her from Tullahoma.

And she'd recently asked him for the recipe. If the woman only knew . . .

He felt around for the piece of jerky, couldn't find it, so finally peered beneath the seat. Something shiny between two floorboards caught his eye. He got down on his knees for a better look. Seeing the bit of meat, he fed it to Jessie, then tried to pry the object free.

Finally, with the help of his pocketknife, it flicked right out. And he couldn't believe his eyes.

41

He studied the thin silver wedding band between his thumb and forefinger, feeling gut punched and realizing with no small disappointment that whatever details Josephine Dunham was holding back about her life, she'd been telling the truth about being married.

A sliver of sun managed to cut through the gray cloud cover and shone on the worn silver band, lending it a sparkle. Struggling with this discovery, weighing how to handle it, he started to put the ring in his pocket when he thought he noticed engraving on the inside of the band. He tilted it toward the light, and squinted, the words worn in places.

"Two are better than one," he read softly, slowly turning the ring, and he again recalled Josephine's response to Bethie's question about leaving town. Yes, Josephine apparently was married and yes, her husband had apparently beaten her. That was beyond acceptable to anyone with morals. But maybe she'd somehow started missing him, however cruel he'd been. Maybe she'd chosen to forgive him and go back to him.

The mere thought soured his stomach.

He released a pent-up breath, the disappointment in him hardening into something akin to anger. He'd foolishly allowed himself to start caring for her in a way he never should have. And the liberties he'd taken . . . He'd acted wrongly toward her in so many ways.

Wishing Bethie had never invited her along today, he slipped the ring into the deep side pocket of his dungarees when he spotted Uncle Jack topping the hill. Uncle Jack waved and Dodge returned the gesture, shoving down the roil of emotion inside him.

"Welcome home, Uncle Jack! How was your trip? Or should I say . . . your visit?"

"It was good. Good to go. Good to come back." Uncle Jack approached the wagon and reached up to the bench to give Jessie a rub.

"Good thinking time on the train, too. Something about those rails passing so quick-like beneath you, the blur of the countryside . . . reminds a man of just how quickly time is passing."

Dodge watched him, then managed a smile. "Wait a minute . . . Don't tell me this visit with whoever it was finally brought you around to the idea of marriage."

Uncle Jack chuckled. "I do enjoy a lady's fine company, but marriage? That's a bit like buying the orchard when you really just want a bite of fruit every now and then."

Dodge shook his head. "You and your sayings about women."

"I've just never met one I've wanted to marry. Leastwise . . . one that was available."

Dodge eyed him, a stab of guilt prodding his conscience. The statement was a little too close to home. He forced a laugh. "Now *that* sounds like a dog that'll hunt."

A smile ghosted Uncle Jack's expression, then his features turned somber. "What if I were to tell you I was thinking of stepping back from running the distillery. Give it to my nephews Lem and Dick. What would you say?"

Dodge stared. "That you'd been tasting a bit too much of the product lately."

They both laughed, but Uncle Jack held his gaze.

"You're serious," Dodge said softly.

"I'm just thinking about it. I'm getting older, Dodge. I've done this near my whole life. Close on to fifty years if you go back to when I first went to live with Dan and Mary Jane Call, and got my first up close lesson about running a still." His expression turned reminiscent. "I stopped going to school early on, but that Miss Mary Jane, she made sure I got my education. She was persistent on that, and I'm grateful for it. Those were good times . . . Living with them, being with Nearest and his family. Nearest and Dan were good men, both of them. First time I ever felt like I really belonged somewhere. Or leastwise, was wanted."

Dodge knew about Uncle Jack's early life, about his mother dying not long after he was born, and his father remarrying. But it was Uncle Nearest who had really put flesh on the bones of Jack's early days, who had told him about how Jack and his stepmother hadn't gotten on, and how Jack—the youngest of ten children and always the smallest—had finally left home at the age of six.

"Those two men taught me far more about life than they even did about making whiskey," Uncle Jack continued. "But they certainly did that, too. I wouldn't be who I am today, nor would I have what I have without them." He gave a quick shake of his head as if to shrug off the memories. "The distillery is growing fast, Dodge. After all, we got the best whiskey around." He winked. "And I've got more money than I'll ever need. I'm not saying the time is right for me to step back at present, but I do think it's coming. And I just wanted you to know."

"I appreciate that, but . . ." Dodge still couldn't wrap his mind around the prospect of Jack Daniel not being at the helm. "You've said this to me before, but I say it back with far more weight . . . This place will not be the same without you."

"Just because I'm stepping back doesn't mean I'm thinking of dying anytime soon."

Dodge laughed along with him.

"I plan on being here for years to come, so I'll be around. Who knows, they still might let me do some tasting every now and then. But what about you, son? What are your plans?"

"What do you mean?"

Something about the way Uncle Jack watched him caused him to think the man knew something he didn't.

"What about your land out west? Got a buyer yet?"

"No. But it'll come. At least that's what I keep telling myself."

"So you're still thinking there's no way you and Bethie can go. Nothing recent that's changed that decision."

Dodge shook his head. "That door has closed. Looks like we'll be here for the duration." He had attempted a positive tone but it came out accepting at best, and he hoped Uncle Jack didn't think him ungrateful. Eager to change the subject, he gave him a brief update on the cattle. "So I'm sorry to say there's been no improvement since you left."

"I figured as much." Uncle Jack stroked his beard. "So while I was in Nashville, I took the opportunity to send a telegram to Washington,

DC, asking for the powers that be to prioritize this. I warned them how quickly it's spreading."

"If anyone can get their attention, Uncle Jack, it's you."

"Well, we'll see. Speaking of which, Mr. Prince will be giving the distillery his undivided attention this week. And my recent visit with him promises the man will be in rare form."

Dodge laughed. "Is he ever in anything else?"

"Is the gauger's book ready for inspection?"

"It is. I looked everything over yesterday and put it back in the safe."

"Good man. I'm sure the inspection will go well. It always does. I—"

The cabin door opened. "Uncle Jack!"

"Hey there, sweet girl!" Uncle Jack called out as Bethie raced down the stairs to him. He gave her a quick hug then chucked her beneath the chin, much as he'd done Kathleen when she'd been that age.

"We're going shooting, Uncle Jack!" She scrambled up to the wagon seat. "Want to go with us?"

"I'd better not today, Miss Bethie. Besides, I haven't done much shooting lately. I'm afraid you'd show me up!"

Bethie beamed. "Mrs. *Citified* is going with us." She lifted her nose in the air, pretending to be a hoity-toity lady.

Uncle Jack turned to Dodge for translation.

"Mrs. Dunham," Dodge supplied and slid Bethie a look that said that was enough on that subject.

"Ah . . ." Uncle Jack nodded slowly. "And just how did that invitation come about? Mrs. Dunham doesn't strike me as a woman who would be familiar with that subject."

"Oh, she's not, Uncle Jack," Bethie said quickly. "She doesn't know the first thing about shooting. That's why I asked her to go." Bethie glanced at Dodge as though to say she knew she was walking a fine line. "She's a teacher, after all, so I figured I'd learn her some things."

"*Teach* her some things," Dodge corrected. "And remember what we talked about."

"I know. I'll be *respectful*." But the mischief in Bethie's eyes indicated that might be a struggle.

"Well, you three have a good time and don't be surprised, Bethie, if

Mrs. Dunham catches on faster than you think she will. She's a mighty smart—and surprising—woman." Uncle Jack looked pointedly at Dodge. "But I'm thinking we all know that by now," he said beneath his breath and headed back toward the office.

Again Dodge sensed the man was hinting at something he should know, but didn't. Or worse, that Uncle Jack had somehow learned about what happened between him and Josephine in the office, and was discreetly chastising him for it. Either way, the guilt already knifing him grew a double blade then did a full quarter turn.

Minutes later, as he guided the wagon up the street to the boarding house, the wedding ring burning a hole in his pants pocket, he hoped Josephine had changed her mind about going with them. Then he caught sight of her.

She was sweeping the front porch, and Miss Mary was seated in one of the rockers watching her. Miss Mary leaned up and pointed toward an area Josephine had just swept, but apparently she'd missed something. Without hesitation, Josephine quickly swept that part of the porch again, then glanced back to see Miss Mary nodding in her typical plain-dealing fashion.

"Whoa, mules." He pulled back on the reins, and Josephine looked up.

She smiled and waved, and a futile thought flashed across his mind. He wished he'd met her first, years back, before her husband, before she'd married, and that he could've taken her west with him, along with Kathleen and Bethie. What a life they would have had together, the four of them. Even if, knowing those three females, the West would have never been the same.

42

"ALWAYS FIGURE THE RIFLE IS LOADED," Bethie said, her voice authoritative. "Because it probably is. Treat it with respect. Never, *ever* point it at anything unless you have a mind to shoot it. And today that means pointing it at me or Uncle Dodge. Or Jessie!"

The dog's ears perked up from where she lay near Dodge as he leaned against the wagon, arms crossed, Stetson pulled low, simply watching.

Sitting on a tree stump and cradling Bethie's rifle, Josephine nodded dutifully, fully aware of how much the girl—standing right in front of her, like a teacher instructing a class—was enjoying telling her what to do.

They'd driven some distance from town to a tree-lined clearing Dodge and Bethie knew well, and the area was lovely. Wildflowers in full bloom swayed with the breeze, and the trickle of a creek whispered nearby.

"And one of the most important things," Bethie continued, "is to keep your finger *off* the trigger until you're ready to let a bullet fly. Else you might kill us all!"

Josephine double-checked. "My finger isn't on the trigger."

"I know, I'm just saying it shouldn't be."

From her peripheral vision, Josephine saw Dodge shake his head. She caught his mouthed "I'm sorry" and waved it off. If he only knew how much she admired Bethie's spunk and how she wished she'd possessed half as much at that age.

Some might have called Bethie bossy or insolent. But Josephine, having taught truly insolent students, and knowing Bethie Coburn's story better than the girl realized, saw it differently. This was a grudge lingering from the incident with her mother's clothing. But more than that, it was a child grasping for control when the rest of her world felt like it was careening downhill.

Josephine knew that feeling well. But she was twenty-four to Bethie's nine, and her heart went out to the girl. When Todd had been killed, then her parents died months later, she'd felt just as lost. Without Sarah—and her students—she didn't know how she would have endured it.

So even as Dodge looked at her with apology, she had all the patience in the world. Bethie was actually a good teacher. Clear, concise, holding eye contact better than most adults Josephine knew. Bethie Coburn wasn't merely a diamond in the rough, she was a rare jewel, and Josephine felt a stir of grief imagining the heartbreak Kathleen Coburn must have experienced departing this world and leaving her precious, incredible daughter behind.

"Are you listening to me, Mrs. Dunham?"

Josephine snapped back. "Yes, Bethie. Of course."

The girl cocked a brow. "Then what did I just say?"

Josephine hid a grin and retraced her steps. "I'm to lean into the rifle. And since I'm right-handed, my left foot goes slightly forward."

Bethie gave a grudging nod. "That's mostly it. This here's my gun. It's a Winchester 1903 .22 caliber semiautomatic. Means you can shoot it without reloading."

Josephine already knew that, thanks to Todd, but simply nodded. Todd had held more than a passing interest in guns, though their father forbade anything to do with them. That hadn't stopped Todd.

"I've already got it loaded." Bethie pointed. "Magazine's in the buttstock. Holds ten cartridges. They just slide right in altogether. That's about it on the gun."

Sensing the end of their lesson, Josephine started to stand.

"Hang on." Bethie held up a hand. "Why don't you let me show you how to do it first?" She walked toward where Dodge had set tin cans along the top of a fence in the distance, paused, and tucked the rifle into her right shoulder, cheek resting easy against the stock. Her movements were smooth, practiced. "Let your eyes move on down the barrel to your sights. Take your time, get a good aim."

The shot cracked. Josephine jumped a little, grateful Bethie wasn't looking. A sharp *ping* followed and a tin can went sailing.

"Good eye, Bethie girl," Dodge said, pride threading his tone.

Cheeks flushed, Bethie handed the rifle back. "Just remember, don't lock up. Stand easy but strong, like you belong out here. Which, of course, *you* don't, but . . ."

Except for that last comment, Josephine heard the clear echo of Dodge's counsel in Bethie's instructions. And the way the girl beamed up at him told her she was likely repeating what he'd said when first teaching her to shoot.

Dodge stepped closer. "That's good teaching, Bethie, but I think it's time for Mrs. Dunham to—"

"Sink or swim!" The grin on Bethie's face revealed her preference.

"I was about to say 'try it herself.' I could be wrong, but Mrs. Dunham doesn't strike me as the sinking kind."

"I don't know . . ." Josephine slid Bethie a look. "There's a chance I'll sink. But you *are* a good teacher."

Bethie just stared back, saying nothing.

"All right, Mrs. Dunham, come stand over here."

Rifle in hand, Josephine did as he asked, certain now the difference she'd sensed in Dodge when she'd climbed into the wagon nearly a half hour ago wasn't imagined. At first, she'd thought it was simply the formality he adopted around Bethie, which she understood—and returned. But it was definitely more than that.

"Take your time," he whispered, giving her room. "It's not a race."

"Unless a cougar's coming at you," Bethie said. "Then time is one thing you ain't got!"

"You *haven't* got," Dodge corrected. "And you know good and well cougars haven't been sighted in these hills for years. Leave Mrs. Dunham be and let her get her first shot off without—"

Josephine took a breath and slowly exhaled—exactly as she'd read yesterday in *A Course of Instruction in Rifle Firing* by Colonel T. T. S. Laidley in the library, Dodge's margin notes fresh in her mind—and squeezed the trigger.

Time stilled. Then *ping.* A can went flying!

It was all she could do not to jump and shout. Instead she turned, heart pounding, to see disbelief on both their faces.

"You've done this before!" Bethie accused.

"I promise, I haven't. But your excellent instruction . . . and Mr. Coburn's notes in the margins of Colonel Laidley's book helped me immensely."

A hesitant smile tipped Dodge's mouth, tugging her thoughts in a direction they had no business going. She looked away.

"Try it again!" Bethie pointed toward the fence.

"Bethie, don't be rude. Mrs. Dunham hit that fair and square. Who knows, maybe she's a natural like you are."

"I don't think so, Uncle Dodge. I think it was luck!"

Bethie stared from Josephine to the cans and back, and Josephine, not at all certain she *could* hit another can, turned back around, took aim and fired. And missed.

"*See?* I told you it was luck! She can't—"

Josephine trained the rifle's sight on the next tin can and fired. It went flying, and Bethie went quiet. The exhilaration of shooting, the feel of the weapon in her grip, and having actually hit *two* of three cans gave her surprising confidence. She glanced at Bethie whose raised brow was clearly a dare to try again, when Jessie started barking.

Josephine turned, expecting to see the dog having spotted a squirrel or even a butterfly. But Jessie stood rigid, hackles raised, staring into the brush. And that's when Josephine heard it.

Deep, guttural grunts. Dry leaves crunching underfoot.

"Bethie, Josephine," Dodge said low. "Get to the wagon!"

They turned to go, but the grunting and snorting sounded again. This time coming from a different direction, louder and closer. Jessie ran toward it, barking.

"Jessie! Come!"

The dog looked back at Dodge, then at the grass near the wagon as it began to stir.

Bethie grabbed the rifle from Josephine and took aim.

"No, Bethie! Your .22 won't stop it. Both of you get to a tree. Run!"

Bethie took off. Josephine followed as snorts and pounding hooves tore through the thicket, feral squeals making her skin crawl.

"Can you climb?" Bethie yelled.

"With the best of them!" Josephine answered, spotting a low-limbed oak. "I'll help you up!"

"I don't need your help!"

In a flash, Bethie scaled a low oak limb, somehow still clutching the rifle. Josephine, skirts hiked, scrambled up beside her—when Bethie slipped and fell, hitting the ground hard, the rifle skidding away.

"Bethie!" Josephine jumped down just as the wild boar burst through the brush a few yards away, tusks flashing.

"Get up there!" Dodge yelled.

Bethie cradled her right arm. "I can't climb up!"

"Oh yes, you can!" Josephine picked her up and shoved her onto the branch. Thin as Bethie was, the girl's weight still proved a challenge. Muscles burning, Josephine hauled herself up just as the crack of a rifle—and Bethie's scream—split the air.

43

A SECOND RIFLE SHOT EXPLODED, and Josephine looked down to see the boar jolt then stumble. Its front legs buckled, and its massive body skidded toward the base of the tree in a spray of dirt and dried leaves. Right where Bethie had fallen.

One last defeated grunt, and the animal lay still. Same as the one crumpled near the wagon, Jessie standing over it barking, the dog's side smeared with blood.

"Jessie!" Bethie screamed, hopping down and clutching her arm.

Josephine climbed down and grabbed the .22, never taking her eyes off the bristled mass and tusks. She backed away, then ran for the wagon, where Bethie knelt by Jessie.

"Uncle Dodge, is she—"

"She's all right. Or will be once we wash the boar's blood off of her. Are you both okay?"

Bethie rubbed Jessie's ears. "I hurt my arm a little, but it's not bad."

Dodge turned to Josephine, question in his eyes.

"I'm fine. But are *you*?" She pointed to the blood darkening his torn pant leg.

"It's nothing. Must've caught it grabbing the Remington. Didn't even notice till it was over."

"But you're okay?" Bethie asked, looking up.

"Absolutely. But that was closer than I'd like." He looked at Josephine. "Thank you," he whispered, glancing at Bethie hugging Jessie again. "For getting to her. I don't know what I would've done if—"

"You would've shot the boar just like you did," Josephine said gently. "And she would have been fine."

He looked down. "Right," he finally said, his voice not convincing.

"Uncle Dodge, I thought you said you weren't bringing the Remington!" Bethie's eyes flashed.

He sighed. "Bethie, what I said was—"

Then her expression softened, and she ran to him.

Dodge caught her up and held her close. "Careful of that arm. Doesn't look broken."

"It's not. I just fell on it wrong, is all."

He looked at Bethie then Josephine, and Josephine sensed what was coming and wished he wouldn't.

"Thank you, Mrs. Dunham," Bethie said, barely meeting her gaze. "For jumping down and getting me. Turns out you're pretty brave. And strong, too. For a citified woman."

Josephine laughed. "Is that what I am? A citified woman?"

Bethie smiled. "Well, you're sure not from around these parts."

Dodge set her down and kissed the top of her head. "I'm going to field dress the boars, starting with the one by the tree, then we'll head on back."

Too late, Josephine realized her expression must have given her away.

"What?" he said, pulling a leather-wrapped bundle from the wagon. "Did you think we'd leave them behind? Those are good eatin'!" He winked. "You ever tasted boar?"

"No, but I've had dinner with a few."

He laughed, and to her surprise, Bethie did, too.

He shook his head. "A citified woman who tells jokes. Not sure we're ready for that." He whistled, and Jessie jumped into the wagon. "You three stay here. This won't take long."

"I'm happy to help, Mr. Coburn. I'm not squeamish and don't mind getting messy."

"I appreciate that, Mrs. Dunham, but I'd rather you and Bethie stay put. Keep watch with Jessie."

"What he means"—Bethie looked over—"is he'll be faster without worrying about you, and he wants you safe instead of watching him cut the boar open and scrape out the innards."

Josephine looked between them.

Dodge gave a little nod. "That's about right. But if you want a lesson—" He gestured toward the driver's bench. "I'll be back for the other one in about twenty minutes, and that'll be the best seat in the house."

Nearly two hours later, as Dodge guided the wagon back through town, Josephine sneaked a look at him—across Bethie, who was sandwiched between them on the bench—and at the blood and mess still staining his clothing, even after he'd washed in the creek.

She'd never seen someone field dress an animal before. Watching Calla kill chickens, while impressive, paled in comparison, and the visuals and stench would long stay with her. She'd gained new respect for butchers and a deeper gratitude for how any kind of meat made it to her plate.

She'd insisted on helping lift the carcasses into the wagon, leaving her skirt and blouse sullied. Each boar weighed at least a hundred pounds, maybe more. Young males, Dodge had said, more tender and less gamey. Despite how quickly he'd worked, buzzards were already circling by the time they pulled out.

He looked over. "You're sure you don't want me to take you back to the boarding house first?"

Bethie discreetly nudged her, as if Josephine could have forgotten the girl's earlier whispered—and surprising—request.

"No, that's all right, I can walk back. There's still plenty of daylight left."

With a nod, he prodded the mules uphill and stopped in front of the cabin. "I might be a while, Bethie. After I drop the boar off with Ol' Pop—" He looked at Josephine. "He's our cook for the farm . . . I need to check on the cattle."

"That's all right, Uncle Dodge. I'll be fine."

Josephine climbed down then turned to help Bethie, bits of twigs, thistle, and dry grass tangled in the back of the girl's blonde hair. Josephine grabbed the .22 along with Bethie's satchel from beneath the bench seat as Dodge released the brake.

"We'll be back in a while. I'll take Jessie with me and wash her up in the creek."

He guided the wagon past the barn and around the corner, the set of his shoulders indicating fatigue, or the weight of what could have happened earlier. Likely both. Josephine followed Bethie up the steps, still curious about the girl's request. She must have landed on her arm harder than she'd admitted.

Bethie closed the front door behind them. "I usually draw my own bath. After all, I am nine."

"Of course you do. Just tell me where everything is, and I'll get the water heating. If we hurry, we'll be done before your uncle gets back." Josephine kept her tone casual. But the fact that Bethie Coburn saw her as an ally instead of an enemy, even briefly, was no small thing.

"We keep the tub in here." Bethie opened a door that revealed a storage room smelling faintly of lye and pine. A galvanized tub, large enough for an adult to sit in with knees bent, leaned against one wall. "I can drag it to my room."

"Oh, I can do that for you. You go ahead and—"

"I can do it."

And she did, using only her left arm. After showing Josephine where the pots were, Bethie disappeared into her bedroom, tugging the tub behind her and closing the door. Josephine remembered that room from her earlier visit.

The woodstove wasn't as large or fancy as Miss Mary's, but it worked much the same. She built the fire, set four pots on the burners, then placed a bucket beneath the pump. She primed it until cold, fresh water finally gushed from the spout, then she filled each pot in turn.

She knocked on the door. "May I come in?"

"Yes."

Josephine opened it to find Bethie sitting on the bed, her overalls hanging loose from her shoulders, her expression pained.

"What's wrong, Bethie?"

"I can't move my arm enough to take off my shirt."

"Well, here . . . Let me help you."

Even before Josephine touched her, Bethie winced.

"It hurts that badly?"

Bethie nodded, clearly hating the dependence. Something they shared.

"Let's take it slow. You just concentrate on keeping your right arm still, and I'll ease the shirt off your left arm, then over your head."

Bethie nodded and drew a steadying breath.

Josephine worked carefully, inching the sleeve up the girl's arm and stretching the fabric as much as she dared. Bethie's breathing grew labored, and when the right sleeve finally slid free, Josephine saw the swelling above the elbow and the dark bruise already blooming beneath the skin.

She winced. The injury was far worse than Bethie had let on. And that didn't surprise her. Sympathy would not be welcome.

"What a tale you have to tell your friends at school!" Josephine said lightly as she carried pots from the stove and poured them into the tub. "Two wild boars charging you! Your uncle shooting them both. But with that arm swelling, we don't want the water too hot. I'll add some cold."

By the time the bath was ready, Bethie had kicked off her overalls, shoes, and socks. Only her knee-length drawers remained.

"I found some Castile soap in the storage room. If you need help washing your hair, I can—"

"I don't." Bethie lifted her chin. "I thank you kindly, Mrs. Dunham. But I can manage from here out."

Josephine smiled. "All right, then." She paused at the door. "If you don't mind, I'm going to heat a bit more water and wash up before I head back to Miss Mary's."

Bethie nodded.

Josephine closed the door, checked the mantel clock, refilled the pots, and set them to heating. The kitchen was simple and utilitarian. She found herself wondering about Kathleen Coburn, what kind of woman she'd been. But she felt certain of one thing: they would have agreed on women's rights.

Fifteen minutes later, just as she'd finished washing up, Josephine heard a faint, "Mrs. Dunham? Are you still here?"

She crossed to the bedroom door. "I am. Do you need anything before I go?"

Silence followed, thick with wounded pride.

"I do need your help again . . . please."

The humility in the request tugged at her. Josephine opened the door to find Bethie turned away, her hair partially wet and partially soaped, twigs and grass still tangled through it.

"How can I help?"

"I think I've got some burrs in my hair. I can't get them out."

"Let me see." Josephine gently ran her fingers through. "Yes, I feel them." She lathered her palms and carefully worked the suds through. More than once, the burrs pricked her fingers. "I'm sorry, honey. I'm being gentle. But they're really stuck."

"Will you have to cut them out?" Dread edged her voice.

Josephine shook her head. "No, no cutting. It'll just take time. Are you cold?"

Bethie gave a small nod.

The remaining two pots of water keeping warm on the stove served their purpose in reheating the bath, and Josephine returned to her task. Twice, the soap slipped from her hands and Bethie had to fish it out. The third time she dropped it, the sudsy water made it hard to find, and they both started giggling. But the fourth time, the soap hit the floor and went sailing.

"Ugh, I'm sorry." Laughing, Josephine wiped her hands on a towel she'd found in the cupboard. "I can't seem to hold on to anything."

Bethie pointed. "I think it went over there."

Josephine peered beneath the bed and spotted the bar of soap. Retrieving it, she noticed other items beneath the bed, too—a sewing basket with scraps of material and spools of thread, a brush and mirror, a small jar of scented water, and—she squinted—a blue metal pitcher holding dried flowers, brittle with age.

She instantly knew who they'd belonged to.

"Found it!" She held up the soap, not wishing to intrude on Bethie's hidden memories of her mother. "Do you know if y'all have castor oil or lard? The soap isn't quite doing the job."

"There's lard in the kitchen. On the bottom shelf."

Josephine returned with it, worked a little between her fingers and gently coaxed it through the tangles. Slowly, one by one, the burrs loosened and slipped free.

"How did you learn to climb trees?" Bethie asked after a minute.

Maybe because Bethie was the one asking, Josephine hesitated only a heartbeat. "My brother taught me."

"You have a brother?" Excitement tinged her voice.

"Yes . . . I did."

Bethie's head turned slightly.

"Todd died about two years ago."

A long moment passed.

"How did he die?"

Unexpected emotion tightened Josephine's throat. "He was trying to help someone, and he got hurt."

Another pause.

"So he didn't teach you about guns? Like Uncle Dodge taught Mama? And then me?"

"Our father and mother were pacifists. Do you know what that is?"

Bethie shook her head.

"A pacifist is someone who believes in avoiding all forms of violence, including war, and sometimes even self-defense. My father didn't approve of guns, so he forbade my brother and me from learning about them." She almost added that Todd had done it anyway, then quickly decided against it.

"Was he older or younger than you?"

"Older. By seven minutes."

Bethie turned fully around, brow furrowed. "You were twins?"

Josephine nodded. "And Todd wasn't just my brother. He was—" She looked away. "My best friend."

"And you miss him." Bethie's voice went soft.

"Every. Single. Day."

Bethie held her gaze then faced forward, but not before Josephine glimpsed the girl's own grief in those beautiful blue eyes.

Josephine worked the last burr free, lathered Bethie's hair once more, then rinsed it clean. "There. I think we got them all." She ran a brush through to be sure, then towel dried Bethie's hair.

"Maybe if your brother had had a gun . . ."

Bethie didn't finish the sentence, but Josephine understood.

"Perhaps that would have made a difference, Bethie, but . . . I don't know."

The devastation surrounding Todd's death replayed, and led, as it always did, back to Mayor Darden. Once men like him decided something, undoing it felt like holding back the tide. And though nothing had appeared in the newspapers yet, she could feel her time here wearing thin.

She held up the towel as Bethie stepped from the tub, then looked away to allow privacy.

"My nightgown's hanging over there . . . please."

Josephine retrieved it from the hook and helped her slip it on.

"I bet your papa feels bad now . . . About not letting your brother learn to shoot."

Josephine held open the left sleeve as Bethie slid her arm through, the movement drawing a grimace.

"My parents are gone now, too. They both died a few months after Todd."

Bethie stilled. "So you ain't got any family left?"

"Haven't got any family," Josephine gently corrected, knowing Dodge would have if he'd been here. "And no, I don't. Except for my husband, of course," she added quickly, hating the lie.

Bethie exhaled. "I'm *never* getting married."

On the verge of asking why, Josephine held back. She knew why. Children saw more than adults realized. Like the way Bethie looked at her now, not seeing her but the violence she'd endured at the hands of a man. She didn't know how to respond. She wondered what Kathleen, or even Dodge, had told Bethie about the situation surrounding her birth. And then it came to her . . .

"Bethie, we shouldn't judge all men by one. There *are* good men in this world. So to judge them as all being the same isn't fair to them. Just like not all women, or girls, are the same." Though she wanted to share more of what Nannie Burroughs and Miss Anthony taught about God creating men and women equally, she didn't. She'd given Dodge her word she'd steer clear of planting any suffrage-related ideas in Bethie's head.

She buttoned the gown as Bethie yawned. "Why don't you leave your right arm inside. It'll hurt too much otherwise, and you don't need to be using it anyway. I can make a sling."

"How do you know about doctoring an arm?"

"I fell out of a tree when I was about your age. Same arm, too."

"So yours got better?"

"Oh, yes, as will yours." Josephine wagged a finger. "But only because I let it heal. Which means resting. I'll find something for a sling. Is there anything else you need?"

"I'm kind of hungry. I've got jerky in my satchel."

"I'll be right back."

She found the bag of jerky and hoped it was the same kind Dodge had shared with her early on because she was hungry, too. A brief search in the cupboard yielded an old flour sack, softened by years of washing.

After a few awkward but humorous moments fitting the sling

beneath Bethie's gown and around her neck, Josephine plumped the pillows on the girl's bed, and Bethie sank back, looking spent.

Josephine handed her a piece of jerky. "Mind if I have some, too?"

"Help yourself," Bethie mumbled as she tore off a piece with her teeth.

The flavors exploded in Josephine's mouth, carrying her back to that wagon ride from Tullahoma with Dodge. Not even three weeks ago, though it felt far longer.

The creak of a door drew their gaze toward the main room, and Bethie quickly pulled the bedsheet up to her chin.

"Bethie, I'm back! Sorry, honey, took longer than I thought."

"We're in here, Uncle Dodge!"

Panting, Jessie, her fur damp, padded in and dropped beside the foot of the bed.

"Mrs. Dunham . . ." Pleasant surprise swept Dodge's expression. "You're still here."

Josephine hurriedly finished chewing. "Yes, but I'm just leaving. I need to get back in time to clean up and help with supper."

He glanced at her skirt. "Miss Mary doesn't like remnants of wild boar on her tenants' clothing?"

Josephine laughed.

"And you've already had your bath," he said, looking at Bethie.

"I just figured I'd get it done." Bethie tore off another piece of jerky.

It was clear Bethie didn't want him to know how badly her arm hurt. But why?

"Bethie was sharing some of her jerky with me, which tastes just like what you gave me before. It's so good!"

"Uncle Dodge makes it himself."

"So I've heard."

He just laughed.

"He's been making it for years!"

"*Mmmm* . . . Well, it's delicious, Mr. Coburn. And I believe I asked for the recipe."

Bethie perked up. "I can tell you what's in it. I help him make it."

Dodge cleared his throat. "We best save that for another time and let Mrs. Dunham be on her way. Here, let me walk you out."

On the porch, Josephine smiled. "You really don't want to share that recipe."

"I will. I promise. It's just a bit . . . detailed and I don't want you to be late." His voice lowered. "Thank you for staying with her. I could tell on the way back she wasn't feeling well. She's a tough little thing. Doesn't like to let on when she's hurting."

"While she didn't tell me outright not to tell you, I sense she doesn't want you to know her arm is worse than she let on. I was surprised when she asked me to stay and help her with her bath. Then when I saw her arm, I—" Suddenly things became clearer. She had to smile. "I think I know why she doesn't want you knowing."

She looked pointedly at him, but he just stared.

"Dodge, she wanted me to help her with her bath . . ."

Slowly, his quizzical look faded and a shy smile took its place. "Ah . . . Say no more. And now I really *do* thank you for staying."

They both laughed, and the genuineness of his reaction was so endearing. So attractive. Even though neither of them moved, she would've sworn the space between them lessened by half, and the warmth in his eyes sparked a flame inside her.

"Josephine, I—"

She moved toward the front steps. "She's in pain, Dodge. There's some swelling and a nasty bruise is forming. I've made her a sling but if there's any way to get Doc Wyatt to look at it tonight, I would."

He didn't respond for a moment, then finally nodded. "He's still in the barn. I'll get him. And . . . I'm sorry about what happened today. In the field. Thank you again for helping Bethie."

"You're welcome again. And there's no need to apologize, about any of it." She let her gaze travel the length of the lush green hills that embraced the town of Lynchburg. "This was actually one of the best days I've had in a very, very long time." She started down the steps, then turned back. "And for the record, you were right."

His brow rose.

"The first day we met you said a rifle could mean the difference between life and death in these hills. I didn't believe you then. But I do now."

44

Running late, Josephine set the dining room table for breakfast then returned to the kitchen. "How can I help you this morning, Calla?"

Calla, standing with her back to her, didn't answer. She'd gone quiet again over the last couple of days, despite Josephine's efforts to draw her out.

"Calla?" she tried again, stepping closer. Only then did she see Calla's hands, trembling uncontrollably.

"I'm trying to stop, Josephine, but—" Her voice caught. "I can hardly do my work for the jitters it's giving me. I dropped a dish yesterday and told Miss Mary I done forgot it was hot." Tears slipped down her cheeks. "I ain't never lied to her before. And her being so good to me. For all the world, I wish the Lord would just take me like I been asking him. I'm so tired of doing what I know I shouldn't . . . all to dull a hurt that seems set on never healing."

Josephine hugged her tight, sorrow and anger battling for dominance. "I wish I knew what to do to help you."

"I think maybe I'm past help," Calla whispered, staring at her clenched hands.

Josephine covered them with her own. She knew the steps for helping women leave men enslaved to drink—had taught them, recited them, believed them. But since she'd fled Atlanta, those steps no longer felt simple. She remembered standing outside saloons with her suffragist sisters, handing out pledge cards, chanting the vow printed in bold black type: *I hereby solemnly promise, by God's help, to abstain from all intoxicating liquors.* Most men, defiant, had tossed the cards back in their faces.

The mere thought of handing Calla a pledge card seemed calloused and cruel. Calla wasn't defiant. She was hurting miserably, desperate to be freed from her addiction. And Josephine wondered, uncomfortably . . . how many of those men in Atlanta had secretly been desperate and hurting, too?

"Oh Jesus, help me," Calla whispered, bowing her head.

"Sit down for a minute." Josephine urged her toward the kitchen table.

"I can't. Gotta get breakfast going."

"Just sit, and I'll get the coffee started. Maybe that will help."

Calla didn't argue, just stared, hollow-eyed.

Minutes later, Josephine handed her a steaming mug. "Drink this and I'll get you something to eat."

"I ain't hungry, but thank you." She sipped the hot coffee, hands wrapped around the warmth. "I don't know how I ended up here." Her shoulders sagged. "And I for sure don't know how to climb back out of this pit."

"I don't either. But we'll figure it out. Together."

Calla pulled an envelope from her apron pocket. "Got this from Nannie yesterday. She writes how proud she is of me." She shook her head. "But she got no idea who I really am."

"Listen to me . . ." Josephine moved to where Calla couldn't look away. "You are so much more than the problem you're having with drinking." She gripped her hands. "You are a kind, caring, wonderful person who, yes, is struggling. You're grieving unimaginable loss, Calla. The death of your husband. Your son." Her eyes filled. "I can hardly fathom that. But you *will* get through this. Impossible as that feels."

Calla didn't respond.

After a minute, she looked up. "I heard about your shooting adventure Sunday. Is it true? Bethie would've been gored if not for you?"

Josephine shook her head. "If not for Dodge shooting the boar, is the real story."

"Way I heard it, she fell from the tree and you jumped down and got her back up just in time." Calla's eyes shone. "I love that girl. Ain't nothing like a child to bring light to the world."

Josephine's heart broke at the loss etched in Calla's features.

The sound of the front door opening carried toward them, as did Miss Mary's voice, and Calla's eyes widened.

Josephine rose. "I'll go talk to her for a few minutes. Give you time to collect yourself."

Gripping her hands tight, Calla nodded.

Josephine poured two more mugs of coffee and met Miss Mary and her husband in the lobby. As they chatted, she hoped—no, she prayed—for Calla, hoping God would listen. *Please Lord, listen . . . For her sake, even if not for mine.*

When she followed Miss Mary back into the kitchen minutes later, Calla was already mixing biscuits, sausage frying on the stove, hands no longer shaking. Calla barely glanced at her before turning away, and Josephine knew. And her chest ached with the awful truth of it. Not so much that Calla had turned to whiskey again for comfort. But the awful truth that as whiskey comforted, it also enslaved.

A while later, her heart still heavy, Josephine approached the distillery office and could hear cursing even before she opened the door. When she did, she saw Mr. Daniel hobbling around on one foot, still cursing up a storm. "Mr. Daniel, are you all right?"

He turned, red-faced. "Do I *look* all right, Mrs. Dunham!" Groaning through clenched teeth, he leaned against the desk and glared at the floor safe. "*Five times* I tried the combination and that confounded thing still won't open! So I hauled off and kicked the good-for-nothing piece of—"

A string of expletives followed that she didn't fully catch and didn't need to. His gaze darted back to her as though he dared her to show even an ounce of humor at his expense.

"Sit down, sir. Please!" Josephine set her purse on the desk and rolled his office chair toward him.

"That dang safe is going to be the death of me!" He tried to put weight on his left foot and winced as he eased into the chair. "I finally have that meeting with Mr. Prince this morning, so I got here early. I need to get the gauger's ledger out of that dad blame—"

"I can help you get whatever you need. And not to worry, we have time. Mr. Prince was still at the boarding house when I left. He's moving very slowly after having been sick for the past two days."

He leaned forward, staring down at his left boot. "I heard he was feeling poorly. What's been ailing him?"

"Between us? I think it's too many buttermilk biscuits and slices of fudge pie. That gentleman loves Calla's cooking and eats to excess, despite his determination not to."

He peered up at her. "At least he's able to work it off by riding that bicycle of his."

Maybe it was his barbed wit or the image of poor Mr. Prince pushing that one-wheeled bicycle all the way through town to the distillery, but Josephine had to laugh.

He managed a smile. "Ah, Mrs. Dunham, if only I could bottle *that*, I'd make a fortune." He shrugged. "Or . . . another one."

It took her a moment to realize what he was referring to. She shook her head. The man was a shameless flirt, even though he meant nothing by it. It seemed to come naturally to him. Yet for all of the differences between them, and there were many, she would actually miss Jack Daniel very much when the time came to leave Lynchburg. His actions toward her had been more than generous, which made what she still intended to do all the more difficult.

"Dodge!" Mr. Daniel called when the front door opened. "Just the man I need to see."

Dodge nodded a "good morning" to Josephine, then frowned when Mr. Daniel rose and started limping toward the safe. "What happened to you, Uncle Jack?"

"I'll tell you what happened to him." Josephine pointed toward the safe. "He finally just hauled off and kicked it!"

"You didn't." Disbelief swept Dodge's face.

"Dodge, this infernal, cast-iron demon has been my nemesis almost from the day I got it!" He grimaced, hand resting on the safe to steady himself. "If you'll get out the gauger's book, I want to look over the figures before Mr. Prince gets here."

Tempted to watch over Dodge's shoulder as he turned the dial on the tumblers, Josephine refrained. A few minutes with that ledger was all she needed. Now if Mr. Daniel would only take his customary morning walk around the distillery.

"How's Bethie doing?" Mr. Daniel asked, easing into one of the chairs in front of his desk. "Everybody in town's talking about what happened."

Dodge handed him the ledger. "She's already much better. Doc said it was a sprain and should heal within a week or two. But she's milking it for all it's worth."

"And how about you, Mrs. Dunham." Mr. Daniel looked over. "Bet that was a first. Wild boars charging at you."

"Yes, it was. I'm glad to hear Bethie's doing well, and I'm *especially* grateful for Mr. Coburn's quick reflexes that day."

Mr. Daniel smirked. "Oh he's got quick reflexes all right. You know that's how he got his name, don't you?"

"She doesn't need to hear that story, Uncle Jack."

"Yes, sirree," Mr. Daniel continued undaunted. "How old were you? About fifteen or so?"

Dodge shook his head. "I'm not contributing to this."

Mr. Daniel's expression turned indulgent. "Bunch of us were up at the farm. It was early fall. I can still smell the crispness in the air and that faint tang of whiskey mash rolling up the hill. A shipment of new bulls had just arrived from nearby Lois, and the hands were unloading them from a rickety old stock cart." He shook his head. "I don't know how that old cart held up under the weight of those three bulls, even for the handful of miles between towns. Anyway, a much younger Mr. Coburn here had been working on the farm for a while, doing odd jobs. But on that particular day, he was helping to get the bulls into the corral."

Josephine glanced at Dodge who seemed intent on not paying attention.

"Anyway, the older hands were shouting orders and swinging ropes, prodding the bulls down the ramp and through the gate when the last bull, a massive brute of a beast, started down. He was snorting, swinging those horns from side to side. Dodge, you remember how big he was?"

"Like I could ever forget. I thought I was going to die that day." He offered a self-deprecating smile.

Mr. Daniel laughed. "I heard the groan of that ramp then a loud crack! The plank snapped and that bull, he reared up and gave a bellow that shook the earth. Then he charged straight for a group of old-timers from town who'd come to watch the unloading. I remember thinking they were done for, and they likely would've been, too. But for Dodge here." Pride softened his tone. "Mrs. Dunham, you should have seen him. In a flash, he ran toward that bull, yelling and waving. That beast skidded to a stop, sent dust and dirt flying everywhere. Men were running, screaming, *Loose bull!*" Mr. Daniel's gaze grew hazy with memory, his focus moving to Dodge. "I'd never seen anything like it before in my life, or since. The way you dove this way and that when that bull charged you. How he didn't gore you five times over, son, I'll never know. Then how you got him into the corral and hopped back over that fence like nothing happened. All the hands were laughing and cheering. *That was some mighty fine dodgin' you did,* they all said. And—" He looked back at Josephine. "The name just stuck."

She stared. "How on earth did you do that?"

Dodge shrugged. "Didn't have much of a choice."

"Oh you had a choice, all right." Mr. Daniel pointed at him. "That was the day I knew you were special. That you had a gift."

"For what?" Dodge laughed. "Dodging bulls?"

"For doing what was best for others despite the cost to yourself." Mr. Daniel's eyes narrowed. "And also a gift with animals. No one else could ever handle Goliath like you did." He glanced at Josephine. "That's what we named that bull. He'd actually let Dodge get close enough to rub his neck."

"He really was a gentle soul," Dodge said.

"Gentle soul, nothing! He looked at everybody else like they were a target ready to be run through. All except for you . . . Hezekiah."

"And there we are." Dodge shook his head, but Josephine caught the hint of a smile, from both him and Mr. Daniel.

"Hezekiah?" she asked.

Nodding, Dodge exhaled through his teeth. "You know, from the Old Testament. My mother, God rest her, loved the story about how he constructed that tunnel to move water through the bedrock beneath the City of David." He shrugged. "Is it any wonder I welcomed the nickname?"

They all shared a laugh until Mr. Daniel opened the ledger and began perusing the columns, then the conversation turned to Mr. Prince's inspection, along with the cattle and Texas fever, and Josephine moved to a side table and continued where she'd left off with correspondence the previous afternoon. But anxiety over her plans made it difficult to concentrate.

Her gaze kept returning to the gauger's book. Changing even one entry so that the amount of barrels filled on any particular day didn't match the number of barrels stamped with that same date in the warehouse would be a minor error. But if she changed several that might be a significant enough error for a revenuer to halt production of whiskey. For a week? A month? That remained to be seen.

Her chest ached with the weight of it all, but one thought of Calla and her resolve strengthened.

Rapid footsteps sounded on the porch. The front door burst open. "Mr. Coburn! There you are! We got us a problem in the stillhouse, sir!"

Josephine recognized the young man as a new worker. He'd had his first payday a week ago.

"What kind of problem?" Dodge asked.

"It's a hissing sound. Like a break in a pipe! Like something's about to blow!"

Dodge was already out the door in the time it took Mr. Daniel to gain his footing.

"Go on, I'm coming!" Mr. Daniel yelled.

Dodge called back, "No need for you to—"

"A hurt foot might slow me down, but it's not going to stop me! I'm right behind you."

As Dodge and the young man took off, Mr. Daniel grabbed his hat and had barely gained the porch when a woman hurried up the steps.

"Oh, begging your pardon, Uncle Jack. I didn't mean to nearly waylay you, sir."

"No harm done, Mrs. Watson. We have us a bit of an emergency, so if there's something you need, I'll be back directly."

"Oh no, sir, I was just . . ."

The woman peered past him, her gaze nervous, almost paranoid, and made eye contact with Josephine, who intuitively knew why she was here.

"Mrs. Watson!" Josephine crossed to the door, never having seen the woman before. "How kind of you to stop by. Please come in, and we can visit for a moment."

Mr. Daniel tipped his hat and made arduous progress in the direction of the stillhouse.

Josephine closed the door behind them, glancing at the gauger's book, knowing time was limited. "Mrs. Watson, how are you this morning?"

"I'm mostly fine, I guess, Mrs. Dunham."

No longer surprised when people she hadn't met knew her name, she invited the woman to sit. No bruises on the young woman's face that she could see, but she had a timidity about her, an undercurrent of trepidation that she recognized.

"Oh no, ma'am. I don't aim to fill up your time. I'm just wondering if—" She briefly bowed her head. "I hate to be asking this and got no right to it, you not even knowing me, but—"

"Do you need food, Mrs. Watson? For you and your children?"

Shame filled her eyes. "Clara Hackett done told me I could come to you for help," she whispered. "I wouldn't be doing it if I had any other way of filling the mouths of my younguns."

"I'm so glad you did come. If you'll wait here, I have a box of food in the back." Having decided to keep some supplies on hand on a lower, out-of-the-way shelf in the storage room, Josephine found an empty box and filled it. She'd bought enough food and other staple items to make another two boxes, hoping Mrs. Carver would send others.

Between what she'd paid Miss Mary, the money she'd set aside to send to Sarah, and the purchases at the mercantile, she'd spent most of her earnings so far. But today was Wednesday. Payday.

She carried the box to the front. "If you know of anyone who needs food, please send them to me. Discreetly, of course. And I'll help as much as I can."

"God bless you for your kindness," Mrs. Watson finished in a whisper. "I'll be praying for you, ma'am."

"Thank you, and I'll be doing the same for you." The commitment felt hypocritical, in a way. But as she'd prayed that morning for Calla, just because she no longer believed God heard prayers on her own behalf didn't mean he wouldn't hear them for someone else.

Mrs. Watson insisted on hugging her before she left, and as soon as the door closed behind her, Josephine hurried back to the desk, grabbed a pencil and opened the ledger, then quickly scanned the most recent entries. Her determination grew stronger by the second.

Each entry recorded the day, month, and year of the measurement of whiskey, along with the barrel location within the warehouse—shelf and position number. Each barrel had been assigned a unique number, then there was the fill date, which she assumed was when the whiskey had been stored in the barrel. Several other columns bore title notations that she wasn't quite certain about, then a column with the title "Tax Paid/ Bonded." Each entry either contained a check mark with a date or had been left blank. But what her gaze snagged on was the column furthest right—where the initials *DC* had been neatly scripted on almost every line.

The pencil in her grip suddenly felt like a dagger. She couldn't do this. Then again, how could she not? When compared to the damage alcohol had done to countless women and children and for so long, this was such a small retribution. She felt like she needed to do it for the cause alone. She'd gleaned enough from her father being an attorney to know she would be breaking a law in changing the figures—tampering with official government records. But Miss Anthony had broken a law too, when she'd voted as a woman. And what if the distillery being shut down even for a brief time gave people opportunity to reconsider? Perhaps even Jack Daniel himself would—

No, she was fooling herself if she thought he would change his mind. But perhaps others might.

Her mind racing, her palms sweaty, she thought of Calla again, the hopelessness in the woman's eyes, and quickly rescanned the columns. She chose four random entries—not bearing the initials DC, but someone else's . . . GC. She quickly checked the payroll roster from the past two weeks. No one with those initials. Perhaps that person no longer worked here. Which was all the better for her.

She carefully changed the numbers in the columns marked Mash Tub/ Still No., Capacity (gallons), Proof Gallons Produced, and Warehouse Entry—then added either a check mark to the empty Tax Paid/Bonded column, or carefully erased the check mark already there.

Reviewing the edited entries, she could hardly tell what she'd changed, so doubted whether anyone else would be—

A forceful knock sounded on the office door and her heart catapulted to her throat. Before she could answer, the door opened just as she slammed the ledger shut.

45

"SHERIFF RIGBY!" Josephine shoved the gauger book off to one side, certain that what she'd just done was clearly written on her face. "How may I help you today, sir?"

Sheriff Rigby glanced at her hand still resting on the ledger. "Jack in?"

"No, sir, he's not." She reached for a stack of bills, wanting to at least give the appearance of being busy. "I'd be happy to take a message for him."

"How about you just tell me where he is."

Condescension layered his tone, but feeling so off-kilter in the moment, she let it pass. "He was headed toward the stillhouse a few moments ago. I imagine he's still there if you'd care to seek him out."

He looked around the office, then back at her. "I got word you're running a little mercantile of your own out of this office. Is that true?"

"A mercantile?" She forced a laugh. "What on earth do you mean by that?"

"I mean that I'm aware of the amount of food and other whatnot you've been buying at the Carvers' mercantile. I'm just wondering what you're doing with it all."

She knew Mrs. Carver would never have divulged that, which left her husband. "Sheriff, as I'm certain you're already aware, I'm staying at the boarding house in town. And the amount of food we go through each week is considerable."

He eyed her. "Think you're pretty high and mighty just waltzing into town and taking this job, don't you?"

She stared. What was it about men in positions of power that made them feel the need to belittle everyone else? She recognized the bait when she saw it—and she'd fallen for it before with men like him. It had cost her dearly. "I'm grateful for this job, Sheriff. And to Mr. Daniel for the opportunity he's given me."

"I'm sure you are." An unpleasant smile curved his mouth. "Question I'm wondering is . . . how grateful."

Heat sluiced through her at his insinuation, and she came to her feet. "I'll be certain to tell Mr. Daniel you stopped by, Sheriff Rigby. Now if you will excuse me, I have work to do."

To her relief, he started for the door, but then he paused.

"Rest assured, Mrs. Dunham, should I get an inquiry about a flighty woman, or if your husband comes looking for you, which I'm sure he will, eventually, it'll be my pleasure to turn over the details of your whereabouts. Good day to you." He tugged on his hat and left the door ajar.

Josephine went cold inside. Here she'd been checking newspapers every day, dreading what *she* might find. It had never occurred to her that Sheriff Rigby might actually volunteer information about her to law enforcement in other towns or cities. As she watched him walk down the street and around the corner, something deep inside her told her to run. *Now.* But to where? And with scarcely any money.

She *was* getting paid again this afternoon but how far would that take her? And the overarching question that gnawed at her—was there anywhere she could run where it would be far enough to escape all this?

Through the window, she spotted Dodge and Mr. Daniel nearly back to the office—Mr. Daniel moving slowly—and she quickly returned the gauger's ledger to the edge of the desk and bent over the stack of bills, every nerve on edge.

Mr. Daniel limped inside and sank down into one of the chairs opposite his desk. "Turns out, it wasn't anything serious. Young Gilbert just got a bit spooked is all."

Dodge picked up the gauger's book. "It was a loose joint in one of the steam lines. We wrapped it with soaked burlap and wire. That'll keep things until the blacksmith can reseal it properly."

Mr. Daniel laughed. "Young Gilbert was afraid to take us inside, scared the whole place was about to go up."

Dodge raised a brow. "Respect for the machinery is never a bad thing. Especially considering what's in that stillhouse."

"True enough." Mr. Daniel nodded. "Let's hope Mr. Prince doesn't fine us for that leak. Speak of the devil . . ."

Josephine trailed Mr. Daniel's gaze out the window and spotted Mr. Prince walking his bicycle up to the porch. Humorous a sight as it usually was, right now it emptied her lungs of air.

"Good afternoon, Distillery Folk!" Mr. Prince said as he walked in. "My apologies, Mr. Daniel, for having to reschedule our meeting from Monday to today. Some sort of illness cast a spell of malaise over my otherwise robust constitution. But I'm much recovered now and appreciate your understanding, as does the United States Department of the Treasury."

Josephine felt Mr. Daniel looking at her, but didn't dare return the attention.

"Well, Mr. Prince—" Dodge held out the ledger. "You might want to take a look at our production since the last revenuer visit, then we can start our walk-through and get as far as we can for today."

Mr. Prince settled in the chair beside Mr. Daniel and opened the book. "Hmmm . . ." His gaze scanned down a page, then another, and another. His eyes narrowed. "Is this figure correct here, Mr. Coburn?"

Josephine's stomach did a somersault.

Dodge leaned over. "Yes, sir. That's correct. We added six more stills since your last visit. Hence, the increase in production on that date."

"Impressive."

"Unfortunately," Dodge continued, "we discovered only this morning that one of the new stills has a loose joint in the steam line. I fixed it temporarily but we'll need to get a blacksmith out to get it properly mended."

Mr. Prince closed the book and stood. "I'd like to inspect the stills first, Mr. Coburn." He returned the book to Dodge. "But bring that with you, if you would. Should questions arise."

"You bet, sir." Dodge gestured toward the door. "After you."

"I'll catch up with you two gentlemen shortly," Mr. Daniel said. "And no sneaking any free samples on the job, Mr. Prince!"

Mr. Prince's laughter carried through the open window, and Josephine watched them as they rounded the building.

"You're not feeling poorly, are you, Mrs. Dunham?" Mr. Daniel asked. "You're looking a mite pale."

"No, sir. I'm fine." Her gaze still following Dodge, she wondered what he would think, how he would react, if he learned what she'd done. Then again, he wouldn't know it was her. They would simply assume an error had been made by GC, whoever that was, it would be corrected, and production would eventually resume. Dodge would be none the wiser.

"How was your visit with Mrs. Watson?"

Hearing the question as though from far away, she looked over at him. "What?"

"Your visit. With Mrs. Watson."

"Oh, yes, sir . . . It was nice. She's a very kind person."

"She is that. You'll remember that her husband, Daryl, works here at the distillery. He's one of our mash men. Handles mashing the grain to begin the fermentation process."

"I didn't know what he did, but yes, of course, I remember seeing Mr. Watson for payroll."

"That's right, that's right." He rose, grimacing as he did. "You know I've been thinking . . . Perhaps we ought to keep a cash tin here in the office somewhere, just to cover incidentals. Things that come up from time to time. You'd be in charge of it, of course. No need to keep a ledger. The money could be used at your discretion. For whoever or whatever you see fit."

Finally having her full attention, Josephine didn't answer immediately. She simply stared until he looked back at her, two and two quickly making four. "Did Dodge tell you?"

"Tell me what?" The barest hint of a smile, not in his expression, but in his voice belied the seriousness of his features.

But she knew he knew. The question was how. "You saw the food in the storage room, didn't you?"

"You're keeping food back there in the storage room?"

"Mr. Daniel." She leveled a stare.

"You are far too easily winkled out, Mrs. Dunham. But we'll fix that immediately once I start teaching you how to play poker."

"As if that day will ever come, Mr. Daniel."

"I'll tell you what day is coming . . . the day you'll call me Uncle Jack."

"Oh please, not this again, sir."

They stared at one another for a long moment. Him smiling. Her scarcely able to breathe for the stranglehold guilt had on her when confronted by this man's generosity.

He glanced toward the door. "I've known Margaret Watson before she was knee-high. Watched her grow up, recall when she and Daryl married, and welcomed their first child, and their next and their next . . ." He smiled. "Then when she buried her folks. Good people who died too young when the influenza swept through here a few years back. But never in all that time has Margaret visited this distillery. Not once. Until you." He pointed in the direction of the stillhouse. "My foot was throbbing so badly, I had to pause for a minute and sit on that old oak stump outside the stillhouse. So I saw Margaret leave."

Josephine looked away.

"No, no. Look at me, please," he said softly.

Culpability weighing heavy, and over so much more than he realized, she did as he asked.

"I knew hiring a suffragist would be a risky business." His trademark charm sparkled in his eyes and somehow deepened his Tennessee drawl. "After all, there's got to be a part of you that would rejoice at seeing this distillery go south, so to speak, which may well happen soon enough, what with all the talk of prohibition. But never did I imagine that the suffragist I hired would end up helping the families of the men who work here. And from her own pocket, no less."

Seeing the sincerity and warmth in Mr. Daniel's expression, she didn't wish to get into an argument with him. But neither could she simply let the compliment stand. "To be frank, Mr. Daniel, I don't view what I'm doing as helping the families of the men who work here. I see it as helping the wives and children of men in this town who drink alcohol—and your whiskey, in particular—to excess. Who choose to spend their wages on liquor instead of feeding and clothing their families. But yes, many of those men, I'm sure, do work for you." She hesitated to share what came next to mind, then decided he should know. "Do you know what one of the women said about the last Friday of each month? The day you give every employee a free bottle of Old No. 7?"

His expression didn't change, yet she sensed silent acknowledgment.

"She said it helps them with having enough to eat that week. Because that's one less bottle her husband has to buy."

A flash of displeasure flickered across his face. "Mrs. Dunham, I don't dispute that some men drink too much. But is that the whiskey's fault or the man's? A hammer in a person's hand can either build or destroy. Should we then outlaw hammers?"

She shook her head. "That's false equivalence. A hammer's purpose is to build. Whiskey's purpose is to intoxicate, to dull a man's senses, to rob him of his faculties."

"Or, perhaps, to help relax a man after a long day's work, to bring comfort to a hurting soul, to help friends celebrate together. And it's to be enjoyed responsibly."

She forced a laugh, but he held up a hand.

"From your perspective, Mrs. Dunham, I realize you see only the drunkard and the abuser. And I cannot—and do not—fault you for that, based on the unconscionable cruelty I believe you have suffered. But what about the hardworking man who sips and enjoys the relaxation my whiskey offers and never raises a hand to anyone?"

"But how many men truly stop at sipping, sir? I've stood outside countless bars and saloons, and have yet to see a man leave one of those places merely having *sipped.* And how do you account for so many women who are begging and marching in the streets for prohibition? Surely you've seen evidence of women in this town who've been beaten and abused by their husbands who were intoxicated."

Mr. Daniel looked across the desk at her, something weary in his eyes. "I will not deny that I've seen women bearing bruises and other, again, indefensible injuries. But I make and sell whiskey, Mrs. Dunham. Not cruelty. Not rage. A good man drinks and continues to be good-hearted. A bad man drinks and turns mean as a snake. It wasn't the drink that made him bad. The drink merely let out what was already inside."

"Does that distinction help Mrs. Watson when her husband comes home full of whiskey and anger?"

A long moment passed.

"No," he finally answered. "It doesn't."

She chose her next words carefully. "You've been very successful in your endeavors, Mr. Daniel. And even though I don't know you well, I know you well enough to know you're not a cruel man. You treat your workers with kindness. Your generosity has touched people all over this town. Including me." She worked to soften her next question, her intention not to accuse, but to provoke thought. "But can you honestly tell me that you've never, not even once, questioned whether the good your business does outweighs the harm?"

He stared at some point beyond her. "Maybe I have. But that doesn't mean the answer is a simple one."

"But it is simple. Stop making whiskey."

"You think if I stop selling whiskey, the men who beat their wives will suddenly become saints? That they'll take up Scripture reading and drink sarsaparilla instead? If it's not my whiskey they drink, it'll be someone else's. And if prohibition becomes law, they'll make whiskey in a barn with fire and lye."

"So because the evil won't be completely eradicated, you choose to continue profiting from it?"

He shook his head. "Mrs. Dunham, I choose to make a product that's the best of its kind in the world. That men—and women, mind you—seek out to enjoy, and I've spent a lifetime getting here. I pay my employees—again, men *and* women—fair salaries. More than they could make anywhere else in this town, or in other towns larger than Lynchburg. Because I know I couldn't be doing what I'm doing without them." His jaw tightened. Earnestness moved into his eyes. "I care about the people who work for me, everyone from the farmers who grow the corn, to the men who drive the wagons crated full of aged whiskey down to Tullahoma. All of them have helped me grow this distillery. I keep them fed and clothed. I also pay taxes, and a lot of them. Shoot, the Federal Treasury has made a fortune off me. If Jack Daniel Distillery is shut down, what happens to my workers? To this town?"

Josephine didn't shy away from his gaze. "And what happens to women like Margaret Watson?"

Sighing, Mr. Daniel stood and moved toward the window, his brow knit tight, his gait hindered. "I don't have all the answers, Mrs. Dunham. Never have claimed to." His next words seemed to come hard. "I have overindulged myself, on occasion. And while I have never raised my hand to a woman, intoxicated or sober, I recognize the dangers, I assure you. I only know that whiskey making was running through my veins before I was even born. My grandmother, Elizabeth Callaway Daniel,

God bless her, made Scotch-Irish whiskey that people say was the best around." He turned back. "You do know that whiskey making originated with women, right? It wasn't men who thought it up first."

Josephine had known that, but somewhere along the way that tidbit of history had fallen by the wayside for her.

"One last question for you, if I might, Mrs. Dunham."

She nodded.

"Do you really believe that prohibition, banning whiskey . . . Do you think it will really stop men from drinking?"

Quiet for a beat, Josephine finally shook her head. "No. But I do think it will stop some men. And women," she added, thinking of Calla and the struggle she might have avoided if whiskey were, indeed, illegal.

"What it comes down to, Mrs. Dunham, is I believe people are responsible for their own actions." He laughed softly. "Take our dear, though slightly odd, Mr. Prince who overindulges on Calla's delicious cooking. You wouldn't want to ban her fudge pie, now would you? Or her buttermilk biscuits with sausage gravy?"

"Again, that's a—"

"False equivalence," he filled in for her. "Yes, yes. But there's truth lingering in there all the same. While I was in Nashville last weekend, I heard a street preacher say that we'll have to give account for everything we do and say in this life. That we all reap what we sow. That's a mighty sobering thought, don't you think?"

Josephine managed a nod, more sobered by that thought than Mr. Daniel could know in that moment.

"Now if you'll excuse me, Mrs. Dunham, I believe I need to catch up with Dodge and Mr. Prince. Shall we continue this lively discussion at a later time?"

"I'll look forward to it."

"As will I." He gave her a last look as he left.

A while later, reticule in hand, Josephine was readying to leave when a mountain of a man walked in. One she would have remembered meeting.

"May I help you, sir?"

He removed his slouch hat and dipped his head, suddenly looking more boy than man. "Uncle Jack around?"

"He's on the grounds. But he's meeting with someone right now."

"Reckon that'd be Mr. Prince, one of them revenuers. About time for that meetin'."

Not knowing him, Josephine was hesitant to agree.

"It's all right, ma'am. I work here. Or I did." He shifted his weight. "'Till I went and did something fool-headed and got myself sent home for a spell. No pay's been awful hard. But I've had time to think on it, and I'm regretful of what I done. Pa says Mr. Coburn was in his rights to fire me straight out." His eyes shone. "But he didn't. And I aim to do better. No more trouble and that's the honest truth."

The man's innocence and guileless sincerity tugged at her. "And you are . . . ?"

"Cartwright." His chest lifted. "Gideon Cartwright. I work the charcoal vats. Drawing off the whiskey, barreling it up. Uncle Jack says that's a right important job."

"Yes, it is. I'm sure Mr. Daniel appreciates your work—"

The words died on her tongue as the pieces slid into place. Gideon Cartwright. GC. She swallowed hard. No wonder the initials in the ledger had meant nothing to her. He hadn't been on payroll since she arrived.

"Well, good day to you, ma'am." He replaced his hat. "I'll be back bright and early come morning."

~

Later that night, unable to sleep, Josephine kept seeing Gideon Cartwright's face. He would most certainly lose his job over this. It was one thing when she thought GC no longer worked there. But to meet Gideon Cartwright in person . . . *Today*. The timing felt almost predetermined.

What Mr. Daniel had said about a person reaping what they sowed returned a hundredfold. As did what Nannie Burroughs had said in her sermon. *What we do with our lives matters. Not only for us, but for generations to come. The seeds we sow will one day manifest themselves in either a harvest of righteousness or a crop of weeds. Which shall it be? It's a question we must ask ourselves every day, and every day we must answer it with honesty and clarity.*

She'd known fellow suffragists determined to force change through any means, whether that meant defacing property or even physically harming someone else. Newspapers reported their outrageous behavior on the front page. And from the start, she had drawn that very hard line in the sand, wanting to follow in the footsteps of Miss Anthony.

Resistance to tyranny is obedience to God, Miss Anthony often said, while encouraging women to break unjust laws and participate in civil disobedience with the goal of furthering the cause for women's rights. That's what she'd been doing by altering the gauger book. It had been like a peaceful protest . . .

Until Gideon Cartwright.

And who was the tyrant in this situation? Whiskey, was her first thought. Mr. Daniel her next. But Jack Daniel was anything but a tyrant. She thought of what he'd said about the men and women who worked for him, along with their families. How he cared about them. Then there was Dodge . . .

What would he think of her? There could never be anything more than friendship between them, but—be it foolish or wise—his friendship, his opinion of her, meant more than she cared to admit. And far more than striking a blow for the suffrage movement.

Tears slid from the corners of her eyes.

She looked across the room at Calla's sleeping form. Calla's hurts, and their remedy, went far deeper than temporarily halting the making of whiskey here in Lynchburg.

Josephine tossed and turned into the night, unable to find rest, Gideon Cartwright and the question of what seeds she was sowing with her life pounding her conscience.

She rose before the sun, having slept fitfully, and hurried to the main house to catch Mr. Prince on his way in to breakfast to casually inquire how the inspection at the distillery was going. To see if he'd reviewed the gauger's ledger yet.

But Miss Mary informed her that Mr. Prince had left early to meet with Dodge and Mr. Daniel. Desperate to get her hands on that ledger before he did, she hurried through her breakfast duties, then ran the entire way to the distillery.

46

By the time Josephine reached the distillery, her side ached and her lungs burned. She paused by the office to catch her breath, then went from building to building, but couldn't find Dodge, Mr. Daniel, or Mr. Prince. Everyone she spoke with said she'd either just missed them or that they hadn't seen them.

Finally, she headed back to the office, knowing that whatever came was by her own hand. But she would not allow Gideon Cartwright to pay for what she'd done. Or attempted to do.

Mr. Daniel had left her a note about the distillery's first gathering of vendors soon to meet in Lynchburg. Only last week, he'd reminded her about his plans to host them for dinner and dancing at his home one evening. And again, she'd kindly but firmly declined, making it clear that while she would work on anything behind the scenes, attending the ball lay far outside her official duties.

His note continued with a list of tasks to be completed, and she read through it, trying to focus, but couldn't. When Bart delivered the mail earlier than usual, her unease only deepened.

She scanned the pile of envelopes, one of them horribly wrinkled and torn on one edge, the ink on the front smeared by what appeared to be water stains. But her first priority was always the newspaper.

Nerves taut, she flipped through the pages, readying herself for the worst. But . . . nothing about Atlanta. She stared. Was it possible that *The Chattanooga Times* had chosen not to report the story? That seemed highly unlikely, given the climate surrounding suffrage and prohibition. But whatever the reason, she was grateful.

After sorting through the envelopes, she looked more closely at the one so damaged. Part of the address the sender had written had been marked through. She could make out the name Jack Daniel's Distillery well enough, but the address itself was—

She exhaled. The sender had mistakenly written Lynchburg, *Virginia,* instead of Lynchburg, Tennessee. No wonder the envelope had gone astray. What a sloppy mistake to make, such lack of attention to detail. Then she read the return address—Department of Agriculture, Washington, DC—and bolted from the chair.

Dodge grabbed the last hay bale from the wagon bed and walked alongside Jake toward the horse barn. Not watching where he was going, Jake stepped into a pile of manure and nearly went down. He mumbled a choice word.

"Careful there," Dodge warned. "If Bethie hears you, she'll make you put another penny in the jar."

Jake laughed. "That niece of yours keeps us all on our toes, that's for sure. I sure am glad y'all are staying around, sir."

"Thanks, Jake. I appreciate that." And he meant it, even if he still hadn't found a way to move past the closed door of Wyoming.

"Want me to take the wagon back, sir?"

"No, I'll get it. I need to pick up Uncle Jack and Mr. Prince. Go ahead and get started in here. I'll send somebody in to help."

"You got it, boss."

Dodge made his way back to the wagon, hoping Mr. Prince's tour of the barrel house was going well. Uncle Jack had insisted on taking him, despite a broken big toe and a slight limp, thanks to the confrontation with the safe. He'd said he wanted to give Prince the full dog and pony show this time, impress upon him how rapidly the distillery was growing.

Dodge wondered if it was because Uncle Jack truly was getting ready to step back and hand control of things over to his nephews. The man didn't seem quite himself these days. Then again, he wasn't the only one.

Dodge climbed up into the wagon, thinking of the ring still buried deep in his pocket. He'd been so busy with Mr. Prince yesterday, and earlier in the week, there'd been no time to talk to Josephine. No, that wasn't true. He could have made the time, sought her out. And he determined to. It was foolish, he knew, but he dreaded sharing with her that he'd found her ring because he feared the discovery would be taken as a sign—a sign that she should go back to her husband.

It didn't help that Bethie had told him all she'd learned about her the other night. About her twin brother and parents dying not too long ago. Perhaps she'd married in haste, and hadn't known the man's true character until it was too late.

Jessie nuzzled close on the driver's seat. Dodge rubbed her ears then released the brake and prodded the mules forward. Whatever the situation with Josephine, he had to give her back the ring.

He'd barely made it a few yards when he heard someone calling his name. He turned on the bench seat and looked behind him to see Josephine running full out toward him. He set the brake and jumped down, wondering if this was God's way of saying, *Do it now.*

"I've looked everywhere for you!" she yelled when she got closer, near breathless. "Someone finally told me they'd seen you head up here. Something came for you. It's from . . . the Department of Agriculture. But instead of addressing it to Lynchburg, Tennessee—" She drew in more air. "They mistakenly addressed it to Lynchburg, *Virginia.* So it took longer to get here."

Dodge tore open the envelope. A single sheet of letterhead with two pages of instructions complete with drawings behind it. *"Dear Sirs,"* he read aloud. *"It has come to our attention that the cattle farm at Jack Daniel Distillery is currently experiencing . . ."* He skipped ahead. *"While there is currently no oral medication proven effective in combating Texas fever in cattle, the US Department of Agriculture is overseeing a cooperative effort with state governments to eradicate cattle ticks."*

He skimmed some more.

"To this end, in coordination with the Bureau of Animal Husbandry, we hereby extend an invitation to your farm to conduct a field test that would consist of tank systems and an experimental dipping solution. Instructions for the dipping stations are included and outlined in detail. Understanding that no guarantee can be offered for its success or against the potential loss of more cattle, limited trials conducted indicate this could be an effective solution in ridding the animals of ticks."

"Could be?" Doubt tinged her voice. "Still, it's more than we have right now."

Appreciating her use of "we," he continued reading. *"Should you agree to participate, your cooperation in reporting your findings would be mandatory . . .*" He skipped on down. "*Sincerely, etc* . . . Then they give the details for the dipping solution."

"Which are?" she asked, peering over the top of the letterhead.

He held the letter where she could read it, too.

Her brow rose. "A mixture of soda, pine tar, and . . . *white arsenic*? Dodge, that's poison. Is that even safe?"

"I don't know. The government claims it is, in regimented doses. But what alternative do we have? We've already lost almost half the herd, and stand to lose the rest if we don't do anything. We already have pine tar on hand. And soda, I can get from one of the dry goods stores here in town."

"What about white arsenic?"

"I'll try an apothecary in Tullahoma. I doubt he'll have enough on hand, but even if he doesn't, I'll need to wire for more from there anyway. Does Uncle Jack know we heard back from them yet?"

"No, I came to you first."

"He'll be encouraged. At least this gives us some hope."

She hesitated, glancing in the direction of the distillery. "Do you know if Mr. Prince has reviewed the entries in the gauger's book yet?"

"He hadn't when I left them earlier. But the ledger's ready to go. I double-checked everything myself."

"I know. I was just—" An odd look came over her face. "Do you know where they are right now?"

"My guess would be the barrel house. But . . . why?"

She seemed intent on not looking at him, the discomfort in her demeanor growing with each passing second.

"I think I'll go check in with them," she continued. "See if there's anything they need." She turned to go.

"Josephine . . ."

She paused. But again, would not meet his gaze.

"Whatever's bothering you, you best say it outright before it burns a hole straight through you."

Jaw tightening, she grimaced. "Oh Dodge . . . I've made a terrible mistake. I—" She placed a hand on her midsection as though about to be ill. "I altered four of the entries in the gauger's book yesterday morning."

He stared. "You did *what*?"

"I made the changes while you and Mr. Daniel were gone to the stillhouse."

"But why? Why would you do such a thing?"

Dread clouded her features. "I did it with the intention of giving Mr. Prince cause to temporarily shut down production here."

He searched her expression, having difficulty believing what he'd just heard, much less reconciling it to the woman he thought he knew. Yet the gravity—and regret—in her eyes said she was telling the truth.

"Dodge, I'm so sorry. I couldn't sleep last night and—"

"Do you have any idea what such an error could cost the distillery? Even more, how it could tarnish Uncle Jack's reputation? And the reputation of this distillery? We're the first—and therefore, the oldest—registered distillery in the country, Josephine. Since 1866, Jack Daniel has been known for his integrity and for paying every last penny of tax due to the government. He's never had the slightest trouble with the Bureau of Internal Revenue."

"Dodge, I feel sick about what I've done."

"But apparently not enough to have not done it. Did you even give a thought as to how this might affect me?"

"I did, in fact—"

"It's *my* responsibility to make sure that ledger is accurate. And what about the rest of the employees and their families?" Anger and disbelief churned inside him.

"I didn't change any of your entries. I changed ones with the initials GC beside them. Dodge, I thought that person no longer worked here. Then I met Gideon Cartwright last night and—" Her throat knotted tight. "I realized I couldn't go through with it. I couldn't do that to him. To any of you."

He exhaled, the muscles in his jaw working. "You say you're set on helping the wives and children of some of the men who work here, yet you do something like this that guarantees they won't see any pay for weeks!"

"I know, I should have thought it through better. I acted out of emotion, based on someone who's hurting terribly and—"

Dodge headed for the wagon.

She followed. "I'm going with you. I'll explain."

"And just how do you plan to do that? Better, I hope, than you've done with me." He climbed into the wagon, and she hurried around and climbed up beside him.

Neither spoke until they reached the barrel house.

He set the brake. "Best if you wait here in the wagon."

She jumped down alongside him, Jessie following. "I did this, Dodge. I'll take the blame. And whatever punishment is coming."

"Easy to say when the punishment will likely be fines you have no possible way of paying."

She flinched, and though he regretted his harsh tone, he didn't take back the words.

"Listen, let me find them and see where we are in the process. If Prince hasn't reviewed the ledger yet, I'll make some excuse to get it from him, then you and I will go back to the office and you will fix this. You remember which transactions you changed?"

"Yes," she said softly.

"Good, then maybe we can get everything resolved without anyone else being the wiser. Anyone other than Uncle Jack, that is. He'll have to be told."

"I know, and I'll tell him." Though she rightly appeared ill at the prospect. "But Dodge, please know how sorry I am. To you . . . especially."

He looked at her—anger and disappointment roiling inside him, and feeling more than a little betrayed. But what bothered him almost as much . . . How could he have been so blind so as not to have seen this coming. How had he missed it—a second time.

47

Seated behind his desk, Mr. Daniel stared between the two of them, his gaze finally fixing on Josephine. She couldn't decide whether he was about to fire her or send for Sheriff Rigby. Or both. The creak of a wagon passing by out front and the clomp of hooves filled the painful silence.

Dodge finally leaned forward. "Uncle Jack, while this could have gone very badly, no lasting harm has been done. At least not that the Treasury Department is privy to. I've corrected the ledger and it's ready for Mr. Prince's inspection."

Mr. Daniel nodded. "I was right when I said that hiring a suffragist would be a risky business. Wasn't I?"

Realizing the question was directed at her, Josephine nodded. "Yes, sir. You were. And again, I deeply apologize for trying to interfere with the—"

"When exactly did you first contemplate doing something like this?" Mr. Daniel asked.

She searched his expression. Usually she could read the man fairly well, but not at the moment. "Shortly after I left your office the day you first offered me the job."

Dodge looked over at her, but said nothing.

"And what changed your mind about following through with your plan?" Mr. Daniel continued.

Emotion threatened to undermine her voice, and it didn't help that Dodge was seated close, watching. She thought of Gideon Cartwright and of how her actions would have affected him. But in the end, she knew the *what*—or *who*—behind changing her mind. "You, Mr. Daniel." Her voice held, but barely. "Namely, your generosity. Not only to me, but to others. I—" She looked down at her hands folded tightly in her lap, then forced her gaze back to his. "I did not expect that. Or more candidly, I didn't expect it from a—"

"Distillery owner," Mr. Daniel stated matter-of-factly.

She nodded again, then could hardly push the next words past the shame gripping her throat. "And you as well . . . Mr. Coburn. Knowing that my actions would also affect you. And this, after you've been remarkably kind to me since my arrival."

She dared look over and the intensity in his blue eyes challenged her composure.

"Mr. Daniel," she continued. "What you said yesterday about reaping what you sow also set me to thinking. Regardless of my opinion about alcohol, I could not repay your overwhelming generosity with such . . . ingratitude."

"I'd hardly call what you almost succeeded in doing mere *ingratitude*, Mrs. Dunham. I'd term it more retaliation. Perhaps even payback on behalf of the American Woman Suffrage Association."

"But it wasn't intended toward you personally, sir. I hope you know that."

"No, you only intended to harm my distillery, my livelihood, and that of everyone who works for me. That makes all the difference." Though his expression was guarded, his sarcasm cut deep.

She struggled for what else she could say or do to convey her regret.

"Earlier . . ." Dodge finally broke the silence. "You said you acted from emotion based on someone who's hurting. Who were you referring to?"

She shook her head. "I can't tell you that."

"I only ask because I think it might help if we understood the motivation behind—"

"I'm sorry, but I can't tell you. It would reveal a confidence that's not mine to share."

Dodge faced forward again, his frustration evident. But what wounded far more was the disappointment she sensed from him. As though she should expect anything different.

"So, Mr. Daniel . . ." She intentionally unknotted her hands. "What are you going to do?"

He looked across the desk at her. "What do you mean?"

"I mean, sir, what happens to me? Are you firing me? Are you going to send for Sheriff Rigby?"

He studied her over steepled hands, then released a slow sigh. "I must confess, Mrs. Dunham, I committed a cardinal sin in relation to you. I did to you what people have been doing to me my entire life . . . I underestimated you. Don't get me wrong, I figured you would try something. After all, you left here that first day all hellfire and brimstonin' me, and not at all impressed with my illustrious gold medal." A touch of humor ghosted his mouth. "Then when I spotted you coming back that next morning, after you'd flat refused the job the day before, I thought to myself, *Here we go, Jack. This spitfire of a female is going to try to take you down.*" He laughed softly.

But Josephine couldn't.

"Your passion for justice—or *perceived* justice"—Mr. Daniel aimed a look she knew only too well—"is admirable, even if I adamantly disagree with your opinion on the matter. And here I was thinking you would choose to conveniently *forget* to order supplies or pay a bill, which would certainly have interrupted production. But your ingenuity to alter the gauger's book—gutsy, too, I admit—would have cost me dearly had you seen it through." His eyes narrowed. "So I'm most grateful, for all our sakes, Mrs. Dunham, that you did not."

Though he didn't say it outright, she clearly heard *or this would be turning out quite differently.*

"While I'm grateful, too," Dodge said, his tone solemn, "I think it's important for us to acknowledge something else. Although I'll admit, I was so angry, I didn't see it at first." He turned to her. "In the end, what prevented this from happening was that you placed Mr. Daniel and me, along with everyone else who would have been negatively affected by your actions, *above* your passion for justice as it relates to drinking. Or more specifically, in this instance, whiskey making. You valued people over strict principle, and that is not at all lost on me . . . Mrs. Dunham."

"Or me," Mr. Daniel echoed quietly. "As one of the finest men I knew used to say, *Hold your principles with conviction, and your neighbor with compassion.*" His gaze slid to Dodge whose expression held gratitude. "

My father," Dodge said softly, glancing over at her.

Josephine looked between the two of them, and swallowed hard. If she'd been close to losing her composure a moment earlier, their unexpected grace all but shattered it. To find such understanding not only from men, but from *these* two men—distillers—and here in these hills. So different from her father's begrudging, often prickly form of grace. Her father's adherence to principle had been unyielding and his interpretation of the letter of the law applied without question.

"So," Dodge continued. "Where do we go from here, Uncle Jack?"

"Forward, of course, but . . ." Mr. Daniel paused, his gaze steady on Josephine. "As the saying goes, *No man ever steps in the same river twice, for it is not the same river and he is not the same man.* Or in this instance, not the same man *or* woman."

She recognized the quote. "Heraclitus," she said—at the same time as Dodge. She looked beside her in surprise.

"I do know how to read, remember," he said in a stage whisper.

She shook her head, appreciating his attempt to lighten the tension. But when Mr. Daniel leaned forward in his leather chair, his expression grave, she braced herself. And sensed Dodge did, too.

"While disciplinary action is certainly appropriate in such situations, Mrs. Dunham, what would mean the most to me right now is for you to look me in the eyes and assure me that, if I agree to keep you on in this position, you will not knowingly do anything to harm this distillery's reputation or the livelihood of the people who work for me. Ever again."

She matched his stare unblinking. "I give you my solemn word, Mr. Daniel. Never again."

He held her gaze a beat longer, then rose. "All right then. That's settled. I trust this matter will stay between the three of us?"

She and Dodge nodded.

"Very good. Now if you'll both excuse me, I've got an appointment." He walked with a slight limp toward the door.

Josephine stood, feeling as though she'd been given a new lease on life. Undeservedly so. "Thank you again, Mr. Daniel. I appreciate this more than you likely realize."

"And I appreciate your honesty and reassurance, Mrs. Dunham. And will hold you to it. Dodge, whatever needs to be done to get those dipping stations for the cattle underway, do it!"

"I'm leaving for Tullahoma shortly. I'll pick up supplies and head back either tonight or in the morning, depending on how long it takes."

"Good man." He'd nearly closed the door when he paused. "Regarding that appropriate disciplinary action, Mrs. Dunham . . . An idea just came to me."

Her mind raced. Would he dock her pay? Require her to work longer hours? Maybe assign her to work elsewhere in the distillery in addition to her normal duties? Then she saw it. That glint of delight in his expression, which told her she wasn't going to like his choice of discipline one bit. But that he would.

48

"I'd be most obliged, Mrs. Dunham," Mr. Daniel continued, "if you would attend the dinner parties at my home when we host the upcoming gatherings for vendors. *All* of the dinners. And you must save a couple of dances for me. Does that sound fair to you?" He tossed her a look of victory as he closed the door.

Josephine just stared after him.

"You know he would've thought of it eventually." The barest hint of humor edged Dodge's tone. "And considering the circumstances, it doesn't seem like too big of a request."

"I suppose not . . ." She slowly peered up. *"Hezekiah."*

He gripped his chest as though mortally wounded. "Oh . . . now that hurts."

She smiled. "I'm only joking. It's not a bad name."

"What about . . . Hezekiah Eustace Coburn?"

"I hope you thanked the bull for sparing you that dreaded fate."

"More times than you would believe."

She laughed softly, and something in his expression, in the way he looked at her, stirred the memory of that kiss. She wondered again what it might have been like to meet him before all of this. Then again, would she have even noticed him while marching at rallies, flanked by suffragist sisters? Something told her she would have. Because Dodge Coburn was a most memorable man, even without his given name.

Breaking their gaze—just as he did—she glanced at the mantel clock and adopted a casual tone. "I think I'll head back to the boarding house. It's a bit early, but supper duties await, and Calla can always use the help. Not that I can cook, mind you."

A look passed across his face that gave her pause, then she realized . . .

"Wait," she said. "Did Uncle Jack tell you about what happened in Miss Mary's kitchen?"

"You mean with your biscuits hard as rocks and sausage gravy a congealed mess? No, he didn't. But Mrs. Gibbs did. Twice. Even after me telling her she'd already told me."

"That woman . . . She absolutely detests me."

"Detests is a pretty strong term." He paused. "Loathe might be better."

She smiled a little. "So you're headed to Tullahoma?"

"Yes, ma'am. For the white arsenic and a few other things."

He walked her outside where Jessie remained dutifully waiting, her tail wagging, and he closed the door behind them. "One last question before you go?"

She paused by the top step.

"Is it someone at the boarding house? Who you referred to before?"

It took her a moment to realize what he was asking. "Dodge, I really can't say who it is. It would reveal a confidence that's not—"

"Yours to share, I understand. But I'd like to help, and think I can. Especially if it's someone I know."

"I appreciate that, and I'm sure they would too, but—"

"Is it Calla?"

She faltered for an instant.

"Because if it is," he continued, "I hope you'll tell me. She's mighty special to us, Bethie and me. And was to Kathleen, too."

Josephine struggled for what to say that wouldn't break a promise but that also wouldn't be another lie. "While I haven't been here long, Dodge, I actually have gotten to know many people, and not all of them are associated with the boarding house. Besides, we both know how Miss Mary feels about drinking, and Calla is the last person in the world who would ever want to go against Miss Mary's wishes. So please, can we just—"

He held up a hand. "All right, I get it. I'll leave it alone."

Relaxing again, she took the porch steps to the street, grateful he'd accepted her response. "Be careful on your trip. Especially if you come back late tonight."

"I know these hills as well in the dark as I do in the day."

"I know, but still. Do you need help with Bethie?"

He shook his head. "I'll ask George Green if she can stay with them for the night. Bethie and his daughter Moriah are fast friends."

They walked to the corner where he gave her a parting salute.

"Dodge?"

He glanced back, and Jessie did too, the cattle dog panting in the afternoon heat.

"Thank you again for your understanding today. It wasn't deserved, from either of you, and I know it."

His smile came slowly. *"I've always found that mercy bears richer fruits than strict justice."*

"That's an easy one. Abraham Lincoln. But I'm impressed. This from a man who barely knows how to read."

His laughter followed her as she turned and walked back in the direction of the boarding house. The upheaval of emotions from the last couple of days gradually caught up with her and, on a whim, she stopped into Velma's Candy for a long-desired purchase. She chose three chocolate-covered caramels and three pralines—with Calla and Miss Mary in mind—and ate her two on the way home. *Delicious* didn't come close, the chocolate silky on her tongue, the pecans rich and buttery.

As she turned onto Miss Mary's street, the late afternoon sun spilled across the blue-green hills, bathing them in a hush of golden light. Thick stands of hardwood forest—hickory, oak, maple, and walnut—boasted hues too numerous to count and, even now, hovering above the highest rise, a shimmer of pink danced against the flawless blue sky. A trick of the heat or humidity perhaps, but still so beautiful, and her vision blurred with unshed tears.

She couldn't deny the beauty of this place or the surprising depth of community she'd found here, and in so short a time. While grateful, she felt unmoored and displaced, another world away from who she was, or had once been. So far from Atlanta, Sarah, her students. Did they even think of her anymore? Sarah did, she knew. But her students . . .

She'd seen enough teachers come and go to know how quickly most students acclimated and moved on. Which was what something inside her told her she needed to do. To move on. But to where? If she knew that, she would have already done it.

As she hurried up the walkway to the boarding house, an idea came as to how she might get the letter she'd written to Sarah delivered, along with the money, while still keeping her whereabouts hidden. Eager to speak with Calla, she reached to open the front door when it opened with force.

Miss Mary, a satchel in each hand and her expression fierce, marched across the porch and down the walkway. "When I say no liquor in my house, I mean *no liquor in my house*!"

Josephine froze. *Calla!* Somehow Miss Mary had found out. Thoughts colliding, she fought for what to say in Calla's defense. Something—anything—that would change Miss Mary's mind.

Then Mr. Morgan, a traveling salesman who'd checked into the boarding house two nights earlier, came running out. "*Please*, Miss Mary, I won't do it again. I-I must've forgotten the bottle was in my bag!"

"Well, maybe this will help you remember." With impressive strength, Miss Mary hefted the satchels and tossed them into the street. One of the bags, apparently not latched, came open, and clothes went flying, along with a half-empty bottle of Jack Daniel's that landed with a thud in the hard-packed dirt. "And don't bother asking to stay here again."

"What if I pour it out right now? Would that change your mind?" Mr. Morgan looked from the street back to Miss Mary. "And even if I can't stay, can I still take my meals here?"

Miss Mary's thunderous glare needed no words.

The man silently gathered his clothes, stuffed them into the open satchel, and trudged toward the town square.

Huffing, Miss Mary strode into the house. "I cannot abide somebody taking shelter in my home while disrespecting my rules."

Josephine followed her into the foyer and found Calla standing just inside, a stricken look on her friend's face.

"And did you hear him?" Miss Mary paused, hands on hips. "Having the nerve to ask for a seat back at my table. My lands, what is this world coming to? People everywhere seem to be losing their minds. Just look at this." She grabbed a newspaper from the side table. "One of them suffragists in New York City attacked a judge right outside his home. All for not voting the way she thought he should. And he was with his young daughter!"

Josephine stiffened. She'd seen that article when scouring Mr. Daniel's newspapers in recent days. Feeling Calla's attention, she hadn't forgotten how Calla had found her suffragist sash beneath the bed, yet had obviously said nothing about it to Miss Mary.

"When did people decide the rules don't apply to them?" Miss Mary continued. "I just can't for the life of me understand how—" Miss Mary suddenly stopped short. Her face paled, and she swallowed hard. She pressed a hand to her waist.

Josephine reached out, recalling the morning she'd seen Miss Mary in the field and wondering again if her hunch then had been right. "Are you unwell, ma'am?"

"No, no, I'm fine." Miss Mary took a deep breath. "Just got myself too worked up, is all. Well, come on, you two. Supper won't finish itself." She disappeared into the kitchen.

But Calla didn't move, her focus moving to the street. "Lord, help me, Josephine. That's gonna be my fate, too, once she finds out."

"She won't find out." Josephine lowered her voice. "You're going to get through this, Calla. And I'm going to help you do it." Although she didn't have the slightest idea how to do that yet.

Later that evening, with supper dishes done, the kitchen set to right, and menus for the next week decided, Miss Mary was saying good night when Josephine remembered her impromptu detour on the way back that afternoon.

"Before you go, Miss Mary, I got you and Calla a little something today." She reached into the cloth bag and handed them each a chocolate-covered caramel along with a praline. "It's from Velma's Candy on the square. Consider it a *very* small token of my appreciation for all you've done for me."

Calla stared at the candy in her palm. "You got any idea how long it's been since I ate anything not of my own making?"

The softness in Calla's voice touched her, as did the look of pleasure when Calla popped the caramel in her mouth. "Oh *my*, that is some kind of good."

But Miss Mary just stared at hers. "I thank you, kindly, Josephine. But I'll save mine for later. I'm a bit full right now."

"Full?" Calla frowned. "I seen your supper plate. You hardly ate a thing." Her eyes narrowed. "You still having that sour stomach?"

Miss Mary waved off the concern as she slipped the candy back into the bag. "Don't waste your worry on me, I'm fine."

"I ain't wasting my worry. I just think you oughta take yourself to Doc Wyatt, is all."

"I don't need to see Doc Wyatt."

"And I think you do! You been having them pains for a while now."

"I'm not having pains, Calla."

"Well, whatever it is you got ailing you, it's been going on too long, and—"

"I'm not ailing."

"Well something ain't right, and a doctor sure enough could—"

"I don't need a doctor to tell me I'm with child!"

Calla stopped cold, her mouth slipping open before a smile that seemed lit from within slowly spread across her face. Josephine shared it.

"You with child, ma'am? *Oh . . .*" Calla gently touched Miss Mary's midsection, emotion tightening her voice. "Why didn't you say something 'fore now?"

Miss Mary shook her head, surprising tears coming to her eyes. "Because I don't want to add to your pain, Calla," she whispered, her voice absent its usual command. "This time of year is always so hard for you. I remember your dear husband and precious son so well. You've been through so much, and I would never do anything to—"

Calla drew Miss Mary to her and Miss Mary's arms came around her. As the two women hugged, Josephine could feel the love between them, the sense of belonging they shared. And as happy as she was for them, emotion of an entirely different kind burned her eyes.

Calla drew back. "You being with child, ma'am . . . And having a precious little one running around here? Well, that just makes my heart sing! What did Mr. Bobo say when you told him? I'm betting he's so proud."

Miss Mary hesitated. "Well, that's just it. I haven't told him yet. Oh I reckon he'll be *right* happy at the news. We've been trying for a family for a while now. But . . ." She briefly looked at Josephine, then away. "You both know he's been in and out of town so much lately, traveling like he is. Still, his recent jobs haven't been as fruitful as he'd hoped. Meanwhile, here I am, proprietress of this boarding house that's doing so well. Not usually something a female manages these days, especially a woman with a child. Or children, if God sees fit. And I just don't know how Mr. Bobo will feel about all that, taken as a whole. But God has blessed us, to be sure. This place is what I've always dreamed of having. And Calla, your cooking is a big part of the reason why tenants stay like they do, and why guests keep coming back. Your fried chicken and that fudge pie."

Calla's smile softened. "You're as much the reason as my food is, ma'am. You got a way of making everybody feel at home here, and so welcome."

Miss Mary laughed. "Well, not everybody. I doubt our Mr. Morgan whose belongings I just tossed into the street would agree."

Calla's smile faltered. Guilt crept in behind her eyes, and Josephine rushed to fill the silence.

"May I offer my own congratulations, Miss Mary. I'm so happy for you, ma'am. And for your husband, who I'm sure will be thrilled."

Miss Mary pursed her lips. "I have a feeling this news doesn't hold the same surprise for you, Josephine. I think you might've heard me in the field one morning before church." Miss Mary glanced at Calla. "Something I'd been craving didn't set too well that particular day."

Understanding gradually dawned in Calla's expression. "It was *you* who ate that last jar of pickled beets!"

Miss Mary smiled. "Guilty, I'm afraid. And while they tasted good going down, I paid for it later."

They all laughed.

"Mr. Bobo's due home in the next couple of days," Miss Mary continued. "I'll tell him the news, and would appreciate your confidence until then."

Josephine nodded, and Calla followed suit.

"Who knows . . ." Miss Mary's smile held doubt. "Maybe my husband will be all right with being married to a woman running a successful boarding house while also raising a family."

Josephine didn't know Mr. Bobo well, by any means, but she knew men in general. In her experience, husbands wanted their wives at home, doting on them, not other people. And most wouldn't want their wives doing better in business than they did.

"Why sure he'll be all right with it," Calla gently offered. "And don't you worry none about raising a child in this boarding house. That little boy or girl will be loved and cared for, and'll have so many doters they won't know what to do with all the kindness."

"I hope so," Miss Mary said softly. "Because I love what I'm doing and think I could stay right here for the rest of my days and live a long and happy life." She grasped Calla's hand. "Providing you stay here with me."

Josephine didn't miss the flicker of uncertainty in Calla's gaze.

"'Course, I will," Calla finally managed. "Where else would I go?"

But Josephine knew what she was thinking, and she hated the painful lie Calla was living, almost as much as the one she was.

49

"THIS TRENCH needs to be five inches deeper, Jake. And an even six feet in height the entire length."

"You got it, boss." Jake and the men with him started digging again.

Dodge worked his way down the twelve-foot-long, four-foot-wide makeshift wooden vat he and others had built over the past two days, measuring as he went. The vat had to be deep enough to fully submerge every cow, bull, steer, and calf. That was the only way to kill the ticks. Concrete would've been better, the agricultural department said, but hauling materials and waiting on curing time would've cost them the herd. So Dodge chose speed over permanence: a wooden vat built from local oak, sealed with pine tar. Once it dried, they'd mix the arsenic solution and begin dipping—experimental, risky, but their last, best hope.

He climbed from the vat and grabbed his shirt from the fence rail. He mopped his forehead, the April sun blazing overhead. So much for March going out like a lamb. The turn of the calendar had brought with it unseasonably dry, scorching heat, which meant the ticks would thrive.

Another day or so and dipping could begin—assuming the arsenic and remaining ingredients arrived by courier as promised in the agricultural department's telegram delivered yesterday.

He took a good, long drink of water from the bucket by the well, then doused himself with the remainder of it, the cool water running down his chest and back.

He glanced toward town, his mind circling Josephine's near-disastrous plan to sabotage the distillery. How different her presence in Lynchburg would feel if she'd gone through with it. She'd come close, despite her last-minute change of heart.

He and Uncle Jack had hashed it out since, agreeing her remorse seemed genuine. And she had given her word. Still, he wasn't finished reckoning with it and decided it would be wise to keep a closer watch where she was concerned, in case her suffrage fervor flared again.

He'd been tempted to tell Uncle Jack about finding her wedding ring, but seeing as he still had it in his possession, he'd thought better of it. He resolved to return it to her the very next time he saw her.

And if that sent her back to her husband—whom he still struggled to believe existed—so be it. He had no right to influence her either way. With effort, he'd laid his desire for her at the foot of the Almighty's throne. Now if he could only leave it there.

"Is it safe to approach?"

Hearing Uncle Jack's voice, Dodge turned to see him—and Josephine—cresting the hill.

"Sure. We haven't mixed the solution yet." He grabbed his shirt from the fence rail and went to meet them, not missing Josephine's lingering look as he pulled it on. Try as he might to curb his desire for her, those looks didn't help.

"Care for a tour of the 'canal of prosperity,' as the government's calling it?" Dodge asked.

"I'm in." Uncle Jack gestured, then looked at Josephine.

"Lead the way, Mr. Coburn."

Dodge walked them through the entire process, answering questions as they went. Minutes later, they ended back where they'd begun.

"One question, Dodge." Uncle Jack stroked his beard. "Any chance this whole dipping process will be finished by next weekend?"

"If the arsenic and other ingredients arrive tomorrow as planned, we'll be done in two days. Three tops. And should see results within a week. Why?"

"Because our first group of vendors arrives next Friday!"

Josephine's head snapped up. "Next weekend? Mr. Daniel, that doesn't leave us time to prepare for everything you want to do."

"We're only showing them the distillery, Mrs. Dunham. Telling them how we make the whiskey. That's what they want to hear about. Then we'll have dinner at my house that night. All very simple."

"But not simple to execute," she countered. "Where will the guests stay? Who's giving the tours? Which buildings will they see? Are the employees prepared? Are the facilities ready for visitors?"

Uncle Jack just smiled. "It never ceases to amaze me how many prodigious thoughts are spinning around in that remarkably capable—and might I add, lovely—head of yours."

She exhaled. "Mr. Daniel, I—"

"I've already put my nephew Lem Motlow on it. Guest lists, schedules, accommodations. All of it."

Josephine paused. "Lem *Motlow* as in Ophelia Motlow's husband? Miss Mary's sister?"

Seeing her confusion, Dodge jumped in. "One and the same. Lem is Uncle Jack's sister's oldest son. Lem recently married Ophelia, Miss Mary's younger sister, after his first wife died a couple of years back. Everybody in town's related somehow, Josephine, so best tread carefully if you gossip."

"So then," Uncle Jack continued, "everything's in hand. It promises to be a grand success. Lem says we even have guests requesting to bring guests!" His full mustache twitched as he smiled. "And if memory serves . . . you promised to attend the dinners, Mrs. Dunham. So I will most favorably anticipate your presence next Friday night."

"I believe she promised to save you a couple of dances as well," Dodge added, fully expecting the glare she tossed him.

"Indeed, she did, Dodge. Now, one more thing . . . I want a shingle made with our motto."

Josephine looked at them. "The distillery has a motto?"

Mr. Daniel cleared his throat. "*Every day we make it, we'll make it the best we can!* What do you think? Better yet!" Uncle Jack snapped his fingers. "Let's have it printed on a big banner we can drape across the side of one of the barrel houses. That way, all the vendors will see it when they arrive."

"I think that's a wonderful idea!" Josephine gave him an enthusiastic smile. "For Mr. Motlow to pursue."

Uncle Jack chuckled. "First time I met you, Mrs. Dunham, I knew I'd met my match. And I have not been disappointed."

The sparkle in her eyes said she appreciated the comment, even if the slight tilt of her head suggested she intended to carry on exactly as she pleased.

"Shall I escort you back to the office, Mrs. Dunham, on the way to my next meeting?"

"You go on ahead, sir. I have something I need to speak with Mr. Coburn about."

Once Uncle Jack was out of earshot, she leaned in slightly. "You said the other day, Dodge, that you'd like to help the person struggling. That you thought you could."

Following her train of thought, he nodded.

"While I'm still not at liberty to share who it is, I'm wondering . . ." Earnestness filled her expression. "How do you help someone who's addicted to liquor? I know all the right things to say. I've stood outside taverns and have handed out pledge cards. I've spoken publicly about the evils of drink and the need to stop." She briefly looked away. "But I have no idea how to practically help someone. But I deeply want to."

More convinced than ever that Calla was that someone, he didn't dare admit it. But if it was her, he hurt for her. And that also meant he'd somehow missed the signs, and that hurt on a whole other level. "First, I know about this because someone I've worked closely with here at the distillery struggled with drinking too much. He quit about six years ago. I remember the time frame because he and I just talked about it the other day."

"I would imagine many people here are plagued with that particular problem."

Accusation layered her tone and apparently she heard it, too.

She winced. "I'm sorry, I didn't mean to sound—"

"I think you might be surprised, Josephine, at how many people work here yet who only drink it on occasion. Some perhaps never. Take me, for example. I'm a regular taster for the distillery and—" He paused for effect. "I enjoy that aspect of my job. And even the taste of it."

She made a face, and he laughed.

"And I will, on rare occasion, have a glass of Old No. 7, and I'll enjoy it. But I don't have to have it, and beyond that, I've made a conscious choice not to have it on a regular basis. Because—"

"Because you've seen what liquor does to people," she interjected. "The misery and trouble it brings."

He held her gaze. "Because I've learned that while a man—and woman—are free to choose, not everything he or she chooses is good for them. And anything we can't control—drink, food, anger, bad habits . . . desires—"

Something flickered in her eyes.

"—those things end up controlling us. And I don't want to be ruled by anything or anyone. Well, except the Almighty."

She searched his gaze, her own so full of honesty and curiosity, then she chuckled beneath her breath. "Underestimated," she whispered.

"Beg your pardon?"

"I'm just saying I underestimated you, yet again. And we'll simply have to agree to disagree on the taste."

"Is that right?" He smiled, remembering the jerky she loved so much. "Remember that recipe you wanted me to share with you?"

"For the jerky you make. *Yes.* Are you finally ready to—" Awareness flickered across her face. "No . . ."

He laughed and looked away for a beat. "I haven't had the heart to tell you, seeing as how you love it, and yet knowing how you feel about Old No. 7."

"And you've let me eat it, even knowing what you do about me."

Hearing both teasing and slight seriousness in her voice, he held up a hand. "All the alcohol cooks out of it during the process. Or mostly all." He winked. "And don't worry, I won't tell anybody."

She tossed him a playful glance of promised retribution, then shielded her eyes from the sun, her expression going serious again. "How did you help that friend? Practically speaking, I mean."

"Mainly I was just there whenever he needed anything. Someone to talk to, to go fishing with, shooting with. Sometimes I'd just sit and listen as he walked back through his life, reliving both the good and the bad. I guess you could say my door was always open. Doc Wyatt helped him a good deal, too, though. Doc mixed up some remedies. Nothing magic, mind you. Nothing like those 'natural tonics' laced with alcohol that swindlers in big cities hawk on street corners. Doc's grandmother was what we used to call a healer. Talk to him. He was here a while ago, but left. He'll be happy to help you . . . and whoever it is you're trying to help."

She nodded, taking it all in. "Thank you, Dodge."

"You're welcome, Josephine."

She turned to go, and he remembered the ring in his pocket.

"I need to talk to you about something, too, Josephine. If you have a minute."

"Sure." She glanced around. "But could we find somewhere out of the sun?"

They walked a short distance down a sloping path through a stand of pines to the creek where the canopy of an old oak provided relief from the heat. Water sluicing over smooth rock and the chatter of birds overhead made a comforting backdrop. He gestured to a fallen log, then sat beside her, keeping a respectable distance, mindful of the solitude around them.

He could feel her watching him as he reached into his pocket. "I found this a few days ago. I keep meaning to give it to you but—" He started to say he hadn't had the opportunity or had forgotten, but didn't want to lie. "It was wedged between the floorboards beneath the driver's seat in the wagon." He opened his palm.

A soft gasp threaded her lips. She took it from him, her eyes filling. She slipped it on her ring finger, then held out her hand to admire it. "Oh Dodge, thank you. I can't tell you what this means to me. I thought I'd lost it forever."

He looked down at her hand, watching her closely. "I'm glad you got it back. It obviously means a lot to you."

"It does. More than I can say." She quickly looked up. "I mean, not because of the marriage so much, of course. Not after what . . . *he* did. But because this belonged to my mother."

He nodded as though understanding what she meant, as though believing her.

"Well . . ." She finally wiped her cheeks. "I'd better get back to the office. But truly, Dodge, thank you for this. And for the tour."

"My pleasure."

She started to rise, but on instinct bolstered by gut hunch, he took hold of her hand and pulled her back down beside him. Her eyes went wide, but she didn't move away. Not an inch.

"Just one question before you go, Josephine."

She swallowed, her breath quickening.

He looked down at the ring, then slowly back up at her. "If you're married, as you say you are . . . why are you wearing your wedding band on the wrong hand?"

50

Josephine looked down at her right hand—and her throat went dry. How could she have been so careless. So thoughtless.

Struggling to see her tangled web of a life from a bird's-eye view, she grasped for any excuse that might make her mistake seem reasonable. But the longer the silence stretched, the more she realized that any explanation she would offer would only sound like the lie it would be. And looking into Dodge's eyes, she knew he saw it, too. She didn't want to lie to him. Not anymore. When his hand closed firmly around hers, she didn't pull away.

"You're not married," he said softly.

She slowly shook her head, and the pleasure in his eyes ignited something inside her.

"For what it's worth, I've always doubted that part of your story. Or maybe it was just wishful thinking on my part."

His gaze lowered to her mouth, and she wanted him to kiss her. Right here, right now. It was all she could do not to lean in first.

"Still, I'd like to hear you say it out loud."

She looked at him, confused. "Say what?"

"That you're not really married."

Whether it was the huskiness of his voice or the faint smolder in his gaze, warmth flooded her body. "I . . . am . . . not . . . married," she whispered. "Nor have I ever been."

"Good to know." He cradled her cheek, his thumb tracing her partially open lips.

She wasn't sure who reached who first or how her hands got into his hair, she only knew that when she deepened the kiss, his response took her breath with it. After a moment, he pulled back slightly, the blue of his eyes far deeper than she remembered.

She ran a hand over his beard. "You trimmed it."

"Just this morning. Bethie got onto me again about it."

"It looks nice." She smiled, taking him in. She could look at him all day long and never tire of it. And although her single suffragist sisters would tell her to run and never look back, another voice inside told her this man was different. That he could be trusted. But could that voice be trusted?

"Josephine . . ." He covered her hand on his chest. "Whoever or whatever you're hiding from, tell me, and I'll help you however I can."

Her pulse still thrumming, she briefly closed her eyes, imagining the disillusionment he would feel when he learned the truth about her. Once he found out she'd killed a man, she feared, in his eyes, she would become just another fanatic suffragist—the very kind he condemned.

She gently tugged her hand from his grip, hoping that would help her to think more clearly. It didn't. "Dodge, I—" All semblance of thought fled, leaving only dread and fear in its place.

He fingered a strand of hair at her temple. "The easiest way to say something hard is usually just to say it."

She gave a nervous laugh. "If I did that, I think you'd run."

"Try me."

The speed of his response and certainty in his voice, the solidness of him beside her . . .

"I killed a man," she said, her voice barely audible.

He didn't move. He didn't flinch. He just waited.

"I was speaking at a suffragist rally." She inhaled then slowly let out the breath. "In Atlanta, where I'm from. Not quite a month ago. Miss Anthony was there and had spoken right before me. It was outside. Hundreds of people had gathered in the street, not all of them supporters."

She recounted every detail she could remember. What she'd said in her speech, how a group of men in the crowd—one man in particular—began heckling her, how he'd thrown that first rotten egg, then the rock, then how a barrage of empty whiskey bottles had been unleashed. "Utter chaos broke out. The police eventually arrived, but instead of stopping the violence, they started arresting the suffragists—who were behaving peacefully!"

She described how she'd avoided being hauled off to jail because of what Todd had taught her. Next, the painful memories of losing Todd poured out, followed by the agony of how he'd died and the crushing blow of losing her parents soon after.

Dodge clasped her hands between his, listening without interrupting. Speaking of Sarah and her fiery Irish spirit brought a fleeting smile to both their faces, but it quickly vanished as she relayed how Clay Darden dragged her into the alley.

Dodge's grip tightened. "Go on," he said quietly, voice strained.

"He . . . got on top of me and started beating me with his belt. I looked for something, anything, to defend myself with and finally found a piece of a brick and—" Reliving the sensation of brick meeting bone sent a shiver through her. "I struck him in the head as *hard* as I could. And he just . . . slumped over. And didn't get up. By then, Sarah had found me, so she saw it all happen. But he never came to. No pulse, nothing. So, we ran."

"You killed that man in self-defense. A man who likely would have killed you." His eyes narrowed. "Do you know who he was? Why he came after you?"

"When he interrupted my speech, I was quick to put him in his place, and some people in the crowd laughed. He didn't like it. I could see he was embarrassed, but I was determined he wouldn't get the best of me." She gave a humorless laugh. "Ironic, isn't it?" She watched a branch being whisked along by the creek's current until the momentum finally pulled the branch under and it disappeared downstream. "What I didn't know until Sarah found me in the alley was that he was the son of Frank Darden, the mayor of Atlanta. A man as anti-suffragist as they come."

Dodge was silent for a moment, looking at the ring on her right hand before turning her hand over. He frowned and traced a forefinger over the healed cuts on her palm. "What's this from?"

"I tried to shield my face from his belt."

Slowly, he brought her hand to his mouth and pressed soft kisses on the faint scars. The gentleness she felt in the act, his understanding and compassion, pushed tears to the surface.

"Josephine, I—" His voice caught. "I've thought so many times about what I'd like to do to the man who did this to you. And even now, part of me wishes he were still alive so I could do it. I'm *so* sorry this happened. I'm sorry we live in a world where a man would do this to a woman."

Josephine stared at their hands, fingers intertwined. "A fellow suffragist, Adelaide Stewart, a good deal older than me, we marched together on several occasions . . . She used to say that the worst thing you could do to a man was to laugh at him, to make fun of him. I always thought she was wrong." Her throat tightened. "I don't anymore."

The distant rumble of a wagon slowly made its way toward them.

He finally looked over. "Surely, if we went to the authorities in Atlanta and explained what happened—"

"Mayor Darden routinely arrests women who support suffrage, and the conditions for them in the prison there are harsh, Dodge. They're treated like criminals. If they refuse food, which some do, hoping to draw attention to the cause, Mayor Darden has them force-fed. Three women I've known personally nearly died from the liquid being pumped into the lungs instead of their stomachs. They suffered cuts to their mouths and their throats, then had high fevers and sickness. Can you fathom what he would do to the woman who killed his son?"

"And so you ran," he said softly.

"With Sarah's help, I got on the first train I could and got out of Atlanta. By the time I got to Chattanooga, authorities were already looking for me in the station. Same for Tullahoma. Slim Poyner helped me get by them and out of the station there and . . . well, you know the rest."

She smiled but he didn't.

"I treated you rudely that first night, Josephine, and I'm sorry. Especially knowing now what you'd been through. But I looked at you and . . . I think I saw all the pain and mistreatment Kathleen had been through. Then when I saw that sash sticking out of your coat pocket . . ."

"That certainly didn't play in my favor, did it?"

That earned her a hint of a smile, at least.

"When we first pulled into Lynchburg that night, and I saw how small a town it was, and how remote, I thought I'd be safe. Especially when I found out there was no newspaper, no telegraph."

"Cut off from the outside world."

"Something like that. Then I learned that a 'very wealthy man in town' had the Chattanooga newspaper delivered to him."

He shook his head. "Good ol' Uncle Jack."

"So after hoping I might be safe, the clock started ticking on that very first night. And every day since, I check *The Chattanooga Times* before Mr. Daniel gets in, hoping nothing about the incident will be in there."

He peered over. "Is that why you took to making sure his newspaper is all nice and pressed?"

She gave him a look.

"Very clever, *Miss* Dunham." He hesitated. "Is that even your real name?"

She nodded. "Something else I wasn't planning on using . . . until Mr. Poyner did, with you. There was no going back after that."

A breeze stirred the trees, and a leaf fluttered and dipped and twirled before finally landing noiselessly at their feet.

"Do you think Mayor Darden had your brother killed?"

"I do, although I have no proof. But my parents believed that, too."

A moment passed, and he started to say something when someone called his name from a good distance away. She turned and looked behind them.

"It's all right." He smiled. "Even in winter, you can't see this spot from up on the hill. But it's probably best if we get back. Just in case anybody saw us coming down here. You're a married woman, after all." He stood and offered his hand, and pulled her up. A slow smile tipped his mouth. "Don't be looking at me like that, Mrs. Dunham. You have no idea what that does to me."

"Oh I think I have some idea."

He closed the distance between them and kissed her, but much more slowly this time, his hand on the nape of her neck, the other tracing a slow path down her back that awakened every nerve in her.

"You not being married," he whispered against her mouth. "That's about the best news I've ever gotten."

She laughed, looking up at him. "And you letting me climb up into your wagon that night . . . *without* assistance, I might add—"

He groaned, which only deepened her smile.

"—you saved me from being caught and taken back to Atlanta, and to prison."

"God saved you from all that. I just happened to be the conveyance he chose at the time."

Hearing the conviction in his tone, she found herself wanting to believe that God still knew the details of her life, and that he cared enough to step into them.

They walked back uphill. Nearly to the top, he paused. "You're going to have to keep being *Mrs.* Dunham, at least until we can figure out next steps."

His use of the word *we*—and even *next steps*—made her feel not so alone. "Yes, I know. And believe me, I've been trying to figure that out."

He looked pointedly down at her right hand, then back at her, and she quickly moved her mother's ring to her left.

"Two are better than one," he said quietly.

It took a minute, but she gathered his meaning. "I never knew that inscription was there until after my mother died. But—" She looked up at him, wondering what Miss Anthony would say if she could hear her now. "I'm beginning to think it may be true, as much as that frightens me."

His laughter was immediate and warm. "Oh, I know it's true. And if it helps, it doesn't frighten me a bit."

When they crested the hill, a farmhand, Jake—Josephine thought his name was—saw them and waved. "Hey boss, I don't know who you talked to—" Jake gestured to a loaded wagon in front of the barn. "But the supplies for dipping got in a day early."

The wagon's driver, an older man with skin well aged by the sun, looked down at Dodge. "You Dodge Coburn, the man in charge of all this?"

"Yes, sir, I am."

"Well I hope you know what you're doing with it, 'cause you could kill 'bout everything in Moore County with this stuff."

"We'll be careful. Jake, get some men and let's get it unloaded. Everybody wears gloves. And every last box or bucket of this goes in the shed like we discussed. Nothing in the barn. Nothing anywhere near living quarters or animals."

"You got it, boss."

Josephine walked with Dodge to the back of the wagon. "I take it this is the arsenic?"

"This ain't just arsenic, ma'am." The driver joined them and lowered the tailboard. "It's almost two hundred pounds of it, along with pine sap, and calcium oxide. Like I said, I hope you all know what you're doing."

Dodge peered at the wagon's contents. "It's for fighting Texas fever. The Department of Agriculture believes it'll rid the cattle of ticks."

"The Department of Agriculture? You mean the gover'ment?" The man spit a dark stream of tobacco. "We'll all be dead by nightfall. Reckon I can't make it outta here fast enough!"

Dodge laughed, and she did too. But the driver scowled.

Dodge gestured to her. "I'm going to be a while. Why don't Bethie and I come by Miss Mary's for supper. Maybe we can talk some more?"

"I'd like that." She also liked the subtle meaning in his eyes, and the fact that he knew the truth about her now. No more pretense. At least with him. "But Dodge . . ." She glanced at the wagonload of chemicals. "Who's going to mix all this up?"

"That would be me."

"Is it even safe?"

The driver cursed. "No, it ain't safe, woman! Ain't you been listening to me talking?"

Dodge shook his head, directing his attention to her. "I know what I'm doing. The Department of Agriculture sent thorough instructions. And don't worry . . ." He winked. "I'm good at holding my breath. Besides, a few of the farmhands around here have been eyeing my position, wanting to take my place. They might just get their chance."

"I 'bout plumb forgot . . ." The driver reached back up to the bench seat and grabbed an envelope. "Man by the name of Poyner from the train asked me to tote this on up to you. Said it looked official."

Dodge took the envelope from him, read the front, and Josephine caught equal parts hopefulness and dread in his features.

"Is it good news?" she asked. "Or bad."

"I don't know yet." He held it up, and she read the words *Department of the Interior, The United States of America* encircling a round emblem in the upper right-hand corner. "I'm assuming it's about my land."

"In Wyoming."

He nodded.

"Perhaps you have a buyer."

"Maybe." He shoved the envelope in the back of his waistband and pulled a pair of gloves from a pants side pocket. "But it'll have to wait." He nodded toward the group of men headed their way. "I'll come by Miss Mary's later."

If his clipped tone didn't signal the end of their conversation, his turning to begin unloading the wagon did.

51

Following supper that evening, with the dishes put away, Josephine joined Bethie and her friend Agnes Preston in the library while Agnes's father conducted business with Mr. Daniel and Dodge in rocking chairs on the front porch. Their conversation—mules, cattle, distillery matters—drifted in through an open window.

She'd come to understand that this was how deals were struck in Lynchburg. Over shared meals and rocking chairs on front porches. It wasn't a bad way to do business.

Despite the open windows, the house remained warm. Bethie had personally invited her to join the girls, so Josephine hadn't dared refuse. Still, the girls' choice of reading—*The Adventures of Pinocchio* by Carlo Collodi—felt uncomfortably apt. Its lessons on honesty and consequence struck too close, especially now that Dodge knew the truth about her. And especially remembering how Bethie had once called her a *liar* in this very room. The thought of the girl eventually learning she'd been right filled her with regret.

Half an hour later, Josephine looked out the window to see Mr. Daniel and Ballard Preston shaking hands.

"Come on, Agnes," her father called. "Sun's fixin' to quit on us."

The girls hugged, and Josephine walked Agnes outside while Bethie disappeared into the kitchen in search of pie. As Mr. Preston and little Agnes headed down the road and Mr. Daniel turned the other way—hardly a limp in his gait—Josephine lifted her face to the breeze, welcoming the cooler air. And the quiet.

Evenings in Lynchburg carried a stillness she hadn't known before. No electric lights, no streetcars clattering toward their final stops. When darkness fell here, it claimed the town outright.

"Join me?" Dodge asked softly.

"It would be my pleasure." She settled into the rocker beside him.

"If you weren't still married," he whispered, eyes forward, "I'd hold your hand right now."

"And if I were still single," she whispered, "I'd let you."

His soft laughter eased something inside her. He'd been subdued all evening. She suspected it had to do with the letter he'd received.

"You told me about your friend Sarah." He glanced toward the front door as though making certain they were still alone. "Have you been in touch with her since you left?"

"I mailed her a letter only yesterday. I had Nannie Burroughs forward it for me."

"The woman who preached. I remember."

She turned toward him. "Do you disapprove of a woman preaching?"

He sighed. "You're relentless, you know that?"

She smiled faintly.

"I'm fine with women preaching, Josephine. Even though I'll be the first to say, it would take some getting used to. I'm fine with women voting and owning land and having their own bank accounts. I think a woman ought to be able to choose her own path in life, just like a man does. If she wants an education, she ought to be able to get one. If she wants to marry and be a mother, she should do that. If she wants to run for Congress, then by all means, run for Congress. But what I can't approve of . . ." He leaned forward in the rocker, forearms resting on his knees. "Is women being thrown in jail and force-fed and nearly dying in the process. Or a woman being dragged into an alley and beaten by a man who's so threatened by her intellect and independence, a man so full of prideful ignorance, that he can't see that woman for who and what God created her to be."

Tears blurred Josephine's vision.

"Is that clear enough? Or do I need to expound further."

She sniffed. "You used *expound* on purpose, just to show off."

"Absolutely I did. Look who I'm talking to." He finally leaned back. "As I've told you, I'm all for change. But it's going to take time. And it's going to take not just women, but men coming alongside to help enable that change. And if it riles you to hear that, then you're just going to have to be riled. But that is the truth, Josephine. Men are largely in charge right now. Be that right or wrong, and frankly, I see a lot of wrong. But just switching which sex is in charge, pardon my bluntness, won't fix the issue either. It's the character of the man or the woman that matters."

The silence lengthened.

"Any other questions on that point?" he asked, the faintest smile coloring his tone.

"Not at present, no. But I appreciate your clarity."

"And I appreciate your relentlessness. Most of the time."

She did her best not to let her smile show. He was so good at masking his humor, which only made what he said seem more humorous. But his words had found their mark, and were already taking root.

Silence surrounded them as she gazed up at the vastness of the dark night sky, every star visible in sharp detail. The moon, a brilliant white, shimmered against the inky backdrop, almost iridescent. She drank it all in, along with the soothing trill of crickets and the soft songs of other midnight serenaders.

"So about that letter you received from the Department of the Interior . . ."

He didn't answer for a moment. "I have a buyer, but it's not the price I was hoping for."

"A bit lower?"

He pointed downward.

"*Much* lower?"

He nodded. "I have to admit, though, it's still a fair-enough price, considering. It's just not what I paid, or what I think the land is really worth. But the offer meets the reserve I set, so I'm legally obligated to sell. I just wish now that I'd never signed the agreement."

He'd originally described the land in Wyoming as wild and breathtaking, his connection to it undeniable. And though the "wild west" had never held appeal—she preferred Europe or even Africa with its ancient wonders, the places she and Sarah had dreamed about traveling to together—his disappointment still tugged at her heart. "I'm so sorry, Dodge." And she meant it. But the words felt weak and flimsy in the moment.

"I wish I could have shown it to you, Josephine. Prime acreage with good water rights and fertile grasslands. Not a day's ride to the railroad. I think you would've fallen in love with it, too."

Perhaps it was the sadness in his voice or the barrier that had lifted between them since she'd revealed the truth about her situation, but it occurred to her that she was still growing accustomed to the possibility of the "we" of them and hadn't looked much beyond that. How could she, considering her situation? But he apparently had. Which told her they weren't just discussing land anymore.

He turned toward her in the fading light. "Does land out west like that not appeal to you?"

Too late, she realized her silence had revealed more than she'd intended. "Dodge, the way you described your dream of Wyoming sounds truly breathtaking—"

"But?"

Another layer of disappointment lined his voice, and she hated having put it there. "There's no 'but' really. It's just that . . . I've studied world history all my life and what I've always dreamed of seeing are the great cathedrals of Europe or the ancient pyramids of Egypt, that's all."

A long moment passed, and the front door opened.

Miss Mary stepped out. "I'm just coming to say good night." She paused for a long moment. "Everything all right out here?"

Dodge stood. "You bet, Miss Mary, everything's fine. Thanks again to you and Calla for supper. It was delicious."

"Want me to send Bethie on out?"

"Please. And tell her no more pie."

"It's a little late for that," Miss Mary said as she closed the door.

Josephine rose, the creak of the rocker overloud in the quiet. "Dodge, I didn't mean to upset you by what I said, I—"

"You didn't." He looked at her, his face hidden in the darkness. "It's just that, when I look at you, I see a woman determined to make her own history, not one content to just walk through someone else's."

52

Josephine hurried from the distillery office to the boarding house, having promised to be on time today. Miss Mary rang that bell at six o'clock sharp every evening and, for some reason, the proprietress had been short-tempered, even terse, this week. Perhaps not feeling well from her pregnancy. Whatever the cause, she wasn't about to be late.

The hectic pace of the last five days was catching up to her. But at least everything appeared ready for the vendors arriving midday tomorrow in time for a tour then the Friday evening dinner party, followed by more activities on Saturday. True to Mr. Daniel's word, his nephew Lem Motlow, a man roughly twenty years her senior, she guessed, had handled the majority of the details. And in true Jack Daniel style, the event promised to be lavish and entertaining.

As she passed Velma's Candy, she waved to Velma inside, thinking about those caramels and pralines again, as well as the fudge she'd purchased two days ago. She'd shared it with Calla who relished every bite. Dodge had been right about Doc Wyatt. She'd spoken with the physician earlier that week, and he was eager to help "her friend."

I see a woman determined to make her own history, not one content to just walk through someone else's . . . Dodge's words echoed in her mind for the thousandth time. He'd captivated her thoughts all week.

She'd seen him several times in the office and when she and Mr. Daniel went to watch the dipping process, which, so far, seemed to be working. But although everything appeared fine on the surface, she sensed a shift in the undercurrent. She'd attempted to sort out her feelings about him.

Her attraction to him was undeniable. She greatly respected him, cared for him deeply, and every time she left his company, she regretted having to. But how he fit into her life—Bethie, too, for that matter, as much as she adored the girl—was what she couldn't come to terms with. Especially with the shadow of Clay Darden's death hanging over her.

As she turned up the walkway to the boarding house, the suffrage mantras she had fast embraced—*Freedom, not marriage. A wife is not a possession. Liberty before love*—marched through her mind again, and didn't help the sorting process. But that was just it . . .

No matter how many times she honestly and unbiasedly viewed Dodge Coburn through a *suffrage lens*, none of those mantras fit the man she knew. None.

She walked through the front door and caught a whiff of fried chicken, candied cinnamon apples, and something else . . . maybe collard greens. For her lunch, Calla had sent a slice of leftover meatloaf with bread and while delicious, that seemed a distant memory now. If she wasn't mistaken, she smelled buttermilk pound cake, too, and was glad Dodge and Bethie were coming for supper.

She rushed into the kitchen with not a moment to spare. "As promised, here I am, ready to work. So tell me what—" She stopped short, seeing Calla and Miss Mary seated at the kitchen table.

Calla's face showed concern, but it was the thunder in Miss Mary's expression—and the newspaper in her hand—that threatened to buckle her knees.

"W-what's wrong?" she asked, and caught the almost imperceptible shake of Calla's head.

"What's wrong?" Miss Mary repeated. "What's *wrong*!? What's wrong is that you lied to me. To us. Straight-faced. Over and over again. And this, after I opened not only my home to you, but my heart." She took a sharp breath. "Calla did the same, and this is how you repay us!"

Miss Mary waved the newspaper clutched in her grip, and Josephine caught the words *Suffragist* and *Murder* in the headline—and the air evaporated from the room.

"I-I can explain," she began, her voice coming out higher pitched. "However the newspaper reported it, it's likely wrong. Or else biased. So *please*, give me the chance to—"

"Biased? You're telling me there's another way to describe this?"

"Yes! There is. I'd been speaking at a rally in Atlanta that morning . . ." The words tumbled out, one after the other, coming faster and faster, until each next breath seemed impossible to take. "He dragged me into the alley. He began beating me. I—"

"Josephine, we're talking about attempted murder here! That's an accusation that's very difficult to get wrong."

"I understand, but if you'll only listen to—" She stilled, Miss Mary's words circling back with force. "*Attempted* murder?"

Miss Mary exhaled. "I'm done with the lying, *Miss* Josephine Dunham. I will no longer abide your—"

Josephine grabbed the newspaper.

"What on earth do you think you're doing? We're in my house and—"

She read the headline. *Atlanta Suffragist Sought for Attempted Murder.* She looked up. "But I killed him. When I left him, he was *dead*."

Miss Mary fell silent.

But Calla moved closer. "What do you mean you *killed* him, Josephine? This newspaper don't say nothing about you killing a man. Only that you tried."

"I didn't *try* to kill him. I was just trying to stop him. He attacked me first. I was only defending myself."

Miss Mary pointed to the newspaper. "This says nothing about self-defense, Josephine. They're saying you acted with forethought!"

Josephine skimmed the front page and sure enough, the article painted a very different picture from the truth. One of a militant female suffragist who had lured a man into an alley under questionable intent but with the real goal of killing him, not only for retribution after he dared to interrupt her speech and publicly deride her opinions, but for revenge against his father's efforts to protect the law-abiding citizens of Atlanta from this *maniacal band of emotionally unstable women*. But all Josephine could think about . . . "Clay Darden is alive."

Calla touched her arm. "But *why* did you think he was dead?"

"Because once I hit him with that brick, he fell on top of me. Blood poured from his head. We couldn't find a pulse and—"

"*We?*" Miss Mary's eyes widened. "Someone else was in on this with you?"

"There was no *this*, Miss Mary, I promise. I—"

"Supper can wait," Miss Mary announced and dragged a kitchen chair from beneath the table. "I want you to sit right down and tell us what happened. And I want the truth."

Glimpsing cautious trust in Miss Mary's eyes, Josephine did as asked and told them everything, same as she had Dodge. They asked questions, and she answered.

When she finally finished, Miss Mary's hard stare portended the reaction Josephine had feared from her. Only, it hurt far more now that she cared so deeply about the woman.

"From the minute I took you into my home, Josephine Dunham, I feared you'd bring trouble. But I did it anyway because I felt the Lord telling me to. And here you did exactly what I thought you would. Only it was trouble bigger than I could ever imagine."

Josephine bowed her head, just as Miss Mary's hand covered hers.

"I'm not saying I agree with all the choices you've made," Miss Mary continued. "All the lying specifically. But given the same circumstances, Lord help me, I reckon I would've done the same."

Calla leaned close. "No wonder you were so scared those first few nights. I heard you in your bed crying, even though I know you didn't mean for me to."

Josephine lifted her gaze, squeezing both their hands. "All this time, I thought I'd killed him. I thought I was wanted for murder. But he's alive."

"Well, don't start celebrating just yet, Josephine." Miss Mary's eyes darted to *The Chattanooga Times* on the table. "Did you read clear to the bottom? That last part? Since they haven't been able to find you, the mayor of Atlanta just put out a reward for anybody who can bring you back to face justice."

"And brace yourself," Calla said. "It's *a lot* of money!"

Josephine read the last paragraph and her stomach dropped.

"What's a lot of money?"

Recognizing his voice, Josephine turned to see Dodge standing in the doorway.

Miss Mary quickly moved to cover the newspaper, but Josephine stopped her.

"It's all right, he knows."

"He knows?" Miss Mary asked.

Dodge looked at them. "What's going on?"

Josephine held out the paper. "He's not dead, Dodge. I didn't kill him. I thought I had, but I didn't."

Dodge glanced at Miss Mary before scanning the front page. "Josephine told me everything a few days back," he said, still reading. "But only after I found her ring in the wagon. When I gave it back to her, she accidentally slipped it on the ring finger of her *right* hand." He finally looked up. "That's when I knew my suspicions were right."

"For what it's worth—" Miss Mary looked over. "I never quite bought that part of your story."

Calla reached for her left hand. "I ain't even noticed you wearing it."

"But a thousand-dollar bounty." Dodge dropped the newspaper on the table. "That's not insignificant."

Josephine checked the date of the newspaper. "This was printed yesterday. How did it get here so quickly?"

"Mr. Bobo got back from his trip a couple of hours ago." Miss Mary gestured to two other newspapers on the chair beside her. "He brought all these with him."

"Any of those papers carrying this story?" Dodge asked.

"No." Miss Mary looked at him, then Josephine. "At least not yet."

Josephine gave a humorless laugh. "I had a feeling Mr. Bobo's traveling and bringing you newspapers wasn't going to work well for me."

"These were all still wrapped tight, though," Miss Mary offered. "So he hasn't read a one of them. And if he'd read it elsewhere, he would've said."

"So as far as we know," Dodge continued, "the four of us are the only ones in Lynchburg who've seen this."

Miss Mary and Calla nodded.

"And can we agree to keep it that way? At least until we can figure out . . . next steps?"

Again, they nodded.

But Josephine caught the familiar words and knew he hadn't said them by mistake. His attention was already on her when she turned, and the concern in his gaze—along with his carefully guarded affection—laid waste every remaining mantra. Now if she could only find a way to escape the far-reaching arm of Mayor Darden's *justice*.

53

The next evening, Josephine arrived for the dinner party at Jack Daniel's residence a little late, not at all surprised to discover he lived in the finest home in town.

The large two-story Victorian house, set back a good distance from the road and a quick walk from the distillery, was flanked on either side with magnolias and crepe myrtles gone a little wild. A muted shade of blue, or what once might have been teal green, covered the weathered wooden siding, and intricate woodwork of gingerbread trim and decorative railings accented the wraparound porch. Hanging ferns and potted geraniums, along with front flower beds overflowing with lilies, irises, and daffodils gave the place a touch of elegance she'd come to expect from Mr. Daniel.

As she climbed the steps to the front porch, soft strains of piano music drifted through the open floor-to-ceiling windows of what appeared to be a ballroom on the main floor. Why was she not surprised. Her thoughts turned to the young woman Mr. Daniel had spoken of—Fannie, he'd called her—the one who had played the piano for his parties. And she felt quite certain, based on the weight of memory in his voice that day, that he still thought of her, too.

She knocked on the door, wishing again she could have foregone this event, especially after yesterday's discovery in the newspaper by Miss Mary. But she had given Mr. Daniel her word, and she was eager to talk to Dodge again. She'd seen him in passing today, but never alone.

She'd worn her best dress, which fell far short of anything remotely formal. But she had taken extra care with her hair. Thanks to Calla's braiding skills, she trusted the elegant chignon borrowed from Miss Mary would hold for the night.

A woman in crisp, formal serving attire answered the door. "How do you do this evening, Mrs. Dunham. Come right on in. Everyone's in the ballroom just there."

"Thank you." She continued in the direction the woman had gestured, then paused just outside the room, wondering at Mr. Daniel's definition of a dinner party. This was a proper Southern social soiree.

At a glance, she estimated at least a hundred people—most already twirling and dancing on the polished marble floor, others gathered in small groups visiting, drinks in hand. The room, a good thirty feet wide and at least fifty feet long, had high ceilings, close to sixteen feet, she guessed. Rich red draperies framed the tall windows, lending an elegance to the room that complemented the grand piano in the corner. If not for the candlelit crystal chandeliers that cast a soft glow over the elegant gathering, she might have believed she was still in Atlanta.

A touch to her elbow brought her around and though she instantly knew those eyes, she still couldn't help but stare. She had considered Dodge Coburn handsome before, but this . . .

He wore a dark single-breasted waistcoat with matching vest, the pieces accentuating his broad shoulders and tapered waist. His white dress shirt with its stiff, starched collar contrasted with his tanned skin, and the formal trousers, night-and-day different from the dungarees he wore every day, were classic straight legged with a crisp crease down the front. But it was his freshly shaven face that caused her mouth to slip open.

"May I have this next dance, *Miss* Dunham," Dodge said where only she could hear, bending slightly at the waist.

"What happened to your beard?"

"I was told it was time to shave it off."

"Bethie?"

He nodded.

"Remind me to thank that girl."

He feigned a hurt look.

"Don't get me wrong. I very much like you with a *tamed* beard. But this is also nice, Mr. Coburn."

He smiled in a way that made her wish they were alone again by the creek.

She glanced around. "But are you certain this is proper under the circumstances?"

"Completely. This is Lynchburg, after all. We're far less formal. Besides, if you haven't noticed, other men are already eyeing you."

She looked around and true enough, a few men were looking in her direction.

"Since you're married," he continued, glancing at the ring on her left hand, "you're a safe dance partner. Meaning they don't have to worry about their attention being misconstrued. Plus, at least to locals, you're an outsider. They see you as temporary and likely gone soon. So best they enjoy the view close-up while they can." His grip tightened on her elbow ever so slightly, and she read hope in his eyes—and wanted to believe it. But a thousand-dollar reward felt impossible to outrun. "Lastly, Mrs. Dunham, the simple fact is . . . you are the most stunning woman in the room, and every man in this room knows it." He glanced toward the dance floor. "Shall we?"

From the pianist at the grand piano, the "Swan Theme" from Tchaikovsky's *Swan Lake* began to fill the hall as he led her to the dance floor. A little rusty, she discovered him to be a confident and steady lead. It had been years since she'd danced like this, but with each step, she felt the rhythm returning.

Dodge kept a respectable distance between them. Still, just touching him—him holding her right hand, while his other rested lightly on her upper back—made her grateful Mr. Daniel had mandated attendance tonight as her *punishment*.

Not missing the occasional glance in their direction, she noticed that most people were simply enjoying themselves.

"You look beautiful tonight," he said softly.

"You're the one who has all the women staring."

He frowned. "There are other women here?"

She playfully swatted his arm, then swallowed against the sheer magic and unlikelihood of this moment. Being in a ballroom, in Jack Daniel's home, in Lynchburg, Tennessee—a place she'd never even heard of a month ago, much less could have found on a map—and in the arms of this man. "Thank you for this, Dodge."

"For what?"

Her eyes watered and it took her a moment to get the words out. "For knowing what you know, and yet still being here. With me. Like this."

His hand caressed her back. "Josephine Dunham, if we weren't on a dance floor . . ."

Her breath quickened at the look in his eyes.

"Later, after the party, if you'll allow me to walk you back, I have some ideas I'd like to share. One, in particular, I hope you'll say yes to. Let's just say it has to do with figuring out a way to make you truly disappear, once and for all."

Whether it was the promise in his eyes or the yearning, bittersweet nature of the melody of the music, she actually started to believe there could be next steps. And with him.

The music gradually ended, and a popular tune—"In the Good Old Summertime"—began. To Josephine's surprise, Mr. Daniel tapped Dodge on the shoulder and cut in. But she didn't mind overmuch. She needed a chance to catch her breath.

If she'd thought that dancing with Jack Daniel, who stood slightly shorter than she did, might have come with some awkwardness, nothing could have been further from the truth. He was an excellent dance partner and never missed a beat. The man was in control on the dance floor. Just as he seemed to be in other parts of life. She, on the other hand, had to concentrate to keep up with him.

"I'm glad you came tonight, Mrs. Dunham."

"I am, too, Mr. Daniel. Thank you for *inviting* me."

He smiled, obviously catching her meaning. "Are you surprised to find such elegance in these hills and hollers?"

"No, not at all."

He looked at her.

"Well, yes, a little. But you have a beautiful home and this is a lovely gathering. Well done to your nephew, Mr. Motlow. That said, I have learned to expect nothing but excellence from you, sir."

"My goodness, high praise, indeed, especially coming from you. And hard-earned, I'll say."

She chuckled. "Judging by the size of this gathering, it looks as though most of New York City showed up."

"It is a good showing. More than half are established vendors already selling Old No. 7 in their establishments. But the rest are potentials we're working on, Lem and me. Just you wait, Mrs. Dunham, they'll be ordering Old No. 7 by the wagonload."

While she couldn't share his enthusiasm for that particular outcome, she had to appreciate his entrepreneurial gift. "You're a natural-born salesman, Mr. Daniel."

"Oh I don't know about natural, Mrs. Dunham. I just learned while I was young how to talk to people. But mainly how to listen. That's the key, I think. That and making the best-tasting whiskey in the world." He wriggled his mustache. "Have you seen my gold medal?"

She laughed, easily understanding why women flocked to this man.

"I do credit most of my success to two men who helped me very early on in life. One a preacher, the other a slave."

"George Green actually told me about them both, sir. Especially his father, Nearest. I would have loved to have known him. Admittedly, though, I found it odd that a preacher would be teaching a young boy about whiskey."

"Oh, Dan and his wife Mary Jane taught me about far more than that. They, along with Nearest and his family, accepted me, gave me a home, a purpose, a place where I felt like I was wanted, and where I could make a difference. That's a mighty hefty gift to give a person in this life."

She looked into Jack Daniel's eyes and, in a blink, saw both the man and the boy, and caught a glimpse of where the seed of his generosity to so many—including her—had been sown. And to people whose opinions differed so vastly from his own.

"Is he still alive?" she asked softly. "Dan Call?"

He shook his head. "He's gone now too. Died last year. Everybody you love eventually seems to leave you, one way or the other, don't they?"

Her throat closed, and it was all she could do to answer. "Yes," she whispered, thinking of her family, of Sarah, her students. And even of him, and the people in this town who, so quickly, had come to mean so much. "It certainly feels that way."

As they danced, she found her attention instinctively drawn to Dodge. At present, he was dancing . . . with Rowena Gibbs. A twinge of jealousy flickered inside her as she watched them together, and she couldn't help but feel an equal twinge of satisfaction at the barely concealed frustration in his expression.

The music ended and everyone applauded. She thanked Mr. Daniel for the dance and turned to go.

"Oh no, Mrs. Dunham. I believe I said two dances, did I not? And I most definitely want to share this next one with you."

The air suddenly filled with the rich, melodic swell of brass instruments, joined soon by woodwind and percussion, and Josephine searched the room until she saw the fully outfitted cornet band situated not far from the grand piano. She looked back at Mr. Daniel and caught that customary twinkle in his eyes.

"Mrs. Dunham, may I present The Silver Cornet Band of Lynchburg, Tennessee."

She shook her head. "Your doing, I take it."

"I might have had a small hand in it. After all, music is my first love. Well, after whiskey and the company of beautiful women." He winked. "We outfitted the whole ensemble from the Sears, Roebuck & Company catalog. Best two hundred and seventy-seven dollars and seventy cents I've ever spent." He grasped her hand. "Now, Mrs. Dunham, I trust you know the waltz."

"I did at one time, sir. But I'll now have to lean heavily on your lead."

"Music to my ears, madam." He swept her along on the dance floor, the melody of "The Merry Widow Waltz" rising and swirling around them.

When the music finally ended, thunderous applause rose, and the band immediately launched into "The Washington Post," a lively, energetic tune. A few couples continued dancing, but most moved off to the side to enjoy the music.

"Thank you for the pleasure of your company, Mrs. Dunham."

"Likewise, Mr. Daniel. It was, indeed, a pleasure."

He looked up at her. "What is it about you that makes me so at ease in your company?"

She smiled. "Perhaps it's because I'm the one woman in this room not *completely* under your spell, sir." She glanced around. "However, you must be aware that women are watching you even now, hoping you'll ask them next."

He sighed and gave his vest a sharp tug. "Yes, there's much to be done in that arena. Enjoy the rest of your evening, Mrs. Dunham."

Inwardly shaking her head at the way he sauntered across the room, Josephine sought out the refreshment table and poured a cup of punch from an ornate crystal bowl, taking a small first sip to make sure it hadn't been spiked. It had not. Parched, she downed it, but before she could pour another, a gentleman approached. One of the visitors from New York City, she felt certain, judging by his manner and attire.

"May I have this dance, madam?"

"Of course, you may, sir."

He held her a little tighter and closer than she would have liked and when the music ended and another man cut in, she quickly wished the former a good evening. There were four more dances with four different partners, two from out of town, and two locals—Mr. Carver from the mercantile who was already a little tipsy and who spent most of his time apologizing for stepping on her feet, then "their dear Mr. Prince" as Miss Mary called him, who discussed tax exemption and documentation the entire time. She was exhausted.

She made her way back to the refreshment table, politely declining two more invitations en route, then poured another cup of punch, took a quick sip, then downed it and two more.

She spotted Dodge dancing with Mrs. Gibbs, forced pleasantness in his features.

"You're not good enough for him, you know."

Josephine turned at the voice, and felt her back stiffen. "Miss Gibbs, how are you this evening?"

"Don't you have any shame at all? We all know the truth about you. How you're with child and just pretending to be married. Well, Mama is making sure right now that he knows everything about you. And she's getting ready to tell everybody else, too. Right here. Tonight. Then we'll see what he thinks. And who he chooses." Rowena pushed past her and maneuvered her way across the dance floor.

Josephine's gaze traveled to Dodge who was still dancing with Mrs. Gibbs, sort of. The woman was talking incessantly, scarcely drawing breath, while Dodge appeared to be losing patience by the second. But what Mrs. Gibbs didn't know, and for what Josephine was so grateful, was that Dodge Coburn already knew the worst about her. Still . . .

She decided it would be best if she took her leave. Perhaps Mrs. Gibbs would forego her public declaration and not ruin the evening for Mr. Daniel and his guests. She motioned to Dodge that she was leaving, and he quickly motioned back. Then she paused, unclear on whether the nod of his head had been meant for her or Mrs. Gibbs.

Finally deciding he'd intended it for her, she slipped from the room and into the foyer where she was confronted with a group of very well-dressed men who had gathered to enjoy a generous supply of cigars and whiskey, as evidenced by the thick haze of smoke and the numerous empty bottles of Old No. 7 lining a side table.

She tried to skirt around them to the front door but the space was too tight and their boisterous conversation far too animated. Looking behind her, she remembered seeing the woman who had greeted her at the door disappearing down this hallway, likely to the kitchen which would most certainly lead to a back door.

The narrow corridor led to another hallway, dim with only candlelit wall sconces. Josephine felt certain she was on the right path, yet despite discovering a coat closet, a storage room, and a very well-supplied pantry, she couldn't locate the kitchen.

Finally, she rounded the corner at the end of the hallway and saw light coming from an open door. The kitchen. And a very nice one. But empty. The staff was probably out serving guests, of which she was grateful not to be one anymore.

Eager to get back to Miss Mary's, she hurried out the back door, closing it behind her—and ran headlong into someone in the dark. She stumbled back and smacked her head against the doorframe.

"Watch where you're going, you ignorant . . ." The man spat out a string of profanities, the scent of liquor sharp on him. But it was the edge in his voice that sent a chill crawling up her spine.

As he stepped closer, pale moonlight fell across his face and the air squeezed from Josephine's lungs. Heart pounding in her ears, she told herself it couldn't be him. But it was. The puckered skin of a gash marked his temple and upper cheek. "Clay Darden . . ."

He eyed her, surprisingly steady on his feet. "Do I know you?" He took another step forward, squinting. "Wait . . . I think I do."

She spun, opened the door behind her, and nearly had it closed when he slammed his full weight against it. She stumbled back and hit her head on something solid before she hit the brick floor. Pain exploded across the base of her skull and shot down her spine and legs. She tried to stand, but couldn't.

Above the screaming pain was the blur of a cornet band, raucous laughter, and people clapping and cheering. She screamed, but her own voice sounded so far away. Seeing the underside of a worktable, she tried to crawl beneath it. But he grabbed her legs and pulled her back. She screamed again and kicked at him.

"Shut your stupid face, you—" Cursing, he slapped her hard across the cheek.

He tried to pull her up but she went limp. He staggered and dropped her. Seeing her chance, she scrambled to her feet and kicked him as hard as she could exactly where Todd had taught her.

He doubled over, clutching himself, curses pouring from his mouth as if something alive was forcing its way out. She raced for the door leading to the hallway, screaming for help, when she felt—and heard—a loud crack across her lower back. Her legs buckled and she went down.

"This time we're gonna finish this . . . Josephine Dunham. Just you and me."

He struck her again with the rolling pin, and she curled into a ball, trying to shield her head with her arms, her lungs screaming for air. He dragged her up by the bodice of her dress, punched her hard in the gut, and everything went black.

54

HOW MUCH TIME HAD PASSED when she finally came to, Josephine didn't know. Her head still fuzzy, she blinked until the world slowly came into focus. He was carrying her, slung over his shoulder, the smell of whiskey still strong, but different from before. Then she saw the slow-burning fires flickering beneath the stills. They were in the stillhouse? At the distillery?

She screamed for help, and he dropped her hard on the plank wood floor, dangerously close to one of the stills. Heat poured from the smoldering embers, and every part of her body hurt. The ceiling of the wooden building swam somewhere far above her.

"Scream all you want. As I told you, we're gonna finish this, just you and me. All you miserable man-haters have caused enough trouble. What you need is to learn what a woman's good for, and I aim to teach you that once and for all." He laughed, unbuckling his belt. "Maybe after you've known a real man, you'll stop trying to act like one."

He dropped down on top of her, the weight of his body a sick memory that caused a cold unlike anything she'd known to grip her head to toe. She clawed and kicked and screamed as he made his intent clear.

Oh, God, please no . . .

Frantic, she searched for a way to stop him as images of Dodge and Bethie flashed through her mind, then Todd, and her parents, their faces clear and vivid. Then she saw the fire beneath the still. As if her body knew what was coming, her stomach roiled as she reached for the flames. Already feeling the scream clawing its way up her throat, she grabbed a handful of embers, the fire searing her flesh, and shoved it hard into the side of his face and neck.

He screamed and rolled to one side, and she got up and ran, cradling her right hand against her chest.

The warehouse was dark, the only light coming from the copper stills, and she couldn't see a way out. Gunfire sounded behind her, and she instinctively hit the floor. After a few seconds, she slowly raised her head and looked at row after row of bubbling, simmering stills all around her.

"Stop shooting!" she yelled. "Don't you know where we are?"

Two consecutive shots rang out, much closer this time, and she ran, hunched over, her body beginning to shake, her palm throbbing. Lightheaded, she sank down against the wall, trembling and holding her hand as she prayed the darkness would swallow her whole. A minute passed, maybe another, and she wondered if maybe—

"I can hear you breathing, you miserable—"

Another shot, this time striking the wall just above her head.

About to move again, she heard a dog barking, then the bang of a door opening hard.

"Josephine! Are you in here?"

Dodge.

"I'm over here!"

Her right hand of little use, she crawled as best she could toward the sound of his voice, and Jessie's barking.

Two more shots rang out, followed by a deep rumbling, then a hiss, and a second later, a still exploded. Metal and wood went flying, and a sudden scream tore through it all.

That's when she saw Dodge running toward her. Struggling to see through the smoke, she moved as fast as she could but he covered the distance first and grabbed her up in his arms.

More hissing, then a deep roil of thunder, and two more stills exploded, sending fireballs toward the ceiling. Dodge was nearly to the door when Clay Darden stepped from behind a still not ten feet from them, gun leveled.

"Dodge, look out!"

"I should have killed you back in Atlanta!"

She braced for the gunshot as Dodge angled his body to shield her. But no shot came. Only the repeated click of an empty chamber before the warehouse erupted in flames.

55

Coughing, struggling for air, Josephine couldn't stop shaking. Her eyes burned and hot throbs of pain pulsed in her right hand.

"Doc Wyatt, over here!" Dodge yelled, his voice strained. He lowered her to the ground as smoke and flames blurred the night sky. Men and women raced back and forth, shouting. Others stood stock-still, watching.

Doc Wyatt knelt beside them. "Was she in the building?"

"Yes, sir, I just carried her out."

The doctor leaned close. "Mrs. Dunham, if you can hear me, can you tell me if you're hurt?"

"My hand," she managed, her throat raw, jaw quivering. Not wanting to, she brought her right arm away from her chest and opened her palm.

Doc's expression was a smooth mask, Dodge's was far less so. Doc Wyatt started rummaging through his bag. Dodge took off his suit coat and draped it over her.

He leaned close, cradling her face, his own smudged with soot. "I'm so sorry, Josephine," he whispered, his voice unusually fragile. "I should have been here for you. But you're safe now. You're going to be all right."

"We need a bucket of water from the spring, Dodge. Fast as you can."

Dodge brushed a kiss to her forehead. "I'll be right back."

She watched him go, not wanting him to leave. Despite having his coat, she couldn't stop shaking. The faint click of glass bottles, the potent scent of camphor, and a sharp metallic odor layered the smoky air.

"Mrs. Dunham, are you still with me?" Doc Wyatt asked.

She blinked, her head swimming but pain keeping her conscious. "Yes . . . I'm here."

"I'm here to help you. If you've been . . . *injured* in any other way, you can tell me."

The hesitance in his voice made her question, and she closed her eyes in an attempt to take inventory. Every part of her hurt, then she remembered. "H-he hit me . . . in the lower back . . . with a rolling pin." Just remembering the pain, and the sound, brought fresh emotion.

A thud and the slosh of water, and she opened her eyes to see Dodge kneeling beside her again. His breath came hard from the run, but something else in him had changed. Anger rolled off him.

"I'd like to give you a thorough examination later, Mrs. Dunham," Doc Wyatt said quietly. "But for now, Dodge, give her a quick drink then I need to cool down the wound."

Dodge held the cup to her lips and she drank, the cold spring water working its way down and reminding her of the first day they'd met, when he'd offered her water from a stream. She saw the same memory in his eyes.

"Now, Mrs. Dunham, please stretch out your arm. Yes, just like that. Dodge, I need you to keep her arm still, please."

She tensed, bracing herself as the doctor ladled a cup of water from the bucket.

"I'll be quick, ma'am."

She gritted her teeth, trying not to scream, and failing. Instinctively, she tried to pull away but Dodge held her arm fast as the doctor poured again and again.

Dodge leaned close. "I know it hurts. It'll be over soon."

Tears slid from the corners of her eyes as stabs of pain pulsed up her arm. "Thank you for coming when you did," she managed, stifling a groan.

"We heard gunshots. I looked for you at Uncle Jack's, but couldn't find you."

She opened her mouth to respond, but pain flared across her hand again, taking her breath with it.

"Soap to clean the wound," Doc Wyatt said softly. "I'm being as gentle as I can."

Dodge reached for her other hand and held it tight.

Drawing strength from his grip, she looked beyond him to the flames devouring the stillhouse and to the partygoers and locals passing buckets of water in a frantic chain. She spotted Mr. Daniel among them, unmistakable even in the chaos, helping alongside everyone else.

Another explosion sounded from within the building, and she flinched. Even knowing Clay Darden could no longer harm her, fear still clung to her. She could feel it on her skin and taste it on her tongue. But she tried to find comfort in—

Something moved in the doorway of the stillhouse, the silhouette of a—

No. It couldn't be . . . She tried to raise up.

"Josephine, you need to lie still. The doc is—"

"It's *him*," she whispered, a chill gripping her chest. "But how? H-how can he—"

Dodge looked back just as Darden staggered through the door of the burning building then collapsed. Men raced to douse the flames on his clothing, then dragged his body clear of the fire.

"Doc!" a man yelled. "We need you over here!"

"Mrs. Dunham, one last step for now. Tincture of iodine. This must be applied carefully. It will not be pleasant, but again, I will be quick."

She gripped Dodge's hand as tightly as she could, the sharp scent of iodine registering just before the pain. She would have screamed if she'd had air left in her lungs.

"There, that should prevent infection in the short term. I'll do more, but the wound needs to air. I do have laudanum if you—"

She shook her head, laudanum containing alcohol. Plus, the last thing she wanted—with Clay Darden still alive—was for her senses to be dulled.

"All right then. I'll be back shortly to apply a salve that'll help with the pain."

He packed his satchel and hurried away, and she struggled to see Clay Darden through the crowd, same as Dodge. Not until Doc Wyatt knelt down beside him could they get a clear view. Darden was not moving.

Dodge leaned down and kissed her forehead, once, twice. "I'm so sorry, Josephine." He brushed the hair back from her face. "I should have been here. Are you . . . all right?"

She nodded. "It *hurts*, but I think what Doc Wyatt did is helping."

"No. What I'm asking is—" Whatever it was, the words didn't seem to want to leave him. "Did Darden *hurt* you?"

Catching the echo of Doc Wyatt's earlier question in Dodge's now, the meaning behind the word swiftly became clear. But it was the unmistakable love in Dodge's voice—in the gentleness with which he touched her—that brought a sob.

"Oh God . . ." He bowed his head. "I'll kill him."

She forced his gaze back to hers. "No, Dodge. He did not hurt me. Not like that."

He stared as if not believing her. "But the bodice of your dress is—it's ripped, so I thought—"

She looked down at his suit jacket as memory tripped back over itself to that moment in the kitchen. "Darden hit me and I fell. I remember him dragging me up by the front of my dress. It must have torn then." She cradled his cheek. "But he did not hurt me in that way." Her chin trembled, and she doubted her voice would hold. "But he did try."

A deep exhale, and he brought her hand clasped in his to his mouth and kissed it hard, then looked back to where Doc Wyatt continued to work on Darden. "Tell me what happened."

The steel in his voice warned her against trying to spare him any detail. "I was leaving the party and tried to leave through the front door, but there were too many people. I couldn't get out. So I decided to find the kitchen and leave that way . . ." She told him everything and he never looked away. Not once.

By the time she finished, she felt empty of tears. Not only from having to relive the experience, but from reliving it through his eyes.

"Uncle Dodge!"

They turned to see Bethie running straight for them, Jessie hot on her heels, and Miss Mary and Calla a short distance behind.

"Would you help me sit up, please?" Josephine asked, and he slowly eased her upright then covered her again with his coat. She painstakingly slipped her injured hand into her lap, clenching her jaw against the pain.

Bethie threw her arms around his neck. "Are you okay, Uncle Dodge?"

"I'm fine, Bethie girl." He held her tight, then gave Jessie a rub. "But Mrs. Dunham is hurt."

Concern knit the girl's brow. "Anything I can do for you, ma'am?"

"You just did, Bethie. Thank you." Her head swam a little, and she took deep breaths, aware of Dodge watching her.

Bethie regaled them with how she and others at Miss Mary's had heard what sounded like a thunderclap. "We were all sitting there in the kitchen, then got up and ran to the street. That's when we saw the smoke."

Miss Mary and Calla joined them, Miss Mary kneeling down. "Josephine, are you all right? Dodge, what happened?"

Calla came alongside. "People saying the stills must've got too hot and blew to—"

A whooshing sound like wind rushing through a tunnel, then a sharp crack—and the roof of the stillhouse collapsed. Flames hissed as embers shot high into the night sky. Boarding house tenants stood a few yards away—Tom Motlow, Roughton Waggoner, Mr. Parks, Miss Livvy, and others—watching it all.

"Some of the stills did blow up," Dodge said. "But we'll need time to sort out all the details." He glanced at Bethie, obviously choosing his words carefully. "Mrs. Dunham's hand got badly burned and—" He paused mid-sentence, his eyes narrowing.

Josephine quickly trailed his gaze and couldn't believe what she was seeing. Clay Darden lifted his head, his arms flailing as though he were trying to fend off some unseen enemy. Doc Wyatt barked an order, and a group of men lifted him and hurriedly carried him toward town.

"Who is *that*?" Bethie asked. "Did he get burned too?"

"My questions exactly," Miss Mary added.

"We can talk more about that after we get Mrs. Dunham back to the boarding house." Dodge carefully helped her up. "I can carry you," he whispered.

"No, I can walk."

"Oh Josephine!" Calla gasped. "Your palm!"

Miss Mary looked down, grimacing.

"Yes, I . . . I burned it inside the stillhouse."

"Josephine, that's not just a burn. What on earth—"

"Miss Mary!" Dodge looked toward town. "Would you please lead the way? Mrs. Dunham has been through a great deal tonight and needs to rest."

Miss Mary, obviously not accustomed to Dodge interrupting her, much less being so terse, nodded. Josephine thanked him with a look.

They hadn't yet reached the town square when she felt the night starting to swirl around her. "Dodge, I don't think I—"

He lifted her in his arms and held her close against his chest, the solid beat of his heart matching the ever-present *tick tick tick* inside her.

56

Dodge lowered her to the bed, and Josephine sank down onto it, the pain in her palm excruciating. But knowing that Clay Darden was somewhere near her, alive—and that God had allowed it—caused a different and somehow even more excruciating pain. If the Almighty did still know the details of her life, so much for him caring enough to step into them.

Dodge picked up the stool by the hearth and placed it by her bedside. "Josephine . . ." He glanced behind him to the open cabin door through which Miss Mary and Calla had just left, Miss Mary's parting glance saying they still wanted details. "This is not at all how I'd planned on saying this to you, but—" He took her left hand, his gaze filled with emotion. "You have captured my heart, and I love you. Every morning when I open my eyes, I'm already thinking of you, and I can't imagine that day without you in it. And I never want to."

The room swayed slightly. Despite his words resonating, blisters now covered her palm, and it felt like it was on fire. "Dodge, I—"

"Please, let me finish. While I don't have what I once did to offer you, the sale of the land in Wyoming will still go a long way in providing for a home and a good life. We could leave tomorrow. I've already thought it through. You, me, and Bethie, we leave in the morning and go someplace where—"

"Dodge . . ." She looked at him through tears, her strength near gone. "I cannot outrun this. There is nowhere I can go to escape it. It will find me, I see that now."

"No . . . You're still thinking in terms of *I*, Josephine. Not *us*. We could do this."

She touched his face, his stubbled jawline, then traced the curve of his mouth. "If I could choose the course for my life, I would choose you," she whispered. "Again and again. But that's not a choice I can make. Not anymore."

"But it is . . ." He kissed her hand and brought it to his chest. "Say the word, and we'll leave at sunup. We—"

Faint footsteps sounded in the breezeway outside Calla's cabin. Josephine didn't even try to pull her hand away, and she sensed he wouldn't have let go, if she had.

"We're back," Miss Mary said softly, her attention on the pitcher of water and basin in her hand, and Calla's on the cup and saucer she carried. Then they looked up.

Calla gave a small gasp.

But Miss Mary stared with her appraising gaze, a hint of pleasure showing. "I *knew* it. Last Saturday night when I stepped onto the porch to say good night, I sensed something between you two. And you still being *married*, Josephine." Understanding softened her features. "But you're perfect for each other. True North, yet still a little lost," she said, looking at Dodge. Her gaze shifted to Josephine. "And knowing where you want to go, but still trying to find your way."

The room tilted hard, and Josephine swayed.

Calla quickly sat and slipped an arm around her waist. "Here, drink some of this. It's tea steeped with slippery elm bark. It'll help clear your throat of all that smoke."

Josephine took a long sip. The brew had a mild, slightly sweet taste and felt soothing going down, at least at first.

"Speaking of . . ." Miss Mary dragged Calla's rocker over, her intent clear. But Josephine didn't have the strength. She looked at Dodge.

"The man you both saw, the one on the ground who'd been badly burned . . . That was Clay Darden."

"No." Miss Mary looked between them. "The man from Atlanta? From the newspaper?"

"But how did he know you were here?" Calla asked, looking at Josephine.

"It was clear he didn't," Dodge continued. "Josephine said he looked as surprised as she was when she first saw him. And although we don't know how, yet, we figure he was somehow part of the group who came for the distillery visit this weekend." Dodge briefly bowed his head. "But it all happened when Josephine was leaving the party . . ."

As he recounted what happened, Josephine sipped on the tea and tried to detach herself from the moment. Her head ached, and she reached back and felt a tender knot at the base of her skull, then remembered hitting a table in the kitchen as she'd fallen. She wished she could just curl into a ball and sleep for days, and wake up to find this was all a bad dream.

Just hearing Clay Darden's name twisted her stomach and stirred a familiar fear. Yet she kept telling herself that he'd been badly burned and couldn't even stand, much less walk. He could no longer physically harm her. Then again, that's what she'd believed before.

As Dodge continued speaking, Calla's arm gradually tightened around her waist and tears slipped down her cheeks. Miss Mary's eyes brimmed with anger and hurt, her hands clutching the arms of the rocker in a white-knuckled grip.

Finally, Calla pulled Josephine close and kissed her temple. "You are one brave woman, I hope you know that."

"A man like that should be whipped." Miss Mary swiped a tear away. "And I'll be first in line."

"You'll have to get behind me," Dodge said, voice hard.

Josephine leaned forward, her hand going to her mouth. "I think I'm going to be sick."

Calla grabbed a bucket from the hearth and made it back just in time. Dodge sat beside her, holding back her hair.

A few moments later, long past embarrassed, Josephine straightened and wiped her face and mouth with a damp rag from Calla, her right hand still cradled in her lap. She tried to move her fingers the slightest bit, but the pain brought lightheadedness. "Do you think Doc Wyatt's coming soon?"

Calla rose. "I can go fetch him."

"No." Dodge stood. "I'll go. It's well past midnight." He kissed the top of Josephine's head. "Try to rest, if at all possible. I'll be back as soon as I can. And please, one of you stay with her. Don't leave her alone."

"Don't you worry." Miss Mary gestured. "I'll run check on Bethie, then come right back down. She was still asleep on the settee in the library, Jessie right by her, when I last looked."

He paused at the door. "I'll check them on my way out." He looked back at Josephine, and as much as she wanted to trust the hope in his eyes, the weight of her circumstances wouldn't let her.

After reheating the water in the pitcher, Miss Mary and Calla helped her clean up and change into a nightgown. Her contribution . . . somehow managing to stand. When they finished, she laid down and curled onto her side, smoke still clinging to her hair. With eyes clenched tight, she counted every heartbeat, wishing Dodge would return with Doc Wyatt. Or at least with the laudanum.

He learned obedience from the things he suffered. The words Nannie had spoken wove a path through her pain and tears pooled in her eyes, but she welcomed the moisture after the sting of smoke and flame. All her life, she'd pursued learning, had prided herself on acquiring knowledge, had devoured every book in her father's library while craving more. So why did she feel more like a student in this moment than ever before?

Finally, footsteps outside the cabin promised the fading hope of relief from pain, and Miss Mary offered her an encouraging smile as she hurried to the door.

"Good evenin', Miss Mary."

"Sheriff Rigby." Miss Mary's voice held confusion, and a trace of distrust. "What brings you by this time of night?"

"I'm here to speak with *Miss* Josephine Dunham."

57

A jolt of fear surged through her, and Josephine struggled to sit up, fighting the irrational, futile urge to run. Calla, who'd been working near the hearth, quickly moved to stand in front of her.

"Miss Dunham—" Sheriff Rigby stepped across the threshold, a deputy with him. "I have a few questions I need to—"

Miss Mary blocked his way. "Hold on there, Sheriff. Josephine is in no condition to answer any questions right now. She's been through a terrible ordeal tonight and needs to rest."

"Oh, I know what she's been through. I've already spoken with Clay Darden, the man she tried to kill in Atlanta—and then again tonight."

"I did not try to kill him. *He* attacked *me*!"

The sheriff pushed past Miss Mary. "What happened in that alley in Atlanta is not for the two of us to debate, ma'am. You can do that when you appear back there before the judge." He nodded at his deputy who pulled handcuffs from his back pocket. "Miss Josephine Dunham," the sheriff continued, "you're under arrest by order of the State of Georgia for the crime of attempted murder. Don't give us any trouble, ma'am, and maybe we won't have to—"

"Don't you go near her, Rigby!" Dodge shoved past the deputy, and Mr. Daniel came in behind him.

Mr. Daniel's gaze connected with Josephine's and, in a glance, she knew Dodge had told him everything.

"Rigby, you're not taking her anywhere." Dodge positioned himself between her and the sheriff. "Clay Darden brutally attacked her tonight in the stillhouse, and *he* will answer for what he's done."

"Coburn, I am *sheriff* of this town and you'll do well to remember that. Besides, Clay Darden is the son of the mayor of Atlanta, and I'm inclined to believe him over some wool-gatherin' woman who's already proven her word can't be trusted. The fact that she's involved with a band of hysterical females back in Atlanta already puts her mental stability into question. Furthermore, according to witnesses who saw you and Miss Dunham earlier tonight, you're not what I would call an unbiased party when it comes to this woman."

Dodge made a move toward him, and Sheriff Rigby's hand went to the gun at his waist.

"Gentlemen, please . . ." Miss Mary stepped between them. "Let's everyone take a deep breath. Sheriff Rigby—*Virgil.* Have you considered that this Clay Darden character could just be spinning a tale to cover his own hide? After all, like you said, his father is the mayor of Atlanta, and this young Darden knows that if his heinous actions came to light, he'd face swift justice. Not to mention the shame it would bring to his family. You have to see that."

"*Heinous* still needs to be proven—*Mary*. But yes, I do see that. Just as I see that this young woman has been deceiving you from the very start. Here in your own home. Telling you she was married and running from a husband who'd beaten her. Am I right on that count?"

Seeing the struggle in Miss Mary's hard stare, with a look, Josephine encouraged her to answer. At the same time, Dodge looked back, and only then did Josephine see the small bottle in his hand. She wished the laudanum were already in her.

"While it's true, Sheriff," Miss Mary began slowly, "that she wasn't fully forthcoming about her situation at first, I think—"

"Here's how it is," Sheriff Rigby cut in, his voice rising. "Miss Dunham is wanted in Georgia for attempted murder, so I'm taking her back to Atlanta to stand trial. I made a promise to the citizens of Lynchburg to uphold the law, and—"

"Uphold the law?" Dodge gave a brittle laugh. "You're doing this for the reward money, aren't you, Rigby."

"That's *Sheriff* Rigby, and I don't know what you're talking about, Coburn."

But the telling look the deputy slid the sheriff confirmed it. The anger in Dodge's expression told her he'd seen it too, and she felt the remaining strength drain from her body.

"Sheriff Rigby, a question or two, if I may." Mr. Daniel's voice held surprising control. "Have you actually laid eyes on that warrant? And don't you need it before hauling this young woman back to Atlanta? Word is, this Clay Darden fellow was severely burned. How can you even trust the claims of a man whose mind is surely so addled by pain?"

"Well, Uncle Jack . . . Fact is, I don't have the warrant in hand. And I haven't seen it yet either. But ever since I met this woman, my gut's told me she's lying about something. But what's convinced me even more that my gut is right—" A slow smile curved his mouth. "Is that not a one of you has challenged me on calling her *Miss* Dunham." His stare moved to Josephine. "Not even you, ma'am."

Jarred by his admission—and her own lack of awareness—Josephine felt her last thread of hope snap clean in two.

"So while I may not have that warrant in hand, under the authority of law, I *do* have the right, Miss Dunham, to take you into custody and hold you for up to seventy-two hours, time to get confirmation of that warrant. Which I'm betting I'll get from Atlanta in record time."

"Excuse me, for interrupting—"

All eyes turned to see Doc Wyatt standing in the doorway. How long he'd been there, Josephine couldn't tell. But the way his gaze moved around the room before quickly settling on her, told her long enough.

"I'm here to see my patient. She needs medical attention, and I need to do a thorough examination. Also, I should tell you . . . Clay Darden just died."

Josephine's eyes fluttered closed, relief and dread welling up inside her.

"Well, seems that arrest warrant just got a little weightier." Sheriff Rigby gestured. "Doc, you got ten minutes."

"Sheriff, I have whatever time I need to tend my patient. You and your deputy—and your promise to uphold the law—can just wait outside until I'm finished."

Begrudgingly, Sheriff Rigby and his deputy left the room, and Calla closed the door firmly behind them.

Dodge knelt by the bed. "Josephine, I will not let him take you back there to stand trial. I'll—"

"Dodge . . ." Doc Wyatt laid a gentle hand on his shoulder. "Let me see to her first. You and Mr. Daniel need to step outside as well."

A short while later, Doc Wyatt straightened.

Calla helped situate her nightgown while Miss Mary pulled up the covers.

"Your lower lumbar is already showing signs of contusion, Miss Dunham. Deep bruising," he added quickly. "Same for your arms. Thankfully, I detect no damage to your kidneys or spine. Which, frankly, surprises me, considering how quickly the bruises are turning. You'll be very sore for a few days. Standing or sitting for long hours will be painful for the next week or so. But you're young and strong, and should make a full recovery." He paused. "And I am thankful to God that the injury I suspected earlier did not occur."

Tears rose to her eyes, and she nodded. "Thank you, doctor."

Surprisingly, emotion rose in his eyes as well. "This world is not a just place," he said softly. "And though I did everything within my power to save that man's life just now, I will admit, if only in this room, I am grateful my efforts failed."

"Amen," Miss Mary whispered behind him.

"Now with your permission," he continued. "I will share your condition with Dodge and Uncle Jack, then will do my best to impress upon the sheriff that gentleness be mandated."

Once he left the room, Josephine managed to sit up with help, the laudanum already taking effect. The poultice he'd applied to her palm before bandaging it was working to ease the fiery pain.

"This ain't right," Calla said, removing a fresh skirt and blouse from the hook by Josephine's bed.

Miss Mary's jaw tightened. "Not right at all. But I can't think of a thing to do to stop it."

Not until after Josephine was almost dressed did she notice that the skirt and blouse Calla had chosen were the ones she'd worn the day she'd fled Atlanta. But she said nothing. Somehow it seemed fitting.

As she glanced in the mirror at her reflection, she felt like she was looking at the same woman who had arrived here scarcely a month earlier. A darkening bruise on her lower jaw, fear and pain in her eyes, and the lingering traces of Clay Darden's first attack. And yet she felt different inside. This place, these people, had changed her. Forever.

Though she couldn't quite define it, she felt somehow less . . . estranged from God. Like the formidable wall erected between them was somehow less so. More lathe and plaster now than stone and mortar. If only the Almighty would see fit to give her one of those *nudges* Todd had told her about. Then again, she wasn't Todd.

"Is this your doll here on the windowsill?" Miss Mary asked.

Josephine glanced back. "No, it's something I found on the way here. I don't need it."

Miss Mary held it for a second, then put it back.

In the darkened walkway outside the cabin, the warm night air carried the faint scent of smoke. Near the stairs leading to the upper deck, Dodge and Mr. Daniel waited. As did Sheriff Rigby and the deputy.

The deputy eagerly stepped forward, handcuffs open.

"Oh, no." Calla held out a hand. "You can put them things away right now, son. That's not happening, you hear me?"

Calla stared him down until the sheriff finally nodded. The deputy backed away.

"Sheriff Rigby—" Mr. Daniel's tone held conciliation. "Dodge and I would like to accompany you as you escort Miss Dunham to the jail, if we may."

"Just stay out of my way. You make trouble—" His focus went to Dodge. "I'll make trouble back."

Miss Mary hugged her first, then Calla, and both times she didn't want to let go. "Thank you both," she whispered, "for opening your hearts to me. And your home."

She attempted to keep pace with Sheriff Rigby and his deputy, but couldn't. Her lower back ached, and she broke out in a sweat. Finally, to their credit, they slowed down. The jail came into view, and it all felt like a horrible dream.

"May I have a moment with Miss Dunham?" Dodge asked when they were nearly to the door.

"You may not." Sheriff Rigby took her by the arm and urged her forward. "And try to come in? I'll arrest you. Don't believe me, just ask Mr. Daniel."

Right before the door closed, its hinges creaking in protest, Josephine looked back. Though darkness hid Dodge's face, his stance bristled with defiance.

"I'll be back in the morning," he called out. "I'll be here at sunup."

And she believed him, even knowing it wouldn't change her fate.

Later, curled on her side atop the foul-smelling, threadbare mattress in the cold, stone cell, her palm and lower back aching, she realized Mayor Darden's *justice* hadn't merely found her. It had won.

58

"Get up!"

Josephine heard the voice from far away, but resisted. Even half asleep, she remembered what awaited. No single dose of laudanum could numb that dread.

"Miss *Dunham*!" The gruff voice grew louder, then a hard shove to her shoulder.

Wincing, she struggled to sit, her back and shoulder muscles screaming. She dragged her gaze to the barred window high on the wall, every movement requiring more calculation, her body slower to obey every command. It was still dark outside.

"Get up. Now. We're leaving."

She blinked. "It's not sunup yet."

"Don't matter. Sheriff says we're leaving now."

He gripped her arm and pulled her to her feet, and it was all she could do to stifle a cry. The deputy slipped the handcuffs on and cinched them tight until the metal pinched her wrists. He motioned her from the cell.

Outside, the night was still. Nothing moved. But as she peered up into the sky, the moon, partially hidden behind clouds, tried its best to give light. A buckboard wagon waited out front, Sheriff Rigby at the reins. So much for waiting three days for the warrant. She looked around for Dodge, for Mr. Daniel. Anyone.

"Get in the back." The deputy gestured, waiting for her to climb up.

She tried, but couldn't manage it. "I can't seem to—"

With a heavy sigh, he grabbed her by the waist and hoisted her up. She stumbled and fell forward into the narrow, wooden bed. Pain exploded across her shoulder and radiated down her back. She rolled onto her side, choking back a sob that threatened to strangle her. But she refused to give them the satisfaction.

The deputy climbed into the wagon bed and tied her ankles with a leather strap before threading it through an iron ring on the side. But after he joined the sheriff and they got underway, she let the tears come, drowned out by the creak and groan of the wagon.

An hour passed, maybe two or three, and she wondered if this was what prison would be like. Time temporarily ceasing to exist. She listened for the sound of another wagon or someone on horseback, anything to tell her she wasn't alone.

The handcuffs chafed her wrists, and she hoped Doc Wyatt's dressing would hold.

The first light of dawn finally touched the horizon, and she imagined Dodge arriving at the jail only to find her gone. Despite her telling him that their being together wasn't a choice anymore, she still believed he would come. He was a man of his word. True North, as Miss Mary said. But he, too, would discover it was too late. Sheriff Rigby and Mayor Darden had seen to that.

By the time they reached the outskirts of Tullahoma, the morning sun blazed hot. The distant blast of a train whistle told her they were close. Sheriff Rigby had found every rock and rut in every twist and turn through the hills, and he'd punished every muscle and bone in her body. His intention, no doubt.

The wagon stopped, and the deputy circled to the back, lowered the tailboard, and untied her. Clenching her jaw, she maneuvered to sit upright—only to find scores of passersby watching her, many pausing to gawk. Avoiding their gazes, she scooted to the end of the wagon bed, trying unsuccessfully to keep her skirt tugged down, when the deputy grabbed her by the wrists and pulled her out.

Walking between them, she kept her eyes lowered as they entered the train station. Once inside, the deputy purchased two coach class tickets then took his leave. She boarded the train with Sheriff Rigby, feeling the weight of every disapproving stare. If his purpose had been to degrade and humiliate, he'd been successful.

"Sit there." He pointed.

She complied, and he claimed the aisle seat across from her. She hoped once the train left the station, he might remove the handcuffs. He did not.

As the miles gathered behind them, she stared out the window, part of her heart still tucked away somewhere in those hills and hollers in the distance. But part of her heart was in Atlanta, too, and she wondered if Sarah had received her letter yet.

Parched, her throat caked with dust, she tried to work up enough moisture in her mouth to speak. "May I have a drink of water?" she managed, having seen the water station as they entered the car.

If he heard her request, he'd opted to ignore it.

"Please," she whispered, hating the desperation in her voice.

He got up and returned a minute later, the cup barely half full. She drained it and a knot formed in her throat, remembering how Dodge—stopping by the stream on the way to Lynchburg that first afternoon—had offered to refill the canteen. That day seemed forever ago.

"Ticket, please," she heard behind them in the car. "We have *Godey's Lady's Book* for women, and *Harper's Weekly* for men." She turned her head when the porter came to their row. "Tickets, please."

"I got them both right here. She's in transport." Sheriff Rigby produced the tickets, and she heard the metallic *click click* as the porter made the punches.

"Would you care for a *Harper's Weekly*, Sheriff?"

A pause. "Sure."

"Ma'am, would you care for a *Godey's Lady's Book*?"

"I said she's in transport. Don't talk to her, talk to me!"

"Beg your pardon, Sheriff. Would your . . . fellow traveler care for a magazine?"

The sheriff looked over.

Josephine nodded. "But may I have a *Harper's Weekly* instead?"

Sheriff Rigby's eyes narrowed. "You'll take what you're offered! Give her the woman's magazine. Maybe it'll teach you to start acting like one."

Josephine's chest tightened as conversation in the passenger car fell quiet. She took the magazine from the porter, trying to manage it with the handcuffs. But dropped it. She leaned down.

"Oh no, ma'am, you stay right there. Let me come to you."

She froze, the kindness in the man's voice, his choice of words . . . She looked to her right. *Slim Poyner.* Emotion flooded her, but Mr. Poyner gave a tiny shake of his head as he bent to retrieve the periodical.

"Yes, sir, Sheriff, *Godey's* is a fine read for a lady." He picked it up and laid it on the vacant bench seat beside her. "Full of fashion, poems, lessons on sewing and knitting." His gaze flicked to Josephine, then darted away. "And don't forget the *recipes*."

"Just give it to her and move on."

"Yes, sir, Sheriff."

Slim Poyner continued to the next car, never looking back.

Her hands trembling, Josephine shifted on the cushioned bench to awkwardly flip the pages, the handcuffs hindering her movements. She finally found the cooking section and turned page by page through the recipes, until . . . Stuck between one of the pages was a slip of paper. A handwritten recipe for Jack Daniel's Old No. 7 jerky.

59

As Sheriff Rigby escorted her into the Fulton County Jail in downtown Atlanta, Josephine scanned the streets for Dodge. He was here. Somewhere. And though knowing she wasn't entirely alone softened the dread of what lay ahead, it couldn't erase her fear.

The jail, a grim five-story brick building, looked more like a fortress with rows of barred windows and a heavy iron gate at the entrance. The cramped foyer was overcrowded, bustling with activity, and the stagnant air reeked of stale sweat, carbolic acid, and unwashed bodies—and stripped away another layer of her courage.

Sheriff Rigby spoke with someone when they entered, and they didn't have to wait long for the desk sergeant. Murdering the mayor's son clearly hastened matters.

"I'll field the questions." Sheriff Rigby's grip on her arm tightened.

Fountain pen in hand, the sergeant logged the details in a ledger. "Lastly, any personal effects on her?"

Sheriff Rigby shook his head, none the wiser to the recipe tucked inside her sleeve.

The sergeant eyed her hand. "That ring's got to go, ma'am." He reached for an envelope. "Put it in here. We'll catalog and file it."

"Will I get it back?" she asked.

"When you're released." He wrote her name and case number on the front.

"So, in other words, no," Sheriff Rigby said beneath his breath.

"And the reward money?" the sergeant inquired. "You collecting that today, Sheriff?"

"Darn right I am." He looked at Josephine. "And my first stop? A tavern for a drink."

Focus forward, she didn't react.

Female jail staff approached, and Sheriff Rigby removed the handcuffs, tipped his hat, and walked away. The women—formidable in height and weight—slipped restraining ties around her wrists and led her to a room where they searched her pockets and the folds of her skirt. One of the women ran a hand over her sleeves and then, apparently feeling nothing, removed her bandage. Part of the cloth had adhered to raw flesh, and Josephine gritted her teeth as the woman tugged it loose.

They led her down a long hallway and up three flights of stairs to the women's section of the prison, and she thought of her suffrage sisters who had walked this same path. Knowing that should have given her strength, but she gained little comfort in the moment.

They moved past cell after cell, most inmates either sleeping or turned away from the corridor. The jail matrons stopped, and Josephine's trembling returned, her feet frozen at the threshold of the open cell. The taller, sterner woman on her left unfastened the restraints and shoved her forward with force, then slammed and locked the door behind her.

"An attorney will be appointed to your case. If bail is granted, you'll hear from him within three days. If not, it'll be longer. And before you ask how much bail will be, that depends on the severity of the charge, whether you're deemed a flight risk, and on your standing in the community. Evening cell check is at seven, lights out at nine, and no talking after that."

The matrons walked away, their keys jangling, and too late, questions flooded her mind. Not that she would have been given answers. She eyed the cell—a stained cot with a tattered straw mattress and thin blanket, a foul sanitation bucket in the corner, and a small barred window. Her panic swelled.

She knew enough about how the system worked, thanks to her father and Todd, to understand that bail would never be granted. The charge was murder. She had already proven to be a flight risk. And her reputation as a suffragist preceded her. But even without all of that, Mayor Darden would see that bail was denied—just as he'd likely arranged every future decision against her.

Exhausted and hurting, she sank down on the cot, hope slipping away. She tried to take comfort in knowing that Dodge was somewhere close, working to find a way to get her out. But the thick masonry walls and the solid iron bars—thick as broom handles and spaced just wide enough for a hand to get through—told her not to trust that possibility.

Later that night, following an uneaten supper of watery cowpeas with what smelled like rancid fatback, she laid on the cot, hungry and shivering, despite the heavy heat. The caged light bulb humming and flickering on the ceiling of her cell had been shut off promptly at nine o'clock, along with all the others, and darkness kept creeping closer, as did the scurry of something in the far corner. Only a faint glow at the end of the corridor remained.

She turned toward the wall. Perhaps not staring at the bars would hasten sleep. She pulled the recipe from her sleeve and though she couldn't see the words in the dark, she'd already committed them to memory. Especially his note at the bottom. *Two are better than one. But I can't be better without you.*

He was the one who had made *her* better. Who had helped her see beyond her own small world and her great big causes. Dodge had—

The tread of footsteps carried down the darkened corridor, and she lay motionless, listening, sensing the same hush settle over the rest of the prisoners, as the steps came closer, closer, then went silent.

"So you're the woman who killed my son."

60

Gooseflesh rose on Josephine's back and arms, and she slowly turned to see Mayor Frank Darden standing outside her cell, feet firmly planted in freedom. She had only ever seen him from afar, but his sharp, angular features—once mirrored in his son—she remembered well, even in the dark.

"Tell me, Miss Dunham, how does it feel? Knowing you've been beaten, once and for all?"

She struggled to sit, weakness from lack of food and rest making standing ill-advised. As she faced him, all the things she'd thought she would say, if given the chance, slipped away. "I won't pretend to think you don't know the truth, Mayor Darden. Both about what happened in the alley a few blocks away and what happened in Lynchburg, which I'm certain you've been told about."

"Yes, the alley where you attacked my son, then the distillery which you burned to the ground in furtherance of your cause, while my son's only misfortune was to be in the wrong place at the wrong time."

Though she couldn't see his smile, she felt it.

"You see, Miss Dunham, there is nothing you can do to rewrite my version of history. In short, once the *illustrious* matrons of your ill-fated cause have died, they and you—along with all the others—will be no more than a slight ripple on the water. Here and gone. Mark my words."

"While I don't believe that's true, it strikes me as odd, as I'm sitting here, looking at you now. If we are only ripples on the water, as you claim, then why the need to jail us? To beat us? To silence us?"

He stepped closer, and a shiver went through her. He wasn't as tall or broad as she remembered, but he was still a man capable of inflicting great harm. And she knew, firsthand, the hatred that drove him.

"Your imprisonment is not merely punishment, Miss Dunham, nor the stamping out of a weak rebellion. It is instruction—an example.

A warning to others not to follow your path. That is how rebellion is crushed at its root. But I don't expect a barren spinster, with notions far above her station, to grasp the logic of it."

Perhaps the iron bars separating them gave her false courage, but she looked him dead-on. "If my imprisonment is meant to instruct, it will. But likely not in the lesson you imagine. Because while you can cage people, you cannot cage ideas. And while you think you are crushing a rebellion, you may, in fact, be fueling it."

"Quite the orator, Miss Dunham." He laughed as he stepped back. "And with a captive audience, no less." He started to turn away, then paused. "I'm told you didn't eat dinner tonight. A shame—I had it made especially for you. We have ways of persuading our guests to eat. In fact, the tenant who occupied your cell up until three days ago discovered that. Sadly, the fare on the menu didn't sit well with her. You might have known her. Adelaide Stewart. Does that name ring a bell?"

Grateful now not to be standing, Josephine felt the remaining strength leave her body.

"Oh, it appears you did know her. Well, I'm sorry your time here didn't overlap." He glanced past her. "I was told she died alone, there on her cot."

As the sound of his footsteps faded down the corridor, Josephine had to consciously draw breath in, then force it out. But nothing could stop the cry building inside her. She ran a shaky hand over the thin straw mattress, recalling Adelaide's smile and her strong alto voice as they sang together as they marched. *The worst thing you can do to a man, Josephine, is to laugh at him.*

She lay back down and turned onto her side, hearing the quiet sobs coming from down the corridor, and soon her own pillow grew damp.

How many tears had she cried? How many had been cried in this place? Nannie had told her the Word of God said he never wasted a tear shed on this earthly journey. "He collects all of them in a bottle," Josephine whispered to the dark, wondering if speaking Nannie's words aloud might make them feel more true. "Do you?" she said softly. "Do you see me? Are you listening?"

Silence filled the air, thick and close. *He learned obedience from the things he suffered.* The words repeated like an inaudible whisper, not grating, not chastising. But softly, tenderly, and she searched the darkness.

"I'm trying to learn," she whispered. "Teach me. Please . . . teach me." The impenetrable stone ceiling loomed above, but somehow she knew her words had reached heaven's throne. Though no answer came.

She drifted from exhaustion only to awaken sometime later to a fragile voice coming from somewhere down the lines of cells, low at first and uncertain, trying to steady itself on the notes of the hymn she hadn't sung since before Todd's death.

"Nearer, my God, to thee. Nearer to thee . . ."

Her breath knotted like a fist in her chest as the memory of Todd singing beside her in church returned, his rich baritone rising, especially on the next line—"E'en though it be a cross that raiseth me"—as if he meant it, every word. "Still all my song shall be, nearer, my God, to thee. Nearer, my God, to thee. Nearer to thee."

Tears slipped down her cheeks as she strained to listen.

"Though like the wanderer, the sun gone down. Darkness be over me, my rest a stone. Yet in my dreams I'd be, nearer, my God, to thee. Nearer, my God, to thee. Nearer to thee . . ."

The hymn continued, fading in parts, the words there but bent beneath suffering. And though she heard no audible voice, she heard *his* voice all the same—clear and deep within her, with eternal truth and unwavering authority she could not deny. Nor did she want to. Is this what Todd had been trying to describe to her when he'd talked about experiencing the hand of God in his life, feeling the unmistakable nudge of his will?

"I hear you, Lord," she whispered, the freedom she felt in that moment making no sense while locked in a jail cell, accused of a crime she did not commit. "And I know you see me. Th-thank you for hearing me . . . and for collecting my tears."

Her cell hadn't changed. No heavenly light pierced the stone walls to chase away the darkness. Yet, within her, light burned—an all-consuming fire that left no room for doubt of God's presence. Or that he would be with her, no matter what.

~

"Take a seat over there." The stern-looking matron who'd shoved her into the cell that first day, pointed to the table in the far corner. "Your attorney should be here soon." The woman marched on past rows of tables where other attorneys met with female prisoners.

Having slept fitfully the first night, Josephine had hardly slept at all the past two. So as she'd been sitting in her cell a while earlier and heard footsteps echoing down the corridor, she'd prayed with everything in her that they would stop at her cell. And they had. Still, she warned herself against hoping.

If Dodge was still trying to help her—and she believed he was, or wanted to believe it—she'd heard nothing from him. Or from Sarah or any other of the suffrage sisters. Did they even know she was here? Or had they tried, only to be turned away?

A door opened at the far end of the room and an older, distinguished-looking, well-dressed man started toward her, and hope raised its weary head. Until he claimed a seat at a table where another inmate waited, and Josephine lowered her gaze. The blisters on her palm, tender and raw, had begun to rupture. The petroleum jelly the nurse hastily smeared on that morning following breakfast did nothing to soothe the burn, though it did protect the open wound.

The door opened again and a young man—no more than eighteen or nineteen—walked in. He headed in her direction as she silently willed him not to. She wanted someone older, with more experience. Someone who stood a chance of—

"Miss Dunham?" he said, his eyes barely meeting hers. "Josephine Dunham?"

"Yes." She tried to mask her disappointment.

"Justin Thacker."

He held out his right hand, and she held up hers.

He grimaced. "I am sorry. That looks recent." He sat across from her and pulled a file from his worn satchel, then unclipped his pocket watch from the chain and set the watch on the table. "We have little time, Miss Dunham, so forgive me for moving through this quickly. I will dispense with pleasantries, which have never come naturally to me. In cases such as yours, which are abjectly straightforward—"

"Wait! It's not straightforward, Mr. Thacker. I am innocent! Clay Darden attacked *me*, and I would appreciate the opportunity to tell you, in detail, what—"

"I beg you to listen, Miss Dunham." Though his tone carried urgency, the calm, measured cadence of his voice never fluctuated. "I have much to say and, as I have expressed, we have little time."

"You're an attorney who swore loyalty to the Constitution, the laws of the state, and to uphold justice, yet you don't want to hear my side of the story?" She tried to capture his gaze, but he seemed intent on avoiding it.

"I would phrase it this way: I have no need to hear your side of the story."

Josephine stared, her confidence in justice, in the legal system, and in any hope of leaving this place crumbling.

61

"To BEGIN AGAIN," Mr. Thacker continued, "in cases such as yours, which are abjectly straightforward—due not to your guilt, but because of the enemies you have made—the prison allocates limited resources. Meaning—"

Josephine looked up. "Due *not* to my guilt? You're saying you don't think I'm guilty?"

His gaze skimmed hers, and he looked genuinely perplexed. "Miss Dunham, we know you are innocent."

"We?"

He glanced at his watch. "I have twice communicated that our time is short. I must insist you allow me to continue uninterrupted."

She found his manner beyond curious and his refusal to meet her gaze maddening, yet she nodded, clinging to *We know you are innocent.*

"To begin again . . . The prison allocates limited resources, meaning legal representation. Namely, me. They assign the least experienced—or those they perceive to be so. Yet, I have an inkling our meeting today has long been in the making." He glanced at his watch again. "To that end, I must share certain information. Some of it will seem superfluous until our conclusion, but some, I trust, you will find heartening. Yet whatever I say, you must appear displeased. As though my words are unwelcome. Do you understand?"

She didn't, but nodded, desperate for hope.

"First, I knew your brother Todd. I—"

"*W-what?* How did you—"

"You are failing at this, Miss Dunham. Displeasure, please."

She tried to frown, but knowing they shared memories of Todd made it impossible.

"Think of Clay Darden and what he did to you," he said, voice low. "And know that he did it not only to you, but to other women who were not as resourceful. *There* we go. That's the anger we need to display for those watching. And they are watching. Not only did I know your brother—" His words fired in rapid succession, as though his mind raced a dozen steps ahead. "He was a remarkable mentor to me. I worked with him, and others, to uncover the corruption we discovered a few years ago in the prison system here. It's still rampant, and not only among the freedmen, but among the women's prison." He glanced at his watch again. "Not much time. The judge assigned to your case has formally denied bail, effectively convicting you before a trial date was even set. The judge based his denial mainly on pressure from Mayor Darden, of course. But also on the fact that you're considered a flight risk. Which, honestly, can you blame him?" His glance flickered to her face. "Oh, nice flash of anger. You've caught on very well, Miss Dunham."

"Because I do not like being wrongly convicted, Mr. Thacker, and I don't appreciate playing games with my freedom. Which is what this meeting is beginning to feel like."

"I assure you, this is no game. The details simply do not make sense to you because you do not yet have all the facts. Now please, stay with me. What you need to know next is that Clay Darden who is now, indeed, dead—yes, we are aware, and thank you for whatever hand you had in that back in Lynchburg." He grimaced. "Very poor choice of words on my part."

Josephine stared. Clearly he'd meant no offense. This young man was obviously intelligent, yet his demeanor bordered on strange. But he was her appointed attorney. "No offense taken, Mr. Thacker. Now please, continue."

"Miss Dunham, I will explain this plainly. Not because it is simple, but because confusion wastes time." He lowered his voice. "There are three men who determine whether you leave this building today—or die in it."

She stilled.

"The first is the judge. The second is Mayor Darden. The third is a group of men who do not wear titles and do not appear in court records. We will call them . . . the organization."

"The organization?" she repeated softly.

"Yes. It is a group of men in this city affiliated with an Italian family and with deep ties to New York, New Orleans, and Chicago. Now, listen carefully. These men advanced a great deal of money to Clay Darden. When young Darden died, his obligations did not. They passed, as such things always do, to his father. Mayor Darden has refused to pay."

"Because he believes himself untouchable," she said.

Thacker nodded once. "Precisely. Power has a way of convincing men that rules apply only to others. This refusal makes Darden the enemy of this organization, and though they conduct their business quietly, they collect their debts unfailingly. And they never forgive."

Her stomach tightened. "But . . . what does all this have to do with me?"

"I'm coming to that. They have decided Mayor Darden should be removed from office. Now they simply need to demonstrate he no longer commands control."

She frowned.

"If a mayor cannot compel a judge," he continued, "then he is not truly a mayor. He is merely a man occupying a chair." He leaned forward slightly, intent sharpening his voice. "By granting your bail—against Darden's express wishes—the judge demonstrates that Darden's reach has ended. Quietly. Efficiently. Without spectacle. And that greatly weakens the mayor."

"It will also enrage him." She drew in a breath. "And the judge? What is his motivation in this?"

"The judge assigned to your case," he continued, "is in debt to the same family—financially and morally. Enough that he cannot repay his debt without assistance. He requires relief. We provide it."

"So I am—" She paused. "The instrument."

Thacker considered this. "You are the occasion."

"So the judge will be offered a bribe?" she whispered.

"A repayment disguised as one," he clarified. "In exchange, he grants bail in your case—over the mayor's objection."

"And if I make bail," she said slowly, "I'm released."

"Temporarily. Long enough to disappear."

Her head spun. "But the judge has already denied bail."

"Which is why it must now be granted in a way that appears lawful."

He leaned forward. "The bail will be excessive. Five thousand dollars. High enough to satisfy public outrage—and wound Mayor Darden."

"Five thousand dollars! I don't have—"

"We know you don't have those funds, Miss Dunham. However, it's being gathered." His eyes flicked past her. "Quietly. From people who remember your family with great admiration and gratitude. Someone who fights for another's freedom isn't soon forgotten. We have three thousand dollars thus far."

Her throat closed.

"However, the bail amount of five thousand is not all that's needed," he continued. "An additional three thousand is required to settle the judge's debt and satisfy the Italian interest."

A cold wind blew through her. "Eight thousand dollars . . ." A staggering sum. Dodge didn't have that amount of money either, she felt sure. And even if he had received the proceeds from the sale of his land—and assuming it brought that much—she could never expect him to just hand it over. Mr. Daniel was wealthy, yes. But she doubted even he had that much in ready cash. And if he did, again, she could never bring herself to ask. "And if, by some miracle, Mr. Thacker, we gather that amount . . . What if the judge refuses the bribe? And refuses to set bail?"

"Then you will remain here until your trial," he said evenly. "And you will not survive it."

A shiver stole through her, and she rubbed her temples. "So to be clear . . . Mayor Darden does not wish me to be freed, and usually, the judge would agree with him. But this judge is beholden to the organization, and the organization wishes to see the mayor weakened. And granting me bail accomplishes that while also paying off the judge's debt."

"Well done, Miss Dunham! And what's more, Mayor Darden will understand at once what has been done—and who has done it."

"He'll be publicly humiliated. And enraged."

"Yes," Thacker replied. "But he'll also know that humiliation is the least of what he should fear. Because power is not lost when it is challenged. It is lost when it is ignored."

She stared. "Are you and your colleagues in league with this organization?"

"In league? Certainly not. In contact with? Without question. That's been essential in exposing the corruption. *If you know the enemy and know yourself*," he quoted.

"You need not fear the result of a hundred battles," she finished with him.

"Yes, Todd said you both enjoyed that book immensely. As did I." He checked his watch a fourth time.

"Mr. Thacker, I—" She took a quick breath. "I want to understand. But who is this *we* you keep referring to?"

He looked past her, then down at the folder in front of him. "The judge has been offered the bribe, which stipulates that he must grant bail in your case. It took longer than hoped because he was on the bench this afternoon."

"What? I—" Josephine shook her head. "But you said *eight* thousand dollars was required, which means we're still five short."

"Correct. At the start of this conversation, I told you I believed our meeting had been long in the making. I don't say that lightly, Miss Dunham. I am not a man inclined to abstractions. I prefer facts, details, and patterns over figurative concepts. Yet, considering the facts, I cannot deny that a power greater than ours seems to have intervened. At noon today I was seated on the courthouse steps with a colleague discussing your situation. Frankly, all seemed bleak. Because as of five o'clock today, the window closes for any reversal of denial of bail. Then a man approached. A bondsman asking for the magistrate's office. He said he intended to post bond for a woman charged three days ago with attempted murder. Then he gave *your* name."

Josephine leaned forward, the thinnest hope stirring, yet mindful someone could be watching.

"We explained to him that bail had not been granted—and likely would not be, given the upgraded murder charge. He still insisted he'd speak with the magistrate himself. Five hundred dollars in cash, he told us, was too much to forfeit without knowing for sure. Miss Dunham, I would wager you know this, but bondsmen generally charge—"

"Ten percent of the total bond for their services," she finished. "Which means he'd be given five thousand dollars!" The words left her in a rush. "Did he say who had given him the money?"

"A bondsman secures future business by *not* revealing his clients."

She nodded, the thin margin of her circumstances becoming razor sharp. "And you said the judge has been offered the bribe."

"Only moments ago. So now, we wait."

She attempted to read the watch on the table but couldn't see the face clearly.

"It's a quarter to five, Miss Dunham."

"Will that be enough time?"

He looked past her again, and she turned to see the matron who had escorted her here walking in their direction.

He stood and picked up his watch and folder. "I'm afraid our meeting has come to an end, Miss Dunham."

"No, no," she whispered, reaching out to him. *"Please."*

"I do apologize for relaying so much information in such haste. I had hoped we would have more time. As it is, we will likely not see each other again. So let me—"

"You won't be my trial attorney? W-what if I request you. Can I do that?"

The matron paused beside her. "Come with me, Miss Dunham."

"Wait, please!" Josephine held up a hand. "If I request you, Mr. Thacker—"

The matron gripped her upper arm, as desperation gripped her by the throat.

"Great change requires great sacrifice, Miss Dunham," he said, rummaging through his satchel, never looking up. "If you and I meet again, it will mean we have failed. This is your only chance to vanish. If Darden, or anyone still loyal to him, finds you, there will be no more options. And the money, regardless of its source, will have been spent in vain. So make the most of this opportunity. It will not come again."

62

"You're not out of this yet," the matron whispered, propelling her down the empty hallway, the ring of keys jangling on her belt. "A few more hurdles await."

Her mind spinning, Josephine struggled to keep up, scarcely believing this was really happening. "So you and Mr. Thacker, you're both part of whatever—"

"I assumed he told you."

"I think he was trying to, but—"

"This is all your brother's doing, Miss Dunham. Or at least the seed of it. It's grown since his death. Inspired by it. Emboldened, you might say."

"But what is *all this*?"

"Todd Dunham had a way of bringing people together. People who would not usually view each other as allies. Your brother found common ground and used it to build unlikely relationships where justice could prevail. Like this—at least we hope."

The matron stopped at two doors opposite each other near the end of the hallway. The door on the left led to the women's cells. She unlocked the one on the right. "Don't say another word until we're outside this building."

She guided Josephine into an office lined with desks behind a waist-high counter. Most were vacant. Three remaining clerks in the back were gathering their things.

The matron approached the counter, Josephine in tow. "One more before you go. A discharge. Bond was made."

The three clerks exchanged looks before one sighed and motioned them forward. The others took their leave.

"Name?" the clerk asked, reaching for a stack of folders.

"Josephine Dunham," the matron answered.

The woman paused, her gaze sliding to Josephine. "I thought bail was denied in that case. That's what the newspapers said."

Josephine's heart pounded, and the matron's grip tightened on her arm.

"I read the same thing. Then I was told bond had been set and posted, so we let her go. I'm just doing my job—and hoping to get home before the day's spent."

"You and me both. But really, what is the world coming to." The clerk flipped through folder after folder, then frowned. "I'm not seeing papers for her. Are you sure—"

A door opened, and an officer walked in. Josephine glimpsed the crowded lobby beyond him, and fought the urge to run. Then recognition set in.

The desk sergeant who had taken her into custody handed the clerk a piece of paper. "Magistrate's office just dropped this by. Thought I'd deliver it before heading out."

The clerk took the form. "Sergeant, your timing is impeccable. And the magistrate's office? Tardy as usual." As she penned a ledger entry, Josephine thought she caught a fleeting exchange between the sergeant and the matron, but couldn't be sure.

A minute later, the matron led her across the lobby, hand still firm on her arm. "Breathe, Miss Dunham," she whispered, opening one of the double doors. "You're almost home free. I'll walk you to the front gate. After that, you're on your own."

But she wouldn't be on her own. Dodge would be there. Somewhere. She knew it. And even if he wasn't—if, for some unfathomable reason, he didn't come—she still wouldn't be alone. Not ever again.

She crossed the threshold into the late afternoon sunshine, and the first breath she took, she knew she'd remember forever.

The streets bustled with traffic and people, and as they walked down the steps, she searched every face for his, her nerves taut. "Thank you," she whispered. "For everything. And please, when you see Mr. Thacker—"

"I know. I will. And Miss Dunham, know this . . ." They paused by the heavy iron gate. "Adelaide Stewart did not die alone. I overheard your conversation with Mayor Darden the other night. I was with her till the very end."

Josephine couldn't have put it into words, but she sensed the confirmation of that deep inside her. "*Thank you,* I'm so grateful to know you were—"

The matron frowned. Her gaze trailed Josephine's toward the street—where Mayor Darden was climbing from a carriage. The matron spun back. "Go. *Now*. He hasn't seen you. Walk to the end of the street. Don't run. Then do as Mr. Thacker said. Vanish!"

The matron left her and, having no choice, Josephine willed one step after another, passing through the iron gates, and walking straight toward Frank Darden. The mayor seemed intent on his conversation with the man beside him, and Josephine kept her head down, though still where she could see him.

Just as she turned left, he looked up—and stopped mid-step.

But she did not. She kept walking, matching the pace of those around her, every nerve screaming for her to look back—and to run. She rounded the corner and quickened her stride, dreading the sound of footsteps behind her. And Darden screaming her name.

Aware of curious glances, she'd tried to make herself presentable for the attorney meeting, but knew she looked as worn and beaten as she felt. A carriage slowed beside her, and she panicked and started to bolt, when someone stepped up behind her and a firm hand closed around her arm. She turned, ready to fight—then froze at the sight of him, and the love in his eyes.

"You make it awfully hard for a man to rescue you when you're rescuing yourself."

Josephine threw her arms around his neck, silently vowing never to let go, and Dodge held her tight. He carried her to the carriage, which lurched forward almost before he'd closed the door. The interior was dim, the curtains mostly drawn.

"I knew you'd come," she whispered.

"I've been watching from across the street all day. I'd almost given up hope, when you walked out. Then just as quick, I saw a look on your face, and spotted the man getting out of the carriage."

"Darden."

"I figured as much. So I followed you until I could get to you without drawing too much attention. But Josephine—" He pressed a lingering kiss to her forehead. "I'm so sorry I couldn't spare you what you went through in there. But I knew if I tried to grab you on the way, Rigby would make good on his threat. And somebody could've been killed." He drew her to him. "I saw you board the train with him. I followed you all the way to the jail, and it—" His voice broke. "—about killed me to watch him walk in there with you. But we had talked it through several times, and—"

"We?"

"Uncle Jack. He's here, so is Bethie. We're headed their way now. But first, tell me the truth. Are you all right?"

"I am now." She touched his face, still needing to be sure he was real. "And this—" She pulled the handwritten jerky recipe still tucked in her sleeve. "—gave me such hope. I've thanked God for you and Slim Poyner so many times in recent days." She quickly told him what he needed to know for the moment, deciding the rest could wait. "But Dodge, the money that was posted for bond. I know it was either you or Mr. Daniel."

"Actually, it was both." He smiled, smoothing the hair back from her face.

She looked down, self-conscious. "I can't imagine what I look like right now."

Thumb beneath her chin, he urged her gaze back to his. "You are, and always will be, the most captivating woman I've ever seen. But Josephine, you need to know . . . While I could never have given you the cathedrals of Europe or the pyramids of Egypt, now I can't even offer you what I once could."

"Dodge, I don't—"

He pressed a finger to her lips. "The bond money took most of the proceeds from the sale of the land, but I would have given every penny. The money's on its way, but Uncle Jack gave me a loan until it comes through." He exhaled. "You need to know that he offered to pay the bond outright, but I aim to take care of the woman I love. The woman I want to be my wife . . . If you'll have me."

"If I'll have you?" She smiled through tears. "Dodge Coburn, I will go anywhere with you. To the farthest ends of the earth. Which is actually preferable at the moment, please."

They both laughed.

"Then that bodes well for what I have to tell you next. Because, while it's a far cry from Wyoming . . . Uncle Jack saw a posting from a rancher out in Colorado needing a foreman. It's a good ways from Denver, I think. It wouldn't be our farm or our cattle, but—"

"I don't need a farm or cattle or a ranch or riches, or even Europe or cathedrals. At least not without you. And Bethie. But . . ." She looked into his eyes. "I know that working another man's ranch isn't what you've dreamed of. Will this be enough for you? Do you think there might ever come a day when you . . . regret what you've done for me? What it's cost you?"

"Regret doing what I've done for—" He blew out a breath. "Look at me closely as I say this. I would give everything I own to be with you. No, working for another man's spread wasn't my dream. But dreams change, Josephine. I used to dream about Wyoming, and cattle, and a stretch of land wide enough that a man could ride half the day and never cross his own tracks. Now . . . I dream about you and me starting a new life, the children we'll have, and how we'll prepare them, along with Bethie, for all the changes coming in this world. Changes we'll work for together."

Josephine's throat tightened as her gaze lowered to his mouth, her love for him stronger than anything she could remember.

He pulled her closer on the bench seat. "Is that an invitation to kiss you, Miss Dunham?"

"Always, Mr. Coburn."

His lips brushed hers, softly, their breath mingling, and his tenderness roused a passion within her, and in her heart—one she prayed they'd have a lifetime to explore together.

"One last thing," he said after a moment. "Uncle Jack managed to track down how Clay Darden was there in Lynchburg. At the last minute, a son of one of the vendors invited Darden to come along as his guest. Uncle Jack feels so bad for what happened."

"It's not his fault. There's no way he could have known."

"That's what I told him, too. Still . . ."

When the carriage finally stopped, Dodge lifted a curtain and peered out. Apparently satisfied, he helped her out and led her through a discreet side door of a hotel and down a short hallway. He paused outside a door. "They're expecting us."

But when he opened it, Josephine could barely believe her eyes.

"There's me Finny girl!" Sarah ran to her and hugged her tight. "Oh, heavens be praised, I wasn't sure if I'd ever be seein' you again." She drew back. "Here I told you not to be trustin' anyone, and you go and put your faith in this motley crew?" She gave a sideways glance at Mr. Daniel and Bethie, who stood to the side smiling.

Josephine hugged her again. "You were the one who told me that when someone shows you who they are, I should believe them the first time." She looked at Dodge, Mr. Daniel, then at Bethie, and even Jessie lying nearby. "So I did."

Mr. Daniel laughed. "Oh, I think it took you more than just a first time for all of us. But little by little—" He winked. "We won her over."

Josephine crossed to him and hugged him tight. "Yes, you did . . . Uncle Jack. And I'm so grateful. For everything."

His arms tightened around her and when he pulled back, his own eyes glistened. "You were worth the challenge, Miss Dunham."

Josephine noticed the mischievous look in Bethie's expression, then the rag doll peeking from the pocket of her dress.

Bethie fingered the doll's yellow yarn hair. "Miss Mary said it was yours, so I just figured I'd keep it safe for you. You can have it back, if you want." She held it out.

"I'd prefer you keep it. She needed a good home, and she found one."

Bethie's eyes widened. "Did Uncle Dodge tell you? We're going to Colorado! All of us! Well, not Uncle Jack, we'll drop him off on the way."

Josephine looked back at Sarah, then at Dodge, and he nodded.

"If it's all right with you, Finny girl. I'm not knowin' that much about cows, but Bethie here tells me she'll be teachin' me good once we get there."

Josephine smiled. "She's a very good teacher, and I can't imagine you not with us."

"Speaking of which," Dodge said. "We have to board the train in less than two hours. We have to leave tonight." As though reading Josephine's mind, he gave her a reassuring look. "But courtesy of Uncle Jack, we'll be traveling in a private Pullman car all the way to Colorado."

"Consider it an early wedding gift," Uncle Jack added in a stage whisper. "Or at least the start of one. After all, *What greater thing is there for two human souls, than to feel that they are joined for life.*"

Josephine returned the smile in his eyes. "George Eliot," she said softly, knowing well the novel, *Adam Bede*, he quoted. But she was surprised that *he* knew it. "But that was a pseudonym for the author's real name, which was?"

Uncle Jack's eyes twinkled. "Mary Ann Evans, of course. I love me a female author."

She laughed, already missing this man. Yet the idea of returning to the train station did not set well. "Dodge, are you sure we'll be all right? Even in a Pullman car?"

"We'll be a family traveling together this time," he said. "Not a woman on her own. Not anymore."

"We got a nice hot bath for you, too, Finny girl, and a fresh change of clothin'. Just in the next room there. And your man got you some food. So you can eat first, if you've a hankering."

The door behind her opened, and not until Bethie stepped out did Josephine realize she'd slipped away. The girl had something draped over her arm.

"I thought maybe you could wear this, Miss Dunham. If you want to, it'd be fine with me."

Looking closer, Josephine recognized the cerulean-blue skirt embroidered with tiny cream-and-pink flowers, and the cream blouse with pearl buttons. Buttons Mrs. Carver at the mercantile had helped Kathleen choose.

Bethie's lower lip trembled the slightest bit. "Mama sewed it when she thought we'd be going to Wyoming. Uncle Dodge came back talking about the wildflowers and how pretty they were. But I'm betting Colorado will have flowers like that, too. Don't you think?"

"Oh yes, I do, Bethie. And I would be honored to wear this. Thank you."

Bethie motioned to something off to the side. "This way we'll be sort of the same, you and me. Uncle Dodge had that made for me special, with little wildflowers tooled into the leather."

Josephine turned. The small saddle, made to fit a young girl but crafted with the same care as any fine Western stock saddle, perched atop a trunk in the corner. Sure enough, delicate wildflowers adorned the supple, chestnut-brown leather, and the love in Bethie's eyes was outdone only by that in Dodge's.

Two hours later, Josephine boarded one of the dark-green Pullman cars with her family, steadied by Dodge's hand at the small of her back and Uncle Jack leading the way. She knew peace wouldn't come until Atlanta lay far behind them. Barely able to stand, she sank down into a plush high-backed seat of burgundy velvet. Thick draperies of green and gold coordinated with the patterned carpet beneath her feet, while electric brass chandeliers with etched glass shades glowed overhead.

She smiled at Sarah and Bethie oohing and aahing at their accommodations, while Dodge shook his head at their antics, Jessie close at his side. Ordinarily, she would have joined them. But after the brief, but luxurious bath and delicious dinner, all she wanted was sleep.

"Oh no, Miss Dunham." Uncle Jack took hold of her hand, then nodded toward the porter at the far end of the car who was folding down a lower berth. "You have a long trip ahead, and a lot to put behind you."

The porter stepped back from the neatly made berth—fresh white linens, a feather pillow, and a blanket tucked in place. "Anything else you need, ma'am, please let me or my colleague know."

Josephine thanked him and sank down with relief.

"I promise I'll let you sleep, Miss Dunham, but one thing I need to—"

"I believe we have surpassed *Miss Dunham*, have we not, Uncle Jack?"

Pleasure lit his face. "*Josephine,* I carry a message from Calla. She asked me to tell you that your friendship—and your example—gave her the courage to tell Miss Mary about the honey . . ." He arched a brow. "And that Miss Mary and Doc Wyatt have pledged to walk this road with her." His gaze sharpened. "I cannot say for certain what she meant, but I have my suspicions. And if I am correct, then a single nod from you will command every resource I possess to aid her. With the greatest discretion, of course."

Josephine took his hand in hers, and nodded.

"Are you trying to steal my girl, Uncle Jack?"

They both laughed, looking up at Dodge.

"Why, you know I'd never try such a thing." Uncle Jack wriggled his mustache. "Besides, she's a mite too tall for me."

Two short whistle blasts signaled departure, and a minute later, the train surged forward.

"Go ahead and lie down," Dodge urged gently. "I'll sit with you for a minute, if you don't mind."

"I'll lie down. But I want you to stay, at least until I'm asleep?"

He bent closer. "Josephine, I never want to leave your side. And don't plan to. Not until we're good and settled in Fountain Creek . . . for at least a decade or two."

She smiled, the rhythm of the train rocking her gently back and forth, and she held tightly to his hand even as her heart slipped to its knees in prayer. She could only marvel at what God had done. He'd led her down a road she would never have chosen for herself, in order to give her the life she never knew she needed—and wanted. But he had known. And despite her ingratitude, doubt, and rebellion, he'd given her blessing after undeserved blessing.

Drifting closer toward sleep and feeling the miles fall away behind them, she turned onto her side and drew his hand to her chest. "I love you . . . Hezekiah Eustace Coburn."

His gentle laugh warmed her. "And I love you, soon-to-be Josephine Dunham Coburn. Rest well, my love."

Epilogue

MAY 1909

FOUNTAIN CREEK, COLORADO

"Finny! We got something from Uncle Jack. It's a package this time!"

At the sound of Bethie's shout, Josephine looked up from the typewriter and out the open window to see her, still some distance away, racing across the meadow toward the cabin, long legs devouring the distance. Eager to hear from Uncle Jack, Josephine also wanted to finish this article while little TJ and Kathleen still played quietly at her feet.

She took another bite of jerky and scanned the last paragraph she'd written.

> "Failure is impossible" is a mantra our beloved Miss Anthony wrote on my heart, and one I hear echoed every day inside me. As we continue to make great strides, we will also face seemingly insurmountable obstacles. Doors will close that we would wish open. But we must stay the course and patiently persevere, holding fast to the eternal truth that God created all men and women equally. He created us to work alongside each other in His Kingdom, and we are not merely "better together," we need each other—women and men partnering together—to bring the change we so desire for this world, and for our daughters and granddaughters. And if it riles you to read that, my dear sisters, then be riled. But it is the truth.

She smiled at the last part, remembering that night with Dodge on Miss Mary's front porch, another lifetime ago. Three years had passed since dear Miss Anthony died, passing the torch to younger leaders, and still the movement pressed forward, gaining momentum. Which reminded her of dear Todd and her parents, and the costly legacy they'd left behind. A legacy orchestrated by God and that had given her another chance at life.

Glancing back out the window, she saw Bethie had stopped to give Honey a rub. Uncle Jack had sent the then-young calf by rail soon after they'd settled, along with a dozen of the distillery's finest heifers and a bull. She feared the man's generosity might one day bankrupt him, and had written him as much, assuring him they had all they needed and more. But still, the gifts came.

Eager to get one last thought on the page, she turned back when her gaze fell to the little blue bottle she kept on her desk. She pulled out the rolled-up piece of paper peeking above the rim and let it unfurl. Though she'd long ago memorized its contents, she treasured the bottle—and Psalm 56:8 that Calla had written in her own words.

"You keep track of all my sorrows," she read aloud. *"You have collected all my tears in your bottle. You have recorded each one in your book."*

Thanking God again for Calla and Nannie and how they'd changed her life, her attention was drawn to Kathleen's blue metal pitcher on the kitchen table. Bethie kept it filled with purple coneflowers planted from seeds Calla had sent them from Lynchburg. Everywhere she looked, she saw reminders of God's faithfulness. Through good times and bad.

She continued typing.

In closing, a dear friend once counseled me not to judge God by my circumstances. I confess with shame that for many years I did just that. But no longer. His faithfulness stretches to the heavens and his compassion knows no end. It is my perspective that skews my earthly lens. I have realized this: If I had the power of God to change my circumstances, I would. But if I had the wisdom of God, I would not. He knows what I need far better than I do. So wherever you are in your life and in this continuing battle for justice, dear sisters, and brothers, take heart. God sees. He knows. He's working.

Bethie raced through the front door of the cabin, nearly tripping over the twins. "Finny, look! It's a package!" She gave Josephine a quick peck on the cheek, her own flushed from the run.

"Be careful, sweetheart!" Josephine laughed and scooped up Todd Jasper and Kathleen, one on each hip. At three years old, TJ was getting especially heavy. And Kathleen, talkative. "Go grab your uncle. He'll want to be here."

"Where's Sarah?"

"She went for a ride with Colin before dinner, but should be back soon. We won't start without her."

Bethie gave her a playful look that Josephine returned. Colin, one of the young hands employed on the Jennings's ranch, routinely called on Sarah these days, making his intentions clear. They all liked him, Sarah especially, and it was good to see her so happy.

Bethie raced out the door toward the barn, fourteen going on twenty and as smart as she was beautiful. By the time they'd traveled from Atlanta to Colorado, four years ago, Bethie had already taken to calling her Finny. Which seemed fitting.

She glanced at the return address on the partially opened package: Nannie Helen Burroughs, National Training School for Women and Girls, 50th Street NE and Lincoln Heights, Northeast Washington, DC. Nannie had accomplished what she'd set out to do, and was changing the world one woman and girl at a time.

All correspondence with Uncle Jack—and anyone else, limited as it was—still went through Nannie, just to be safe. Their home, their world, was here now. All of her writing was done under a pseudonym as well. Veritas Aequitas. Dodge's idea. Latin for Truth and Justice.

Josephine recognized Uncle Jack's decorative script on the package within, and realized how Bethie knew it was from him.

"Come here, Kitty Kat." Dodge came through the door, Bethie in tow with Jessie trotting behind them. He took little Kathleen and planted kisses all over her face until the girl dissolved into giggles. Then he placed a kiss on Josephine's lips that stirred memories of the wee hours together that morning. She saw the memory of it in his eyes, too.

Bethie took TJ from her and tickled his little tummy. "You grin just like your Uncle Jack, you know that? But Finny, we can't start without Sarah. She'll be givin' us all a good tongue lashin', if we did."

Bethie had Sarah's accent down to a T, and it always made Josephine laugh.

Dodge glanced out the window toward the snow-covered peaks. "I saw them coming down the ridge a while ago. She shouldn't be long."

Josephine reached down and gave Jessie a rub. The cattle dog was showing gray on her muzzle but a more faithful and loving companion couldn't be found. And still, every time it rained, Jessie slept on the end of their bed, wanting to be close.

Josephine cut the remaining string from the package and opened the box, then smiled. *Read this first, Josephine, before opening the gift within. And I will know if you don't!* was written on the outside of the letter. She would follow Uncle Jack's wishes.

Dodge and Bethie's laughter as they played with the twins drew her focus, and it still caused emotion to well inside her when she thought of what her life might have been like had she not been forced to flee Atlanta that day after the rally, and had dear Slim Poyner not offered to help her. What wealth of treasures she would have missed.

The rhythm of horse hooves sounded from outside and a minute later, Sarah burst into the cabin, cheeks flushed and blue eyes radiant. "Don't be tellin' me you're havin' a family meetin' without me!" She gave the twins a quick peck each on the cheek, then eyed the letter in Josephine's hand. "Oh! Is that from Uncle Jack? Have I missed anything, Finny girl?"

"No, we were waiting for all the family to be here."

Sarah's eyes went soft, as they always did when they mentioned family.

Josephine unfolded the letter, and just seeing Uncle Jack's beautifully scripted handwriting brought him closer somehow. *"Dearest Colorado Family, I trust this finds you well and enjoying spring in those beautiful mountains. The pictures you last sent of that rocky range filled me with awe. A regret I will long carry with me is that I failed to travel west to see you and your home when I could. Thank you also for the picture of the twins. Kathleen is precious, as was her namesake, and Todd Jasper is a right handsome lad. Good to see he doesn't take after his father."*

Everyone laughed, Josephine catching the warmth of memory in Dodge's expression.

"I don't have much to do with the distillery anymore," she continued reading. *"Not that there is much to do with our state now officially locked down by the law of prohibition. No making or selling of whiskey in Tennessee. You won, Josephine. If you were still here, I'd salute you with a shot of Old No. 7."*

She met Dodge's gaze, knowing he followed these events as closely as she did. Public sentiment had shifted after a shocking Nashville murder the previous November, when former US Senator and newspaper editor Edward Carmack was gunned down in the street by Robin Cooper, the son of a man Carmack had once called friend. Years of bitter politics and the rising heat over prohibition had turned the men into enemies. The killing—and the swift release and pardon of the man responsible—ignited outrage across Tennessee. Carmack became a martyr, and by January the General Assembly passed statewide prohibition.

Josephine grieved the violence that led there, but she thanked God for the outcome. She found her place in the letter and continued.

"Lem is considering moving the distillery to Missouri and Alabama to make the whiskey there, even though we poor souls in Lynchburg cannot buy it. Do not tell anyone, but I might have a few barrels squirreled away. Mine is simply to enjoy life and bring joy where I can. Sometimes I think back to our debates on the issues and wish we could have them all over again. I have not changed my stance, mind you, and I know you remain the same. But I would welcome our banter."

Josephine's eyes watered, and it took a minute to continue.

"Miss Mary tells me to send you her love and that you owe her a letter." Josephine smiled, able to hear the woman saying it even now. *"Young Louise, four years old, has everyone at the boarding house wrapped around her little finger. Miss Mary has her hands quite full, especially being with child again, but she and Calla make a good team. Calla is doing so well, and every time we are together, we speak of you all."*

"I wish we could see them," Bethie said softly, and Dodge pulled her close.

"Calla sends her love," Josephine continued, memories tugging at her heart. *"She recently wrote down a collection of recipes and I have told her we should get them published and call it Miss Mary Bobo's Boarding House Cookbook. But Miss Mary is not for it. Miss Mary fears it will only bring more business to the boarding house, and she says she already has more than she can handle. But everybody knows she'll always make room at her table."*

"Finny," Bethie interrupted. "Why don't you write down your recipe for sausage gravy and biscuits and mail that to her? She could put that in."

They all laughed, and Josephine continued reading.

"Mrs. Carver at the mercantile sends her best as well. She's continuing your work, and I told her to use as many shelves in the back storage room as she needs. I should probably bring this letter to a close. But one thing before I do. I was baptized last Sunday in Mulberry Creek. Now don't start thinking that I'm regretting my whiskey-making days. I am still most proud of what we all built together here in Lynchburg. Be sure and tell Dodge that. Lord knows I miss him and the talks we used to have."

"I miss you too, Uncle Jack," Dodge whispered, his voice soft.

Josephine took a steadying breath. *"I'm so grateful for the success I've had in my life. I only wish I'd known sooner what true contentedness was and that it can be found only in Christ. He is what matters most. Nothing else comes close."*

Josephine scanned the next lines and winced. *"As you already know, that dang safe that broke my toe cost me my foot and nigh on up to my knee a couple of years back. But the doctor recently took my leg clear up to the hip. So last Sunday, men had to carry me down into those cold waters, then heft me back out. And while I miss my leg and would gladly have it back, I could feel nothing but joy and peace not my own. God is good, is he not?"*

Josephine nodded. "Yes, he is," she whispered. "Better than I ever knew." She glanced up. "Almost done."

"Along this same vein, please find the enclosed gift. It is something I know you have long admired, Josephine, and even coveted when you worked with me, so I want you to have it. Especially seeing that my treasure is now laid up in heaven where moth does not corrupt and where thieves cannot break in and steal."

Josephine paused and looked at Dodge. "No, he wouldn't."

"Can I open it?" Bethie asked.

Josephine nodded. "Be my guest."

Bethie unwrapped the paper and gasped. "It's his gold medal! The one he had framed in his office!"

Dodge laughed. "Uncle Jack, you are one for the books, sir."

Josephine's gaze returned to the letter. *"Give my love to everyone and please, let me hear from you in return at your earliest opportunity. Yours most sincerely, Uncle Jack."*

Josephine started to read the postscript aloud, then realized she'd never be able to. Besides, it was really intended for her and Dodge alone.

"What a good letter!" Sarah said, chasing little TJ out the front door. Kathleen quickly followed and Bethie ran in pursuit.

As if sensing there was more, Dodge came alongside her. She handed the letter to him.

"P.S." Dodge read, *"I'm not sure which one will do me in first, Josephine. The love of the ladies, as you used to tease me about, or the plague of that blasted broken toe. But know that whatever takes me from this world, I will die a better man for having known that lanky young boy who saved us from that massive beast of a bull and that fiery young suffragist who waltzed into my office and gave me what for. I think I saw the love between you two before either of you ever knew it. And just for the record, though you might not want to tell Dodge this, I never considered you too tall."*

Dodge laughed. "Why that ol' scoundrel."

"He's quite the man, that's for sure."

Dodge brought her scarred palm to his lips and kissed it, once, twice, as he often did. She wrapped her arms around him, thinking of Lynchburg and Mulberry Creek, of the distillery and Miss Mary's, the places where their love began, and she knew part of her heart would forever belong in those hills.

A Note from the Author

Dear Reader,

Nestled among the hills and hollers of Middle Tennessee's Highland Rim lies the town of Lynchburg—home to the world-famous Jack Daniel Distillery, Miss Mary Bobo's Boarding House, and many cherished childhood memories of my own.

This story, long in the making, weaves fact with fiction and features characters inspired by real people (such as Nannie Helen Burroughs). To serve the narrative, I've taken some artistic license with timelines and ages, though these individuals truly did know one another and shared life in Lynchburg. Among them are Jack Daniel, Miss Mary Bobo, Nearest Green, Dan and Mary Jane Call, Lem Motlow, my great-great-grandfather Ballard Preston, and my great-grandmother Agnes Preston Tripp Gattis, among others.

Jack Daniel enjoyed many a meal at Miss Mary's table, and some of Miss Mary's boarders portrayed in the story lived for decades in her home—well into their nineties—enjoying her legendary hospitality and unruffled spirit, and even breathing their last earthly breath within those walls. Thank you for allowing me to bend time a little while remaining faithful to the spirit of this place and its people.

Though I was born and raised in Atlanta, my late father Douglas Wayne Gattis hailed from Gattistown and Lois, small communities just a stone's throw from Lynchburg. Lynchburg was a familiar destination for our family, especially when out-of-town guests wanted to tour the distillery or visit the graves of loved ones buried nearby in Lois cemetery. Several of my relatives worked for the distillery at the turn of the century, including my great-great-grandfather Ballard Preston who broke mules for the operation. The original Preston homestead is not far from Lynchburg proper, and I've had the pleasure of walking those dirt roads and gazing across the beautiful hills that remain largely unchanged more than a century later.

One of my most vivid girlhood memories of Lynchburg is the distillery tour—specifically when the guide would open the lid of one of those massive sour-mash vats, causing the "aroma" to waft toward me, nearly taking me down. It's a sensory experience you never forget, and one you're still welcome to experience today, if you're game.

My connection to Miss Mary Bobo's Boarding House runs almost as far back. Miss Mary died in 1983, just one month shy of her 102nd birthday, but her entrepreneurial spirit and business savvy made her a woman well ahead of her time. Although I portray her as owning the house in 1905, she and her husband actually leased it from Dr. Salmon in 1908, naming it the Bobo Hotel, and they purchased it outright in 1914. After her husband's death in 1948, Miss Mary continued running the boarding house until her own passing in 1983. Today the house remains under the care of the Jack Daniel Distillery, and Miss Mary's legacy of Southern comfort food and storytelling lives on.

Each year, more than 300,000 visitors from all fifty states and over thirty countries make their way to Lynchburg to tour the distillery, many making time to pull up a chair at Miss Mary's table—where you're fed full up, as we say here in the South. If you visit (and I hope you do), be sure to make a reservation ahead of time. It's a popular place! And whatever you do, don't leave without sampling the fried chicken, candied apples, and the chocolate fudge pie. Those are my favorites, and Miss Mary would approve.

Though this story concludes in 1909, the movements for women's suffrage and prohibition pressed forward. In 1919, Congress approved the Eighteenth and Nineteenth Amendments, enacting national Prohibition and guaranteeing women the right to vote. Tennessee women played a pivotal role in both causes, and in 1920, Tennessee became the decisive thirty-sixth state to ratify the Nineteenth Amendment—securing a hard-won victory born of decades of sacrifice and perseverance.

Thank you, friend, for taking another historical journey with me, one especially dear to my heart. And if you're new to my books, thank you for choosing to read this story. Your time is a gift I never take for granted.

Most gratefully,
Tamera

Acknowledgments

My heartfelt thanks to the wonderful people of Lynchburg, Jack Daniel's Distillery, and Miss Mary Bobo's Boarding House for their kind and generous assistance as I wrote *In These Hills*.

Special thanks to Mike Northcutt, Lynchburg/Moore County Tennessee historian and President of the Lynchburg/Moore County Tennessee Historical Genealogical Society; Marsha Hale, longtime employee of Jack Daniel's Distillery and president of Lynchburg's Chamber of Commerce; and Lynne Tolley, great-grandniece of Jack Daniel and former proprietress of Miss Mary Bobo's Boarding House, for sharing the lesser-known history of this remarkable place—and to Mike for reading an early draft and helping ensure the historical accuracy of the story.

Lynne, your book *Miss Mary Bobo's Boarding House Cookbook* is an absolute treasure. Bless you—and the late Pat Mitchamore—for preserving and recording the rich history of Lynchburg and Miss Mary's for generations to come.

Discussion Questions

1. When she first arrives in Lynchburg, Josephine believes she has no choice but to lie to Miss Mary and the others about her situation. But Miss Mary challenges her, saying "We *always* have a choice, no matter how hard the road is." Do you agree?
2. Josephine is surprised to learn that Jack Daniel and Miss Mary are such good friends, when their views on alcohol are so diametrically opposed. Do you have friends who hold different views on certain things than you do?
3. Dodge challenges Bethie to pray about something and let God change her mind if he chooses to. Do you find it difficult to let God change your mind about things you feel strongly about?
4. Dodge wonders if he is building anything—the way Jack Daniel and Nearest Green did—that will outlast them all. What are you building that could outlast you?
5. Josephine tells Nannie that she's not sure God is listening to her. When is a time you weren't sure God was listening to you? How did it eventually work out, or are you still waiting for an answer?
6. On her deathbed, Kathleen told Dodge he was going to have to learn how to entrust Bethie to God. Do you find it hard to trust your loved ones to God's care?
7. Josephine gains a new perspective with more empathy for those addicted to alcohol because of her friendship with Calla. Have you experienced anything like this? How did God grow your heart in that situation?
8. Jack Daniel and Josephine have heated discussions about the positives and negatives of alcohol. What messages about alcohol did you grow up with? Has your perspective changed at all?

9. Jack Daniel quotes Dodge's father, saying, "Hold your principles with conviction, and your neighbor with compassion." What do you think about this advice?

10. Dodge turns over his desire for Josephine to God but has a hard time leaving it there. Have you ever struggled to let go of a desire and leave it with God?

11. Josephine wonders, if God cares enough to collect our tears in a bottle, why doesn't he simply prevent bad things from happening in the first place? Do you have an answer for her, or is this something you also struggle with?

12. Looking back over her life, Josephine writes, "If I had the power of God to change my circumstances, I would. But if I had the wisdom of God, I would not." Do you agree with her?

About the Author

Tamera Alexander is a *USA Today* bestselling novelist and one of today's most beloved authors of inspirational historical romance and women's contemporary fiction. While being Gram Tam is her current favorite role, she'll never turn down a stroll through an old cemetery or browsing through antique shops.

Her works have been awarded numerous industry-leading honors—among them the Christy Award, the RITA Award, the Carol Award, and *Library Journal's* top honors—and have earned the distinction of *Publisher's Weekly* Starred Reviews. In 2020 she was inducted into the Christy Award Hall of Fame which recognizes authors for their legacy and contribution to Christian fiction. Her deeply drawn characters and thought-provoking plots have earned her devoted readers worldwide.

Tamera and her husband love living in Nashville, Tennessee, and treasure the time spent with their grown children and grandchildren. They live a short distance from the Southern mansions that serve as the backdrop for many of her critically acclaimed novels. Tamera views her writing as a way to grow closer to the Lord Jesus Christ—and her deepest desire is that those who read her novels will take steps closer to him as well.

Tamera invites you to connect with her at TameraAlexander.com.